ZEBRA BOOKS
KENSINGTON PUBLISHING CORP.

ZEBRA BOOKS

are published by

Kensington Publishing Corp.
475 Park Avenue South
New York, NY 10016

Copyright © 1988 by Lynette Vinet

All rights reserved. No part of this book may be reproduced in any form or by any means without the prior written consent of the Publisher, excepting brief quotes used in reviews.

First printing: July, 1988

Printed in the United States of America

As always,
To Martin and my two boys.
To my parents and my sisters.

A special thanks to my editor, Pesha Finkelstein, who remembered me and gave me the opportunity.

To my agent, Pamela Gray Ahearn, who is always there to listen and to help.

To Cassie Edwards, my thanks and gratitude for your support and friendship.

Chapter One

New Orleans, January 1858

"Miss Laurel, now you stop peepin' out of that window all evenin' long. If your cousin said she'd be here by six, you can count on her to be here at seven. That girl just ain't got the sense the Lord gave to her when she was born. Take old Gincie's word on that."

Laurel Delaney took one last look down Chestnut Street, her view partially blocked by the large, white Corinthian columns that were connected by an iron-lacework railing on the lower gallery. Turning from the window of the Garden District mansion, she allowed the edge of the white lace curtain to fall gently from her fingertips. She gave a small smile to Gincie, the old black woman who now dusted the mahogany tabletop in the parlor, and sighed.

"I wish just once I could rely on Lavinia to be punctual. Why I bother to finish dressing so early for the opera is a mystery to me. She is always late."

Gincie shook her head, her gray hair hidden by a green turban. "That's because you is a lady, Miss Laurel, and not like your cousin who ain't got no regard for folks' feelin's. Ever since she arrived from San Antonio, she ain't said more than two words to you. Always off gallivantin' somewhere and comin' home loaded down with boxes. Where do you think she gets all that money from anyway?"

"Now don't start picking on Lavinia again," Laurel gently chided Gincie, though not sure why she felt protective of Lavinia. Gincie was right about Lavinia. She didn't seem to have much regard for people's feelings, especially not for her younger cousin's. Laurel smoothed down her high-necked peach satin gown. "I suppose Uncle Arthur is doing very well on his cattle ranch. Lavinia has been keeping the New Orleans shopkeepers busy since her arrival, hasn't she?"

Gincie stopped polishing the Queen Anne table and gave her full attention to the young dark-haired woman who was framed by the gold-edged mirror behind her. "That Miss Lavinia don't fool old Gincie. I saw her shoes that first day she pranced in here. The soles were all worn out. You can always tell a lady by her shoes; I always say that."

Laurel sat down on the Louis Quinze sofa and lightly fingered the gold-and-green brocade material. "You're being much too harsh on her, Gincie. Lavinia is high-strung, I think."

"Hmph!" Gincie turned away in a huff. "That fancy Yankee school Mr. Anderson sent you to after your parents died didn't teach you nothin' about people. Miss Lavinia is usin' you, and you're just too good-hearted to know it. That Miss Lavinia is up to no good. Just you wait and see."

Laurel didn't suppress the smile that rose to her strawberry-tinted lips when Gincie departed the parlor. She wished she could be more like Gincie, either hating or loving passionately . . . even like Lavinia who had a flair for the dramatic, a *joie de vivre*. Laurel doubted that she had any passion within her; the fire that coursed through Lavinia's veins was lacking in her own.

At twenty years old, she was still unwed, still a virgin, and likely to remain both until her dying day. She had been told by various gentlemen that she was comely, almost regal in appearance when she entered a room. "Coolly regal" was how her best friend's brother had described her once. She still didn't know if he had meant that as a compliment or a criticism. Laurel was in no hurry to wed, having found that the few kisses she had received from her friend's brother, and other overamorous suitors, had left her cold.

She felt herself to be a proper young woman, perhaps staid. Sometimes Laurel did wish to be more like Lavinia, who was uninhibited and could charm a man with the arch of a finely made brow or the tilt of her auburn head. Laurel hated to admit to herself that she envied Lavinia's wild, untamed beauty and felt overshadowed by her cousin's physical brilliance.

Laurel's thoughts drifted back to the time, some seven years earlier, when she had been thirteen and Lavinia fifteen. Uncle Arthur had paid a surprise but brief visit to her father. Lavinia had sat in the carriage with the curtains drawn the whole time. Laurel's mother had forbidden her to speak to her cousin, and Laurel had had only a quick glimpse of her cousin's pale face when Uncle Arthur entered the carriage. Then they had driven away, and for the next six months Laurel's family hadn't visited their upriver plantation.

The only explanation offered to Laurel had been that Lavinia was ill, and even then Lavinia's name had been mentioned in hushed tones as if she had died or when Laurel's parents thought Laurel wasn't within hearing distance. She remembered her father saying that Lavinia was wanton and spoiled. Her mother had whispered that Arthur had taken a shotgun to a boy who disappeared from the ranch, never to be found, that it was a tragic situation. Laurel had had no idea whom or what situation they meant.

A year later the yellow fever epidemic had hit, and Laurel's parents had died. Laurel, herself, had become very ill and would have succumbed to the fever if not for Gincie's ministrations and prayers. She had survived, and shortly afterward, John Anderson, her parents' lawyer and Laurel's acting guardian, had made arrangements for her to be sent to school in Boston. Laurel had remained at the prestigious girls' school until her graduation.

Now she was home again and making the round of boring parties, escorted by a fawning Philbert Anderson, John's son, whom Laurel assumed was more interested in her fortune than in her herself. Other young men were kind to her, considerate, but Laurel guessed her money caused them to gravitate toward her. This assumption was always driven home with a vengeance whenever Lavinia arrived, unescorted. Their attentions turned upon her, and Laurel found herself sitting alone in a corner or in conversation with a boring dowager.

No matter how much she wished to dislike Lavinia, she couldn't. A waiflike quality surrounded her. Laurel thought this strange since Lavinia had been raised by an indulgent father and stepmother whereas Laurel had grown up virtually alone. However, Laurel decided that Gincie was correct about Lavinia. Ever since her arrival some two months ago, she had expected Gincie and the servants to wait upon her and treat her like a princess.

If Emily and Sylvester Delaney were alive, Laurel had no doubt that Lavinia wouldn't have been invited to the house, much less have been able to order around the servants. Laurel knew she should set down stern rules for her cousin to follow, but she couldn't begrudge Lavinia her hospitality and didn't have the heart to turn her out.

Though Lavinia didn't rise until noon and then left the house after a large lunch, only to appear near dark loaded down with packages, Laurel never inquired into her personal affairs. She had recently heard that her uncle had suffered a financial setback, but evidently the situation had reversed itself. Lavinia wore expensive gowns and each day arrived home with more. The daughter of a man in financial trouble couldn't spend money like water.

As dusk descended and the carriage rolled onto the circular drive for the trip to the opera, Lavinia still hadn't returned. A cool breeze whistled through the treetops as Laurel stood up and peered into the encroaching darkness.

The street was empty and quiet except for the unending cacophony of locusts.

"Where are you, Lavinia?" she grumbled aloud.

"Auguste, do you hear me?"

Lavinia Delaney's long hair cascaded onto the pillow in auburn strands. Her deep-set blue eyes widened as she gazed at the man beside her on the bed. Auguste was so still, so pale, whiter than the sheet atop his imposing frame.

"Answer me," she pleaded, rising terror in her voice.

Touching the arm of Auguste St. Julian, one of

the wealthiest planters along Bayou Teche, Lavinia drew instantly away. His skin felt so cold, and she knew he was dead. A harsh ragged sob rose in her throat as she attempted to gather her wits. She scrambled from the bed and reached for her dress.

"God, help me," she said, almost choking on the words, praying for the first time since her childhood. Only half an hour earlier Auguste had been strong and healthy, an insatiable lover for a man well past fifty. What had happened to him after she fell asleep? Had his heart failed?

Lavinia trembled so much that she could barely button her gown. Her breathing sounded ragged to her own ears, and her heart felt about to burst.

Should she summon help? She dismissed the thought immediately since Auguste was past saving now, but mostly since she dreaded becoming the object of wagging tongues in such a sordid scandal. For years to come she would be unable to live down the stigma of having been with St. Julian when he died. Lavinia possessed few scruples, but she knew that if she informed the authorities, other wealthy New Orleans men might shy away from her if the truth were known. Auguste was a married man and had taken an apartment in New Orleans two weeks after meeting Lavinia. Not even the landlord was aware of Lavinia's existence or the secret afternoon trysts.

Now Auguste was dead.

As he lay there before her, Lavinia felt her dreams die, too. Not that she had been in love with Auguste. He had been very much in love with her, but she had been only fond of him. Perhaps fonder of his money still, of the many presents he bought for her. However, she wasn't so cold-hearted as not to feel anything for the man. She wondered why nothing ever worked out for her, why she seemed to have been born under a black cloud. Her first love had been destroyed by her father, and now poor Auguste had been taken from her by death.

A bitter sob escaped her as she finished dressing. She foresaw a bleak future for herself and her father's ranch, the Little L. The ranch was in dire need of money to survive the coming year, her father having lost quite a few head of cattle during a drought last year. She would do anything to save the ranch, anything. Ever practical, a plan formed in her mind, offering her a ray of hope. Though her father would dislike the plan, Lavinia decided that whatever must be done would be done.

Quietly she picked up her reticule and pulled the black webbed veil of her hat over her face. Then she crossed the room, not glancing in Auguste's direction, and opened the door. Making certain that no one was in the courtyard, she stealthily made her way to the sidewalk.

The dusk-shrouded street was empty at this time of evening. The carriage Lavinia had borrowed from Laurel still waited on the other side of Jackson Square. Before she got into the vehicle, Jonas, Laurel's driver, looked suspiciously at her. Lavinia shrugged as she settled herself onto the leather-upholstered seat. She knew Jonas would remain silent even if Laurel questioned him as to where she went everyday. He didn't know much of anything, so his opinion would be conjecture. Always a person who loved attracting attention and basking in admiring male glances, Lavinia was for the first time grateful that she had used discretion where Auguste was concerned. No one could fault her or question her about his death.

She smiled to herself and hoped she would arrive

home in time to join her dear cousin at the opera. Softly chiding herself for neglecting Laurel, Lavinia decided she must make it all up to her by convincing Laurel to accompany her home to San Antonio. After all, that had been the main reason she had come to visit her cousin. But then she had met Auguste and realized he would marry her and give her the money to save her father's ranch without question or reservation. Now that plan was ended, and she must bring Laurel home with her. Of course, Lavinia's father would be less than overjoyed to see the daughter of his deceased brother since Arthur Delaney and Sylvester had never gotten along. But Laurel's visit would change his mind about the past. Lavinia was certain of that.

Because of Laurel Delaney, the Little L would be saved.

The dark fire in the man's eyes momentarily disconcerted Monsieur Henri Maurice, but he assured himself that his client's anger wasn't about his handling of the delicate matter they now discussed. He had been most circumspect in his questioning of the residents of the Esplanade Avenue apartment where Auguste St. Julian had died. In fact Henri was always amused by how eager people were to speak about crimes in general, to discourse on what they believe happened. However, St. Julian's death wasn't a murder or a crime . . . except to the dark-clad man who sat across the desk from him.

The man crumpled a piece of white paper in his hand, his eyes never leaving Henri's face. "So you are telling me, Monsieur Maurice, that no one saw this woman on the day of my uncle's death."

Henri inclined his head. "But that is not to say she

wasn't at your uncle's apartment. A resident across the courtyard did see a woman with your uncle one afternoon, coming out of the apartment. However, she was veiled."

"So that is all you discovered? That a woman was with him? That's not enough!"

The investigator involuntarily jumped. This nephew of St. Julian's was a formidable man, a man who inspired fear at times. Taking a kerchief out of his pocket, he wiped his sweating palms on it, and noticed that even in the unseasonable February heat, his client didn't perspire. He appeared cool, but Henri had dealt with enough people to realize this man boiled inside.

"Please, monsieur," Henri cajoled. "Many of St. Julian's neighbors are men like himself. Wealthy men from out of town who rent apartments, town houses, and entertain lady friends, keep mistresses. The personal matters of other men aren't of interest to them. Anyway, no crime has been committed. Your uncle's heart failed. The lady did not kill him."

"Lady!" The man stood up and paced the small office. "Mademoiselle Lavinia Delaney doesn't deserve such a title. She is a whore, a woman who was sequestered for over six months on her uncle's plantation while she bore an illegitimate child."

"Or so it is believed, monsieur. None of the servants would discuss Mademoiselle Delaney with me."

"So then you are telling me that no one will speak about this woman."

"Perhaps her cousin."

"No," Henri's client said and shook his head. "She is family and no doubt protective of her. Your investigation disclosed that the cousin is a woman of refinement. I don't wish to involve her in such an unseemly affair." He grew silent, then held out his hand to Henri. "I thank you for your investigation."

"I wish I could have done more for you, gotten you the information you wished."

"You have, Henri."

After St. Julian's nephew departed Henri's office and walked briskly down the street of Vermillionville to visit his Aunt Clotilde, he knew he did have all the information he needed on Lavinia Delaney.

A scowl deepened the grooved lines of his face. So, his Uncle Auguste had fancied himself in love with a whore. And what was worse, she was an American from Texas, not a Frenchwoman. In his hand he still held Auguste's last letter to him, written two days before his death. The words were ingrained on his mind.

"My nephew," it had begun. "I am in love with a beautiful young woman named Lavinia Delaney. You have known that Clotilde and I haven't been married in the true sense for some time. When I confided my marital state to you last year, you insisted I should take a mistress. I cannot love in that way, my boy. My heart must belong to one woman. So, I am going to ask your aunt for a divorce. *Mon Dieu!* The repercussions I dread to think about. However, I will marry Lavinia. Don't worry. So far we have been discreet. Soon you shall receive a bill for items which I have purchased for her in your name, so no one can trace them to me. I shall reimburse you. I wish your blessing and please don't think your uncle is a foolish old man. If you knew my Lavinia, you would love her, too."

The letter had been signed in Auguste's flowing

penmanship. The bills for Lavinia Delaney's extravagances began arriving three days after Auguste's funeral. Bills his nephew intended to pay, a debt he also intended to be repaid by the woman in question.

When he arrived at the St. Julian plantation and saw the tears still streaming freely from his aunt's eyes for her dead husband, he swore vengeance on the cold-hearted Delaney woman.

Chapter Two

February 1858

"Lavinia, whatever is the matter?"

Laurel's worried question, spoken in a gentle tone of voice, seemed to cause Lavinia's tears to flow freely. The two cousins sat on the sofa in the elegantly furnished parlor of the Delaney Garden District mansion. A warm breeze wafted through the tall windows that opened onto the veranda at the front of the white-columned house. Laurel noticed that Lavinia's hands shook, her face as pale as the taffeta gown she wore.

"It's Papa," Lavinia choked, her tears trickling prettily down her cheeks. "A letter arrived from Seth this morning. Papa has been taken suddenly ill."

"I'm so sorry. What does your stepbrother say is wrong with Uncle Arthur?"

Laurel's brow puckered into a worried frown as she asked this question. She knew how devastating a sudden illness could be, how totally unprepared most people were for such news. She remembered how quickly her own parents had died and hoped Arthur Delaney's illness wasn't serious.

Lavinia's large blue eyes lifted from the letter in her trembling hands to focus on Laurel's face.

"The doctors aren't certain. Seth believes I should return home, that Papa may not have—oh, I can't bear to say it—much time." Her voice broke again. "I admit I haven't been the most dutiful daughter, but I love my father."

Placing a slender arm around Lavinia's shoulder, Laurel hugged her. "I'm sure your father knows you love him, Lavinia. Seth is right. Your place is by his side."

Lavinia grabbed Laurel's hand in her own. "Would you consider returning to Texas with me? Please? I know Papa would want to see you again."

"Our fathers weren't very friendly," Laurel reminded her.

"I'm aware of that. However, I think papa would like to make peace with you since your father is gone. Believe me, Laurel, Papa suffered a great deal after the breakup of his partnership with Uncle Sylvester. More than once I heard him bemoan the fact that he never told your father how sorry he felt over the whole incident. By the time he married my stepmother, he had long since gotten over his infatuation with your own mother. But your father never forgave him for falling in love with his wife."

Laurel pulled away from her. "If you're saying that my mother loved Uncle Arthur and led him to believe that she would have left my father for—"

"No, no," Lavinia broke her off. "Papa knew your parents loved one another and accepted that fact. It's just that his pride forbade him to admit he had made a monumental fool of himself where your mother was concerned. I know he would have liked to have made amends, but your parents died before he extended the olive branch." Lavinia's blue eyes narrowed. "You see, that time I was in ill health and arrived here with Papa to ask Uncle Sylvester if I might stay at the plantation, Papa was quite concerned about me and never got around to apologizing for his past mistakes before he returned to Texas."

"I see," Laurel said and disentangled her hand from Lavinia's. Standing up, she crossed the room to the window and gazed out at the tranquil street scene. White-pillared mansions, as large as her own, stood majestically on both sides of Chestnut Street. From the moment she had been born, she had lived in this house, except for the summers on the plantation that she had sold last year, and the Boston boarding school. In truth she knew no existence other than this and was totally happy here. Now Lavinia wanted her to go to San Antonio because she feared Arthur Delaney might die and wanted to make amends.

Laurel didn't understand why Arthur should care at all about her. When her parents died, he hadn't offered to provide a home for her, and Laurel would have welcomed the gesture, though an empty one at best. Any family, even one with unresolved problems, was better than living in a boarding school and depending upon the good will of friends to ask her home for the holidays. She had spent a total of four Christmases with Anne Talbot's family in New York. At school, Anne had been her best and dearest friend, and for the rest of her life Laurel would be grateful to Anne's parents for providing a warm holiday for an orphaned girl.

And now, after all these years, Arthur Delaney wished to make amends. Laurel had no inkling as to what had transpired between her parents and Arthur. She only knew that Arthur had been left a widower with an infant daughter and that her own mother, Emily Delaney, had recently married her father. Evidently Arthur had loved Emily before his wife's death and had pursued her. This pursuit had caused the rift between the brothers and ended the partnership of the Little L Ranch before it had even started.

The afternoon sun spilled into the parlor and highlighted the auburn strands in Laurel's dark hair, casting a golden hue across her porcelain complexion. Lavinia wiped her eyes with a kerchief, and Laurel wondered if her tears were real. Could Lavinia be using her for her own reasons? Emily had always proclaimed that Lavinia could be deceptive. Laurel, however, could think of no reason why Lavinia would lie to her about such a serious matter as Arthur's health.

"Will you come with me?" Laurel heard Lavinia ask.

Laurel gave thought to this question as once again the familiar street scene outside caught her attention. She swung her gaze away from the window to her elegant parlor, which was also familiar. She could walk blindfolded through it and the house, and not bump into a single piece of furniture. Nothing had changed since her parents' deaths. Last year Laurel had returned home to the stuffy parties and dull young men eager to marry an heiress. But Lavinia with her bold blue eyes and flaming hair lived in an untamed land where convention and decorum could be set aside for the most part. How she envied Lavinia her freedom.

Suddenly Laurel realized that she was of age, her own woman, and no longer needed John Anderson's reluctant approval. She surmised that Anderson wanted her to marry his Philbert, but Laurel found nothing attractive about the young man with clammy hands.

A wild longing overcame her. Her blood surged through her veins. Perhaps she did possess some of Lavinia's fire. Why shouldn't she be reckless and not think of the consequences just once in her life? When she returned from Texas, the house would still be here, and the same dull young men would vie for her favor. And if Arthur Delaney were ill and wished to make up for all the years he had barely acknowledged her existence, then she would allow him to apologize to her.

Turning to face Lavinia, Laurel said, "We shall make arrangements to leave for San Antonio immediately."

"Wonderful!" Lavinia purred and watched Laurel leave the parlor in search of Gincie.

Lavinia clapped her hands together and crushed Seth's letter to her bosom. What a coincidence that Seth would happen to write at this particular time. She thought it was a wonder that he could tear himself away from the tarts he frequented long enough to pen the letter. But the fact that he had written only served to make Lavinia aware of the grave situation at home. Granted, of course, her father wasn't that ill. Seth said he had suffered a spell of sickness that had soon passed. Laurel didn't need to know his illness wasn't that serious, Lavinia decided, but Arthur Delaney might lose the Little L, and neither Lavinia nor Seth wanted that. His financial situation wasn't the best, and if things didn't turn around soon, he would lose the ranch.

Seth might be Lavinia's stepbrother, but both of them couldn't bear the thought of being poor.

"Well, that won't happen," Lavinia assured herself. "Not if Seth and Laurel marry."

She smiled to herself and decided to begin packing.

The days before departure were busy ones for Laurel. Since she had no idea how long she would be in Texas, she made arrangements to close the house. Though Gincie didn't wish to go and Laurel told her she could remain at the house with the few servants, Gincie staunchly refused.

"Where you go, I go, Miss Laurel." Gincie stood with arms folded, not about to be deterred from accompanying her "baby," as she referred to Laurel.

Laurel was glad Gincie would accompany her and Lavinia on the trip. She had been so long without Gincie that she dreaded to be separated from her again.

A few days before the *Cotton Blossom* was due to leave New Orleans for the meandering trek through the bayous, Laurel and Lavinia, followed by Gincie, made last-minute purchases.

The shopkeeper welcomed Laurel warmly but grew stony-faced at the list of clothes Laurel wished to purchase. "Mademoiselle Delaney, these clothes are not fit for a lady like yourself. I suggest satins and silks rather than . . . calico." Madame Daphne could barely say the word. Laurel hid her smile behind her gloved hand.

"I have all the satins I need," Laurel assured the woman. "I should like to be comfortable on my trip to Texas. The weather, so far this year, has been unseasonably warm. However, if you can't oblige me . . ."

"*Oui,* I shall immediately have gowns sewn for you," the Frenchwoman said hurriedly. Her eyes skimmed with interest over Lavinia. "And what about you, mademoiselle? If I recall, you appreciate

23

the finest silks. Why, when you and the gentleman were in here last month, I told you we'd soon receive a French silk. It has arrived, and the color will perfectly complement your eyes."

"No, thank you." Lavinia spoke icily and made a hasty retreat from the shop.

Laurel thanked the flustered Madame Daphne. Before she joined Lavinia on the street, Gincie whispered, "Miss Lavinia's up to somethin'."

Laurel realized Gincie was most probably correct, but what Lavinia did with her time and with whom she spent it were none of her concern. Still, Laurel felt curiosity as to the man's identity.

"Shall we go?" Lavinia asked brusquely and flounced down the street ahead of Laurel and Gincie.

Later they stopped at the French Market. Laurel helped Gincie choose fresh fruits and vegetables for supper while Lavinia stood at a distance. As Laurel walked among the stalls of colorful and fragrant-smelling produce, she noticed a young man approach Lavinia and engage her in conversation. At this moment Gincie asked a question about the menu for the next day, and Laurel turned her attention to her servant. By the time she cast a glance back in Lavinia's direction, the man was gone and Lavinia stood transfixed.

Lavinia's face was as white as the lace on the edge of her green bonnet. Immediately Laurel realized something was wrong with her cousin. She rushed headlong through the throng of bustling people and past the stalls until she reached Lavinia.

"Lavinia, whatever is the matter?"

Blue eyes, filled with an unfathomable fear, flickered over Laurel. Laurel repeated her question, but Lavinia seemed barely able to speak.

"I . . . must get home," she said at last through pale, trembling lips.

Gincie joined them as Laurel helped Lavinia into the carriage. At home, Lavinia sat on the sofa and refused to drink the tea offered to her by Gincie.

"You're acting real peculiar," Gincie frankly told her.

"Leave me alone, both of you! I don't need your forced solicitations."

Lavinia jumped off the sofa and paced the room like a caged tigress. Laurel nodded to Gincie to leave them alone.

"When are you going to tell me what's troubling you?" Laurel asked after Gincie's departure.

Lavinia attempted to feign ignorance. "I don't know what you're talking about. Nothing is wrong with me."

Sighing in exasperation, Laurel poured some tea into a teacup. "I noticed a young man speaking to you at the market. After his departure you looked ready to faint. Do me the courtesy of telling me the truth, dear Cousin. I'm beginning to wonder if you've ever been truthful about anything. I have never asked you about all those afternoons when you left the house and returned with packages, or about the expensive gowns you're suddenly wearing. Evidently you spent your time with a more than generous man. Madame Daphne mentioned that today."

"That woman and her big mouth! I'd like to ram one of her bolts of French silk down her throat."

Laurel couldn't help smiling. At least Lavinia was her feisty self again, and color had invaded her cheeks. "Why don't you tell me everything, Lavinia, and no lies?"

When Lavinia finished telling Laurel about her affair with Auguste St. Julian and his subsequent death, Laurel remained silent. She had no idea what to say to Lavinia. Never had she imagined something so tragic had befallen her cousin, but she felt that Lavinia's headstrong attitude had caused her own misery.

"Are you going to lecture me now, Laurel, tell me what a wicked woman I am for becoming involved with a married man?"

Laurel shook her head and gently patted Lavinia's hand. "I don't believe you're wicked, and I won't judge you. All I hope is that in the future, you'll give more thought to the men you become involved with."

Twisting the kerchief in her hands, Lavinia gave a nasty laugh. "Thank you for that."

"You didn't mention the young man at the market. Who was he?"

"He was Auguste's driver when he stayed in the city. He said he wished to warn me about a private investigation by a family member into Auguste's death. Someone in the St. Julian family has discovered my identity and holds me accountable for Auguste's sudden demise."

"But you didn't kill the man. He died of natural causes," Laurel remarked.

Lavinia got up and moved restlessly about the room. "Evidently this person wants revenge of some kind." After a few moments she stopped, and her face was wreathed in fear. "We must travel by steamboat through the bayous before we take the coach into Texas. The St. Julians are quite powerful in the bayou country. Laurel, anything could happen to me before I arrive home. I can't leave for San Antonio now. I can't risk entering the bayou country. My life is at stake!"

"Hush!" Laurel attempted to calm her and pulled

her down beside her on the sofa again. "I admit your situation is a serious one, but no one is going to harm you. Did St. Julian's driver give you the person's name?"

Lavinia shook her auburn head. Fear still gleamed in her eyes.

"Then perhaps all he heard was a rumor of vengeance. Maybe this investigator was only checking into the facts, and now that the police have ruled St. Julian's death was from a natural cause, I doubt very much if you're in danger. You might be guilty of being indiscreet, Lavinia, of dallying with a married man, but murder, no. No one can hold you accountable for such a thing."

Lavinia longed to believe Laurel, but she couldn't stop her mind from running away with her. "I can't go to San Antonio. I shall be harmed if I do, I know I will."

"Stop it! We will go to San Antonio. Your father needs you. We'll simply come up with a plan to protect you."

"What sort of plan?" Lavinia asked, immediately interested.

"I'm not certain." Laurel shrugged her shoulders and contemplated her cousin. Lavinia was extremely beautiful in a wild sort of way. She was the type of woman people noticed immediately, but if her hair were worn more severely and she dressed in darker clothing, then whoever was searching for Lavinia Delaney would be put off . . . at least until they reached Texas.

Laurel grabbed Lavinia's hand and pulled her up. "Come upstairs with me," she told her cousin. "We're going to change a silk purse into the proverbial sow's ear."

As Laurel and Lavinia boarded the *Cotton Blossom* nearly a week later, Gincie, who walked behind them, shook her turban-clad head in dismay. "Ain't right, Miss Laurel," she muttered.

"Hush, Gincie," Laurel rebuked the woman. "We're doing this for Lavinia."

From the levee, the busy hum of labor reached Laurel when she stood on deck while the trunks were taken from the carriage and brought to the boat. People of all tongues, all races and nationalities buzzed on the dock in Babel-like confusion. Despite the strangeness of the circumstance, Laurel looked forward to her Texas journey; however, she didn't believe she could say the same for Lavinia.

"How long do I have to stand out here with all eyes upon me?" Lavinia asked in agitation. "I feel quite ridiculous. Did you actually wear this hideous dress once?"

The "hideous dress" Lavinia referred to was a dark-brown calico that Laurel had worn to church on Sundays when she was in Boston. The dress was plain but serviceable, and Laurel thought Lavinia resembled the part she played rather well. With her thick auburn hair pulled tightly back into a coil at the base of her neck, the prim brown bonnet on her head, and the pair of spectacles that had belonged to Laurel's mother perched on her nose, she indeed resembled a lady's companion. No one would be able to identify her as the wildly beautiful Lavinia Delaney. Until they reached Texas, Lavinia would be known as Agatha Malone.

"You look quite respectable," Laurel told her in lieu of another description.

"I look like hell, and you know it. I believe you're enjoying my humiliation, Cousin Laurel."

Perhaps she was at that. For the first time in her life, Lavinia's beauty paled alongside her own. Laurel only smiled. "If you want to change, you may do so. But if a relative of St. Julian's should be searching for you, you'll be safe in your disguise. Remember, I'm not the one who has to travel incognito."

"Oh, bother! I'm going to the cabin and wait until supper." Lavinia stalked off after Gincie, leaving Laurel on deck with an amused grin on her face.

It was then she saw him out of the corner of her eye. The man must have been watching her for some time. He leaned on the railing and shot her a penetrating glance that sent shock waves down to her toes. Never had any man looked at her with such a degree of arrogance. He appraised her as if she were a tasty confection in a sweet shop, yet he seemed to find her not at all to his liking. She noticed his eyes, which were blacker and harder than granite, flickered over her steadily.

Laurel felt herself color under his intense perusal. Briefly she wondered if her lace petticoat showed beneath the rose-colored satin crinoline. Her matching bodice with white lace at the square neckline, she knew, wasn't cut indecently low, but she wondered if her bonnet were askew. The thought occurred to her that this man found nothing lacking in her physical appearance. Indeed, the hungry look in his eyes was testament to that fact, but he evidently didn't think much of her as a person. Laurel didn't care for such rudeness from a stranger.

Lifting her chin high, she attempted to pass him without glancing in his direction, but he blocked her way and bowed formally. The river breeze ruffled the strands of his curly black hair when he straightened. "Good morning," he said in a silky voice.

She caught the scent of fresh tobacco, mingled

with his own musky male scent. This man cut a dashing figure in a dark frock coat with matching trousers. Many women would melt willingly into this man's arms, if given half a chance. Laurel might be inexperienced in the ways of passion, but she was well aware that some men could ruin a woman with a glance. She felt this man was one of those.

"We haven't been formally introduced, sir." She sounded curt, very cold. The man only smiled, but there was no warmth in his eyes.

"I am a stranger to New Orleans, mademoiselle. I hope not to be a stranger to you much longer. I shall make it a point to be properly introduced to you."

With that remark, he bowed again and then quickly walked away. Laurel thought he was an odd man and didn't care for the way her heart thumped in her chest. But when she was in Boston she had been approached by men who were less than gentlemen, and her frosty manner had deterred them. She didn't believe an icy approach would matter to this man. Already she sensed he was a hunter, and she the prey, and not about to be stopped until he had made his kill.

Laurel shivered in the warm morning air and went to her cabin where she decided to put the stranger and his bad manners from her mind.

She hoped she wouldn't run into the man again.

Chapter Three

Laurel had just finished dressing for dinner when she entered Lavinia's adjoining cabin. Before her stood Lavinia in a golden silk creation that took away Laurel's breath. Her cousin's auburn locks were pulled atop her head and cascaded in ringlets down her back. Compared to the prim dark-green gown Laurel wore, Lavinia resembled a fairy princess.

"Well, how do I look?" Lavinia asked and swirled around the cabin. Gincie stood with her arms folded, a disapproving frown on her face.

"You're a breath-taking sight, Lavinia," Laurel spoke truthfully. "But you can't have dinner in the dining room dressed like that."

"Why not?"

"Because I thought you feared the St. Julian family. You're supposed to be my dour-faced companion, Agatha Malone."

"Oh, her." Lavinia laughed and preened before the mirror. "I've given old Agatha the night off. I'm not about to have my evening spoiled. I can go back to being plain Agatha in the morning."

Lavinia never ceased to baffle Laurel. Only the

week before she had cried in fear of her life, and now because she was apparently bored with her masquerade, she had decided to drop the pretense for a while. Laurel didn't care one way or the other what Lavinia did, but she wasn't about to allow Lavinia to use her.

"I booked passage for a Miss Agatha Malone, companion to Miss Delaney. And now it seems that I'm to look like a fool in front of the captain and everyone else who saw you board the boat this morning. Truly, I don't care if you drop the charade, but from now on I shall tell everyone who you really are. That news should delight St. Julian's relative, if such a person actually is trying to find you. You may as well place a large sign on your person, proclaiming your identity."

For an instant Lavinia's chin trembled, but only for an instant. Then she lifted her head high and flashed Laurel a dazzling smile.

"I wonder if you really care about me, Cousin Laurel, or if you enjoy my disguise. Sometimes I think you dislike me a great deal."

There was a grain of truth in Lavinia's statement, and Laurel hated to admit she did get some enjoyment out of the beautiful Lavinia playing the plain Jane. For most of her life she had mentally compared herself to Lavinia and found herself lacking, though her mother had constantly assured her she was beautiful but in a quiet sort of way.

She didn't dislike Lavinia. In fact Laurel felt rather protective of her and couldn't fathom why.

"I care about you very much," Laurel found herself saying. "If you wish to wear your new gown, I won't stop you. I shall introduce you as my beautiful traveling companion."

Lavinia silently considered Laurel. She sighed her

defeat. With a furrowed brow, she began to fiddle with the buttons on the back of the gown. "Help me with this, Gincie, and get that plain blue gown of Laurel's. I shall wear that tonight."

When Lavinia stepped out of the gold silk gown, she handed it to Laurel. "I want you to wear this dress. I think the color will suit you and bring out the green of your eyes."

Lavinia's thoughtfulness brought unexpected tears to Laurel's eyes. "I can't wear your gown."

"Yes, you can and you will. Auguste had it especially made for me, and there is a golden dove on a chain that complements the dress. I think he'd have been most pleased for you to wear this gown. You know, Laurel, in your way, you're much more beautiful than I ever could hope to be. If you dressed in more vibrant colors, in gowns with a bit more daring, and wore your hair differently . . ."

Lavinia began to gather the thick strands of Laurel's dark hair atop her head, allowing a few cascading curls to fall gently across her shoulders. "What do you think, Gincie?"

"I think my baby is the most beautiful lady on this here boat."

All eyes turned upon Laurel when she entered the dining room. The multitude of candles of the elaborate chandeliers cast a golden glow over her. She shimmered in the gown, which drank in the lights' reflection. As she floated across the Brussels carpet to her table, followed by a prim-looking Lavinia, she caught a glimpse of the man who had accosted her on deck that morning.

Lavinia noticed him, too.

"What a handsome man," she whispered across

the table to Laurel. "He hasn't taken his eyes off us since we sat down. Do you know who he is?"

Laurel didn't bother to cast a glance in the man's direction. "No. He approached me on deck this morning and was too familiar."

"I hope you didn't sound as frosty then as you do now. You'll never catch a husband like that, Laurel. A man doesn't want to be frostbitten."

"I don't intend to marry, Lavinia."

Lavinia's mouth fell open. "Whyever not? I'd have married Auguste except . . . Well, you know what happened there."

Straightening her spine against her chair, Laurel said, "I think men are a great bother. The ones I've met were only interested in my fortune. I have no use for such a man and prefer to spend my own money rather than be at a man's mercy and have to beg for it."

Lavinia began to eat the salad placed in front of her. "I wouldn't mind begging anything from such a man as him," she said and smiled in the direction of the dark-eyed stranger, who was still watching them.

"You're incorrigible," Laurel said and proceeded to eat her dinner.

After a main course of fish, covered with melted butter, and a dessert of strawberries and cream, Laurel couldn't avoid the man who had watched them from across the dining room. He suddenly stood before them, the captain by his side.

"Miss Delaney," Captain Steele began hesitantly, not at all sure he should interrupt her meal, "this gentleman wishes an introduction."

Because the captain seemed so uncertain and his face was slightly red with embarrassment, Laurel hoped to put him at ease. but inwardly she cursed the dark-clad man who had attempted again to intrude upon her life. However, she smiled up at the captain and the man beside him.

"By all means," she said.

"May I present Antoine Duvalier to you, Miss Delaney? And this is"—the captain turned to Lavinia, and Laurel introduced her by the name Agatha Malone—"Miss Malone," he uttered and quickly departed.

Duvalier stood, seemingly waiting for an invitation to sit, which Lavinia quickly dispensed. Laurel gave her a condemning look as Duvalier took a seat next to Laurel's.

"Do you travel often by steamboat?" Lavinia asked.

He lit a cheroot and leaned back in his chair. "I had business in New Orleans. I very seldom leave my plantation, Petit Coteau."

"A plantation, how divine!"

Laurel couldn't miss the flash of excitement in her cousin's eyes. She thought that Lavinia was being much too forward with the man.

"Agatha, I believe it's time we turned in for the night. I'm certain Mr. Duvalier will understand. We have a long trip ahead of us and must rest."

"What is your destination?"

"San Antonio," Lavinia chimed in.

"I'm certain Mr. Duvalier isn't interested in our itinerary." Laurel rose from her chair. Duvalier followed suit and strode after them when they left the dining room.

He took Lavinia's hand and kissed it. Then, before Laurel could protest, he captured hers also. His lips felt like flames on her flesh, and she pulled away.

"You'd be very surprised at my interests, Miss Delaney. I assure you they are many and varied."

Then he turned and leisurely sauntered away.

"Laurel, the man is so handsome and cultured! I think he likes you."

"Me? You're the one he spoke to. He barely glanced at me at all."

Lavinia laughed. "You're jealous."

A blush stained Laurel's cheeks. "I am not. Let's go to bed, Lavinia. We have a long journey in front of us."

When Laurel was ensconced in her cabin, she discovered she wasn't tired at all. Instead she found a book and began to read but decided the book bored her. From Lavinia's cabin she heard Gincie's soft snores, and looking in, she noticed that Lavinia was also fast asleep.

Returning to her cabin, she heard the gentle lapping of the water against the steamboat and saw the brilliant moon in the star-dappled sky from her window. Suddenly she left her room, without throwing on the shawl Gincie always insisted she wear for protection against the night air.

Outside, she walked slowly along the deck and breathed in the jasmine-perfumed night air. On the shoreline dark images of trees blended together. The moonlight spilled onto her figure and highlighted the gleaming material of her gown, the alabaster beauty of her shoulders and arms. The night air felt pleasant upon her naked flesh, and for the first time in her life, she didn't feel embarrassed that her bosom was less than half covered.

She fingered the golden dove that hung at her neck on the matching chain and was swallowed in the valley of her breasts. A man who had loved Lavinia had given her the dove as a symbol of his love. Laurel briefly wondered if she would ever know such love but dismissed the thought. All she had known over the past seven years had been a sense of loneliness, of isolation. Few people had cared about her, and the young men she had met were no exception. Lavinia was wrong, she told herself. She wasn't beautiful. None of those men had wanted her for herself or any looks she might possess. They had wanted her for her money.

A sigh escaped from between her lips, and she bent a trifle further over the railing than she had intended. Panic seized her for an instant because she thought she was about to fall into the swirling, dark waters, but suddenly warm, strong hands grabbed her about her waist and pulled her back.

Grasping her rescuer's hands, she leaned for an instant against a hard, masculine body. "Thank you," she gasped. "I would have fallen if you hadn't—"

Her voice silenced when she turned and looked up into the dark visage of Antoine Duvalier. Instantly her pallor gave way to high spots of color on her cheeks. "You!"

"Me? Yes, it's me, Miss Delaney. Is that all you can say to the man who just saved your life?"

Why did this man have the power to turn her from a pleasant human being into a haughty-sounding schoolmarm? She wasn't haughty at all, not really. What was there about Antoine Duvalier that rankled her?

Attempting to pull away from him, she felt herself actually trembling. "I'm sorry. I didn't realize it was you. Thank you, Mr. Duvalier."

He flashed a blindingly white smile. "Call me Tony."

"I can't."

"You sound almost horrified, Miss Delaney. Why not?"

"It isn't proper."

"Proper, is it?" His eyes narrowed, taking in her large, luminous eyes that shone like twin emeralds in the moonlight, the heaving, partially gold clad bosom, the dove resting contentedly between her breasts. A long curl draped enticingly across her right shoulder to wind its way over the swell of her bosom, then to end at her small waistline where Tony felt it brush gently against his hand.

He had known many women in his life and found love with none. Eventually he knew he must marry and sire an heir for his plantation, but from his own experience with women, he had found them to be conniving schemers. The ones he trusted the least were the women who appeared innocent to the untrained eye. They gave the impression that if they were thoroughly kissed, they would swoon in his arms. When he did kiss them, he always discovered what he had already suspected. They might pretend to be innocent but in reality knew what a man wanted and were prepared to give it to him.

Tony had to remind himself that this was one of those women. She might tremble in his embrace and pretend her lips didn't ache to be kissed, but Tony Duvalier knew differently. The golden dove snuggled in its lush resting place was proof of that, as was the thin silk evening gown that so clearly outlined every voluptuous curve. He had paid the bills and was well aware of the cost of the trappings she wore and what they had cost his uncle. He would take great delight in humiliating this woman with a burning kiss, then in glaring at her when she responded like the whore he believed her to be.

"I doubt very much if you're concerned about propriety, Miss Delaney."

Before Laurel was fully aware of his intention, she felt his hands tightening on her waist and bringing her closer against him. His sensual mouth swooped down upon hers in a punishing kiss. She started to pull away, to break free. She felt unable to breathe. Suddenly the pressure of his mouth lifted, and his lips claimed hers in a gentle kiss, devoid of pain.

A velvet mist swirled around them, something dark and so achingly pleasant that Laurel couldn't move, didn't want to break the enchanted spell. Never had anyone kissed her with such passion and sudden tenderness. She felt uncertain how to respond at first. A sweet burning sensation had begun in the pit of her stomach and wound through her veins like liquid heat. She felt him release her hands. Unaware of her own actions, Laurel slid her fingers along his chest, then upward to stop at the broadness of his shoulders.

A groan escaped from Tony and brought Laurel back to awareness. Her eyes flew open. She trembled at the intimacy of her action and pulled away, feeling her cheeks burn with shame in the moonlight.

Tony's ebony gaze pierced through her. He wore an odd expression on his face, almost as if her drawing away had surprised him. "I can't figure you out, Miss Delaney, but I will, know that I will." Gently he caressed her face with a warm finger before he turned from her and headed away.

Laurel stayed on deck for some minutes, shivering not from any chill but from a surging emotion of wanting unlike anything she had ever before experienced.

Chapter Four

The Saturday before Mardi Gras the *Cotton Blossom* docked by the Water Street steamboat turnaround on Bayou Cortableau. The passengers disembarked to the pungent aroma of fresh bananas, oranges, and grapes. Laurel noticed that some of the passengers, who apparently had been waiting for the boat's arrival, played poker and drank Sazeracs. On the piers were cargoes of hides, syrup, cotton, molasses, and lumber, all packed and ready for the return trip down the watery passageway to New Orleans.

Laurel, with Lavinia and Gincie beside her, waited on the pier in search of a carriage. When Tony Duvalier sauntered over to them, Laurel felt her heart beat erratically.

"May I assist you ladies in some way?" he gallantly offered and made a sweeping bow.

Lavinia laughed and dimpled prettily despite the glasses on her nose and the dowdy, brown calico gown she wore. "We're in need of a carriage to take us to—"

Laurel interrupted her, her green eyes flashing. "We can manage quite well by ourselves to get to the hotel. Thank you anyway for your offer, Mr. Duvalier."

Duvalier folded his arms across the front of his brown frock coat. "Ah, that would be the Garland Hotel. I know the place quite well. Perhaps I could escort you."

"Would you?" Lavinia gushed and batted her lashes. "We'd be most grateful."

"No!" Laurel's vehement objection startled herself as well as the others. She sent Lavinia a chastising look.

Since Duvalier had kissed her two nights ago, she hadn't seen him. Instead she had stayed in her cabin, forced to listen to Lavinia's pitiful wails about being confined. When Laurel snapped at her, telling her she should consider herself lucky that no member of the St. Julian family had the opportunity to discover her whereabouts, Lavinia had given her a peculiar glance. It was almost as if she hadn't realized until that moment that her docile cousin had a temper or a tongue. Lavinia had silently retreated to her own cabin.

Laurel had spent the rest of the her time reading, and at times recalling Duvalier's kiss and her wanton response to it. She had been only vaguely aware that Gincie was moving slowly while putting things in order and didn't notice that Gincie's usual chatter was absent.

"I didn't ask if you'd consent to a breach of propriety, Miss Delaney." Duvalier's voice intruded upon her thoughts, and she found herself blushing, not failing to miss his amused grin.

"I'm sorry," she said, aware that Lavinia's gaze darted suspiciously between herself and Duvalier. "I shouldn't have snapped at you."

"Apology accepted." His expression changed from one to amusement to seriousness. "However, your slave appears to be about to faint." Bounding forward, Tony reached for and grabbed the swooning Gincie in his arms.

"Gincie, what's wrong?" Laurel asked worriedly. Beneath Gincie's dark complexion, her skin was ashen, and her eyes were puppy dog sick.

"Just feelin' poorly. Nothin' to worry about. I'll be fine."

Laurel knew that Gincie was seldom ill, that whatever ailed her might be serious. "We must find you a doctor."

Tony whistled, still holding Gincie against him. A carriage that had been parked at the curb rolled onto the pier at the summons. Gently he placed Gincie inside. When Laurel and Lavinia joined them, he gave orders in French to the driver, and the carriage traveled down the street. Soon it was beyond the town, finally stopping at a small house. The house was in the Acadian style with a low roofline and a long porch across the front. A small but well-tendred garden ran the length and width of the house on all four sides.

Tony carried Gincie from the carriage, as she protested she was fine. He seemed not to hear her and pushed open the white picket fence with his foot before entering the yard.

"Gaston! Gaston!"

Immediately a black man, respectably dressed in a white shirt and gray trousers, ran out the front door onto the porch. "I have a patient for you," Tony said to the gray-haired man.

"Bring her in, Master Tony," the man said and motioned them into the house.

Laurel began to walk inside, but Lavinia grabbed her arm. "I'll stay in the carriage. I don't like sickness."

Once inside the house Tony introduced Laurel to

Doctor Gaston Mornay and his wife Tillie, a plump, cheerful black woman who made Gincie comfortable on a small cot.

"I'll be fine," Gincie insisted and gave a deep cough, but the doctor frowned as he checked her throat and chest. He turned to Laurel.

"Do you have a place for Miss Gincie to stay? I'm afraid she's caught a bad chill and must rest for a week or so. If not, she's welcome to stay here with me and my wife."

"That's very kind of you, Doctor. I do appreciate your kindness. I'm traveling to San Antonio, but I shall stay at the hotel until Gincie is well."

From the cot Gincie's voice came strong and clear. "No, you go on ahead without me. I'll manage fine. Besides, old Gincie ain't too happy to be goin' to San Antonio anyway."

Laurel knelt by the cot, aware of Duvalier's eyes upon her. "I can't leave you here. I won't. When you're better, you're coming with me or we'll make arrangements to send you back to New Orleans."

Gincie shook her head tiredly. "I'm too sick. You have to go and you know it. Time to make peace."

Laurel realized the truth in Gincie's words. She must see her uncle before he died. It was up to her to put things right. She felt the doctor would care for Gincie, but she wasn't ready to leave at that moment. She had to know Gincie would be all right. Lavinia was really the one who needed to reach San Antonio.

Patting Gincie's hand, she said to the woman, "I'll stop by in the morning to see how you're doing."

On the return trip to town Duvalier sat with a perplexed look on his face while Lavinia twisted a kerchief in her hands. "You treat your slave very well," he said to Laurel, sounding surprised.

"Gincie isn't my slave. She's free and has been since I freed her last year. I personally don't believe in slavery. Gincie stays with me because she loves me, and I love her."

Duvalier cocked an eyebrow. "Such liberal thinking might get you into trouble in the South."

Laurel shrugged her blue-satin-clad shoulders. "My ideas about slavery are Northern in concept, probably because I was schooled in the East, but love and kindness are universal."

He shot her another surprised but appraising glance.

Lavinia fidgeted. "Can we go any faster?" she asked. "I should like to rest."

"We'll be at the hotel soon, Miss Malone."

Laurel didn't miss the assessing glance he threw at Lavinia. Soon the carriage stopped in front of the red-brick Garland Hotel. Lavinia left the carriage in a flurry of skirts and hurried inside. Laurel started to follow but stopped and lingered on the street, still holding Duvalier's proffered hand.

"Thank you for taking Gincie to the doctor. That was kind of you. Doctor Gaston seems a competent man."

Tony nodded. "Gaston was one of my father's slaves. He took care of all the sick on Petit Coteau. My father realized Gaston had a gift for healing. He freed him and sent Gaston north to medical school. We thought Gaston would stay and practice up there, but he didn't. Instead he returned home, a free man, and practices among his own people. Do believe me when I say that he is the best physician I've ever known."

Now it was Laurel's turn to be surprised. She had assumed Tony Duvalier had no heart, but she was now learning that he did. She wasn't so sure she liked knowing this fact. It made her much more vulnerable to him.

She felt the warmth of his hand, then the pressure of his lips on her flesh.

"I will see you soon," he said confidently, almost as if he knew something she didn't. Then he entered the carriage. She watched as he drove away, her heart tripping to the beat of the carriage wheels. She would have stayed staring at the street except Lavinia came out of the hotel and glared at her.

"Come on, Laurel. I can't register without you, and I don't want to be in public for too long a time. Remember this is St. Julian territory."

"Yes, yes," Laurel said and reluctantly went inside with her cousin. She had forgotten that.

"Then I suppose I shall have to return home without you."

Laurel noticed that Lavinia sounded very relieved the next morning when she told her that she would have to travel to Texas alone. As Lavinia sipped her tea, her hands shook. Laurel decided the strain of the past weeks, of wondering if a St. Julian relative was on her trail, was finally wearing her thin. Plus the fact that she had to hide her light under a bushel so to speak. Sitting on the small sofa in the hotel room in her blue silk wrapper that clung to every curve of her body, her long red mane of hair hanging down her back and over her shoulders like a sunset, caused Laurel to decide that Lavinia should go home as quickly as possible. She definitely couldn't keep up the pretense of being a homely spinster companion much longer.

"A coach leaves at noon," Laurel told her and poured herself a cup of tea. "I'll stay on until Gincie is better. Perhaps she should return to New Orleans. I think she already misses it."

"Gincie is faithful to you," Lavinia commented somewhat jealously. "Almost like a little dog following after you all the time."

"I'll ignore that comment," Laurel said bitingly. "Now I must dress." Her deep-green wrapper made a swishing sound as she left the room.

Lavinia had just finished drinking her tea when a knock sounded on the door. She went to it and opened it a crack, rather amazed to see Tony Duvalier so early in the morning but even more aware of how handsome he looked in a cream-colored frock coat and brown trousers.

He bowed to her. "Miss Malone, I'm sorry to be here so early. I had hoped to see Miss Delaney. Is she up yet?"

"Yes, but she's dressing," Lavinia said and opened the door wider, allowing him to see her in all her early morning beauty. "She takes quite a long time to dress. May I help you?"

Her eyes filled with eagerness and drank in Tony Duvalier's handsomeness. She wondered what he wanted with Laurel anyway. She was so drab sometimes and so proper. Lavinia guessed that Duvalier was a man of fire, of passion. The two were entirely mismatched, she believed.

Tony's eyes scanned Lavinia's luscious body, taking in her delicious state of dishabille, the tousled red curls he would never have believed had been hidden in the tightly rolled chignon she had worn. Without the glasses he realized her eyes were a piercing blue, and he caught his breath. This woman couldn't be Agatha Malone, but she was the same woman who had traveled from New Orleans with the beautiful brunette who had perversely bewitched him.

"I wondered when Miss Delaney might be leaving for San Antonio."

"Oh." Lavinia's hope-filled eyes lowered, then she lifted them to Duvalier's face. "Miss Delaney will not be leaving today, but I shall."

"Is it usual for a traveling companion to go on ahead?" he asked.

"I have much to attend to there before Miss Delaney arrives. Now if that is all," Lavinia finished, a bit peeved that Duvalier's interest was only in Laurel.

"Thank you. Please tell her I shall call on her later in the day."

The door abruptly closed in his face. Tony stood outside, his gaze on the dark oak wood. He had sensed Agatha Malone's interest in him and thought this woman was a chameleon. As he walked down the stairs to the main floor, it wasn't the red-haired siren his mind dwelled on. It was a woman with dark hair and green eyes, a woman who might have caused his uncle's death, a woman who had caused his aunt much pain.

He left the hotel, wondering how someone with the face of an angel, the prim disposition of a schoolteacher, could possibly be a heartless witch. He had kissed her only a few days ago and had felt the desire within her for him.

He walked along the piers and knew he must quench this desire for that dark-haired vixen, Lavinia Delaney. Soon she would be at his mercy, and he would make her suffer for his uncle's shame. She would feel great humiliation for what she had done, for loving a married man old enough to be her father. For killing him with her passion, her greed, and giving nothing in return.

Still the actual impression he had received of Lavinia Delaney was different from the one he had built in his mind. The two images were at such odds that, as he glanced at the waters of Bayou Cortableau, he felt almost as if Lavinia were two different people. He even felt remorse for having to hurt the vulnerable side of her, the one that would capture his heart if he weren't careful.

Unwillingly his loins tightened in recall of the way her hand had slid onto his chest that night on the boat. Her lips had tasted like nectar, drugging him with their sweetness, almost causing him to forget his purpose. Her body had molded to his, and he remembered thinking how well their bodies fit together.

Tony shook himself to drive the memory from his mind. He could almost understand how his uncle had been taken in by this deceiving temptress, who appeared fragile and trusting and inexperienced. He still remembered the crimson stains on her cheeks when she drew away from him. He would have believed Lavinia was innocent if he didn't know better. The reports from the investigator had been thorough. Lavinia Delaney led a wild existence, and her father had been glad to be rid of her. Tony had discovered that she would be on the *Cotton Blossom,* and he had followed her. The woman he had met was nothing like what he expected, but beneath her pristine exterior beat the heart of a wanton woman. His uncle was proof of that.

Squaring his broad shoulders, he walked away from the bayou. He must drive the angel image from his mind and replace it with the one of the whore. When he did so, he wouldn't feel so guilty, he decided, because soon his plan would be set in motion.

Lavinia disappeared in a flurry of dark taffeta skirts and delighted blue eyes as the coach door closed behind her. She barely managed a wave to Laurel before the coach sped away, leaving Laurel standing alongside the street.

The afternoon sun disappeared behind a large gray cloud, bringing a gentle breeze in its wake. But seconds later the cloud skittered away, and once again the sun shone brightly in the heavens and warmed Laurel with its intensity.

"We could do with some rain."

She turned at the sound of Tony Duvalier's voice behind her. "It is rather warm for this time of year," Laurel remarked.

He fell into step with her and walked in the direction of the hotel. She felt terribly small alongside of his six-foot frame, and when he gallantly took her elbow to escort her across the street, she realized how strong his hand felt. In her mind flashed the picture of his face bent to hers, his mouth devouring hers in a kiss, and caused her to feel much warmer than the weather actually was. A wanton kiss. A kiss that even now made her heart beat faster just to recall.

She saw he was looking down at her with an amused glint in his eyes, and she flushed. It was almost as if the man could read her mind. "Am I so amusing to you, Mr. Duvalier?" she asked somewhat waspishly. "Or is my bonnet on crooked?"

Tony stopped walking and peered down at her. His hand snaked out and touched a wayward dark curl that rested near her cheek. "Your bonnet is fine, but I think you'd be more comfortable without one. You do have beautiful hair."

Her voice sounded breathy, almost catching in her

throat when she said, "Thank you."

A warm smile engulfed his face. "I appreciate a woman who can take an honest compliment and not pretend modesty." He took her elbow again and escorted her back to the hotel. When they were in the lobby, he turned to her. "I have plans for us tonight."

She blinked. "What plans?"

"A surprise, but I expect you to be ready at seven."

He started to turn away as if the matter were settled. She tugged at his coat sleeve. "I can't make plans for this evening. I must pack for my trip, and I have to check on Gincie."

"I was just at Doctor Mornay's. Gincie has a touch of pneumonia, and he thinks it best that she not travel right now."

"Oh, my!" Laurel placed a gloved hand to her lips. "I must see her."

"Don't worry," he consoled her. "I'll take you out there if you wish."

She nodded, and soon they were in Tony's carriage heading for the Mornay cottage. When Laurel entered the house and saw Gincie, she realized that the woman wouldn't be able to travel to San Antonio with her. Though Gincie was talkative, she coughed, a deep aching sort of cough that sounded painful.

"Don't worry over me, Miss Laurel," Gincie told her when they were alone. Gincie sat on a cot with a pillow propped behind her back. "Doctor Mornay and his wife take real good care of me. I ain't goin' too far with the way I been feelin' lately. But you got to get to San Antonio and see your uncle before the Lord takes him. You have to go."

Laurel sighed, realizing again that Gincie was right. She had to go. "I'll visit Uncle Arthur for a while, then on my way home, I'll come get you, and we'll both return to New Orleans."

Gincie's dark eyes settled on Laurel's face. "You don't have to do that, my baby girl. I know how you been lookin' forward to this visit. Just take your time. If I ain't here when you start for home, either I went on ahead to New Orleans or the good Lord took me. Either way, you don't worry over old Gincie."

Tears misted Laurel's eyes, and she hugged Gincie. "What am I going to do with you? But I know one thing, you better not go off to heaven now or in the near future. I need you to look after my children one day."

This comment brought a grin to Gincie's lips. "You figurin' on marryin' and havin' babies soon, Miss Laurel? You considerin' marryin' that handsome Mr. Duvalier?"

"No, well, hush now, Gincie. It was just a comment. Don't start making anything over it." Her face grew warm, and she fiddled with the string on her reticule.

After she had hugged Gincie again and paid Doctor Mornay for her care, Tony rode with her to the hotel. During the ride back she could barely look at him. Each time she did, she remembered Gincie's question about marrying Tony Duvalier. It was absurd even to consider such a thing. She barely knew the man, had kissed him only once, but that one kiss she wouldn't soon forget.

Soon the carriage halted at the hotel, and when he helped her out, he said again, "Seven o'clock," before she had the time to protest.

Chapter Five

Before Laurel went to her room, she spoke to the hotel manager and inquired about the availability of another coach.

"There won't be one until the day after tomorrow. Because of Mardi Gras and the riffraff who plague the roads, no coaches will leave until then. We've had some trouble with the criminal element in the prairie area, and after some people celebrate for too long . . ." His voice drifted off. "Let's just say it's better to be safe than sorry."

"I understand," she said, though she felt impatient to be on her way to San Antonio. It seemed events had conspired against her and that she was to remain in the bustling town of Washington along Bayou Cortableau longer than she had planned. She decided that she might as well enjoy herself and avail herself of Tony's company.

She had been in her room for half an hour when a knock sounded on the door. On opening it, she saw a plump woman with graying hair and a broad smile. Over her arm was what appeared to be a skirt and a blouse. Without saying a word, she pushed past Laurel and entered the room.

"Who are you?" Laurel asked indignantly. "I didn't invite you in here. If you don't leave, I'll call the manager."

The woman turned to her, the smile still on her face. "You are Mademoiselle Delaney? Oui?"

Laurel nodded. The woman nodded.

"I am in the right place. Monsieur Duvalier sent me to dress you for the masquerade dance tonight."

Laurel looked at her uncomprehendingly. "Dance?"

"You know," the woman said and hummed a few notes of music, moving her suprisingly tiny feet in time to the rhythm. "A dance, mademoiselle, in honor of Mardi Gras."

Laurel now recalled Tony's mentioning something about a surprise, but she was caught off guard when the woman, who identified herself only as Lulubelle, ordered up a bath for Laurel. Laurel glanced hesitantly at the skimpy-appearing garments that the woman laid on the bed. Her parents had gone to a number of elaborate carnival balls, and she could recall the beautiful gowns her mother had worn, the feeling of heady excitement that had pervaded the house as her parents came down the stairs in their formal regalia, and how awestruck she had been. But she had never attended any dances, and certainly not in costume. In fact, if Lavinia hadn't arrived with trouble in tow and if Uncle Arthur hadn't become ill, Laurel knew that she would have been on the arm of Philbert Anderson this very night at an elegant but stuffy affair.

The thought of Philbert with his long, thin fingers resembling the legs of a crab caused her to giggle. If she had to choose between Tony and Philbert as escorts, she would choose Tony any day.

When Laurel had finished her bath and was attired in her costume, she looked at herself in the cheval glass and wasn't certain she should be seen in public. The costume was fashioned in the gypsy style, and Laurel thought she resembled a woman of loose morals. The skirt fell to just above her ankles in a swirl of lavender-and-gold-printed silk, the hem edged with golden beads, and a split up the side revealed a shapely thigh. Her breasts, usually well concealed, now strained against the thin, cream-colored peasant top and swelled high above the white lace edging of the low neckline. She had never worn such an outfit before and felt indecent.

Lulubelle didn't catch the shocked look on Laurel's face as she made clucking sounds of approval and clapped her hands in delight. She then brushed Laurel's waist-length hair and pulled up the right side and fastened it with a pink rose. Next she clipped large golden loops to Laurel's ears.

"*Magnifique!*" Lulubelle exclaimed and stood back to view her handiwork. "Monsieur Duvalier will be so pleased."

"Are you certain he chose this outfit for me?"

"*Oui*, mademoiselle. That Tony has an eye for pretty ladies, and you are the prettiest of them all."

"Monsieur Duvalier has a great many lady friends?" Laurel asked, turning from the mirror.

"Of course. He is a Duvalier, and like his father and grandfather, he is the heartbreaker." Lulubelle smiled impishly. "I was Tony's nurse, and I can tell you that he was a scamp even as a child and twisted poor Lulubelle around his finger."

Laurel wasn't certain why this news about Tony's love for the ladies distressed her. She wondered why he had picked such a daring costume for her.

"I can't wear this," Laurel told the woman. "It

isn't decent."

"Pooh, mademoiselle! A lady is a lady, no matter her clothes. A whore will always be a whore even dressed in the finest silks. I have a feeling that you are hesitant about enjoying life. Am I not right?"

Laurel nodded, fastening her eye on her reflection again.

"Then it is time you lived a bit. Here. Wear this and no one shall recognize you." Lulubelle took a small black mask from a bag that rested on her ample hip. She turned Laurel to her and positioned it on Laurel's face, then tied the strings at the back of Laurel's head. "Voilà, look in the mirror again."

Laurel swung around to see her reflection. The woman in the mirror couldn't be herself. She appeared so mysterious, so unlike the proper young woman she really was. Seeing herself like this caused a tiny, half-wicked smile to form on Laurel's mouth. The feeling that had originally possessed her to accompany Lavinia to Texas rose once again within her. A recklessness filled her, a strange wild yearning to taste life, to cast aside propriety. Dare she risk living for the moment?

She dared.

"What about shoes?" she asked Lulubelle.

The woman shrugged. "Wear them or not, but the costume looks better without the shoes. No true gypsy woman owns a pair of shoes, mademoiselle."

"Then I won't either," Laurel laughed and twirled around the room, loving the swishing movement of the skirt against her bare legs. She stopped at the sound of a knock on the door.

"Monsieur Duvalier," Lulubelle said knowingly and winked.

Suddenly Laurel's palms perspired. What would Tony think of her? she wondered. But then, he had chosen this gypsy costume, and she was determined to enjoy herself tonight. For once in her life she would be reckless and throw caution to the four winds.

Lulubelle opened the door. "The mademoiselle is ready," she said to Tony.

Tony was dressed as a pirate of the high seas in a red shirt, dark pants and boots, and a gold sash tied around his waist. A black patch covered one eye. Lulubelle winked and laughed huskily as she left the room.

Tony entered and then faltered at the sight of Laurel. He hadn't expected the gypsy costume to mold against her curves so distractingly or the peasant blouse to reveal her lush breasts so temptingly. He suddenly ached to touch the rosy tips of her nipples that strained against the thin material. Most distracting of all was the slit up the side of the skirt, revealing an ivory thigh that caused his breath to catch in his throat as he imagined the satiny feeling of her flesh as his fingers ran the length of her leg, and stopped at the apex between her thighs.

"Is something wrong?"

Laurel's voice brought Tony out of his reverie. "I was thinking you look quite different."

"I know," she admitted and flitted around the room. "Thank you so much for the costume. I love it!"

A wry smile played around his mouth. He realized he had chosen the correct costume for Lavinia Delaney. Finally after all the ladylike pretense, her true colors were starting to show. He presented her with his arm.

"Shall we go?"

Laurel caught a slight hardness to his voice. Moments before, he had appeared stunned, almost paralyzed at the sight of her. She could have sworn she had seen a flame within his eyes for her, but she must have been mistaken, she told herself. Perhaps he wasn't pleased with how she looked. Suddenly she didn't care as the heady feeling of daring renewed itself.

Laurel laughed up into his face and took his red-silk-covered arm.

"Indeed, I am ready to go, sir!"

Tony turned his head. He had been contemplating the velvet black night through the window of the carriage, and now his gaze rested on the woman who sat across from him. Her features were obliterated in the darkness, but he didn't need to see her to know she was beautiful, breathtakingly wanton in her gypsy costume. He silently cursed himself for having chosen such a revealing creation, thinking that she would somehow understand the implication behind his choice. Once again this woman had caught him off guard. Instead of a woman shamed and humiliated, she absolutely glowed with sensuality, an excitement that seemed to reach out and touch him in the carriage.

Even now he felt himself harden to think of her voluptuous beauty, to hear the rhythmic cadence of her breathing. Somehow, though he wasn't certain when, this wanton creature had woven a spell over him, the same spell she had apparently cast upon his poor uncle. The thought of Auguste St. Julian and the vengeance Tony intended to wreak upon Lavinia Delaney caused his fists to curl into balls. Beautiful she might be, but she was not the innocent she pretended to be. He wouldn't allow her beauty and his desire to sway him from his plan.

* * *

Laurel heard his sharp voice that cut knifelike across the short distance between them. "We're heading for my home, Petit Coteau."

"Lulubelle told me there is to be a dance there. You've never mentioned your family or your plantation very much. Are you involved in cotton growing?"

"I doubt very much if you'd be interested, but I do grow some cotton. However, my prime interest is cattle."

She caught the unmistakable hint of scorn in his voice. He sounded almost patronizing, as if she wouldn't know anything about plantations or cotton growing. Why, if he only knew her father had owned one of the most lucrative plantations along the river. Laurel had sold it last year, and she could tell him a thing or two about cotton growing, but she kept quiet, not wanting to get into an unpleasant discussion that was sure to follow.

She expected him to speak further, but he didn't. Instead, in a surly mood, he retreated into a stony and puzzling silence. Again, Laurel wondered if he was displeased with her or the costume. Had she done anything to cause him to be barely civil to her?

Finally, after a ride unbroken by further speech, they swung off Grand Prairie Road onto a drive that led to a house blazing with lights. From Laurel's vantage point, she could see many carriages parked in front of the large two-storied structure with six large columns and two dormered windows on the third floor. White balustrades trimmed in green enclosed the upper and lower galleries.

Inside the house was a large front hallway with a curved stairway that wound up to the third floor.

From the ceiling hung a huge chandelier, its crystal teardrops sparkling and reflecting a myriad of prismatic colors on the walls. Tony led her into a double parlor where guests had already assembled. Ornate chandeliers twinkled in the parlor, also, in direct contrast to the iron reproduction of the Duvalier cattle brand above the fireplace.

When Laurel caught sight of herself in an exquisitely carved Venetian mirror, she nearly cringed. The other women guests were attired in silks and satins, some with glittering masks over their faces, but none of the costumes were as simple or revealing as her own. She even noticed a woman dressed as Marie Antoinette, another as Elizabeth I . . . the sort of costumes she would have chosen. Suddenly she wondered if Tony Duvalier had wanted to make her appear foolish in front of his guests.

She swung around and faced him, her hair falling across her creamy shoulders. "Is the reason you chose this costume, the reason you brought me here, to make me look obviously out of place?"

Tony arched a dark brow and shot her a penetrating look. "Do you feel that way?"

Laurel guessed that for some reason unknown to her he might be testing her. However, she wouldn't allow herself to be used as an amusement for his warped sense of humor. She couldn't fathom this man. Sometimes he was so kind and gentle, other times she didn't know what to think about him. Like now when his handsome face was scowling at her in disapproval, a disapproval she didn't feel she had earned.

Rising to her full height of five feet and three inches, she straightened her shoulders and stared him down. "I feel confident, Mr. Duvalier. I'm not quite certain what you're up to, but understand, sir, that nothing you do can destroy the good time I expect to have tonight. I have decided to enjoy myself."

And before his amazed eyes she did just that. Within seconds of walking proudly away from him, she was surrounded by men who begged her for a dance, much to the vexation of the other women in the room. A lively French tune played by two fiddlers drifted through the parlors, and before they ceased playing to indulge in some wine, Laurel had danced with every costumed duke, king, and clown. But not with the tanned frowning pirate who watched her from across the room.

"You are beautiful, mademoiselle," the young man dressed as a clown told her. He said his name was Jean DuLac. "Tell me your name, please. Remove your mask so that I may gaze upon your most lovely face."

Laurel, though not used to receiving attention from men, knew she had nothing to fear from DuLac or any of the other men in the room. All of them seemed to be neighbors and friends of Duvalier's, and since she had arrived with Tony, she received the impression that no one would make an untoward comment to her, almost as if they respected and feared him. Throughout the evening she had noticed her partners casting wary glances in Tony's direction, and DuLac unwittingly gave her the answer.

"Perhaps Tony wishes to keep your identity secret and wants you all to himself."

"Is that what you think?" Laurel asked and watched as the woman dressed as Marie Antoinette familiarly hung on Tony's arm.

"Oui, but you see I thought he was to wed—"

"What?" Laurel's head snapped back to DuLac's

face.

The man placed a long, thin hand to his mouth, dismay on his face. "Pardon, mademoiselle, I said nothing."

"Tell me."

Apparently DuLac noticed the fire emanating from Laurel's eyes, framed by the black mask, and knew it would do no good to lie. "The lady with him is Simone Lancier. It is expected they will marry as soon as her father recovers from an illness."

Suddenly the room felt stifling to Laurel. She had to get away from these people and the music, which was starting up again. Until she learned about Tony and this Simone woman, she had enjoyed herself and had basked in the unaccustomed male attention. Now, she felt a strange sensation like a hand squeezing her heart. Inwardly, she cursed herself for being a fool to get involved with Duvalier in the first place. The man was a womanizer, but that was no reason to single her out on the boat, to kiss her the way he had, and now to choose a revealing costume he had known would humiliate her in front of his friends.

Why was he doing this to her?

"I should like some air," she murmured to Jean DuLac.

"Certainly." As he took her arm and escorted her outside onto the gallery, Laurel was aware that Tony watched her leave with Jean and saw Simone plant a loving kiss on Tony's lips.

Outside, the sound of locusts crying for rain filled the air. A rush of wind rustled the leaves of the large oak trees nearby, and a jagged streak of lightning scorched the sky, followed by the inevitable rumble of thunder.

"Ah, I think we shall get some rain," Jean noted.

"Perhaps there will be a change in the weather, too. I hope so since it has been very warm lately."

Laurel barely heard him, her mind not on the weather. Everything could have been so wonderful tonight, she thought, if only Tony hadn't been so distant suddenly. If only he wasn't getting married. But what difference did that make? she asked herself. She had no hold on him and would never see him again after she departed for San Antonio in a day's time. Sometimes Tony was so insufferable she could barely tolerate him. Unable to decipher his motive for wanting to embarrass her with the costume, Laurel willed herself to stop dwelling on Tony.

She removed her mask as an unbidden tear slid down her cheek. Quickly she wiped it away, convincing herself she was more angry than hurt at Duvalier's strange behavior. After all, he didn't know her, and most certainly she didn't want to know anything more about him. So why should she be upset over the news that he and Simone Lancier were to be married?"

"Here, mademoiselle." Jean handed her a kerchief. He placed an arm around her shoulders. "I think Tony has hurt you."

"No. I'm worried over my uncle who hasn't been well. I must see him soon before it's too late."

Jean shot her a pitying look, but he apparently didn't believe her sadness was entirely over her uncle's health. His embrace grew tighter, and he smiled in a brotherly fashion. "A lady as beautiful as yourself should smile."

The sound of booted feet scraping on the wooden gallery drew their attention. Tony loomed over them like a dark specter. He had removed his patch, and now a black fury caused his eyes to appear blacker than usual. "Would you please leave us alone,

Jean?"

Jean hesitated, but Laurel smiled at him, assuring him she would be all right. After Jean made a reluctant departure, Tony moved in front of her, blocking her view of the inside parlor where people danced to the fiddlers' music.

"You should congratulate yourself," Tony told her. "My cousin Jean isn't easily swayed by women."

"What do you mean?"

"Let's just say he's drawn to young men rather than young ladies."

"Oh," she said, immediately comprehending. "I still think he is very nice."

"Yes, he is, but then he's the only man in the room I'd have allowed to escort you outside. If any other man had taken it into his head to bring you out here, I might be tempted to call him out. Every man in the room is half in love with you."

"I can take care of myself," she said, not quite believing what Tony said about the men or the duel. Her gaze turned upward to his, wondering what game he was playing with her.

Laurel was inexperienced with men, but an awakening of her own sexuality had begun this night, a sense of power. Every man but Tony had complimented her on her beauty, had secretly desired her. She had acted the coquette, the flirt, to rile him and get even with him for bringing her here to humiliate her.

For some reason he wanted to believe the worst of her and see her in a bad light. She decided she could give as good as she got. Duvalier had dressed her as a creature with no morals, flaunted her before his friends, but she had turned his game to her own advantage by unwittingly making him jealous. And he was jealous. Why he should be, she didn't know.

After all, he was going to marry someone else. Yet she wouldn't leave for San Antonio until she had gotten some revenge on Tony Duvalier. The perfect way to do that, she realized, was to act the role he had written for her.

Through long, sooty lashes, Laurel fastened her gaze on Tony's full, sensual lips. "Are you half in love with me, too?"

Black eyes measured her for a moment before he said, "You'd like that, wouldn't you?"

She shrugged a bare shoulder. Lifting her hand, Laurel ran her fingertips over the deep vee of his red shirt; then slowly, so slowly that she felt Tony catch his breath, her nails stroked the soft down of hair on his chest. She knew her actions were brazen, but dressed in the gypsy costume, she no longer felt herself to be the proper and staid Laurel Delaney, the woman who regally entered a room with her head held high. A shiver at her own daring coursed through her. However, she wouldn't stop and took perverted delight in knowing that this time she was the one affecting Tony Duvalier.

"I think I'd be immensely pleased if you were in love with me, but I can have any man I want. I left a pack of drooling men in the drawing room. Why aren't you drooling?"

Brazenly, almost as if she were someone else, her mouth lowered to his chest, and she planted a warm, moist kiss on the spot where her fingertip had just been.

As Tony sucked in his breath, she felt the rapid beating of his heart against his rib cage. His skin tasted slightly salty and was hard and smooth beneath her lips. Delighting in Tony's rapid breathing, she trailed tiny kisses up the fur-planed expanse to the hollow of his throat.

A groan of intense pleasure mingled with a sound of pain escaped from Tony. In one motion he pulled her to him, trapping her with an arm around her waist, and with the other hand he grabbed a handful of silky tresses so she would be forced to gaze upward at him.

"I'm not like the others here," he ground out. "I'm not so easily taken in by a beautiful face, a voluptuous body. But I know what you are, though you pretend to be virginal and innocent." He laughed hoarsely. "In fact, I'd probably have let you alone and never touched you again. However, my gypsy temptress, I am only a man, and you've ignited the spark."

His mouth came down upon hers in a searing kiss that took her breath from her. The world spun crazily. Laurel realized she had gone too far with this man. What did she know about men? Nothing. Not even enough not to tempt one, especially not this one. She broke away from his mouth's possession, knowing she had to stop the inevitable.

"Please, please," she croaked when he moved his head to the valley of her breasts and buried his tongue within the hollow. "Stop. I was playing a game, Tony. I'm not what you think."

"You're everything I thought you'd be and more," he said in a muffled voice. "I intend to quench my desire for you. I have to." He scooped her up into his arms just as lightning streaked the night sky.

Laurel struggled to escape. "Put me down, Tony. I apologize."

His voice sounded ragged and harsh when he spoke. "Maybe this will teach you not to play games."

He carried her from the gallery into a dark grove of oak trees that blotted out the sky and lowered her onto the soft grass. Realizing that her skirt had ridden up to her upper thighs, she attempted to pull it down and sit up, but Tony held her fast.

When another streak of lightning flashed, she saw his face, the agony and desire in his eyes, as if he warred within himself. She began to plead again but stopped when he moved and his body covered the length of hers. His hardness rested against the spot between her legs, and a searing heat spread through her body and lodged in that area. Involuntarily she strained against him, aching for something only he could fulfill.

Tony laughed bitterly. "You're not fooling me, you never did. I knew from the moment I met you that you'd belong to me, that I'd do the dishonorable thing by making love to you. You do want me, don't you?"

He nipped at her lips, his hands moving over the material of her blouse, then sliding inside to cup a warm, full breast. His tongue drifted downward to the nipple, which he gently sucked.

Hot lava flowed through Laurel. Never in her life had she felt such intense pleasure, an insane longing to forget propriety, to be a woman at last and wrap her legs in wanton abandon around Tony as he filled her with his love. The thunder overhead was lost in the beating of her heart as Tony's hand moved over her rib cage, then downward to the velvety smoothness of her naked thigh.

Her arms wound around his neck, and she whispered his name in a husky voice that she barely identified as her own. Pulling him closer, she trailed fiery fingers over the broadness of his back and then kneaded the warm, hard flesh of his chest.

"I've never desired a woman as much as you," he said in a tortured voice. "I can't resist you. God help me, I can't!"

His mouth ground down upon hers. Laurel felt his tongue collide with hers, swirling and tasting the sweetness of her mouth. Her breath quickened. Exquisite and pleasurable sensations shot through her body, and not even the piercing white lightning that flashed hotly above them or the rumble of the thunder disturbed her.

"Love me, Tony. Love me, love me," she whispered in a passion-laced voice.

"Oh, God forgive me!" he cried and started to pull off his pants. Suddenly the sound of alarmed voices and bright torches filled the night.

"Monsieur Tony! Monsieur Tony!"

Tony cursed under his breath. "That's Rabelais, my foreman. What can he want now of all times?" He began to stand, but instead he tenderly kissed her lips again. "Wait for me, my temptress," he whispered before leaving her.

Laurel lay upon the wet grass, feeling a slight mist settle upon her flesh. Her pulse beat hard. It was only when she heard the cries of "Lightning has struck the barn! Get the buckets!" that her senses returned. Standing up, she arranged her clothing and smoothed down her touseled locks and then walked toward the sound. She found that the barn was bathed in a red-orange glow. The male guests were lined up from a well to the fire and were passing heavy wooden buckets of water to Tony at the front of the line. The taut muscles of Tony's back strained with the movement each time he emptied one onto the flames.

"Isn't this exciting?" a guest dressed as Aphrodite whispered to no one in particular.

"Clarice, you must lead a boring life to enjoy such a spectacle," the husky voice of Simone Lancier commented. "Tony and I are never bored, if you understand my meaning." Simone and the woman giggled; but Simone's flashing blue eyes were directed in Laurel's direction.

Because the fire had been discovered immediately, the barn and the horses housed inside were saved. The men stopped passing the buckets. A hissing sound and the odor of burning wood permeated the air. A perspiring Jean DuLac in his soot-covered, green-and-red clown costume saw Laurel. He wiped his brow with a kerchief. "That Tony is a lucky devil, *chérie,* with life and the ladies." He winked and went inside the house.

Laurel lost sight of Tony and Simone as the guests began milling about to inspect the damage. Then she saw them at a distance, standing beside the charred ruins, arm in arm.

Laurel's face burned with humiliation, anger, and pain. If not for the fire, Tony would have used her like the worst trollop. To think she had begged the man to make love to her, had writhed beneath him on the grass like a whore. Her hands flew to her face, unsure of what she had been thinking to allow such liberties. Yet she couldn't deny that her traitorous body had desired him. Tears flooded her eyes.

Then Tony turned in her direction and made a movement to rush after her, but she spun around and ran down the gravel driveway.

"Where are you going?" Simone clutched at his shirt sleeve.

Tony didn't relish possessive women and shrugged off her hold. "Wherever I choose."

"We're going to be married, Tony. I suggest you remember that."

He cocked an eyebrow, his face smeared with soot. "I haven't asked you, Simone. You've just assumed we would." Bounding away, he left Simone in a snit.

By the time he reached the front of the house, he saw the carriage that he and Laurel had arrived in earlier speeding down the drive. So, he thought wryly with a degree of anger at himself for falling prey to her charms, the little tease was running away again just as she had done the day of Auguste's death. Well, she wouldn't get away this time. He would be damned if she led him a merry chase as she had done with his uncle. He vowed that Lavinia Delaney would not be the death of him. However, he couldn't help but think, with a degree of contempt for himself, about what would have happened if the fire hadn't started. Would she now have been in his bed?

He attempted unsuccessfully to shrug the thought away. His loins tightened just to imagine her hair spread fanlike across his pillow, the feel of the soft ivory body writhing in ecstasy beneath his own, the sweet taste of her strawberry lips. "God!" he moaned aloud and broke the spell by turning and heading for the porch at the back of the house. He couldn't let the woman do this to him, wouldn't allow himself to fall further under her spell. He had to convince himself that she was like any other woman and could easily be replaced. So many women had vied for his kisses, had begged for his touch over the years, that Tony could no longer remember their faces or the bodies that had attracted him. But this woman was different. This woman was dangerous. He had started to feel something for her, a sweet but burning desire he had never known, a melting sensation when he first kissed her. She mustn't get to him, he decided. She wouldn't pull *him* into her enchanted web.

Only servants remained outside now to clean up

the charred remains of the fire. From inside the main house, the laughter and singing of his guests drifted through the windows and lingered on the night air, disturbed only by the rumble of thunder. He went to his room and changed into a black silk shirt. Pouring himself a glass of Courvoisier, Napoleon's brandy, he fortified himself for what was to come.

When he mounted his horse, raindrops splattered across the silken material of his shirt, leaving wet splotches on his broad back. Almost as an afterthought before he kicked at the horse, he withdrew a black hood from his pants pocket, crumpling the cotton material in his large hand.

Suddenly Jean DuLac appeared on the porch and hailed Tony as he rode swiftly past. "Where are you going? Where is the pretty gypsy girl?" he cried.

Tony barely glanced at him, steadfast purpose shining in his black eyes. Spurring the stallion, he galloped down the drive onto the road that led through the prairie area back to Washington. Rain pelted him, but he only rode harder, faster. Then through the rivulets of rain blinding his eyes, he noticed the wavering flickers of light from the carriage lanterns.

His prey was up ahead.

Nimbly he pulled the hood over his head, enclosing his stony features. Soon his revenge upon the woman he believed to be Lavinia would commence in earnest. But not until he had held her in his arms, branded every inch of her ivory flesh with hot kisses, and felt waves of ecstasy wash over her when he entered her writhing body would his vengeance be fulfilled. Only when she had surrendered her body to a nameless, faceless man would she realize what a harlot he thought her to be, know the pain she had caused him by killing his uncle with her greedy passion.

Soon, very soon, his uncle would be avenged.

Spurring his horse anew, he broke into a wild gallop and followed the midnight flame.

Chapter Six

Within the interior of the leather-upholstered coach, Laurel reclined against the seat. She folded her arms across her breasts in a protective gesture and hurriedly wiped away a tear that threatened to fall from one of her emerald eyes. She willed herself not to cry. Crying never accomplished anything. She had cried countless tears for herself and her parents when she was away at school. The tears had never brought back her parents but gave her a red nose, which her friend, Anne, had gently told her made her resemble a circus clown.

"Well, I won't look like a carnival clown because of Tony Duvalier," she groused aloud. But for all her low-voiced mutterings and the staunch way Laurel bit down upon her lower lip to keep the tears at bay, she felt foolish. Duvalier had ensnared her in a sensuous trap, one in which she had willingly participated. Unable to rid herself of the image of Tony with Simone Lancier, she dimly realized she shouldn't have run away. Their embrace meant nothing to her. She could be as cavalier as Tony about the drugging kisses he had rained upon her face, the way his warm hands had boldly cupped her breasts and snaked up the length of her inner thighs to touch her until she was so besotted that she had wrapped her legs around his back and begged to be taken like the worst whore.

She should have proved to him that women could enjoy passion as well as any man.

But the blood rushed to her face to recall what had nearly happened between them, and the memory of it, the way her flesh still tingled from his touch, caused Laurel to place her hands on her heated cheeks. She couldn't be nonchalent about lovemaking. It wasn't in her nature to take such an intimate act lightly. Duvalier had intended to make love to her, and afterward he would have left her to seek the arms of Simone Lancier, his fiancée.

"The conceited bastard won't have a chance to humiliate me again," she spoke aloud and wished Tony's driver would hurry the coach along. The sooner she returned to her room at the hotel and packed her bags for her journey to San Antonio, the better off she would be, she decided. She would forget Tony Duvalier and her wanton response to him. Yet not to remember his dark passion-laced eyes, the sensual stroking of his strong hands on her flesh, would be almost impossible. Even now her traitorous body tingled from the experience.

"Forget him!" The vehemence of her own words startled her, and sanity returned.

Rain pounded heavily upon the roof of the vehicle. Lightning illuminated the passing countryside, allowing Laurel to see the wind-whipped trees that swayed on each side before blackness enveloped them.

Would she never reach the town? Inwardly she cursed Tony Duvalier for luring her to his Mardi Gras dance, for choosing her revealing costume, and then using it against her. His motive still bewildered her, and she cursed herself all the more for her own stupidity in believing she even possesed a fatal charm. She laughed aloud at her own folly. Fatal charm, indeed. Her charms had fueled Tony's ardor to such a degree that he would have made love to her on the lawn if the fire hadn't started—and she would have let him. Thank the fates for the bolt of lightning that struck the barn. She couldn't imagine anything worse than becoming another one of Duvalier's easy conquests. And Laurel had no doubt that she would have been one.

Wild winds and pounding rain besieged the coach, rocking it unsteadily. Laurel held tightly to the edge of her seat, encased in utter darkness, except for the faint flicker of the outside carriage lanterns that sputtered and then were extinguished completely. Still the horses raced onward.

The coach wheels rolled slickly along Grand Prairie Road toward town. From far off she heard what she assumed to be a peal of thunder, but shortly she realized it was the steady beat of a horse's hoofs behind the coach.

"Halt!"

A man's voice penetrated the darkness, followed by the sound of a pistol shot. The coach jerked to a sudden and jolting stop.

Giving a small cry, Laurel nearly slipped from her seat. She braced herself against the door, and in the brief instant when a flash of lightning emblazoned the night sky, she saw him, attired all in black with an equally dark hood over his head, on an ebony stallion. Both were silhouetted against the suddenly incandescent night, and in that quick flash of light the gleaming pistol was also outlined.

Above the din of the rain she heard him shout to

the driver not to move, to remain seated. The pulse in Laurel's throat throbbed an irregular beat, and she could barely swallow. Did this man intend to rob them? She vaguely remembered the hotel clerk informing her that at Mardi Gras time ruffians sometimes traveled the roads. Just her luck, she thought through a haze of fear and dread, to be caught in such a situation. And all because of Tony Duvalier, the arrogant bastard. One more reason to hate him.

Should she run or put up a fight? The man had turned his horse toward the coach. For a brief instant she froze, poised on the brink of indecision. Before she had time to react, the door was abruptly thrown open. A long, black-clad arm reached into the interior and plucked her from the coach as if she were a rose in a garden.

Her fear prevented her from screaming. In fact she seemed to have no voice at all as the man positioned her in front of him on his horse and coiled his arms, ropelike, around her waist. Tony's driver sat immobile, his face obliterated in the darkness. When she felt the man behind her spur the stallion, she knew she had to do something to stop him.

"Let me go!" she cried and attempted to break free, to somehow throw herself from the horse and run anywhere, anywhere away from this man who held her so tightly against him, so close against his powerful chest that she could feel the beating of his heart against her back. But his hold wouldn't be loosened, and her entreaty had no effect upon him.

After flailing against him, she realized her struggles were for nothing. There was no way she could escape from him, and she doubted he was even listening to her pleas for release. She had to keep all her strength and wits about her. However, seconds later, when he veered onto a side road that seemed to appear from nowhere and rushed headlong into a densely forested area, she wondered if she would ever find her way out of this even if he did release her unharmed.

Through the rain-sodden night they rode. Rivulets of water streamed freely down Laurel's face, nearly blinding her. Her hair was plastered to her head, as were her clothes against her body. But she realized these discomforts were nothing to the tortures this man probably planned for her. Yet she must quell her fear and concentrate if she hoped to escape alive and tell the authorities.

Quieting down and being forced to lean unwillingly against her kidnapper's hard chest, a musky male scent assailed her nostrils. She found his scent disturbing, strangely familiar, but it was the slight smell of alcohol upon his breath that made the most impression upon her. Was it brandy? A not unpleasant whiff stirred past her nose, and she recognized it as Napoleon's brandy, a liquor her father had drunk many times. Such an expensive drink seemed somehow out of character with the highwayman behind her. Another, more disturbing scent made an impression upon her. There was a lingering trace of woodsmoke about him.

A shiver of fear coursed through her again when she felt the horse change direction. No longer were they on the side road. Now they were gingerly making their way through an area filled with palmetto. The bayou? She practically choked on her fear. She would never survive here. Or did this man intend her to survive at all?

The rain had slackened. Low overhanging vines became visible when a sliver of a moon appeared from behind a cloud. Moss-draped trees dripped steady drops of water onto the ground. From far off the growl of a panther cut through the night, followed by the cry of its victim. Laurel compared herself to the hapless creature and the man behind her to the panther. She was the prey who had just been snared by the hunter.

The thought occurred to her that she might bargain for her freedom. He must be desperate to have kidnapped her. Perhaps money was what he wanted, and she had plenty of that. She must swallow her fear and speak to him, to make him believe she wasn't at his mercy, although she knew very well that she was. As much as she had wanted to flee Duvalier earlier, she now wished she had never foolishly run away. At least, she would have been safe at Petit Coteau. She felt no security in this man's arms.

Turning her face slightly to the right, she glanced up at him, but was unable to discern anything behind the slits in his hood. However, she felt his gaze upon her and wondered if he had been watching her for a long time to gauge her reaction.

"Kidnapping me will avail you nothing. I haven't any money on me." Damn! Did her voice sound as terrified to him as it did to her? She must hide her fear. "But if you will take me to my hotel, I'll get you some." There. That sounded better, more confident he would have a change of heart and release her. "Take me back, and I'll give you whatever you want."

Laurel winced when a bitter laugh escaped him, his scorn evident in its rich timbre. His wet hand snaked below the neckline of her blouse and gently massaged a pouting nipple. Did she imagine that his eyes blazed with a fire behind his hood?

"I want no money," he whispered raspily. "The treasure I seek is within my arms."

His meaning was clear. He intended to ravish her.

For some unaccountable reason, he wanted her, not money.

A warm hand still caressed her breast, swirling the nipple between his fingers and triggering a melting sensation within her not unlike that which she had experienced in Duvalier's arms earlier. What was wrong with her? she asked herself. Was she a wanton, eager for any man who touched her?

"Don't do that," she entreated.

"What?" he whispered against her ear.

"Touch me like that!"

"I think you like my hands upon you, and I don't intend to stop."

His voice was so husky and low she barely heard him, but his intentions were obvious. This dark-clad stranger was going to have his way with her, and all her protests would avail her nothing. He had her at his mercy in this wild and untamed setting. True to his word, his hand remained in her blouse, gently rubbing the throbbing peak of one breast before snaking over and finding the other.

The feel of his hand upon her, the sensations his touch produced, weren't unpleasant to Laurel. She knew she should fend him off somehow, but she was trapped within his grasp. From somewhere deep inside her throat, she emitted a low moan of pleasure.

"Wanton witch," he intoned in her ear.

"Please leave me alone. Take me back to the main road."

She hadn't intended to plead like this, but she understood that he wasn't going to release her until he was finished with her—if he did intend to free her. The thought that he might kill her entered her head for the first time, and she visibly trembled. She wasn't ready to die yet. God, she had barely started to live.

"You're shivering," the man noted in his raspy voice, and his arms tightened around her like a protective covering when he withdrew his hand from her bodice. A tiny surge of hope rose in Laurel at the thought that he felt remorse for what he was doing to her, and this bit of physical comfort was his way of making amends, that he might have a change of heart and release her. But her hopes were dashed when he said, "I don't want you to fall ill on me. That would take all the enjoyment out of my plans for you."

"I hope you catch your death, you filthy beast!"

Where the courage to utter such words came from, Laurel didn't know. When she felt him stiffen behind her, she expected he would strike her. Instead he laughed again and slid a hand along the swelling curves of her breasts, almost as a perverse reminder that she was his captive and he had the right to intimately touch her.

"Believe me, my sharp-tongued temptress, I don't intend to die and deny myself your luscious body. Until I decide your fate, you belong to me."

"Have you no conscience?" she asked, not willing to resign herself to the fate he had decreed for her.

His hand moved down to her waist, then lower until his fingers gently grazed the soft flesh of her inner thigh. "Not where you're concerned."

"I'll never give in to your lust."

"Yes, you will, my delightful beauty. Indeed, you will beg me to love you. Admit to yourself that you're more than the smallest bit excited by this kidnapping, by my hands stroking your satiny flesh. Before this night is finished, you'll be on your hands and knees to me."

"Never!"

Her objection vibrated through the moss-laden

trees and across the water, which rippled with slithering and swimming creatures. He said nothing else, and Laurel knew any further protests would go unheeded. Somehow, she resolutely decided, she would escape.

The horse had traveled along a shore path the entire distance and now crossed a shallow body of water to the opposite shoreline. This side of the bayou wasn't as dense with trees and undergrowth, and soon the dark silhouette of a small cabin came into view. Supported above the ground by four rough-hewn logs, the cabin rested half over the water and half over the shore. The horse approached the shore side and stopped to graze on the furling edge of a fern.

The black-clad man jumped down and unceremoniously hauled Laurel from the horse. Dragging her protesting form, he pulled her up the wooden steps onto a rickety porch. Then, pushing back the thick iron latch from its sheath on the cabin door, he propelled her into the inky-black room.

She spun around from the force. When her head stopped spinning, she attempted to focus her gaze. At the moment she could see little, only a vague outline of a table and chair against the wall and a cot near the window. But when the moon peeped through the clouds, she saw very clearly that the window was barred. What sort of place was this makeshift prison?

"You can't make me stay here!" she declared.

"You'll do whatever I decree," he stated with such deadly calm that she shrank away from his voice in the darkness.

"Someone will find me. I was a guest tonight at Petit Coteau, and the carriage you abducted me from belongs to Tony Duvalier. His driver will tell him about you, and the authorities will be called in. You'll never get away with this."

His raspy tone held a hint of a smile. "I already have. Granted, Duvalier may search for you, but he won't find you. You're in the bayou, and access to the road is long and arduous. But we're wasting time with such foolish talk. I brought you here for a purpose. Take off your clothes."

Laurel backed away. Even in the room's darkness she felt his eyes upon her, almost imagined she could see them flare like twin flames. She sensed his approach toward her; then his hands, heavy upon her arms, lifted her up as if she weighed nothing and threw her on the cot. Her mind reeled with the realization that he was going to rape her and rape her now. She wouldn't be able to plan an escape. She must act.

Lifting her legs, she kicked out, not certain that her knee had reached its mark until she heard him groan. Pushing herself off the cot, she gained a moment to run across the room toward the door, eager to be outside, not caring that the bayou was filled with harmful creatures. Those creatures would do her less harm than this man, and at the moment she wanted to get out of the cabin and find the horse. She would flee the hooded stranger and somehow find her way to the road.

But that was not to be. No sooner had Laurel reached the door than it was roughly pushed shut with a thud, and once again she was thrashing against the man's chest, attempting to break the grip of his steel-vise arms around her.

"No! I won't let you do this to me. I'll kill you first!"

Her rantings only seemed to incite his passion as he held her in midair. He was as strong as a Titan.

"Why do you insist on fighting? You know you can't win against me, and you also know you don't want to fight. Give in to me. Give in." His voice was huskily soft and suddenly seductive against her cheek.

The fight died within her when his warm, moist lips touched hers in a kiss that deepened when his tongue slid between her teeth to connect with her own. A strange melting sensation uncoiled within her abdomen and seeped into her legs before winding its way to center in her pulsing womanhood. The feeling excited and frightened her. This was how she had felt in Tony's arms, and she ached for the same sort of fulfillment, for something she wasn't even certain existed.

The man seemed to take her sudden quietness in his arms for acquiescence, and a slight moan escaped him. With one long stride, he put her on the cot and was on top of her. His hands slid up her thighs to seek the throbbing peak of her desire. Long, sure fingers stroked her softness, and Laurel whimpered in mounting passion against his mouth.

"This is how I've thought of you for so long," he said lowly. "In my arms whimpering and aching for me. You are a tempting tease, a vixenish whore."

Laurel's eyes flew open. His words threw cold water over her increasing ardor. For an insane moment she had thought she was in Tony's arms, again succumbing to her desire for him, a desire for a man who had only intended to use her and cast her aside. Now, her mind cleared, and she realized this man was far more dangerous than Tony. He was a stranger, who had kidnapped her and intended to force her to respond to him. Not rape her. She had fallen into her kidnapper's trap as easily as into Duvalier's. What was wrong with her? She had to stop this or become no better than a whore in her kidnapper's eyes and, worst of all, her own.

She rested submissively against him, allowing his hands to wander freely over her flesh. Once again she smelled the faint odor of smoke surrounding him. His black hood suddenly made Laurel realize that for some reason he didn't want her to know his identity, that he intended to humiliate her by her response to an unknown man. But, she thought, his plan would fail if she removed the hood.

With a surprising quickness, her hand bolted upward, and she grabbed a handful of the wet, coarse material and began to yank it from him. Before she had a chance to reveal her kidnapper's face, he had swiftly wrenched her hand away and held her arm between them in a vicious grip. His other arm firmly pinned her to the cot.

"Nice try, my wanton miss."

Tears of rage and disappointment welled in her eyes. She had failed to see his face or even something to identify him. The cabin was too dark, and her only clue was his voice. Even that was disguised.

"I know what you're trying to do. You want to humiliate me, to obtain a response from me. Why, I don't know, but it won't work. You'll have to rape me because I won't give you the satisfaction of making this easy for you."

"You're wrong," he said jeeringly. "I'll prove you wrong."

With that he proceeded to kiss her again, to attempt to tantalize her with his lips, his tongue. Hot, eager hands stroked her breasts, her thighs that lay bared to him. But Laurel had willed herself to lie still, not to react in any way to this man's lovemaking. Yet she found it difficult not to whimper in growing desire. Something about this man's touch excited her perversely, and she wondered if she was a wanton. Even now his hardened manhood rested against her lower body, and he ground into her in an attempt to elicit a passionate response.

Nothing happened.

Soon he stopped his movements and removed his weight from her. Standing up, he towered over her half-naked and wet form. When he heaved a sigh, she felt more than saw that he had come to some sort of a decision.

"You think you've won," he said at length.

"Yes," she whispered lowly.

His voice came out harsher and raspier than ever. "You're wrong. The game isn't over yet."

With that terse remark hanging on the air, he made for the door. Laurel scampered off the cot just as he exited, but when she reached the door, she heard the latch being sheathed.

"Let me out!" she cried and pounded on the heavy pine door. "You can't keep me here! Take me back!"

For a moment all was silent as she wondered if he were considering, but when his booted feet scraped against the porch flooring only to be followed by the steady clip-clop of the horse's hoofs, she knew he had left her.

She slid to the floor and huddled against the door, drawing her knees up to her chest. The tears she had suppressed flowed freely now. Never in her life had she felt so weak and wet and cold. And alone.

Chapter Seven

Early the next morning, bright sunshine streaming in through the barred window roused Laurel. She wakened, shivering in her still damp costume, to a suddenly cold morning to discover that she had fallen asleep on the floor beside the door. A few times during the night she had wakened, cold and wet, but had been so exhausted she could not summon the strength to crawl to the cot. Now her clothes and hair were not yet dry, and the skirt and blouse were dirty from lying upon the floor.

Slowly she stood up, every muscle aching in her body, and hugged herself for warmth while surveying the room. It was small. Two large steps would take her from the door to the cot and barely three feet to the left was the table and chair. Nothing else. No blanket to warm her, no food. What did the blasted man who had kidnapped her expect her to do? she ranted inwardly. The whole incident seemed like a nightmare, and while she had slept, she had dreamed she was safe and warm in her own home, in her own parlor, pouring tea for Philbert Anderson. Being with Philbert, at the moment, held far more appeal than this place she now inhabited. Yet this was no dream from which she could waken, but a living nightmare.

Again she wondered, why had the masked man chosen her? A prickle of fear coursed up her spine when she thought he would soon return and finish what he had started last night. Though relieved at having escaped his lovemaking, she couldn't help but wonder why he had stopped. Certainly, he could have finished the act without her participation, but he had wanted her to respond. That was why she had been brought to this place.

"I'll be gone before he comes back," she vowed aloud. "I'll find some way out of here."

A surge of strength flowed through her, and she walked to the window and wrapped her hands around the bars. The bayou was breathtakingly beautiful, and if she hadn't been forced here under duress, she might have taken pleasure in the peach-gold sky that was now turning a light blue, in the fluffy clouds skittering overhead and seeming to touch the tall cypress trees that surrounded her. Two egrets basking in the warming rays of the sun stood like sentinels on the shoreline. Birds twittered in the trees, and she saw the flash of a fish as it jumped from the water, only to dive back into the silvery depths.

How free they all were, and how she envied these creatures their freedom—a freedom that she vowed would soon be hers.

Pulling at the thick iron bars accomplished nothing. They wouldn't budge, nor would the door give way when she pushed her weight against it. She then picked up the chair and rammed it against the center of the door, but the door was much too thick, and the chair barely caused an indentation in the solid pine planks.

In frustration, Laurel threw herself upon the cot and quelled the urge to cry. She had cried enough last night and did not wish to shed any more tears. She already found it difficult to breathe, and her throat felt slightly raw. Probably from all the dust in the room, she thought and coughed. Putting her feet under her, she leaned backward against the wall and pondered her situation. Had this cabin served as some sort of a prison? Perhaps for wayward slaves? She remembered her kidnapper telling her that she was in the middle of the bayou, so he may have had need of such a place for his slaves. But why choose her? None of it made any sense. If her kidnapper owned this property and had slaves, he must be quite wealthy and not in need of money, a fact she had already guessed. He had made it quite clear that he had made no mistake about her. He meant her to be here.

But why? She had never been in this area of the parish before and knew no one except Tony Duvalier. Her only other connection with the bayou country was Lavinia's tragic association with Auguste St. Julian . . .

Laurel sat straight up, her heart hammering in her ears. "I can't risk entering bayou country. My life is at stake!" Lavinia had cried to her before their departure. A relative of St. Julian's had investigated the old man's death, held Lavinia personally responsible. There was no other answer to why she, herself, had been kidnapped and left in a cabin in the middle of the swamp. St. Julian's relative didn't want *her*. He wanted Lavinia and believed he now had her at his mercy, that his uncle's death would be avenged.

"That's the answer!" Laurel blurted out, her excitement mounting. She jumped off the cot and stood in the center of the dust-covered floor, a becoming rosy flush staining her cheeks. She would convince the man he had kidnapped the wrong person, and then he would release her. Certainly he could be made to see his mistake. She wasn't Lavinia Delaney but Laurel Delaney. How easy it would be. She would simply inform him of his mistake when he returned.

Yet when the morning sun climbed higher in the sky, she wondered if he intended to return or if she were to stay in this cabin until she died from starvation or froze to death. Once more she found her way to the cot and lay down, huddling against the wall. She had just dozed off when the sound of footsteps on the porch outside followed by the creaking of the latch as it was pulled from the sheath woke her.

Sitting up with her hair all atumble and her clothes wrinkled and dirty, she watched as an old black woman entered, carrying a basket. The cabin was suddenly filled with the delicious aroma of smoked sausage and freshly baked biscuits. Without glancing in Laurel's direction, the woman headed for the table, placed the basket in the center, and unpacked the food. As she busily set the smoked sausage on a china plate, Laurel rose from the cot.

The smell of the food caused Laurel's stomach to growl. Never in her life had she felt such hunger, and the sausage beckoned to her empty stomach. However, this woman must have ridden here or come by pirogue, Laurel reasoned, and the cabin door was ajar. Freedom was only a few feet away, and right now escaping this place meant more to her than a full stomach.

The woman turned her back to Laurel and placed a fluffy biscuit on Laurel's plate. Laurel inched toward the door, which blew gently in the cool breeze. Another foot and she would be free. The woman was much too old and moved too slowly to be able to stop Laurel from escaping. So far Laurel saw no evidence that her kidnapper was nearby. Evidently the woman had arrived alone and would present no threat to her.

Grabbing the door handle, Laurel swung the door back and scampered onto the porch, expecting the old woman to hobble after her. What she didn't expect was the tall and broad-shouldered black man who blocked her way. Easily holding her in his grasp, he hauled her struggling and screaming back into the cabin. He said something in French to the old woman, who just shrugged her shoulders before he wrenched the door closed.

"You shouldn't have done that, mademoiselle," the woman admonished her. "If you had escaped, the monsieur would have been very angry with me and my son. My son is a good boy and deserves no punishment because of your foolishness." She went back to the basket and withdrew a bowl of custard and a spoon, followed by a pot of tea, still warm, to judge by the curling steam rising from the pot.

The woman's nonchalance riled Laurel. How could she pretend nothing was wrong? "Who are you?" Laurel demanded.

"My name is unimportant," she answered calmly.

"Tell me who is your master, the monsieur of whom you speak."

She shook her head. "Do not ask me such a question. I cannot answer you."

"Can you tell me if he is a relative of Auguste St. Julian?" Laurel implored.

Continuing her chore at the table, she didn't glance in Laurel's direction, giving Laurel the impression that she had guessed correctly. Her kidnapper was St. Julian's relation.

She motioned to Laurel to sit. "Please eat, mademoiselle."

Laurel was ravenous, but at the moment she wanted to impress upon her that her master had made a grave mistake. "Don't you think it strange that I am here? Don't you wonder why your master kidnapped me and threw me in here? Don't you care?"

The old woman stiffened her back. A look of indignation appeared on her face. "I never question monsieur. Never!"

"You like being a slave then, a virtual prisoner? Well, I don't, and I demand my freedom. I implore you and your son to help me escape. I'll make it worth your while. I have plenty of money."

Laurel could tell her pleas fell on deaf ears as the women refused to even acknowledge Laurel's comment. The woman sniffed in disdain. Not even money or simple human kindness would make her relent and help Laurel. What sort of a hold did this monsieur have over her to exact such loyalty after the monstrous thing he had done? She appeared to be an intelligent woman. She must realize that her master had kidnapped an innocent woman.

"Eat, mademoiselle."

Laurel moved forward, drawn by the aroma of the food in spite of herself, and the sounds emanating from her stomach demanded to be stilled. Laurel looked at the food, still warm on her plate, and then at the woman. Apparently it was important to her that she eat as a way of appeasing her master.

"I'm not here of my own free will, and you do realize that."

"I realize that monsieur will be very angry if you do not eat."

Laurel looked down at the food again, unable to pull her gaze away, but with a strength of will she did. She settled her eyes upon the woman's worried and lined face. "Tell monsieur that I will not eat until he releases me. Also tell him that he made a mistake. I am not Lavinia Delaney but her cousin, Laurel, and I demand my release. I refuse to eat one bite of this delicious fare until he comes here and apologizes for what he has done to me. Otherwise, he'll have a corpse on his hands. Someone will start searching for me when they realize I've disappeared."

"Mademoiselle, no." She wrung her hands in frustration. "Monsieur will not like this."

Despite the fact that Laurel felt drawn to the food like a magnet, she moved toward the cot and sat down. "Return the food to monsieur with my message."

The old woman opened her mouth to protest anew, but Laurel stopped her with a severe look. In defeat the woman began to repack the food, but Laurel noticed she didn't reach for the custard and the spoon. When she picked up the basket, Laurel saw a neatly folded blanket that she must have placed on the table earlier.

"To keep you warm, mademoiselle," she said and inclined her head to the blanket.

Laurel picked up the soft wool coverlet and uttered her thanks to the old woman. "Be certain to tell your master that I'm not who he thinks I am," Laurel reminded her. Nodding her head, the woman left and closed the door behind her.

Then came the ominous sound of the bolt.

Left alone, Laurel reached for the custard, grateful to the woman for purposely leaving the creamy concoction. Deciding that her kidnapper didn't have to know she had eaten anything, she defiantly shoved the spoon into her mouth but found no pleasure in the dessert although she was hungry. Her throat hurt, and the mid-morning sun that warmed the cabin didn't dispel the sudden chill that settled over her. Placing the half-eaten custard on the table, she wrapped herself in the blanket, lay on the cot, and drifted into a fitful sleep.

"I'm very upset with you, Tony. I think you could act the gentleman and apologize for your sudden absence last night. I looked quite foolish to your guests after your departure." Simone stirred the tea a servant had recently placed in front of her, adding five lumps of sugar to the steaming brew.

"Careful, Simone, or you'll get fat," Tony warned from across the black walnut dining room table where he lazed in a rococo-style chair, calmly smoking a cheroot. He watched as Simone lifted her fluffy blond head, framed by French doors and fan-shaped leaded glass windows behind her. The golden sun emphasized her beauty, which, he guessed, would become overblown in a few years. She would most probably grow quite plump like her mother, but Tony had never cared about a woman's physical appearance—not if he loved her. And he didn't love Simone Lancier. They had grown up together, and Simone had even shared his bed on a number of occasions. In fact she would now be gracing his bed if it hadn't been for the dark-haired temptress he had hidden in the bayou.

When he returned home last night, blaming Lavinia Delaney for her deviousness and himself for being forced into such a predicament, he had been tempted to seek out Simone, who was sleeping in the guest bedchamber. He had almost knocked on her door but had abruptly turned away, nearly bumping into Jean DuLac in the hallway. Tony realized he disliked the intrusion of overnight guests and vowed that he would not throw another party too soon.

Simone shot him a waspish smile. "My darling Tony, I worry much less about gaining weight than looking positively skeletal like your little friend last night. What was her name? You never did introduce your gypsy girl. I would think she was quite unhealthy. There wasn't an ounce of extra flesh on her, and I know you prefer a woman with a good appetite . . . you who are filled with an appetite to taste life."

She purposely leaned over her breakfast plate of eggs and sausages, giving him an unencumbered view of her flawless bosom in the tight-waisted and low-cut gown. The seamstress had done wonders showing off Simone's physical assets to advantage. The gown suited Simone perfectly, and the blue color matched he eyes. Tony guessed she was trying to lure him upstairs to bed, and at any other time, he would have gone.

But Simone had raised the topic of the woman he had brought to the dance last night, and he couldn't get her off his mind. He hoped Zelie and Emmanuel hadn't had much trouble with the tempestuous miss. Zelie was much too kind-hearted for such an undertaking, and no doubt she might be taken in by Lavinia's silken lies. Emmanuel, however, wouldn't be so amenable to the emerald-eyed beauty. He was a trusted servant and never questioned Tony's actions.

The sound of Simone's lulling voice brought him out of his reverie, and he silently cursed himself for even now being under Lavinia Delaney's spell.

"After we're married, darling," Simone was saying, "you'll never want any other woman but me, you'll never even look at any other woman. I can make you happy, Tony, I know I can. All you have to do is name the date of our wedding. I saw the perfect pattern for my wedding dress in the latest issue of *Godey's Lady's Book*."

Simone's words caused Tony to feel trapped. The thought of marriage to Simone, to any woman at the present time, was out of the question. He would never marry until he found the perfect woman with whom to share his life.

He stumped out his cheroot in his breakfast plate and stood up. His expression was utterly bored. Beneath his well-dressed exterior of white shirt, brown frock coat, and matching trousers, his insides grew cold at the thought of marriage to Simone, but he smiled at her disarmingly, his smile brilliant.

"I thought you wanted to wait until your father had completely recovered from his illness," Tony said smoothly.

Coming to stand beside him, Simone reached up and fiddled with a gold button on his shirt. "You know very well that Papa is always ill, Tony, because he drinks too much. He'll die from the effects of alcohol one day and will never stop drinking until death closes his eyes. I don't want to wait any longer to become your wife. Let's announce our engagement soon."

The manipulative little minx. Until last night Simone, claiming her father's health, hadn't been that eager to marry him, but Tony knew she wavered because she enjoyed flirting with all the men and probably bedding some of them, too. Her virtue, or lack of it, had never bothered him—he was quite knowledgeable on that score himself—but now she felt she had a rival in Lavinia Delaney. He laughed aloud. If only she knew to what extent he had gone to avenge his uncle's death on her supposed rival for his affections.

"Whatever are you laughing at?" Simone asked somewhat huffily.

"I'm sorry," he answered and disentangled her hand from his shirt button, "but I can't think of two more mismatched individuals than you and me."

"Mismatched? We're very much alike, Tony."

"Exactly why we'd never be happy, Simone. I want a woman I can trust, and you, my pet, are not that woman." His forefinger touched the tip of her nose, and his expression softened.

"I can't marry you, and whether you realize it or not, I'm doing you a favor by not marrying you. Anyway, I've never encouraged you. You've taken it for granted that we'd marry because our fathers were friends. Your father may already wonder why I've never pressed my suit of you or formally asked for you. I don't love you, Simone, and have no intention of taking you to wife. I'm sorry to hurt you, but I've done you an injustice by not having already told you how I feel. Look elsewhere for a husband, for I'm not about to become one soon."

Her mouth fell open, and her eyes clouded with forced tears. She had never been refused anything, or anyone, she had wanted in her life. And now here was Tony Duvalier, one of the wealthiest men in the parish, spurning her. To be honest, she didn't love Tony, but she loved making love to him and reveled in the way he made her feel. She couldn't imagine not marrying him. Her father wished the match, and she loved her father despite his weakness for liquor. How would she explain to all her neighbors, her friends in Vermillionville and New Orleans that Tony Duvalier didn't want to marry her? It was inconceivable to her that he didn't want to marry her, and oh, so humiliating.

Simone pulled away from him. "It's because of

that woman you no longer want to marry me," she said with what she considered to be just the correct amount of pain in her voice.

Tony pretended not to know whom she meant and started to walk past her, but her hand shot out and stilled him. "You belong to me, Tony."

"What a possessive cat you are," he said and shrugged off her hand before opening the French doors and going outside into the bright morning.

The endless expanse of fields stretched before him, and he watched the servants as they tilled the long rows of the cotton fields. Then, walking beyond the house, he stopped at a distance and leaned against a barbed-wire fence that separated the grazing land from the rest of the plantation. Cattle contentedly munched on the sweet, green grass. Tony smiled. Not many other plantations in the area could boast such hearty, well-fed cattle. He had recently introduced the Brahman breed into his stock, hoping that by crossbreeding, he would produce a heartier breed of cattle than had previously existed in the prairie area.

In the past Tony had lost some heads to tick fever, flies and mosquitoes, and drought that sometimes lasted for weeks. But the Brahman was a sturdy breed, used to surviving in hot country and able to live through periods of famine. So far, things had worked out well, and the cattle had thrived except for the loss of an occasional cow to a cattle thief. That seemed to be happening more often in the prairie area, and Tony knew he would have to put an end to that eventually.

But now a wanton, dark-haired beauty filled his thoughts, and he wasn't certain he liked expending so much time and energy on such a woman. He knew he would visit her again, maybe this very night, but first, he would let her stew a while until she became completely pliant and would melt in his arms at his touch. He wanted Lavinia to beg for him before taking her in a rush of passion, he ached to humiliate her by making her confess her desire for him. Then after he had spent himself within her and made her realize what a wanton she truly was, he would release her. The plan was quite simple, but the ease with which he had trapped her, of kidnapping her, disturbed him. For such a conniving woman, everything had gone his way too easily. Instead of feeling that Lavinia had gotten her just deserts, he almost felt she was a victim—more disturbingly, *his* victim.

As Tony sauntered back to the house, he noticed Jean DuLac waving to him in the distance. When they came within speaking distance, Jean smiled at his cousin.

"You slept very late, Tony, but then you were out until past three in the morning. Were you with your gypsy girl?" Jean nudged Tony knowingly. "You looked quite flushed when I saw you in the hallway early this morning."

Probably from that damn hood I wore over my head, Tony thought in aggravation. He patted Jean heartily upon the back. "The wench was insatiable, *mon cousin*."

"Really?" Jean said in surprise, a bit curious about the woman. "She didn't seem to be that type of female. I mean she was nothing like Simone and acted more of a lady."

"Looks and mannerisms can be deceiving," Tony uttered harshly.

Jean grew quiet and followed Tony into the house. When they entered the back parlor, Zelie practically flew into the room after them.

"I must speak with you alone, Monsieur Tony," she said, wringing her hands; an urgency in her voice.

Jean left the room without being asked, and Tony calmly poured himself a snifter of Courvoisier. "How is my prisoner?" he asked.

Zelie came forward, her brow furrowed, and she lifted her turban-clad head to look into his eyes. "The mademoiselle refuses to eat. She is strong-willed and won't eat a bite until you come to her and apologize for what you have done to her."

Tony practically choked on the brandy. "The woman is mad! Let her starve before I offer her an apology for anything."

"Monsieur, I fear you have done her an injustice." Zelie wiped her perspiring palms on the front of her apron. "She knows her kidnapping is related to your uncle's death."

All color drained from Tony's tanned face. "Does she know I'm behind it?"

Shaking her head, Zelie assured him that his captive had no idea he was involved. "However, monsieur, she is not a stupid woman; she may realize this fact very soon. She told me to tell you that she is not Lavinia Delaney but her cousin Laurel, I think she said her name was. She said you have made a grave mistake."

Tony tightened his hand around the brandy snifter. Laurel Delaney? Was it possible he had kidnapped the wrong woman? The thought of such a mistake momentarily caused a wave of alarm to course through his veins. But such a wanton couldn't be Laurel Delaney. A woman like Laurel Delaney, reputed to be an elegant if a somewhat cold woman, would be unable to make his passion flare. Not a lofty ice queen as his investigation into Lavinia Delaney's relative had shown. He preferred a willing, flesh-and-blood woman in his arms — someone who responded to his kisses, his embraces.

A smile quirked around his lips. That Lavinia was such a woman, and he would congratulate her the next time they met on how easily lies rose to those luscious, strawberry-tinted lips. No, he convinced himself, he had kidnapped the right woman. He waved a tanned hand at Zelie.

"She is lying to you. You mustn't believe anything this woman says. She killed my uncle, and I know you wish to see this woman punished."

Zelie nodded slowly, but her old hands trembled. "You told me this Lavinia Delaney was cruel and dangerous, monsieur. You said she had hurt Auguste, and for that I will not forgive her. I took care of your Uncle Auguste when he was a little boy and loved him dearly. But this woman I saw today has no evil within her. She is frightened, and I think she means to starve herself. You must go to her, monsieur."

So, Tony thought, Lavinia had deceived old Zelie. How crafty she was to enlist Zelie on her side. Well, he wasn't an old woman with a soft heart. He would make Lavinia Delaney sorry she had ever met Auguste St. Julian.

"Don't worry about her," he spoke softly. "She'll eat when she gets hungry enough. Just keep bringing her food."

Zelie started to say something else but apparently thought better of it. *"Oui,* monsieur," she said and shuffled from the room.

The brandy slid like silk down Tony's throat, and that drink was quickly followed by two more until he felt sufficiently calm. Taking a deep breath; he turned away from the sideboard and stalked out the house to the barn where he gruffly ordered his horse saddled. Within minutes he was flying down Grand Prairie Road, not at all certain where he was headed until he noticed the cottage of Gaston Mornay.

Reining his horse in, he hesitated, overcome by a momentary qualm of guilt that he had kidnapped the wrong woman. Could it be that he had unwittingly kidnapped Laurel Delaney and not the treacherous Lavinia? Tony shook himself and decided he must learn the truth. The only person who could provide that truth now was Gincie.

After Tony had been solicitously handed a cup of coffee with chicory by Tillie Mornay and had conversed at length with Gaston about the disappearance of another cattle the night before, he and Gincie were left alone. Tony suddenly felt ill at ease with the woman but hid his discomfiture by lounging in a cane-backed chair as he slowly sipped the steaming brew.

"You're looking much better," Tony noted and smiled approvingly. Gincie's cheeks had a healthy glow about them, her eyes shone like onyx stars in her lined but happy face. She flashed her sparkling teeth at him.

"I sho' do feel better, sir. Doctor Mornay's been takin' real good care of me, and Tillie is as kind and good as they come." A slight frown, however, crept across her brow, and she fiddled with the tiny bow on her white nightdress. "But I'd feel a lot more at peace if I had seen my baby before she left for San Antonio today. I thought she'd have told me good-bye, but I guess she was in a fuss to be gone. Her uncle's been ailing, you know."

"I didn't know that," Tony muttered, raising his eyebrows in an answering frown. "However, I did see Miss Malone when she boarded the coach the other day. Strange that she went on ahead without your mistress."

Gincie lifted her head from the pillow propped behind her, and devilment danced in her eyes. She gave a chuckle and waved her hand in the air in amusement. "That Miss Lavinia is somethin', I tell you that. Since Miss Laurel is gone now, I guess she wouldn't mind if I told you the truth about what those two girls did."

"What truth is that?" Tony's face turned ashen, somehow knowing what Gincie was about to impart. He nonchalantly took a sip of coffee but found it tasteless and was unable to swallow.

Gincie laughed lightly, eager to tell someone about the Delaney cousins and their charade. Tony listened, and by the time she had finished recounting how Miss Lavinia had thrown a temper tantrum on the steamboat because she was forced to look dowdy and unattractive, and how Miss Laurel was the one to remind her that she had better act the part of a lady's companion or she would have nothing else to do with Lavinia's problem, Tony hid his quaking hands in the pockets of his frock coat.

"That Miss Lavinia with her flamin' hair can't hide her looks if she wanted to, but I always did think my baby was the prettiest. Don't you think so, Mr. Duvalier?"

Tony barely heard Gincie's question, his mind was still registering the fact that the woman he had sequestered in the bayou wasn't Lavinia Delaney at all. He glanced up to see a perplexed Gincie.

"Don't you think my baby is the prettiest lady you ever did see?" Gincie asked again to be certain Tony had heard her.

"Yes," he answered in a rush. "She is the most beautiful woman in the world." And he meant it.

Pleased, Gincie grinned.

"I told Miss Laurel you were the man for her."

Standing up abruptly, Tony scraped his chair against the floor. He appeared disoriented, as if his mind were a thousand miles away. Tillie appeared and inquired if something was wrong.

"Tell Gaston to take good care of Gincie," he muttered, then turned his attention to the woman on the bed and absently patted her head. "I have a feeling you'll see your Laurel very soon." Then he was gone and viciously spurring his stallion down the road in the direction of the bayou before either woman could say another word.

Sweat poured from Tony's brow and down his face, but he felt cold, dreadfully cold. His fingers felt so chilled he could barely hold the reins. The pounding of the stallion's hoofs upon the road beat a wild cadence in Tony's brain—Laurel Delaney, Laurel Delaney, Laurel Delaney.

He had kidnapped the wrong woman!

By the time he entered the forest and could see the cabin through the trees, he had cursed himself a hundredfold. He should have made inquiries into Lavinia Delaney's appearance, should have asked the investigator, Henri Maurice, the color of Lavinia's hair. Then again, if, as Maurice had told him, the woman was always veiled during her trysts with his uncle, the man wouldn't have been aware of such a fact. Gincie had said Lavinia had flaming hair, and his prisoner was a brunette, a most enchanting and beautiful brunette, who caused his blood to stir with her innocent kisses.

"Damn!" His curse hung upon the air like the Spanish moss on the nearby trees. The woman in the cabin was an innocent. He was worldly enough to have sensed this, and he had, but he had been so caught up in his stupid plan for revenge that he had purposely blinded himself to her inexperience, thinking it only a ruse to ease his conscience.

He had much to make amends for to Laurel Delaney. Just before reaching the cabin, he halted. He couldn't simply rush in and drag her from the cabin, though he ached to do so, and ensconce her at Petit Coteau. She would know immediately that he was her kidnapper, and her scorn and hatred would be more than he could bear.

Why this was so, he couldn't fathom. He had never felt protective toward a woman before and had never cared what a woman thought about his callous behavior once their affair was over. But Laurel was different, he reminded himself. She was a lady and a woman of impeccable character, though she did have the reputation of being an ice queen. Tony knew better, but right now he couldn't dwell on Laurel's passion. He must release her from her prison. But again—how? He didn't want her to discover he was the one who had locked her in and thereby lose his chance of making it up to her.

The stallion pawed at the soft earth, eager to move onward. Instead, Tony turned the horse away from the cabin and headed out of the forest. A plan was forming in his mind, and if everything fell into place, he would have his chance to make up to Laurel for his transgression against her. And maybe, just maybe, she would fall in love with him in the process. This thought startled him and pleased him at the same time. He would like nothing better than to have Laurel Delaney's love. In fact, if he were a different type of man and not so jaded in affairs of the heart, he could love her, too.

Chapter Eight

Shafts of late afternoon sunlight wove gold and orange highlights resembling a brilliant tapestry into the silver ripples of the shallow bayou. A slight cool breeze soughed through the upper reaches of the cypress trees and gently ruffled the Spanish moss that hung from the branches like an old man's beard. From where Tony stood on the opposite shoreline from the cabin, he noticed a streak of black slithering across the watery expanse. A moccasin and a potentially dangerous snake. For the first time in a long time, Tony offered up a small prayer that no harm would befall Laurel when she crossed the bayou. If anything happened to her, it would be his fault, and he would be unable to live with himself.

From his vantage point behind a clump of underbrush, he watched as Zelie was paddled across the swamp by Emmanuel. In her lap she held a basket filled with freshly fried chicken and homemade grits—something he had decided that a hungry Laurel would be unable to resist. From Zelie's tightly drawn mouth, he reasoned that Zelie's disapproval of the whole affair came from the fact that she thought he should be the one to enter the cabin and free Laurel Delaney, not use the ruse of delivering a hot meal and forgetting to lock the cabin door.

Tony felt as much of a coward at that moment as Zelie must have thought him. But he couldn't risk Laurel's discovery that he had been the one to kidnap her. If she learned the truth, the hard-headed miss wouldn't deign to glance in his direction except with icy scorn in her eyes, and he wanted her gaze to be filled with desire and love for him. No, this was the only way to free her, he decided, and to achieve her love.

The plan seemed simple, too simple, a part of him thought, but he had no alternative. Just moments before he had ordered Zelie not to speak to Laurel, to leave the basket on the table, and to conveniently forget to sheath the latch on the door. Knowing Laurel had tried to escape earlier in the day, Tony had no doubt that she would try the door again and escape after Zelie and Emmanuel had paddled away. Then once she had waded across the water to the opposite shoreline and had trekked through the wilderness for half an hour or more, he would suddenly appear and rescue her. Of course, she would probably ask questions, but he had all the answers. He would simply tell her that his driver had arrived at Petit Coteau, relating the details of the kidnapping. Because of the delicacy of the situation, Tony, himself, had started a private search. After all, her reputation was at stake.

A smile slanted his mouth, and his dark eyes danced, their amber flecks lighting up like beacons to think of how grateful Laurel would be. To imagine the sweet kiss she would bestow upon him, a kiss that would erupt into hot ecstasy, promising a night of smoldering passion, caused a burning ache in his loins. God, he wanted her with a fierceness he had never experienced for any woman. Was it her innocence? he wondered. Or the fact that he now realized she would never experience desire for any man but himself? Whatever the reason, he would enjoy tutoring her in the art of lovemaking.

Now if only things worked out as he had planned.

A distance away he heard the two horses that he had brought with him whinny lowly. As soon as Zelie and Emmanuel had paddled across the swamp, they would find the horses and ride to Petit Coteau where the buggy waited to take them into Vermillionville. Tony couldn't afford to let Laurel discover the two servants at the plantation, so he had ordered them to go to the town house, something for which Zelie didn't care but which Emmanuel took in his stride.

Tony shifted on his boot-encased legs, brushing against a tree stump. The gold buttons on his ebony-colored shirt reflected the dying sunlight, and he breathed a sigh of relief to see that Zelie had already brought in the basket and was now being helped into the pirogue by Emmanuel. Soon the pirogue nudged the shoreline, only ten feet away from Tony's hiding place. Emmanuel caught his eye and nodded, and Zelie attempted to say something, but Emmanuel pushed her ahead of him, toward the right of Tony. Within minutes Tony heard the soft gallop of the horses drifting away on the sweet evening air.

All had gone well so far. He gave a sigh of relief and waited. Soon Laurel would rush from the cabin. Soon she would kiss him in gratitude for rescuing her. But the sun set, and a heavy fog began to settle over the bayou until all was enveloped in a gray haze. If she didn't come out of the cabin soon, she would not be able to find her way across the murky water when the dark of night enfolded the area like a black cloak.

"What the hell is wrong?" he muttered out loud, growing more impatient by the second.

When fifteen minutes had passed and still Laurel hadn't made her desperate bid for freedom, Tony had had enough. He must discover what had gone wrong with his plan. As he strode across the creature-filled bayou, he didn't stop to think what would happen once he entered the cabin. He only knew that a heavy sense of foreboding had filled him and that something was very wrong.

When he reached the cabin, he noticed that the door gently swayed on its hinges in the evening breeze. Pushing back the door to allow entrance of his broad frame, Tony peered into the shadowy room. He vaguely made out the shapes of the chair and table before his gaze centered upon the cot against the barred window. He blinked, not able to find Laurel at first, until he realized that her slight form rested on the cot, covered by a blanket.

"Laurel," Tony whispered and moved into the depths of the room until he stood above her, looking down at her. In the semidarkness her eyes rested on his face, and a shock went through him that now she would know he was the one. But when he bent down, again murmuring her name, he heard no response except a low agonized moan.

Her head turned away from him, her long, raven tresses spilling over the edge of the cot to fall onto the floor. The profile of her was barely visible, and he reached out a hand to stroke her cheek, expecting her to thrash out at him, to berate him for what he had done to her. Instead his fingers felt singed by her flesh, and he drew back as the knowledge flooded over him. Laurel was sick, very sick. Turning her head toward him, she issued another moan, and he realized that her emerald gaze was filled with fire, not from anger, but from a high fever. In fact, she didn't seem to see him at all or to respond to the caress of his cool hand upon her face when his fingers grazed her skin again.

"Laurel, you're very ill," he said, still not quite able to believe her condition. She shivered under the blanket, totally unaware of him. Then when she mumbled for her mother, for Gincie, he knew she was delirious.

"Damn!" he swore under his breath and stood up. Nothing had gone right. He had thought the plan so simple that his allowing her to escape would pose no problem. Instead he now had a worse problem than before. Laurel needed medical help, something he couldn't provide. More importantly, he couldn't bring her to Petit Coteau but must leave her here until she was well. Or until she died.

His heart almost stopped its steady thump. He knew he must get a physician, but he was unable to walk through the forest at night, the distance was too great and perilous without a torch. And he didn't have the heart to leave her alone. If only he had brought his stallion, then he could ride for help. What a perplexing dilemma he had gotten himself into. Everything was his fault, and if Laurel Delaney died, that would be his fault, also.

But he wouldn't allow Laurel to die. From the mists of time he recalled Zelie rambling off about a certain grass that grew in the bayou, that when the grass was mixed with water and strained, then administered to the sick person, the fever would break. Tony had always discounted Zelie's cures, believing them to be mostly superstition, but now he had no choice. He would have to be the one to save Laurel Delaney's life.

* * *

"Drink this down, *chérie*. It will make you well."

That voice was there again. Laurel shut her eyes tighter, shivering beneath the blanket, not wanting to be disturbed. All she wanted was to go back to sleep and dream lovely, sweet dreams. But that voice wouldn't let her. The voice constantly invaded the warm fog that shrouded her mind. Was that her mother's voice whispering to her, or her father's? Why wouldn't the voice allow her to slip away to that peaceful realm she had glimpsed, a place of beauty and lush flowers. But it harped at her until she muttered "Go away!"

But the voice didn't stop. Once again it demanded that she drink, and she felt herself being lifted and forced to swallow a vile-tasting brew. She made a face, and the voice said, *"Bien,* Laurel. Rest now." Then a hand stroked her forehead, followed by a cool cloth in its stead.

Whose voice was that? she vaguely wondered. Was it Gincie? She managed to open her eyes a crack. A deep, dark velvet blackness met her. Though she couldn't see anyone, she sensed a person nearby. In her mind she felt as though she were twelve years old again and very sick from the fever. Of course, she decided, she was ill with yellow fever, and Gincie was taking care of her. That was why she felt so awful, why she shivered so. She was so tired, so very sleepy, but once again the voice intruded on her when she began to fall asleep, and someone pulled off her clothes, and she felt a coolness settling across her body. That Gincie! Why wouldn't she leave her alone? She wasn't going to die from anything. She would survive the fever. Didn't Gincie remember that?

"Leave me alone Gincie," Laurel mumbled and swatted weakly at the hand that stroked her brow. "Bronze John isn't going to get me. You know that."

Was that a laugh she heard? Well, when she was better again, she would tell her mother how Gincie had laughed at her and wouldn't leave her alone when she felt so sick. But where was her mother? she wondered and began to sob. Where was she?

Sometimes, when she opened her eyes, there was light, but such a harsh light that she closed them again. At one point when she focused her eyes; she saw a man bending over her, a handsome man with dark, probing eyes. Who was he? But, of course, he must be her father, though he looked nothing like him. She wanted to smile at him, but her face hurt. Everything hurt, and she shook so horribly.

All she could manage to say was a very low, "Papa" before slipping away to a place that no longer held visions of bright flowers and rainbows but of distorted memories from her childhood, of a strange man who forced her to drink something that made her gag.

Sometimes loving hands stroked her face and body, bringing a welcome coolness to her. At other times she was cold, so terribly cold that her teeth clicked against each other like dice. She cried for her mother, for Gincie, for her father, feeling alone and frightened in a strange place, and no one came for her. No one but him, the stranger, who held her against him in a warm and comforting embrace.

Laurel's long lashes fluttered open uncertainly, and once more her eyes beheld darkness, not a strong ebony darkness where one saw nothing, but more like a soft, velvet black cloud where shapes were outlined and the night held no terror. Was she dead? She wasn't certain, still unable to grasp where she was and that she had survived the fever that had racked her through the long day and into the night. Now she felt warm and safe, protected.

A contented sigh escaped from between her lips, and Laurel snuggled deeper into the enveloping warmth that seemed to seep into her very bones, infusing her fever-racked body with renewed life. She still felt sleepy but was no longer weak and welcomed the enveloping warmth of the blanket and the strong arms that held her closely against a broad, fur-planed chest.

She startled at realizing she wasn't alone, discovering that someone held her, lazily stroking the silky flesh over her spinal column. She felt strong but gentle fingers drifting from her neck to the base of her spine, then stopping as if to consider exploring the fullness of her buttocks, only to retrace the same path. Her breasts, Laurel realized, were pressed against the man's chest. Sprigs of chest hair cushioned her rose-tipped nipples against his powerful pectoral muscles. Even in the dark she felt the muscles flex and strain against her as if he wanted to draw her very body into his own. His shirt was open, though the collar scratched her cheek, and she felt his breath ruffle the strands of her hair. An intimate gesture, but not as intimate as the fact that her naked legs were entwined around his pant-clad ones. In the darkness Laurel colored, thinking she should draw away from this man's embrace but not wanting to be left alone in the void she felt certain his leaving would herald.

Her mind was only beginning to clear. She recalled she had been sick, probably delirious, and though she didn't actually remember seeing the man's face, she felt he had been with her and nursed her through her delirium. And then the events of the night of the Mardi Gras dance washed over her, and she stifled a tiny gasp to realize that the man who held her now, the man who had saved her life, was the same person who had kidnapped her. A silent laugh bubbled up to her throat to think of the irony of the situation. Her kidnapper had become her savior.

A strange calm possessed her. His intimate presence didn't frighten her. She lay in his arms, listening to his heartbeat, feeling the tensing of his muscles when his arms pulled her protectively toward him. A sweet melting sensation flowed through her, only to be trapped in a tight coil in the center of her abdomen, seeming to build and claw at her, begging for some sort of a release she could scarcely imagine. Somehow she knew that this man wouldn't hurt her, wouldn't take unfair advantage of an ill woman. Perhaps she had been mistaken about him from the beginning. The man wasn't an ogre, intent upon raping her. He was the man who had saved her life, and a bond had been forged between them. Nothing in her prim and proper past had prepared her for the rush of emotion that now threatened to consume her. She could feign sleep in his arms until he left her, or she could make him aware she was awake, but somehow she sensed he already knew this.

In years to come Laurel would never quite know why she lifted her head to look into eyes that she felt watched her in the darkness. She only knew that if she didn't, her life would take a different course. Her lips were even with his because she felt his breath upon her mouth when she murmured, "Thank you for saving my life."

When he didn't reply, she wondered if he had heard her, but his answer, whatever it would have been, no longer mattered, for his lips descended upon hers to taste the warm honey of her mouth. The kiss was tentative, exploratory at first, then grew bolder, filled with the promise of his desire. Laurel moaned low in her throat as a spark ignited and slowly melted the coil within her abdomen until hot liquid coursed through her body, only to wind its way back to the lush, warm center of her womanhood.

The practical part of her nature demanded she stop at once. The man had undressed her and had had the nerve to lie next to her in an intimate embrace. But the blossoming woman within her refused to heed. For the first time in her life, she didn't care about the consequences of her actions, only about the man next to her, who did wonderful, wanton things to her flesh.

Lowly he whispered her name, and it seemed to hang on the air like a morning mist. Laurel shivered from excitement and desire, meeting his kisses with her own, arching her body toward his . . . aching for him but not knowing what it was she wanted. All reason and logical thought stopped for her. This man was now her world. For one night she would belong to someone and give herself up to the ecstasy of loving a stranger. But he wasn't a stranger, not when her body responded so to his touch. With each feathery stroke of his hands across her body, the hot kisses he rained across her breasts, Laurel recognized him as the part of herself that had been missing. Only in this man's arms did she feel complete and alive.

By agonizing and tantalizing degrees, his hands moved from her hips to the moist and warm core of her womanhood. A moan of pleasure caught and died in her throat. Sharp pinpoints of pleasure shot through her when his fingers gently stroked her, readying her. Laurel ran her hands up his hard chest, burying her fingers in the mat of chest hair, then skirting to his broad shoulders. She wanted to feel all of him in the same way his hands explored her. Suddenly the once ladylike Laurel pulled at the confining shirt, ripping it from his massive shoulders and running her fingertips over the rippling muscles of his back before he began to tug at his pants.

The cot grew instantly lighter, and she gave a fearful cry that he had left her. Then she heard his pants dropping to the floor, and quickly he was beside her again, naked and hard. His tongue plundered the deep recess of her mouth, swirling in the dark cavity until her tongue joined his in a frenzied assault upon her senses. Threading her arms around his neck, she pulled him closer to her and reveled in the feel of his hot skin against her own. Molten kisses left their mark upon her as his mouth drifted from her swanlike throat to the taunting rose-hued nipples that ached for his lips.

He spoke in a low voice, mumbling words in French, which Laurel barely understood but instinctively knew told how much he wanted her. Words weren't needed between them. Laurel felt as if she were being guided by a primitive force as old as time itself and was helpless to stop it — didn't want to stop it. The blanket that had covered her earlier now lay sprawled on the floor along with his pants and shirt. Nothing covered her from his hot gaze, which even in the darkness seemed to scorch her and brand her as his. The tide of desire washed over them, threatening to consume them. And when she felt his burgeoning manhood pressed intimately against her lower body, she was ready for his entry and wrapped her legs around his hips when he thrust into her. The moments of pleasure vanished, and she cried out with the pain of his joining, bringing her back to reality. "Stop, please no more," she whispered with tears in her voice.

He stopped his thrusting movements and lay still atop her. "There is much more to come, *chérie*. Much more pleasure." He quieted her protest with a deep kiss that left her clinging and breathless, wanting him to stop but now growing aroused when he started to gently grind his hips in a circular movement against her. Spears of white heat built by degrees in the center of her womanhood, threatening to flare and inundate her in flames of ecstasy. The pressure became so pleasurable, so unbearable, that Laurel knew she must be released or go insane. Her arms wrapped around his shoulders and pulled him close against her, so close they felt as one, and she would have sworn that his frantic heartbeat matched her own.

"Please, please," she cried, not knowing what she called for, but he knew. He tensed, then withdrew for a second before thrusting into her and causing the breath to leave her body. The white-hot heat that had flared within her loins now exploded in a golden, shimmering liquid and flowed through every nerve and artery of her body. Without realizing it, she writhed against him, and in that instant she felt the throbbing warmth of his release.

Chapter Nine

Late the next morning the gentle patter of rain awoke Laurel. She stretched catlike beneath the blanket and yawned as her emerald gaze settled on the gray sky outside the window. Translucent drops hung from the eaves of the cabin and clung to the iron bars before slithering down the black length to the window sill. For the first time in two days she felt strong enough to sit up and survey the scene outside. Trees swayed like graceful dancers in the breeze, the limbs swathed in skirts of wet Spanish moss, and the steady stance of an egret on the opposite side of the bayou reminded her that she was denied the freedom the bird enjoyed.

Laurel sighed and fell back onto the cot. How long was she to be kept here? she mused and raked a slender hand through her long hair. She felt she would slowly go insane if freedom was denied her any longer. As it was, she thought she was being driven to the brink of insanity. She had had the most peculiar dream the night before, a wonderfully wanton dream, in which her kidnapper had made passionate love to her, and she had responded to his kisses and his embrace like a whore. But though her cheeks pinkened to recall the dream, which must have occurred in the height of her delirium, a sense of complete satisfaction filled her. Such dreams and thoughts were wrong, a part of her protested, but she couldn't stop dwelling on how the man's hard body had felt beneath her fingers, how his kisses had scorched her flesh, and how she wished she would dream such fantasy again.

"I *am* going crazy!" Laurel objected to her own musings and sat up. "If I don't escape from here soon, I'll become a stark, raving lunatic." However, she couldn't help recalling that her kidnapper had nursed her through her illness. She remembered the awful brew he had forced down her throat and his surprisingly gentle treatment of her. Color washed her cheeks anew when she gazed down at her body that was bare beneath the blanket's wrapping. The man had had the audacity to undress her, but then again she shouldn't be surprised where such a man was concerned.

Glancing toward the table, Laurel noticed a basket there with a note lying next to it. Still weaker than a sick puppy, she stood up gingerly and walked the few feet to the table. With trembling hands, she opened the ivory paper.

"Please eat, mademoiselle. I shall be back later."

There was no signature. Instinctively Laurel realized her kidnapper had written this terse message and left the basket for her. And he *would* be back.

Opening the straw top, she smelled the odor of freshly prepared soup and homemade biscuits that wafted up to her and caused her stomach to growl like a jungle cat. How long had it been since she had eaten? She could barely remember, but out of principle, she wanted to forgo the food. The man must be arrogant to believe she would do whatever he wanted after he had kidnapped her. But her resolve deteriorated under the wonderful aromas, and she found herself salivating. Sitting down on the chair, she took out the silver bowl that contained the soup and began noisily slurping down the warm broth, heedless of the spoon in the bottom of the basket. She would worry about decorum another time, she decided.

After the soup and a flaky biscuit had been consumed and filled her empty stomach, Laurel felt content. Still clutching the blanket around her, she vowed that when the man returned, she would stop acting like such a ninny and demand her freedom. Had the servant woman not told him that she wasn't Lavinia? Was that why he still held her captive? In her dream she remembered him calling her by her own name in the heat of passion. But again, that was only a dream.

The creaking of the door alerted her. She thought her kidnapper was coming and flew out of the chair, holding the blanket tightly against her, waiting for him to enter. The door slowly opened a crack, but no one stood there. Laurel blinked, unable to believe her good fortune. He had forgotten to lock the door. She was free.

Unmindful of her state of undress, she flew to the door, ready to depart, but then stopped. She needed clothes. Turning quickly back, she spotted the gypsy costume lying on the edge of the cot. Hurriedly she threw off the blanket and pulled on the skirt before reaching for the blouse, which rested in a tangle on the mattress. When she picked it up, something gold and round fell onto the dusty floor. Holding the blouse in front of her exposed breasts, she stooped down and picked up the object.

A gold button with an engraved *A* in the center gleamed in the palm of her hand. Where had it come from? she asked herself. "From him" was the answer that resounded in her head like an echo. Suddenly feeling weak, she sat down on the cot and clutched the button tightly. The memory of her "dream" washed over her. She had pulled at the man's shirt, nearly ripping it from his powerful shoulders. She could still recall the softness of the fabric and the hard, rippling muscles beneath her fingertips. She gasped, and her heart nearly stopped beating. It was no dream.

She unfurled her palm and gazed at the button, a reminder of a passion-laced night. What must the man think of her? she cried silently. And when he returned, he would no doubt expect her to act like a whore again. She swore under her breath at the outrageous situation in which this man had placed her. When he first kidnapped her, she had expected him to rape her. Instead she had freely given him her virginity and loved every moment of wanton abandon in his arms. She couldn't claim rape. Yet she didn't want to face the dark, hooded visage of her lover. She couldn't face him and allow him to think she had freely given herself to him, though this was, indeed, the case. No doubt he would expect her to play the tart again, and she wouldn't. How could she admit that she had wanted this man to make love to her, and that if he approached her again, she would fall willingly into his arms?

"No, never again," she breathed and pulled the peasant top over her head. Freedom was only a few feet away, and she would never have to tell anyone what had happened to her, or even to remember the night of desire she had spent in the arms of a stranger. But when she went to toss the button on the cot, she couldn't. It represented a night of sweet, unbidden passion—something she might never experience again.

Laurel swayed for a brief moment, overcome by tiredness and fear that her lover would return before she chanced the escape. However, she took the button and slipped it into the hem of her skirt and scurried from the cabin.

Once outside, Laurel leaned weakly on the porch railing, shielding her face from the sun as it slipped from behind a cloud to beam its warmth onto the silent bayou. Soon her eyes adjusted to the shimmering light, and she took a deep breath to steady herself. Surveying her surroundings, she looked in the direction of the shoreline from which she thought the man had entered on the rainy night of her kidnapping. A small section of shore jutted out like an arm and which, she felt certain, led though the wooded area to the road beyond. But she had to wade across the bayou to obtain her freedom.

Propelled by the innate desire to be away from the cabin that had been her prison and the place where the stranger had branded her as his woman, she stood in waist-deep water before she realized thick, rich mud enveloped her feet with each tentative step she took. When she reached the opposite side, feeling fortunate that nothing had slithered in her direction, she dropped for a moment to her knees, fatigued and breathing shallowly. But she had to go on, had to escape the memories of the past few days . . . if ever she could.

Rising to her feet, she smoothed out the wet cloth of her clinging gypsy costume. Then she moved onward into the dark forested area, which she hoped would lead her to help, salvation. But how will I explain this? she asked herself and felt herself blush as she began to walk beneath a canopy of low-hanging trees. She had been kidnapped, nursed back to health by her kidnapper, only to give herself to him—willingly. Would anyone believe such a preposterous tale, and if someone did, would she still be accepted or would she be treated like a harlot? She didn't wish to dwell on such a possibility now, or even think about the man who had taken her freedom, her love, only to disappear after having apparently suffered a twinge of conscience and having brought her some food. He hadn't been man enough to wait until she woke up this morning, to admit to her that he had wronged her. But he hadn't really wronged her. That was the problem. She had given herself body and soul to a virtual stranger.

A pulsating headache started to pound out a torturous rhythm with each step she took. Her bare feet, unused to being unshod, already felt raw, as she meandered down the wooded trail. Luckily the mud cushioned them against the larger pebbles and protruding vines that littered the way. Not only did Laurel have to watch where she stepped but on what she stepped. The thought of disturbing any reptilian life sent shivers coursing through her. It was minutes later that her teeth began to chatter, and she realized no fear of snakes had done that. She was sick again, and she knew it. If only she could get through this tropical maze of croaking frogs, fluttering birds overhead, and moss-laden trees that blocked out the sunlight, she would improvise some story to her rescuer. However, she had no idea how far the road was or even if she was headed in the right direction, for other trails branched off, God only knew where.

Laurel followed a thin, winding path, overrun with weeds, but after what seemed like hours, she was still in the heart of the forest and apparently no closer to the road. She must have taken the wrong trail. Was this how her life would end—on a lonely and forgotten trail in the middle of a forest with only birds to mark her passing? How tired she was, how cold and weak in the knees. She barely had the strength to go on, much less to retrace her steps to try another trail.

A sob rose in her throat. Sinking to the ground, she relished the softness of the dew-covered grass, which felt as soft as the finest feather mattress she had ever slept on. She supposed this was as good a place as any to end her life, a life that had barely begun. And all because she had wanted to sample the wild and untamed existence of Texas, to be like Lavinia. She wondered if Lavinia and Uncle Arthur would miss her. Probably not for long, she decided. But Gincie would miss her. Sweet, dear Gincie. Tears began to trickle down Laurel's cheek to think how Gincie would suffer when Laurel didn't return for her. More than anything, she mourned this aspect of her own death. How would Gincie fare without her?

Thunder sounded in the distance, though a spot of sunlight danced across her face. She would miss the sun, and everything that was now denied her. Not so long ago she had told Lavinia she would never marry a man who wanted her only for her money, that she would rather be alone. A strangled laugh bordering on hysteria bubbled up in her throat. Well, she had received her wish. She was going to be alone now forever. Her life would end beneath a canopy of tall moss-hung trees.

The thunder seemed to be growing louder until it nearly deafened her. With all the strength Laurel could muster, she opened her eyes and peered up at the sky beyond the pines and oaks. "Why, the sky is blue," she muttered stupidly, expecting the rain to start. Her strength had failed her, and now thunder reverberated in her head until she wanted to scream from the pain. Then it stopped to be replaced by the gentle sound of a horse's whinny.

She heard her name being called in a wrenching, agonized voice and felt herself being lifted and held in a man's arms. Cushioned against a hard chest, she could feel the rapid beating of a heart against her arm. For a moment she expected to see the dark, hooded countenance of the man who had caused her to be here in the first place, of the man she had shamelessly loved the night before. Instead she saw Tony Duvalier's handsome and concerned face bending over her, blocking out the sun, the sky, and the trees.

"Would Mademoiselle like the curtains drawn?"

Laurel glanced from her position on the bed and shook her head at the pretty, young woman with skin the color of light chocolate.

"I think not, Pauline. I want the curtains always opened from now on. I like the sunshine," Laurel amended, seeing the peculiar glance the servant girl sent her way. She couldn't explain to one of Tony Duvalier's slaves how she had come to love the sun after her imprisonment.

She wondered if Duvalier had informed anyone about what had happened to her. Most certainly she hadn't told him anything other than what the driver must have told him. A man had kidnapped her from the coach. Only Tony knew where she had been kept prisoner, and if he assumed the worst, he hadn't said anything to her so far. In fact, over the last week, since she had been at Petit Coteau and under a physician's care, Tony had been very kind and behaved as a perfect gentleman should. If not for Tony's private search for her, she would have certainly died.

But as Laurel sipped the warm tea offered her by Pauline, she again wondered why he hadn't found her before she escaped. Surely he was familiar with the territory. He had lived in the area all his life. When she gathered the courage to ask him who the man might have been, even going so far as to admit the truth about Lavinia's deception to him, he had remained strangely silent. She had feared he would condemn her, but he had gently told her to forget the whole incident, that she was safe with him.

She stretched luxuriously against the linen sheets, the frills at the neckline of her nightdress tickling her chin. Tony Duvalier had thought of everything, even to going back to the Garland Hotel and claiming her trunks so she would have her own things. She grudgingly admitted that she was liking him more and more each day. Another man, given the strange circumstances of her disappearance, might not have offered her a room in his home in which to recuperate. But then again, she had known from the very first that Tony Duvalier wasn't like other men.

A knock sounded on the door. She nodded to Pauline to admit Tony, who always visited her at the same time each afternoon after lunch. At the dismissive wave of his hand, Pauline scampered away, leaving the two of them alone. Today, Tony wore a pair of dark-brown trousers, a tan shirt, and black riding boots. The color emphasized his deep bronze coloring and the raven head of curly hair. Laurel had never seen a blacker pair of eyes than Tony's and for a fleeting second she recalled how they had flared with passion the night they had nearly made love at the Mardi Gras dance. She blinked rapidly to dispel the image. After all that had happened to her in the last ten days, she didn't want to become bewitched by Tony Duvalier. Besides he had a fiancée.

Moving a Queen Anne chair closer to the tester bed, whose sheer white hangings were tied to the four mahogany bedposts, Tony sat down and handed her a book. "I thought you might like to read, since you look as though you're feeling better."

She took the thin volume from him, amazed at how Tony always made it seem as if he had just left the room for a brief instant, when actually it had been a whole day. Why was it that suddenly she felt she knew him so much better since he had found her and brought her here? Probably because he *had* found her and didn't question her about what had happened between her and "that man," as she now thought of her kidnapper.

"*Aurora Leigh*," Laurel said and noticed it was a comparatively new work by Elizabeth Barrett Browning. "Thank you so very much, Tony. I loved her *Sonnets from the Portuguese*. I do feel quite well now and shall start reading this today."

He spread his long legs out in front of him. "Don't expect too much from this work. It isn't that good of a story, but it does have its moments. I thought you might be interested in reading the latest literary rage."

A dimple deepened in one of Laurel's cheeks. "I had no idea you were such a learned fellow."

"I suppose there's quite a bit you don't know about me, Laurel."

"I don't doubt that for a minute."

A long stretch of silence passed between them. She heard his steady breathing and felt his gaze upon her face when she turned away to sip at her tea. His intense perusal of her caused her to feel apprehensive, edgy, and she felt that stupid stain of color rising to her cheeks. Why couldn't she be like Lavinia more and accept a man's gaze without blushing like a silly fool? The thought flashed across her mind that the man who had loved her for that one wild, mind-drugging night could be very close-by. Her hand shook and caused the cup and saucer to rattle. Immediately Tony was up and took it from her. He placed it on the table beside the bed and looked down at her.

"You're very beautiful, Laurel."

In fact, Tony thought, she was more than beautiful. Just looking at her caused him to yearn for her. He ached to hold her again, to inflame her passions for him whereby she would melt shamelessly in his arms. But he must tread slowly with Laurel or lose her forever.

"I wish you wouldn't say things like that," she whispered and tried to avert her gaze from his penetrating eyes, but he tilted her face up to his. "Once I might have welcomed your attentions, but, Tony, things are different now. Things have changed."

Her honesty took him aback, and he didn't understand at first. Then the light dawned. For the first time she was admitting in her shy but subtle way that something had happened in that cabin on the bayou. Why now and why to him? Did this vague confession mean she could never give her heart to him now?

Tears misted her eyes, turning them into sparkling green pools. The hurt, the raw pain reflected in their watery depths tore at his very soul.

"I'm not the same person I was before that man, and I . . ." She could barely say the words as a sob shook her. "Oh, why am I telling you this? I swore

I'd never tell another person what happened to me."

Tony could tell she longed to cry, and he sat next to her on the bed, drawing her into his arms as she finally broke down and sobbed out the painful truth, which was much more painful for him to hear than for her to tell. She had no idea of the guilt he carried, how he longed to make it all up to her. When she had finished reciting her tale and wiped her eyes with one of his silk kerchiefs, she even managed a timid smile, which tugged at his heart, black cursed thing that it was.

"So, you see, Tony, I'm unfit for any man," he heard her say. "There can never be anything between us now. That man must live nearby, and for the rest of my life, I'll be haunted by his image. For all anyone knows, he could be an acquaintance of yours. What if he comes here for me?"

"You're safe here now, Laurel." His voice sounded ragged, and his large hands clasped her upper arms, keeping her in place when she sought to move away. "I can make you forget what happened—all of it—if you'll let me try."

Laurel had no doubt that Tony would endeavor to make her forget. But could she ever stop remembering the feel of the man's lips upon her body, the way she had wantonly arched herself upward to meet that first heart-stopping thrust when their bodies joined? Could Tony really make her forget? Did she want to forget?

"Oh, God, Tony, I don't know anything anymore!"

He was pushing her too hard. Time was what she needed, but he didn't know how long he could wait for her. The intoxicating scent of violets drifted from her hair, and beneath the thin, frilly gown he could see the rise and fall of her full breasts with each breath she took. He longed to throw her on her back, to admit he was the one who had loved her and that he was going to love her again. No doubt, she would respond to him. He was certain enough of his prowess to know what her reaction would be. It was what would come later that bothered him. She would be repulsed by what he had done, and he couldn't bear to harm her again. No, time was the best he could do for now.

Letting her go, he stood up. "I'm sorry about everything," he said, his voice laced with meanings she couldn't fathom. "You need your rest, and I'm badgering you about things you can't deal with at the moment." Bending down, he kissed the top of her head. "Ring for Pauline if you need anything."

Then he was gone.

Laurel gazed at the closed door for a long time afterward. Her thoughts whirled in her head like leaves in a windstorm. She really ought to leave Petit Coteau for San Antonio. Her uncle needed her. But she couldn't leave yet, not with the feeling that her life was unsettled. Too much had happened in too short a time. She couldn't think straight. Perhaps the best remedy was to remain in Tony's home until she could decide what to do. But beneath the rational musings was an irrational thought that her kidnapper was still nearby, and this knowledge brought a rapid heat to her body, almost consuming her with forbidden desire.

From beneath her pillow she withdrew the shiny gold button and clasped it to her breasts. Pauline had been quite upset with her when Laurel felt well enough to demand to know what had been done with her gypsy costume. Pauline had grudgingly retrieved it from the trash to be burned. When the torn and dirty, gold-and-purple skirt was again in her hands, Laurel had clawed at the hem until the button popped out. The gold button was all she had to convince her that the night she had lain in a stranger's arm hadn't been a dream.

It had been paradise.

Chapter Ten

Two days later Laurel was surprised by the unexpected arrival of Gincie. The woman flew into the room and embraced Laurel against her ample bosom, stroking her hair as though she were a little girl and calling her "my baby." In the doorway stood Tony with a huge grin on his handsome face and an unaccountable softness in his eyes.

"When Mister Duvalier came to tell me that you had been sick, Miss Laurel, I just up and told Doctor Mornay that I didn't feel poorly anymore. My place is with my baby, I told him. I done thought you left for Texas, but you ain't gonna get rid of me now. I'm stayin' with you until you get your strength back to travel on to San Antonio." Gincie folded her arms across her chest in a gesture of loving defiance. Laurel laughed and grabbed one of her hands.

"I wouldn't think of going anywhere without you, Gincie. I've missed you so. Are you really feeling better?"

"I sure am," Gincie said, eyeing the opened chifforobe in distaste. With much hustle and bustle she marched over to it and withdrew three of Laurel's best gowns, declaring that that uppity French girl didn't know anything about taking care of a lady's dresses, which were in need of pressing. With the gowns laid over her arms, Gincie hurried from the room in a whirl of rainbow-colored silks and satins to teach Pauline a thing or two.

Tony sauntered leisurely into the room and took his accustomed place in the chair by her bed. "I think Pauline has finally met her match," he observed and shot Laurel a devastatingly handsome smile.

"Do you mind if Gincie takes over looking after me?" Laurel leaned back against the propped-up pillows and drew the sheet up a bit. Something about Tony's covetous glance caused her to flush.

"Not at all. That's why I brought her here. I knew you missed her, and she certainly has missed you." The smile faded and deepened into something more serious as he observed Laurel, whose long, dark hair spilled in silken waves across her shoulders. Even the ruffles of the gown at the neck couldn't conceal the swell of her breasts beneath the thin material. An ache started in Tony's loins. God, he would grow crazy if he couldn't have her warm, willing body beneath his again.

"Laurel," he began in a husky breath, then cleared his throat. "Do you really intend to head on to San Antonio when you're recovered enough to travel?"

"Yes, I must. My uncle is ill. I told you all about that."

"I wish you'd wait a while."

Her eyebrows arched, and he continued hurriedly. "Until I know you won't fall ill again. I'd like to show you Petit Coteau, if I may."

Somehow she felt he had wanted to say something else. Perhaps he wanted her to stay because he had come to care about her? But if she stayed, then what? He couldn't offer her marriage. Tony was engaged to Simone Lancier, and the memory of Simone's clinging to him, the embrace she had seen between the two, caused Laurel to know that she hadn't a chance with Tony Duvalier. He might desire her, as he had proved the night of the dance when she had nearly abandoned herself to him on the lawn. But Laurel could foresee no future with a womanizer like Tony. Granted, he had rescued her and been incredibly kind and solicitous to her. She owed him a great deal, but she didn't owe him her heart and vowed she wouldn't be swayed by Tony's ardor again. Not when she had tasted true passion in the arms of a stranger, a man she would never see again, an experience that would be forever denied her in the future.

"Tony," she began slowly. For some stupid reason she relished the feel of his name on her tongue. "I told you already there can be nothing between us. Staying here much longer won't change my mind about you. I admit you turned my head the night of the Mardi Gras dance, but there—"

He broke off her words by the harsh scraping of chair legs against the highly waxed wooden floor. Standing up, he towered over her, and Laurel noticed a hot flame in his eyes, not from passion but anger. "Dammit, Laurel, I asked if you wanted to see my plantation, not sleep in my bed! I know you think I've just crawled out from under a rock, though you're too much of a lady to say that to my face. But you didn't care what you told me the other day about your seamy little tryst in the bayou when you needed a shoulder to cry on, did you?"

Laurel gasped in outrage. How dare he throw that back in her face. She had been overwrought, emotionally drained, and she had wanted to talk to someone about what had happened. She had made a monumental mistake in telling Tony. She knew that now.

"Arrogant bastard!" she screamed at him. "You're not a gentleman to bring that up to me."

"And you, miss, are not a lady to crave a stranger's hands upon your body." The fiery depths of his eyes held her to the spot for a moment before he grabbed her and pulled her from the mattress into the circle of his arms. His head came down in one fell swoop, and his mouth claimed hers, drowning out any protests she was about to utter.

Laurel felt his tongue invading her mouth, joining with hers in an age-old combat of wills. He wanted her response, and she wouldn't give it to him. Once again, as on the night of the dance, when he had nearly claimed her beneath a rain-filled sky, she felt her traitorous body start to respond. She almost raised her hand to slap his face but stopped herself. Tony was the sort of man who enjoyed making women mewl from pleasure in his arms. Well, not this time, she told herself and willed herself to remain quiescent in his embrace. Did he think because she had given herself to that man in the cabin that he had the right to expect the same thing from her? Tears started in her eyes. Tony had treated her shabbily from the very first, insinuating things about her that weren't true. And now just when she was beginning to like him, to think he had some redeeming qualities, he acted the brute. If he wanted a response, he certainly in hell wouldn't get one from her. Simone would be more than willing. Let him go to her, for Laurel Delaney was no whore.

"Kiss me, Laurel," he ground out savagely between mind-drugging kisses that threatened to turn her legs to jelly. "Kiss me back."

She didn't.

His hold loosened, and she fell weakly onto the bed. Tony glared at her for a few seconds, then started to walk away. She halted him with her voice.

"I would appreciate a tour of your plantation, however. My father owned one, and I should like to see how well yours compares with his."

A slight sneer curled his lips, but his eyes held a glimmer of respect for her. He left the room, slamming the door behind him.

Laurel wiped her eyes free of the threatening tears, but even after Gincie had returned and helped her dress, she still felt like weeping.

Downstairs in the parlor, Tony poured a huge glass of whiskey from a crystal decanter on the sideboard. Never much of a whiskey drinker, he, however, enjoyed the feel of the liquid as it burned a path down his throat. Despite the fact that the clock in the foyer chimed ten times, he didn't care that it was too early to indulge. He needed something to take the edge off his own pain, a pain that threatened to consume his very soul.

He cursed under his breath and sprawled on a small Empire chair, appearing incongruous with his long legs spread out before him. Tony swirled the liquid in the amber-colored glass and saw Laurel's face within the golden depths. He hadn't meant their conversation to take such a nasty turn. It seemed to him that ever since he had met her, nothing worked out to his advantage. Perhaps being denied Laurel's love was his punishment for seeking vengeance upon Lavinia Delaney. And he wanted Laurel with an unquenchable passion as much as he still wished Lavinia to pay for his uncle's death.

Downing the contents of the glass in one large gulp, he got up and poured another drink. Still he felt on edge. Didn't Laurel realize how much he cared for her? Of course not. He hadn't told her. Most certainly he could never tell her he was the man in the cabin. And the most absurd thing in the whole situation was that she couldn't respond to him because she thought she loved another. A bitter, harsh laugh escaped him as he once more took his seat. Laurel was enamored of a phantom lover—who was himself.

Damn, he moaned to himself and swallowed the whiskey. What was he going to do? She would leave for San Antonio if she didn't come to realize that she could very easily care for him, Tony Duvalier. He couldn't let her leave now. He was protective of her. He had followed her the whole distance she had traveled in the woods when she escaped from the cabin. But she didn't know that and would have to remain in the dark about that, just as she could never know he was the one who had nursed her back to health.

Laurel presented a challenge to him, and Tony appreciated a good challenge where women were concerned. Most of them gave in to his physical demands too easily. Laurel was different. She was in his blood, and he wouldn't rest until she was in his bed.

The sound of footsteps on the gallery alerted Tony to Jean DuLac's coming. Jean poked his head around the doorframe like a turtle in its shell.

"Ah, Tony, so you are in here," Jean said and entered the parlor. "I thought your time would be taken up with your pretty gypsy girl."

Tony motioned him to an identical chair beside him. "How do you know about Laurel?"

"Ah, such a pretty name. All of your neighbors know about her illness by now. Word travels fast among the slaves who are only too happy to tell their masters . . . and mistresses. Simone is much put out, *mon cousin*. I expect you'll receive a visit from her shortly."

Tony shrugged and stood up to pour Jean a drink. "Let her come. What Simone thinks is of little consequence to me."

Jean looked surprised. "I thought you and Simone were to marry."

"Simone would like everyone to believe that, but no, I have no intention of marrying her."

Taking the glass offered to him by Tony, Jean surveyed his cousin. Tony looked worried, not at all like the devil-may-care man who could have any woman in the parish with a snap of his fingers. Something troubled him, and Jean was astute enough to realize the trouble was probably in an upstairs bedroom.

"I think you should impress upon Simone that there is to be no marriage. She can stir up a great deal of trouble if she puts her fluffy blond head to it. However, she appears to be the least of your worries now. Is this Laurel the reason for the sadness I see in your face?"

Tony grimaced and surveyed Jean in turn. They had grown up together, almost as close as brothers. Jean's mother had been a Duvalier before her marriage to Jean's father, and more than one duel had been fought over her. Hot blood had always run in the Duvaliers. It seems that Jean's hot-bloodedness ran in the opposite direction than Tony's. Tony never could understand why Jean wasn't swayed by a woman's charms. Many women had expressed interest in his fair-haired cousin, and Jean always treated them reverently, respectfully, and managed to keep them as friends. Something Tony couldn't imagine, especially not with Laurel Delaney. He wanted her as his lover, not as a friend. But Jean was a good judge of character, and Tony valued his opinion.

"Laurel doesn't seem to care for me. I'd give almost anything to make her want me."

"Ah, I see. I spoke to her on the night of the Mardi Gras dance, and she seemed to care for you, Tony. Something must have happened to cause her feelings to change."

If you only knew, Tony thought and turned away so Jean wouldn't see the guilt he felt certain flooded his face. He heard Jean continue.

"Laurel is a lady, a true lady. She has values and will not be taken lightly by any man. You say you want her. What do you want her for?"

Tony turned to Jean. "I want her for my lover, of course."

"Of course," Jean said, a scoffing note in his voice. "You haven't heard a word I just said. Laurel is not the type of woman to be your lover, or any man's. She deserves much more, Tony. Have you considered marriage to her?"

Utter shock wreathed Tony's face. Marriage? Jean must be mad. All the women he had ever known had been untrue, only wanting his money, his name, his reputation in the community, and his elegant home. He would never consider marriage before he was ready.

"Wedded bliss isn't for me now, Jean."

Jean shook his head and sipped his whiskey. "Then you shall never have your Laurel. Marriage is what she will require."

"Why do all women have to have a price?" Tony intoned and stuffed his hands in his pants pockets.

"We all have a price, *mon cousin*. Even you. One day you will marry Laurel. Let's wager, say, your best stallion, Domino."

Tony cocked a dark brow. "What do you want if you lose?"

Jean considered a moment before a huge smile lit up his face like a brilliant candle. "I request your first son be named after me. Either way, I win."

"Not an unreasonable demand." Tony laughed and patted Jean on the back. The laugh quickly faded when he saw Laurel standing by the open doorway to the parlor, dressed in a pink-and-white-sprigged muslin day dress that molded to her curves. Her beauty nearly took away his breath; he had never seen a more beautiful and enchanting sight. She was silhouetted in the doorway, and he found himself thinking that she belonged to Petit Coteau, that the house had never looked so lovely until she stood there. He shook his head at the absurdity of the thought when she extended a slender hand to Jean. He wasn't going to marry, if he could help it. That crazy, romantic Jean had put silly ideas in his head.

Jean bestowed a gallant kiss upon Laurel's hand and put her arm through his, walking her onto the gallery, much to Tony's chagrin. After a few moments of polite conversation, Jean departed but not without a whispered remark to Tony.

"I think you are jealous of me, *mon cousin*. But don't worry. The lady is in love with you. I can tell these things."

After Jean's departure, Laurel turned to Tony. He leaned against the white railing, watching her with deep black eyes, and her heart speeded up a bit.

"You promised to show me Petit Coteau, I believe."

"And so I shall if you feel up to it."

She nodded she did, and within minutes Tony was lifting her into an open carriage and then taking the seat beside her and grabbing the reins.

The plantation was larger than Laurel had imagined, stretching in all four directions. The people working in the fields impressed her with their diligence and appeared well cared for. "No one is ever beaten on Petit Coteau," Tony told her, reading her mind:

Wispy traces of hair curled around Laurel's cheeks in the midday breeze. "I'm pleased to hear that, Tony. My father used an overseer to mete out punishment. That was the only part of the whole system he couldn't stand. Papa couldn't harm a fly, but someone had to discipline unruly slaves, he was told. When I sold the plantation last year, I freed all of them. Most stayed on to work for the new owners since they knew no other life. Soon all of this will come to an end if the Northern states have a say. You know, when I was away at school, some of the girls shunned me and called me horrible names. I had a friend who defended me, and I shall be indebted to her for the rest of my days." Laurel grew silent as his eyes came to rest on her. "How do you punish the slaves?" she dared to ask.

"Years ago, during my father's time, the wayward ones, as he liked to call them, were imprisoned for a few days in a tiny house. When their punishment was up, they usually settled down and gave no more trouble. However, there were ones who ran away."

"Were they ever caught?"

Shaking his head, Tony urged the horse along the dusty road that ran through the cotton field. "Not if we could prevent their return. My father didn't have a liking for brutality, and he knew that if a runaway slave was found, he'd have to use severe punishment.

So, he did the only thing he could. He freed all of them."

Pleased surprise surfaced on Laurel's face. "Why didn't you tell me your people were free?"

"They're not 'my people.' They belong to themselves. I suppose I'm lucky they work for me. Paying wages can take quite a bit out of the running of this plantation. But without the wages, there would be no Petit Coteau, and I couldn't exist without this place."

Laurel couldn't help thinking, what an unusual man was this Tony Duvalier.

Soon they came to a large expanse of land, about thirty acres, on which Laurel saw a number of small Acadian houses. They stopped in front of one which was surrounded by a wagon and a buggy and an assorted mixture of cows, pigs, and chickens roaming about the place. A thin woman appeared on the porch, toting a crying baby on her hip. Her homespun dress was covered by a white apron, and on her head she wore a matching bonnet.

"Monsieur Tony," the woman said and smiled. Laurel could see she had lost two of her front teeth, but that didn't detract from the warmth that shone on her face. "Would you care for some tea?"

"Merci, Madame Dauzet." He helped Laurel down from the carriage, and they entered the small but tidy house and were instantly seated on two of the best chairs. Tony introduced Laurel to the woman, who served them both tea without removing the baby from her hip.

"Octave is in the fields," Madam Dauzet told them. "The rain last week was so heavy that the crops almost drowned, but thank the *bon dieu* that all shall be well. Octave will bring you the yield as soon as he can."

Tony waved a hand in a dismissive gesture and chucked the baby under the chin. When Madame Dauzet asked him if he would like to hold her son, Tony eagerly reached for the child, surprising and delighting Laurel. He had a way with children. No sooner had he situated the baby on his lap, then the baby stopped crying.

Madame Dauzet laughed. "You always made my little ones smile, Monsieur Tony. When my Hippolyte was a baby, he would hold out his arms to you each time he saw you. Now that boy is almost a man and such a trial at times."

"What's the problem with Hippolyte? He's nearly seventeen now and must be eyeing all the girls."

Madame Dauzet shook her head. "It is nothing." She smiled gently at the baby in Tony's arms and patted the dark head of her son. "You shall make a good father one day."

Tony coughed and handed the baby boy back to his mother, aware of Laurel's soft gaze upon him. They bade her adieu and once more toured the plantation.

"Do the Dauzets work for you?" Laurel asked as they rode past a field where some men furrowed the land.

"More or less. They crop on thirds. I supply the land, which is used for pasture, the house and barn, and the livestock. Each family gives me a third of their produce, and I pay the taxes. Most of the families have been here for generations. Many of them are like my own family. Octave Dauzet and I played together as children."

"Then you're also a landlord?"

Tony nodded.

"And a lover of children?"

Tony colored but covered up this apparent fondness by saying, "You'd have seen what a lover of children I am if the child had wet on me. He'd have been tossed into his *maman*'s arms but fast."

Something in the warmth of Tony's voice, the slight smile that crimped the edges of his mouth, tugged at Laurel's heartstrings. She couldn't help but think that Madame Dauzet was correct. Tony Duvalier would make a good father. She looked away when he glanced in her direction, hating the way her heartbeat speeded up. She expected him to say something to her, perhaps to mention the incident that morning in her bedroom. He didn't. Instead he grinned at her, softening the anger she had felt toward him earlier.

The carriage leisurely covered the distance around the plantation. Large elm trees shading the gravellined road cast soft splotches of shadows across their faces as Tony urged the horse along. Laurel felt contented, more at peace then she had been in the last two weeks. She didn't understand her reactions to Tony. Sometimes he could infuriate her with just a glance; other times, like now, just a flicker of his dark gaze, wreathed in warmth, could set her silly heart to pounding. What was wrong with her? she worried again. Was she a foolish woman like Lavinia? Or wanton like her? Why was it that she couldn't separate the coursing sensations of warmth flowing through her body each time Tony looked at her from the passionate memories of the night with a stranger in the bayou cabin? She knew she couldn't go on like this much longer. Perhaps if she left soon for San Antonio, she could bury these feelings and get on with her life.

After Tony had stopped and showed her his cattle, giving her a lengthy dissertation on the merits of the Brahman breed, and after she had been introduced to his foreman, Leon Rabelais, Laurel noticed a cluster of ramshackle dwellings across the fence line. On the porch sat shabbily dressed men and women, who fanned themselves with torn dishrags. In the yard scantily attired and dirty children played with a thin-looking mongrel.

"Tony, who are they?" Laurel asked, instantly pitying them, especially the children.

Glancing in the direction of her gaze, Tony's face hardened. "Poor white trash. Don't bother with them or offer them your sympathy, Laurel. The men don't work, nor want to work. They swill wine all day long and wonder why their children go hungry, why their wives and daughters must wear rags for clothing. If they would get off their behinds and make a decent living, they could buy food and clothes. But they don't care."

Tony's harsh attitude bothered Laurel. "Aren't these people part of your plantation?"

"No. My property line ends there. I'm not responsible for any one of them, nor do I intend to be."

"But, Tony, the children are so thin and dirty."

"Don't waste your sympathies on them. Their fathers could work to take care of them, but they don't. There's been quite a bit of stealing in the area lately. In fact the Vermillionville area has been plagued by cattle thefts. A few of my own herd have disappeared. I wouldn't be the least bit surprised if one of those ne'er-do-wells on the porch had committed the crimes. Believe me, if I ever catch one of those thieves, it will be his last theft. Something is going to have to be done soon. Crime is rampant in the area." He led her back to the carriage and, without a backward glance, headed for the house.

But Laurel couldn't forget the faces of the children or the hardened, poverty-stricken ones of their parents. Something must be done for the children, at least. Yet Tony's words about the crime element struck a worried note in her brain. Could one of those men, or a man like one of them, have kidnapped her? After a moment's thought, she decided that was unlikely. The man who had kidnapped her and made love to her had been a man of refinement. A vengeful man, no doubt, but a man with a strict code of honor.

As they drove by the fence line that divided the house from the fields, Tony abruptly stopped the carriage and jumped down, only to cross to one of the white posts and pick a handful of spring wildflowers. As he sauntered back to her, Laurel felt the quickening beat of her heart. Tony looked so handsome in his shirt, which was unbuttoned almost to the navel and revealed a great deal of dark furplaned chest. His broad shoulders defined his lean hips and powerful legs, which were encased in tight-fitting pants. With his ebony hair blowing gently in the breeze, Tony's handsomeness wasn't to be denied. Too bad he could be so arrogant at times that he set her teeth on edge.

Jumping into the carriage, he pressed the wildflower bouquet into her hands. "Accept these flowers and my apologies for my behavior this morning, Laurel. I'm sorry. I know how hard it was for you to tell me about the incident. I shouldn't have said what I did."

Laurel was touched by the flowers, by the hope she saw in his expression that she would forgive him. Would she ever understand Tony Duvalier? He constantly kept her off guard. The slight breeze that passed over them ruffled the wisps of hair around her face, framing the large, green eyes and delicate features. A tremulous smile touched her strawberry-colored mouth.

"I accept your apology, Tony."

Her simple, straightforward words, coupled with the fact that Tony found her to be unbelievably beautiful, sent a shock wave through Tony's masculine frame. Her luscious red-tinged lips were but inches away from his. The enticing swell of her breasts were only a hand's length out of reach. He ached to pull her to him, to feel her body pressed against his, and to taste the sweetness of her mouth again. However, Tony decided not to touch her. Somehow he must woo her and win her love for himself, not as the nameless, faceless man who captured her heart.

"Thank you, Miss Delaney. I shall endeavor not to upset you again." He squeezed her hand, and Laurel laughed.

"So serious suddenly, Tony? You haven't called me 'Miss Delaney' since before you found me in the woods."

That was true, and Tony flushed. He had never called her by her own name because he had thought she was Lavinia, and that name had sounded too vile to even utter. But now as he gazed into her trusting face, green eyes dancing with amusement and warmth, Tony knew he wanted Laurel Delaney. And if Jean's prophecy turned out to be correct, Tony would be out a fine horse, but he would come out the winner in the end.

Chapter Eleven

Tony waited on the veranda, puffing on a Cuban cigar, until he heard Doctor Fusilier's footsteps descending the marble staircase. Hurrying inside, he lifted his eyes inquiringly at the physician. Doctor Fusilier shook his head.

"I'm sorry, Tony, but there is nothing else to be done."

Tony cleared his throat. "You mean Miss Delaney is completely recovered."

Nodding, Doctor Fusilier took his coat from the rack alongside the stairs. "Don't look so distraught, *mon ami*. You should be pleased the young lady is well again. Her throat infection was quite severe, but now all is clear. There is no reason for her to remain at Petit Coteau. Her health is good, and she is quite eager to be on her way to San Antonio."

"I thought you were my friend, Alphonse."

Alphonse Fusilier cocked an eyebrow in Tony's direction and pushed his arms into his coat. "Indeed, I am. I delivered you, remember, and soundly spanked your bottom, which I think might be a good idea under the present circumstances. For some reason, known only to yourself, you wanted Miss Delaney sequestered here as long as possible. Well, she has been under my care for almost three weeks now, and she is recovered. My job is finished. In all good conscience, I cannot tell her she must not leave. That is your problem to overcome. And believe me, my young friend, you have no easy task. Miss Delaney is one headstrong mademoiselle."

"She must remain at Petit Coteau," Tony persisted.

Alphonse shrugged. "As I said, she is your problem, but I suggest the direct approach with her. Evidently you're enamored of her. Tell her how you feel."

Tony could see he was butting his head against a brick wall as far as Alphonse was concerned. The man had ethics and had completed his job. Laurel was headstrong and determined to leave for San Antonio as soon as the doctor gave his consent. Now she knew she was well again, and Tony knew she would soon leave. He had tried everything to change her mind. He had been kind and gentle, left flowers in her room, accepted her warm thanks as graciously as he could, and refrained from sweeping her into his arms and kissing her luscious lips. So far, nothing had worked. Laurel still wasn't his lover. Tony groaned under the burden of knowing that soon she would bid him adieu.

"A fine friend you turned out to be. In matters of the heart, Alphonse, you have no feelings," Tony groused.

Alphonse laughed and headed out the front door to his waiting buggy.

Tony glanced up the winding stairway to the elaborately carved balustrade that overlooked the vestibule. The door to Laurel's bedroom remained closed like a white sentinel guarding the ice princess. He was tempted to believe she had no feelings, no heart, where he was concerned, but he knew differently. That night in the cabin when they both had lain drenched in sweat, clinging to each other and finding earth-shattering fulfillment, had proved to him that Laurel Delaney overflowed with fiery passion for him. Well, not for himself, Tony silently amended, but for her kidnapper. What was he going to do now? He couldn't let her leave for San Antonio.

Tony went to stand outside again, his dark gaze taking in the green, lush sweep of his fields. The last week he had practically begged her to remain on the plantation until she was completely recovered, and perhaps for a longer time afterward. She had smiled at him, her face full of warmth, but her green eyes had held determination. "We'll see, Tony." she had told him, giving him a grain of hope that she would see fit to remain. Now, he realized she had never meant to stay here but had already made up her mind to catch the stagecoach to Texas.

A lot of wasted breath and energy on his part, he decided.

In the distance he noticed his foreman going through the paces with an Arabian mare Tony had recently purchased. He remembered when he bought her the horse had been skittish, allowing no one near her and bucking each time he managed to climb onto her back. What a challenge the horse had been. He had even named her Challenge. But then one day he had approached her in a no-nonsense way, with no more cajoling words, no more loving pats. Challenge had allowed him to ride her, and ever since she had recognized Tony as her owner. If only women could be trained as easily as horses, Tony mused.

Taking a long puff on his cigar, he suddenly realized that perhaps Laurel was a great deal like Challenge. The horse hadn't taken well to loving gestures but had responded to a firm, nonchalant hand, and maybe Laurel felt the same way. She wanted to make up her own mind and not feel she was being tugged to make a decision. Could the whole answer be to allow her to decide for herself without his interference, and then, he hoped, she would come around to his way of thinking? It was worth a try. From now on, he would quit pestering her to remain at Petit Coteau. He would leave all up to Laurel.

Yet he worried she would still leave for San Antonio before he could entice her into his bed. Such was life, he realized, and shrugged. However, this was one woman he didn't intend to let get away.

"That Mr. Duvalier is a true gentleman," Gincie pronounced after Doctor Fusilier's visit. "I think he likes you. Why ain't you encouragin' him back?"

Laurel glanced up from the window seat where she sat, gazing down at the tranquil scene below her. She had been watching Tony walk away from the house to the fields and realized that she had been staring at him for quite a while. It was only Gincie's voice that caused her to end her reverie.

Gincie busied herself with pulling Laurel's gowns from the chifforobe and shaking out the wrinkles before going downstairs to press them. Laurel left the window seat and sat before the vanity mirror, unable to answer Gincie's question. She couldn't tell dear Gincie why she didn't encourage Tony's attentions or any man's. Gincie would be shocked, horrified no doubt, if she learned the truth about the kidnapping. Things were better left alone, Laurel decided. Though she did welcome Tony's attentiveness and his kindness, she sometimes wanted to scream at him to stop badgering her about San Antonio.

Gincie paused in the doorway. "Are we or ain't we goin' to San Antonio?"

This time Laurel did answer. "I can't say, Gincie. Soon, I think. We can't stay here forever."

"You better make up your mind, 'cause I'm gettin' tired havin' to oversee that that clumsy Pauline don't burn your pretty dresses."

No sooner had Gincie departed than Pauline came to the door. "You have a guest in the parlor. Mademoiselle Simone Lancier wishes to see you."

Laurel told her to tell Simone she would be right down. What did the woman want? Laurel asked herself. She hadn't seen her since the night of the Mardi Gras dance and had no great desire to see her now. Laurel went to the cheval mirror and appraised her appearance. She found her cheeks to be a trifle pale, and she had grown thin due to her illness. Her hair hung in long dark waves down her back, and she now wished she had the time to pull it into a chignon. With her hair hanging around her face she always looked like a child. Her eyes flickered down the expanse of her body, not particularly caring for the green-and-white-striped gown that made her look more slender. Compared to Simone's lush curves, she looked like a boy. She had only just regained her appetite, and it would take a few weeks to be back to her former weight. By then Simone Lancier wouldn't be sitting in Tony's parlor, waiting for her like a cat ready to pounce on the unsuspecting mouse.

"Oh, the devil with her!" Laurel muttered and turned in a rush, her skirts billowing behind her like a green-and-white parasol. She wouldn't allow Simone's perfectly manicured beauty to intimidate her. As a guest in Tony's house, she did owe it to his fiancée to be pleasant to her.

Downstairs Laurel found Simone in the parlor, sipping tea. Upon seeing her, Simone stood up and kissed Laurel on both cheeks. The woman stepped back, appraising Laurel against her own low-cut gown, which rivaled yellow jonquils in the springtime and set off her golden hair and milky-white skin. Apparently Simone found Laurel lacking, for she flashed her a smile whose brilliance was only diminished by the diamond necklace at her neck.

"I've come to see how you are doing. Tony's cousin, Jean, told me you had been ill. Tony never properly introduced us at the dance, and I thought we should become better acquainted." Simone sat down on the sofa and patted a place next to her almost as if she owned the furnishings and the house. Laurel purposely chose a chair next to the sofa, not missing the daggerlike glare that Simone threw her. However, when she spoke, her voice sounded honey smooth.

"You're aware that I am Simone Lancier and have been a neighbor and friend of Tony's for years. A very special friend," Simone reminded Laurel.

"Tony has never mentioned you."

Laurel's quick response caused Simone to redden with anger or embarrassment, or a combination of the two. But she waved away her discomfort with a hand and made a twittering sound as if she were greatly amused.

"That Tony is such a ladies' man, *chérie*. He has the habit of making a woman feel that she is special. I suppose it would be very ungentlemanly of him to mention me and our 'special relationship' to you.

You are, after all, only recuperating in his house. Am I to understand that you shall soon be departing Petit Coteau?" Simone sipped her tea and eyed Laurel warily.

Concealing her aggravation at Simone's drilling her for information about her status in Tony's life, Laurel casually stood up and walked to the fireplace. With a possessive hand she stroked the edge of the mantelpiece.

"I've grown quite fond of this house . . . and Tony. He has been most kind to me during my illness, and I can think of but one way to repay such generosity."

Simone's cup clattered to the floor. Tea splattered on the material of her gown, staining it an ugly shade of brown. She rose quickly, heedless of the gown's condition.

"And just how do you intend to repay him, Mademoiselle Delaney?"

Simone was breathing hard, her bosom nearly popping out of her low bodice.

"Be warned that I can be a formidable opponent where Tony is concerned."

"I had no idea we were in some sort of a game, Simone, but I fail to see what that has to do with the party?"

"Party?"

"Yes, the party I intend to throw for Tony," Laurel said, relishing Simone's discomfort. "What did you think I was going to do? Seduce him?"

The color had drained from Simone's face, leaving it pale and pasty looking. "Don't try such a tactic with him, otherwise, I shall—"

The sound of Tony's voice interrupted Simone. He entered the room, taking in the sight of Simone with tea stains on her gown, and Laurel looking like a candy stick.

"I believe a party is a wonderful idea. How are you, Simone?" He bent and dutifully kissed her cheek. "I overheard your conversation, and you shall be first on the guest list. Now, I really think you should hurry on home, *chérie*, before those stains set."

"Tony," Simone began but bit her lip. She shot Laurel a withering glance and nearly ran from the room. When the front door was slammed with a bang, Tony laughed aloud.

"Simone is up to her old tricks, I see."

"She seems to care about you, Tony." Laurel felt suddenly deflated by this knowledge. Simone must have some feeling for Tony to come here and warn her away from him.

"Mademoiselle Simone Lancier is a proprietary female, Laurel."

"Why shouldn't she be? You are going to marry her."

"No, I'm not."

"But Jean told me you were."

"Jean was wrong, and I have already told Simone I didn't want to marry her. Have you believed that all this time?"

Laurel nodded, so numb with relief that he wasn't going to marry such a woman that she felt giddy and light-headed. She clutched at the back of the chair as the room began to spin and would have fallen except for Tony's picking her up in his arms.

"Tony, put me down," she begged and was forced to wrap her arms around his neck.

"I told that fool of a doctor that you weren't well yet. You're going upstairs to bed."

"I am not!"

"*Oui, chérie,* you are, and you won't be allowed

downstairs until I say so."

"I'll come downstairs when I damn well please!"

Tony's mirthful laugh echoed through the vestibule and up the stairs to Laurel's room.

Gently he laid her on the bed, but she sat up quickly and started to bound from the mattress a large restraining hand on her waist hindered her.

"Let me up, you bully," Laurel ranted and strained against his hand. "I won't be treated like a child."

Her gown rode low across her shoulders, revealing the creamy swell of her breasts to Tony's heated gaze. Laurel watched as the amusement on his face disappeared and desire took its place. She shivered from the intense longing she saw there and was rocked to the core of her being to realize that she felt it, too. Her mind whirled when he sat beside her and stroked her cheek, her neck. Then his hand hovered at the valley between her breasts, and she heard little, throaty sounds of anticipation emanting not from Tony but from herself.

"You're definitely not a child, Laurel," he whispered. "You're a woman. I want you to be my woman."

Slowly, so slowly she felt as if she were watching him in slow motion, his dark head descended to claim the spot, where his hand had hovered, with an earth-shattering possession of his mouth. An arc of sunlight spilled through the window and enveloped them in a golden hue. Laurel felt as if her blood had turned to molten gold. Each kiss, each flick of his tongue across the lush curves of her breasts made her weak. One of his hands pushed away the bodice of her gown, and she felt her breast cupped in a warm embrace. She moaned as his hand discovered a taut nipple and gently caressed it between his strong, sure fingers.

Tiny gasps of pleasure escaped her. She writhed against him, closing her eyes, and gave herself up to feelings of desire that spiraled within her, seeming to cloud her reason. His mouth soon replaced his hand, and the gentle tugging of his lips against the stiff, rose-hued peaks caused her to clutch at his broad shoulders. Her passion threatened to drown her when his hands moved wantonly down her hips, her thighs, and then she realized he had hiked up her skirt. Her desire-shrouded brain registered that his hand had found that part of her that only one man had fondled, had loved. Tony's fingers stroked her softness until she thought she would scream with the ecstasy of sensations coursing through her and building to a climax in the moist center of her being. A part of her didn't want him to continue, but part didn't want him to stop. She knew this was wrong, yet she felt unable to mutter the words to push him away.

As on the night of the dance, Tony held her in his thrall. She heard him whisper her name, felt the hot kisses he brandished upon her breasts, and when his fingers entered her, she wantonly arched her back, eagerly meeting them. Somehow, some way, Laurel was transported to the bayou cabin and the hooded man who had made her a woman. With her eyes tightly shut, she imagined that Tony and the man had merged to become one. Somehow the memory of that encounter made the exquisite sensations that gathered in a liquid heat, threatening to inundate her in spiraling hot flames, permissible. Her body was helpless against the man who now worked his sensual magic over her. She wanted to experience the same jolting quivers of ecstasy again. In her mind Tony had ceased to exist, and she was once more writhing in wanton abandon beneath a stranger's hands.

And then when the wild pleasure she sought finally crested, her body exploded. Her cries of ecstasy were smothered against Tony's mouth. His kiss was deep and shook her to the very essence of her being. When she opened her eyes, the image of her phantom lover disappeared. She found Tony staring at her. Laurel colored a vivid shade of red to realize what had just happened between them. Tony's hand was still joined to her, and he probably could still feel the pleasurable waves of her traitorous body lapping at his fingertips.

Covering her face with her hands, Laurel felt tears of humiliation gathering in her eyes. What had she done? What must Tony think of her? She couldn't bear to look at him, because his own face was wreathed in desire for her, a desire she knew could never be fulfilled. She had given her heart to a stranger, and this was the main reason she cried. Tony wasn't that man.

Without her fully realizing it, Tony's fingers slipped away. He gently moved her hands from her face and sat holding them before he spoke.

"Laurel, do you want me to make love to you?"

Heaven help her, she thought, but she did. And she couldn't. Her heart had betrayed her as well. She realized she could respond to Tony, but without love there was nothing. Her heart belonged to another man.

"I'm sorry, Tony. I can't."

"Because of that man? You want him to make love to you?"

"Yes." The word sounded as if it had been wrenched from her, and Tony sighed, dropping her hands.

"I still want you, Laurel. I want to marry you."

He felt as surprised by this admission as Laurel looked. Why he had said such a preposterous thing, he didn't know. Yet that was what he wanted at the moment. With her lovely eyes awash with tears, the way her dark hair spilled onto her naked breasts, and the memory of her response to him, he could envision her as his wife and the mother of his children. For the first time in his life, he believed he had fallen in love and wanted marriage. Damn that romantic Jean for putting the insane idea in his head in the first place!

"Will you marry me, Laurel?"

Laurel considered Tony for a moment. He loved her, and she could see that love on his face for her. When had all of this happened? she wondered. A handsome, wealthy man wanted to marry her. And she knew that she more than likely would come to like making love to him. The past few minutes were proof of that. But she didn't love him and wouldn't marry him. She would have to hold part of herself from him, and she decided she must be fair with Tony. He deserved a woman who would give her whole heart to him.

"I can't," she said softly.

At her answer, he appeared resigned, seeming to sense that the situation was hopeless. Laurel, however, didn't know that he warred within himself whether or not to tell her that he was her kidnapper. He decided once again that nothing would be gained by this information. She would only hate him when she learned the truth, and he still wouldn't have won her love.

Standing up, Tony grinned. "You're the first woman I've ever asked to marry me."

"I'm honored," Laurel told him and with his help pulled down her skirt and fixed her bodice before standing up. "I'm leaving for San Antonio soon. I assure you I feel quite well."

"The party is off then. I was looking forward to telling Simone that you and I were to be married."

Her beauty took his breath away when she gave him a tiny smile. He thought he would love her for the rest of his life; in fact he knew he would. After meeting Laurel Delaney, he would *never* marry now. No woman could make him feel the way she did. But she didn't deserve such a cad for a husband. That was the main reason why he didn't take her in his arms again or try to change her mind. Perhaps in San Antonio she would meet a nice man and get married and have the children he had hoped to have with her. And this knowledge caused his eyes to harden for a second. He couldn't bear any man touching her but himself.

"I hope you'll be very happy in Texas," he said coolly and so formally that Laurel wondered what had happened to the man who had so recently had love on his face for her. "When you are ready to leave, tell Picard, my groom. He'll have a carriage waiting to take you to the stage line. Good-bye, Laurel."

Tony turned away and left the room, closing the door stiffly behind him. Laurel stood in the center of the bedroom, her pulse racing. Part of her wanted to run after Tony to agree to his proposal because she had hurt him, and she knew it. But then she couldn't marry him. He must realize eventually that she had done him a favor.

Yet, if it hadn't been for the man who kidnapped her and loved her, she would probably have accepted Tony as her husband. This realization caused her tears to flow, and she cursed that nameless, faceless man for robbing her of her happiness.

* * *

Laurel had intended to leave as soon as possible, but an early spring thunderstorm, threatening in its intensity, had delayed travel. One week later Laurel was still at Petit Coteau. Her relationship with Tony was friendly but distant. Some nights when Jean visited, she sat in the parlor after supper, but as soon as Tony appeared, dressed in his formal attire, off the two cousins would go to Plonsky's Opera House. Tony never returned until dawn, and she cursed herself for not being able to fall asleep until she heard his horse's hoofs on the driveway. Probably, she decided, he had spent the night at Simone's or at a brothel, and she hated herself for being disturbed by this thought. She would almost think she was in love with him.

To counteract his offhanded treatment of her, she began to take her meals in her room. Gincie wasn't the least bit pleased by this.

"You ain't gonna get a husband by eatin' in here," she told her sternly. "Bees get caught with honey, not vinegar. Those hard looks I done seen on your face and Mr. Tony's ain't the way to make peace."

Laurel had said nothing to her. She couldn't say anything in her own defense because Gincie wouldn't have understood she loved a man who had kidnapped her. She had never told Gincie about the incident and wouldn't do so now. She was too close to leaving for Texas and putting the whole incident from her mind.

One afternoon Laurel woke from a nap to Pauline's gentle tap at her door. Gincie immediately opened it.

"What do you want?" Gincie asked. "You done woke Miss Laurel."

Pauline's face reddened, and she curtseyed to Laurel who sat up.

"I'm sorry, mademoiselle. The man at the stagecoach office sent word that a stage will be leaving tomorrow at noon. The roads are cleared for travel."

Laurel thanked her and got off the bed. She sat by the dressing table, and Gincie came to stand behind her. Gincie picked up her brush and ran the soft bristles through the long strands of Laurel's hair.

"Looks like we'll be leavin' tomorrow, Miss Laurel."

"Yes, it does."

"Ain't you gonna tell Mr. Tony good-bye?"

"I suppose I shall if he's around. He seems to sleep during the days now and leaves at night with Monsieur DuLac. It seems as if he's becoming quite a wastrel."

"That man's hurtin'. You ain't told me what happened between you two, but I got eyes, and that man loves you. You love him, too."

"No, I don't."

Gincie finished brushing Laurel's hair and stood back with the brush clutched in her hand. "If you was a little girl, I'd be tempted to use this here brush on your bottom. But you ain't a little girl. You is a grown woman, Miss Laurel, and about high time you started actin' like one."

"I don't need you to chastise me."

Laurel whirled away from the mirror and sat down by a small table. In front of her was a tray the cook had prepared for her. Roasted duck with rice and a garden salad were there to tempt her, but Laurel only picked at the food. She wasn't the least bit hungry, nor had she been able to eat lately. In fact she always felt nauseated, and Gincie was forced to go the kitchen to make a mint brew. Still, she couldn't shake this sickish feeling, especially in the evenings.

"You ain't eatin' again." Gincie's sharp eyes took in the uneaten food and the sudden whiteness of Laurel's face. "You feel sick again, don't you?"

Laurel took a deep breath to keep the sick feeling at bay. "It will pass. It must be the aftereffects of my illness."

"Like hell it is. Don't you know what's ailin' you, Miss Laurel? Haven't you figured it out yet?"

Gincie's probing caused a wave of alarm in Laurel. She didn't want to think about what Gincie's questions might mean. "I have a slight indisposition, that's all."

"An indisposition that lasts nine months, and you know I'm right. I think you got the evenin' sickness instead of the mornin' sickness. You ain't got your monthlies yet."

Laurel groaned and held her head in her hand. "Isn't there anything about me you don't know, Gincie?"

Gincie came and touched her shoulder, and her voice was gentle.

"You is my baby, Miss Laurel. You took the place of my little Annie who died when she was just a year old. I know as much about you as I did her, and myself. I know when you're happy and when you're scared and hurtin'. You is scared now. Did you tell Mr. Duvalier about the baby?"

Laurel lifted her head. "No. There's no reason to tell him anything. I might not be pregnant at all. This is none of his business."

"Ha! That man gets you in the family way, and it ain't his business. Miss Laurel, what is wrong with you?"

Grabbing one of Gincie's work-worn hands, Laurel said, "Don't mention any of this to Tony. Please."

"Don't you want him to do the right thin' and marry you?"

How could she tell Gincie that the right thing wasn't to marry her? If she was pregnant, the child wasn't his. But Gincie could never know that.

"He already asked to marry me, and I turned him down. Now forget about this. I can assure you I'm not having a baby. We have to leave for Texas tomorrow and have quite a lot to do."

Gincie started to say something else but didn't. She didn't like the warning look in Laurel's eyes and had decided not to mention anything to Tony. But half an hour later Laurel had the worst case of evening sickness so far, and Gincie decided to find Tony Duvalier, even if she had to storm a house of ill repute to do it.

Chapter Twelve

The longer Gincie dwelled on Laurel's problem, the more upset she grew. By the time Laurel drifted off to sleep, she was in a dither to find Tony. Convincing Tony's groom to take her into town at nearly midnight was no easy task, but she made the job easier by giving him a small butterfly brooch that Laurel had given her as a birthday gift. She hated parting with the piece of jewelry, but if it insured Laurel's happiness, Gincie was content.

However, by the time they reached Washington, the opera house was closed. Picard, the groom, even went to a brothel on the edge of town, but Tony wasn't there. By now, Gincie was filled with panic that she would never find Tony before the stage left at noon. Then she remembered Jean DuLac, and within minutes she was waiting on the porch of the white-columned house in the center of town.

A dim light glowed in the parlor when a servant let her inside. To her delight she found that Jean was still awake and entertained a sweet-faced young man.

At her appearance in the doorway, he stood up and asked her what she was doing there. After a few hesitant starts, Gincie whispered in Jean's ear that she needed to find Mr. Duvalier.

"Is Miss Delaney in some sort of trouble?" he asked.

"The biggest trouble a lady can get herself in," she answered.

Jean realized the gravity of the situation immediately and told her he would have Tony home long before the noon departure.

But that wasn't as easy to do as Jean had originally figured. He went to Tony's usual haunts in town, but he was nowhere to be found. Then he took his horse and rode in the opposite direction, away from Washington, to Clermont, home of the Lanciers.

A sleepy servant answered his summons, and within minutes Simone rushed down the stairs, a thin wrapper clasped to her voluptuous body. Her golden hair hung down her back like sunlight, and Jean couldn't help but appreciate what an angelic-appearing beauty she was.

However, when she spoke, her shrewish voice broke the image. "What is the matter, Jean? I was sound asleep. My father has been ill, and you're here in the middle of the night. In need of some company? Well, I'm not to your taste."

Simone smirked, and Jean managed a tight laugh. "I'm looking for Tony. Have you seen him?"

"After the way he has treated me since that American trollop has been under his roof? You're mad to think that I'd even speak to him. Did she send you here? Is that why you're here? You're so enamored of the little witch that maybe there's hope for you yet."

Jean held up a restraining hand. "There's no need to get nasty, Simone. I have to find him as soon as possible. If you see him, tell him that he is wanted at home immediately."

Simone nodded she would, then went upstairs after Jean's departure. Such a simple request, she thought. But one she would never deliver. Stepping into her bedroom, the soft glow of the candle by her bedside illumined Tony's large frame, spread-eagled across her bed. She stopped to admire the broadness of his shoulders, the thick pelt of hair on his chest as it tapered to his waist, only to disappear and then bush out across the area of his body that had always held such fascination for her. What a man!

Her hand snaked out, and her fingers gently stroked his naked thigh, feeling the soft hairs on his leg tickle her flesh. Then the exploring trail led to that part of him she wanted to drive deep into her own body, to know again the delights of being Tony's woman. Her hand grasped it, enfolding it in a soft but firm caress. Almost miraculously she felt the stiffening of his shaft in her hand, and knew that he was hers, that she could do anything she wanted with him. Tony had arrived earlier in a drunken stupor and attempted to make love to her, only to fall asleep soon after he had undressed. She had spent the last two hours waiting for him to wake up and claim her. And now was the moment for which she had waited.

"Tony, *mon amour*," she whispered. "I am ready for you."

For a brief instant he lifted his head. "Laurel?" His eyes fastened on Simone. "You're not Laurel." Then his head hit the pillow, and he began to snore.

The object that Simone so coveted fell limply in her hand.

* * *

Laurel's trunks were already in the stagecoach when Jean found her moments before departure.

"Please wait until Tony can be located before leaving," he implored.

Jean appeared so helpless and boylike with his light blond hair glinting in the sunlight that Laurel almost wished she could grant him this favor and wait for Tony. But she couldn't. There was nothing else to say to him, and she wouldn't tell him about the baby. She wasn't certain if Jean tried to prevent her from leaving out of a sense of loyalty to Tony or if he somehow had guessed she was pregnant. Either way, it didn't matter any longer. Soon, Tony Duvalier would be out of her life completely as was the man who had captured her heart in the bayou cabin.

"Give Tony my regards," Laurel told Jean before kissing him on the cheek. She stepped into the Wells Fargo stagecoach as Gincie lumbered in beside her with a worried look in her eyes. With a crack of the whip, the horses started into action, and soon the stagecoach, which contained three other passengers besides Laurel and Gincie, sped down Grand Prairie Road.

"You're makin' a bad mistake, Miss Laurel," Gincie bemoaned.

"Well, it's my mistake to make," Laurel said sharply and dismissed the ache that gnawed at her soul. She would have to raise her child alone, but she was better off than many women in her circumstances, she found herself thinking. At least she was wealthy and could give the child all the love she posessed and material wealth. However, a father was something her baby would simply have to do without. She dreaded the thought that society might ostracize her child and they would both have to deal with that fact of life. The path she had set for herself and the life she carried within her would be rocky and hard, and she prayed they would survive. Still a part of Laurel wished she had accepted Tony's proposal. Things would have been so much simpler. But he didn't know she carried the child of the man who had kidnapped her, and if he did, would he still have wanted to marry her?

Laurel shook her head to stop the whirling thoughts and patted Gincie's hand. "We'll be fine, Gincie. Wait and see."

"I hope so, Miss Laurel," Gincie said with a catch in her voice. "For your sake, I do hope so."

The afternoon sunlight spilled onto the bed, waking Tony with its brightness. He sat up slowly, trying to orient himself to his surroundings. A porcelain clock on the mantel chimed the noon hour, and he realized he was in Simone's bedroom, ensconced in her bed with a thin sheet to cover his naked body. He groaned.

How in the hell had he gotten here? He didn't remember anything about the previous night. He had left the house about eight, gone to Plonsky's Opera House for half an hour before making his way to the local saloon, quickly downing three bourbons and countless whiskeys. After that, he recalled nothing. And Simone, where was she? he asked himself and started to get up to dress, but a dull headache prevented him from moving too quickly.

From down the hall he heard the faint tinkle of the bell Monsieur Lancier used to summon the servants. He wondered if he should look in on the old man but dismissed the idea. He doubted the very stern and strict Pierre Lancier would wish to know that his daughter had bedded a man in his home. Of course Tony and Simone had made love many times in this room, but that had been when Simone thought they would be married. Her father, sick as he was, had probably been aware of their trysts and ignored them. But now there wasn't going to be a wedding, and he didn't think Lancier would ignore his presence in his daughter's bed without the possibility of marriage.

Tony sighed and slipped out of bed just as Simone entered the room. His nakedness brought a sly smile to her mouth, and she licked her lips at such an enticing and arousing sight. Tony grudgingly admitted that she looked quite pretty in a simple blue-and-white frock with a slip of lace at the low neckline. With the sun shining on her golden hair, Simone resembled an angelic being. But Simone was far from being a saint.

"I trust you slept well," she said with a smile, but he heard a slight edge to her voice.

"Like a rock, Simone. Thank you for your hospitality."

Tony began pulling on his discarded pants, trying not to give in to the pounding of his head and lie back down on the soft bed. He had to get back to Petit Coteau. He wasn't certain why. Most probably Laurel wouldn't even leave her room, but he liked knowing she was nearby and that at any moment she would appear to brighten his day. However, since she had rejected him, his days and nights had been less than bright.

Simone walked over to him after she had picked up his shirt, drawn by the sight of his powerful chest. She splayed her fingers over the fur-planed expanse and lifted her ruby-colored mouth to his.

"You don't have to leave so soon Tony. Stay and have something to eat. I know you must be hungry after last night."

A giggle escaped her, and Tony's eyes narrowed. "Nothing happened last night."

"You slept in my bed, *chéri*."

Tony shrugged and grabbed the shirt, his muscles flexing as he slipped into the silken garment. "That doesn't mean a thing, Simone. You know I was too drunk last night to do anything other than sleep. I might have been very drunk and don't recall a thing, but I know for a fact that I was unable to make love to you."

Simone's eyes shot blue slivers in his direction. "What makes you so sure nothing happened, Tony? Am I not woman enough for you any longer? Or perhaps you are less than a man."

Tony laughed and buttoned his shirt before sitting on the side of the bed and pulling on his boots.

"Let's stop playing games. Both of us know how we used to be together, and I don't have to prove anything to you about my manhood. And you are quite a woman, Simone, but things are different now."

"Because I'm not Laurel," Simone grumbled.

Tony's dark brows rose a fraction of an inch. He stood up and grabbed his jacket.

"I'll leave now, and believe me, I won't be back. My apologies for last night. If things had been different—"

"Don't apologize!" Simone interrupted. "You insult me with your feeble apology. I cared for you once, and you've cast me aside for a woman who makes you miserable. And you are miserable. Why else would you get so stinking drunk that you really don't know if we slept together or not? I pity you."

Simone stung Tony with her criticism, and he couldn't deny her words. He *was* miserable. Though he knew she didn't truly care for him, he felt badly about his callous treatment of her. Simone was a promiscuous bitch, but she had provided him with moments of ecstasy in the past. He grabbed the doorknob, yanking open the large oak door, and gave her a smile.

"You're quite correct that I am miserable. I only hope that you never feel the pain I'm experiencing right now."

His broad back filled the doorway, then he was gone. Simone trembled and clasped her arms around her waist. Already she felt pain at his polite dismissal of her affections. Granted, she had never loved Tony, but she did covet his wealth and his perfect male body. She thought they could have made a perfectly acceptable marriage. Her father's illness had drained their money, and she knew that when he died she would have to sell the plantation to pay off the bills, plus her own extravagances. She would have precious little to live on then, and all because of Tony Duvalier and his Laurel.

She would never forgive Tony for not wanting her.

"I'll have you yet, Tony," she whispered to the closed door. "And if I can't, I shall make your life worse than miserable."

When Tony stopped his horse before the house half an hour later, Jean hurried outside and motioned furiously to him.

"Where have you been, Tony? I've been searching for you since last night."

Tony glanced down into Jean's flushed face. "Is something wrong with Laurel?" He made a move to get off the horse, but Jean stopped him.

"She left on the noon coach for Texas."

"Oh," was Tony's only comment, feeling as if a tree had fallen on his chest. He felt unable to breathe.

"Go after her," Jean ordered.

"Things are best this way."

"Laurel is pregnant, Tony."

Jean's words barely sunk into Tony's brain. Laurel was having a child? Why hadn't she told him? But then again, why should she tell him when she didn't know the child she carried was his own.

"Follow me in the buggy to bring Gincie back to the house. I'm going after the coach to get Laurel." Tony spurred the horse around and stirred up dust as he galloped down the lane and onto Grand Prairie Road.

Large trees shaded the road and offered a degree of coolness to the occupants in the cramped quarters of the coach. One of the women, who sat across from Laurel, rested her chin on her ample bosom, already dozing. The woman's husband read the daily newspaper, and the other woman traveler had begun to knit. Laurel wished she had something to keep her mind occupied. All she could think about was the man who had claimed her in the dark of night, a night she knew couldn't be put behind her. She would soon have a living, breathing reminder of their brief passionate encounter.

And she couldn't forget Tony Duvalier, try as she might. Leaning her head against the leather seat, she tried to stop the thoughts swarming in her mind like honey bees. The swaying and jostling of the coach soon lulled her into a light sleep, and she was jarred awake by Gincie clasping her hand, followed by the sudden stopping of the coach.

Outside she heard voices, and a sense of d*éjà vu* filled her. She had been kidnapped from a coach once before. Could it be him?

"It's Mister Tony," Gincie said in disbelief, but her lips turned upward into a delighted smile.

"Did you have anything to do with this?" Laurel asked in a frantic whisper.

"Ain't sayin' I did and ain't sayin' I didn't." Gincie resolutely folded her arms across her chest. "But if you know what's good for you, you'll marry that man."

Laurel peered out the window, aware of the curious gazes of the coach's occupants when Tony slid from his horse to open the coach door.

"I want to talk to you, Laurel," he told her and held out his hand for her to take.

Her first instinct was to refuse, but she didn't want to cause a scene. She extended her hand to his, and he helped her out of the coach.

"I ain't got all day," the driver mumbled to them. Tony nodded and drew Laurel away from everyone's prying eyes to a shaded cluster of trees on the side of the road. He stared down at her, a dark angry look on his face. Laurel didn't flinch, meeting his gaze with a challenging one of her own.

"You have your nerve to pull me off the stage, Tony. The driver has a schedule to meet."

"To hell with his schedule! You're running away from me."

"I am not! I'm going to Texas. You already knew that I would leave Petit Coteau sooner or later. I don't know why you're acting so upset. My problems have nothing to do with you, and I told you that."

"You didn't tell me you were having a baby."

So he had found out, and Gincie had to have been the one to tell Jean, who had wasted little time in informing Tony. Everyone thought the child was his, but he knew better than that. Still Tony had come after her. A warmth spread through her for no logical explanation at this realization.

"The child is my own business."

"Do you intend to have it?"

"Certainly. How can you suggest such a thing?"

"How will you take care of it alone?"

"Tony, I'm far from alone. I have Gincie, and I am quite wealthy. My baby shall never want for anything."

"Except a father."

The sting of his retort caused her to falter, and Laurel found support by reaching out a hand to steady herself against a towering oak. Lifting wide, troubled eyes to him she spoke more confidently than she felt.

"I'll give my baby enough love to take the place of two parents."

Tony raked his hand through his thick glossy hair. His face possessed a haunting quality that Laurel had never before seen, and his eyes were filled with quiet desperation. He started to reach out for her but stopped himself.

"I want to be your baby's father," he said so lowly that Laurel at first wasn't sure he had spoken at all. But he repeated himself, and something stirred within her like a butterfly's wings in the pit of her stomach.

His offer touched her. Tears formed in her eyes, and she shook her head when he stroked her cheek.

"Don't touch me, Tony. I don't deserve your kindness, and I can't accept your offer. I . . . can't . . . forget."

Tony's sigh fanned her face. He knew she meant that night in the cabin, and he cursed himself anew for what he had done. They were both enslaved by a memory, only she didn't know that. Determination steeled him for her refusal, but he wouldn't allow her to leave for Texas, not with his child growing within her.

"None of that matters to me, Laurel. If I can forget, so can you. We can begin over again. Your baby deserves a father. I don't think you realize what problems await you and the child in the future. I won't allow you to have a child alone and without a husband to protect you. If you don't care for me, think of the baby. I can give this child as much love as you. And with both of us loving him, he'll be one happy baby boy."

"Or girl," Laurel said, the tears finally slipping down her cheeks. Once again, it seemed as if Tony Duvalier was rescuing her. He had saved her from falling over the side of the riverboat and had found her in the bayou. Now, he wanted to save her reputation and to give her baby a name. No other person, save her parents, Gincie, and her schoolfriend, had ever been so kind to her. Tony was offering her himself, and his unselfishness caused her to nod numbly.

"I don't know if I can be a true wife to you right now," she said. "But if you still want me as your wife, I accept your proposal."

A soft, cool breeze wafted over them. Tony reached out and gently touched a wispy curl that rested at her temple. Pure joy filled him, and in that moment he had never been happier. He was going to marry Laurel and raise their child. She was his, his alone.

"You won't be sorry, Laurel. I promise you I'll be a good husband and father."

Taking her hand, he kissed her fingertips, then led her to the waiting stagecoach. The driver and the other passengers were aggravated when Laurel's trunks were hauled down from the top of the stage, but Gincie was smiling.

Soon Jean arrived and situated Gincie in the buggy beside him while Tony pulled Laurel up beside him on the horse. The returned to Petit Coteau to plan their future together, but in Tony's happiness to finally have the woman he loved, he had forgotten her words to him under the tree. The thought never entered his head that once they were married, she would be unable to be his wife in the truest sense of the word.

Chapter Thirteen

"Any word from our 'dear' cousin?"

Lavinia looked up at her stepbrother's entrance into the parlor. Then her gaze flew back to the telegram in her hand, which she had received from Laurel that morning. Upon first reading it, she hadn't believed the words. She had been stunned and sat in one spot for a long time, waiting for and dreading this moment. But apparently Laurel had married none other than Tony Duvalier. If she hadn't been in such a state of shock, she would have laughed in amusement at Seth's hopeful expression. He wanted Laurel's money as much as she did. Probably more. However, she wouldn't allow Seth to know he unnerved her with those cold and calculating eyes of his.

Clearing her throat, she gave a nervous laugh and handed the telegram to Seth. His blond eyebrows bunched together as the import of Laurel's news hit home.

"The idiot! The stupid fool! How could she have done this to us?" he asked, clearly distraught.

Lavinia smothered another laugh, silently congratulating Laurel on upsetting Seth. Sometimes he seemed so self-assured, so cocky. He believed that because Arthur Delaney had married his mother, most of Arthur's money would pass to him. Well, Seth was wrong. If Arthur died, both she and Seth might very well become paupers. So far, Arthur had been able to make good on only a few of Seth's outstanding debts. She, however, didn't care a hoot if Seth's creditors ever received a penny. She was more concerned about the Little L's financial condition and what would happen to the ranch if her father should die. He hadn't looked well the last weeks. Laurel had been her last hope to save the ranch, and now all was lost because Laurel had married the handsome and very rich Tony Duvalier.

"You mean how could she do that to you? Well, I guess Cupid shot his arrow into her fourteen-carat gold heart, dear brother." Lavinia practically sneered as she stood up and brushed the wrinkles from her navy-blue taffeta gown. "I doubt very much if Laurel will visit now."

Seth stuck the telegram into the pocket of his Levis, the scarlet color of his shirt rivaling the high splotches of color on his cheeks. He stomped a boot-clad foot on the hardwood floor. "Damn!" he intoned, and sent his cold blue eyes, which now brimmed over with hot anger, in Lavinia's direction. "It's all your fault Laurel didn't come. You should have waited for her and not been so hot to get back here. Not once have you mentioned what the hurry was. Didn't you tell her that your father was desperately ill?"

"I did," Lavinia said, immediately on the defensive with Seth. She hated it when he became angry. His temper could take such an ugly turn, as it had the day he informed her father that she was in love with a "dirty half-breed Mex," his way of referring to Jim Castille. Even seven years later she didn't know what difference her love affair with Jim could have made to Seth. But apparently he had been correct when he told Arthur Jim wasn't to be trusted. That same day Arthur had discovered that Jim had stolen a few gold pieces, and had run him off the ranch. Part of her would never forgive Seth for destroying her happiness, just as another part of her would never stop loving Jim Castille.

"Laurel is a grown woman and had the right to marry the man she loves."

Seth cocked an eyebrow, a sprig of blond hair falling over his forehead. "How protective you are of her suddenly. Before you left for New Orleans a few months ago, you were ready to milk her dry. You're not softening up, are you, Lavinia? I mean you're such a romantic."

"Go to hell!" she snapped and crossed in front of him to leave the room. Seth stopped her with a large hand on her arm and pushed her onto a leather sofa.

He towered over her, a purplish color rising into his face. "You failed in our plan. I sent you to New Orleans to bring Miss Moneybags to San Antonio, and even that you couldn't achieve." He gestured with his other hand to the practical but comfortably furnished parlor in which they now found themselves, and his breath, fanning her cheek, seemed filled with fire. "What will you do because of this failure, my dear? You like comfort, and though I admit the Little L must go a long way to rival the Delaney mansion, I'm certain you don't want to go begging on the streets. I don't even think you'd make an adequate whore."

Lavinia winced. She did love comfort and pretty things, and Seth knew this. He also knew she would never sell herself on the streets. Being a man's mistress was one thing, but a prostitute another. She couldn't even find a suitable wealthy man in San Antonio who would have her. The scandal with Jim Castille was still remembered and whispered about. No decent man would want her as his wife. Mistress, perhaps, but never a wife. That was why Auguste St. Julian had appealed to her. He had known nothing of her past, her disgrace.

Her large, blue eyes implored Seth to loosen his unrelenting hold on her arm. She wondered how her late stepmother, Anna Renquist, who had been a kind and affable woman, could have produced such a cold, unfeeling man?

"What do you want me to do, Seth?"

"Nothing!" he spat back, causing her to jump. "It's up to me now. All of it falls onto my shoulders because you're so inept at things which require use of your brain rather than your body."

"How could I know Laurel was going to marry?"

"Your feeble excuses are too late." He dropped her arm and looked around the large parlor. A mahogany staircase led to an open balcony on the second floor where all the bedrooms were situated. He would hate losing such a nice home. As a child, in Germany with his mother and real father, he had lived in a tiny room over a fish market where his father worked. He remembered their sturdy and serviceable clothes, the smell of pine from the constant cleaning of the floors by his mother, and how she would get down on her hands and knees to scrub. What a life! The best thing that had ever happened to him had been when his father died and he and his mother came to live with his Uncle Johann in San Antonio and worked in his bakery. As luck would have it, Arthur Delaney's eyes had fallen upon his still pretty and young mother. With the ensuing marriage had come prosperity, and Arthur had treated him as his own son. Had Lavinia not already claimed Arthur's heart, Seth knew he could have entirely won over the old man, but she was his daughter from Arthur's first wife. And just a daughter who could be easily disposed of in marriage . . . that was if anyone would ever want the harlot.

Seth had considered marrying her himself once. Of course, she was his stepsister, but that wouldn't have deterred Seth. He would have found a way to marry Lavinia Delaney, heiress to the Little L, but Lavinia had done the unforgivable in Seth's mind by giving herself to a half-breed Mexican. Seth had dealt with that by planting evidence that Castille had stolen from the Little L. He had been quite pleased by Arthur's ready action. In his mind he could still see the seventeen-year-old Jim Castille running like a frightened coyote from Arthur's shotgun, which had been pointed in the center of his back. If the choice had been up to Seth, Seth would have shot him. He had wondered later if Arthur regretted not shooting the boy when Lavinia turned up pregnant. That had been when Seth decided Lavinia wasn't suited to be his wife. The day Arthur left for New Orleans with his wayward daughter to confine her on Sylvester Delaney's plantation had been greeted with rejoicing by Seth. He had thought Lavinia was out of the way. He had been wrong.

A few years later she returned home, after spending much time in Europe and wasting precious Little L money, money that Seth felt was his by right. He had taken care of ranch business and ingratiated himself with Arthur to such an extent that he knew that when the old man died, he would receive the lion's share of the ranch. He had run up gambling debts, clothing debts, and creditors had hounded him until Arthur was forced to pay some of them off. Things had been going smoothly until Lavinia returned home, and they had both discovered that the Little L was headed for financial trouble.

Things had looked bleak, but then Lavinia had mentioned her rich cousin Laurel, having received a letter from her upon her graduation from some prissy, Northern finishing school. And so he had easily convinced Lavinia to bring home Laurel Delaney. Such a rich young woman would have made a wonderful wife. He had thought she would probably be homely and skinny as hell, but he had wanted Laurel Delaney as his bride.

His eyes slid now to Lavinia, taking in her wide, frightened blue orbs, the exquisitely made taffeta gown, which he guessed had cost a pretty penny. Where the money had come for that extravagance and the other gowns she had worn since returning home, he hadn't a clue. She had never wanted to speak about her New Orleans sojourn or indicated why she had rushed home without her cousin. Whatever the reason, it didn't matter now. He must take matters into his own hands if he wanted to breathe easy at night and not worry over creditors or ending up in some tiny room above a fish market again.

"I'm going to Louisiana," he stated emphatically.

Lavinia's mouth dropped open. "You're going to ask my cousin for the money? I doubt her husband will allow it."

Seth shook his head at Lavinia's stupidity. "I'm not going there to beg money from the bitch or get on my knees to that Cajun husband of hers. I do have more finesse than that, Lavinia."

Finesse. Lavinia nearly laughed. If Seth possessed

finesse, she had never seen evidence of any. "Then I don't understand, Seth."

"Of course you don't because you're a dolt, my dear. But I tell you this: as quickly as marriages are made, they can be undone. Understand my meaning?"

Seth strode up the stairs, a delighted smirk on his face, and called to Rosita, one of the house servants, to help him pack. He had a stagecoach to catch.

Chapter Fourteen

"Ain't right, Miss Laurel. Just ain't right for you to be sleepin' alone. I don't know what's ailin' you, child, but if you ain't careful, you gonna lose Mr. Tony. Any other man would have found himself a lady friend by now. Mark my words, you gonna lose him if you don't act like a wife to him."

Gincie's warning sent a shiver up Laurel's spine. The soft calico gown that Gincie pulled over Laurel's head to fall into green waves at Laurel's feet didn't dispel the chill. Granted, the morning was warm and a bit muggy, but she felt unprepared for the cold feeling that clutched at her stomach as the import of Gincie's words hit her. She *might* very well lose Tony.

"I know you mean well," Laurel said, opening her bedroom door, "but my relationship with my husband is my own business.

Gincie appeared hurt, and Laurel's tone softened. "Don't worry about me so much."

When Laurel entered the dining room seconds later, she expected to see Tony seated at the head of the table. Each morning for the last six weeks, since the day after their wedding, they had breakfasted together. This morning he was absent.

Essie, a servant girl, appeared and set a plate of eggs and bacon before Laurel. Her stomach growled in hunger as she picked up her fork.

"Has my husband gone out already?" Laurel inquired of the dark-eyed girl.

"Oh, no, ma'am. Mr. Tony's still asleep. He done got home at five o'clock this mornin'. I expect he won't be up till noon today."

Essie sent Laurel a perplexed look as she left the room, almost as if she didn't understand why the mistress wouldn't know the master was still asleep. And Laurel felt as foolish as she probably looked to learn that Tony had evidently left the house last night after she had retired. Why hadn't he told her he was leaving? Where had he gone?

Gincie's warning filled her mind again. Had Tony taken a mistress? Perhaps he and Simone had been together. Laurel's appetite faded, and she laid down her fork on the table beside the uneaten breakfast. She really couldn't blame him if he had found sexual satisfaction elsewhere. Since the day they had married, they had shared separate rooms. Though Tony had been thoughtful to her and considerate of her pregnancy, she realized now that he must have always wanted a normal marriage. She had been so caught up in what she wanted that she hadn't really acknowledged his needs.

Her mind drifted back to their wedding. The ceremony had taken place in the parlor with Jean as Tony's best man and Jean's sister, Denise Abadie, a widow from Vermillionville, as her matron of honor. After the priest had pronounced her Tony's wife, Tony's warm, amber gaze had settled on her face as he toasted her with a glass of champagne. His smile had contained hope, she recalled, and his kiss had been tender. Even now she could still feel his hand in hers as he led up the stairs to her room that night, after Jean and Denise had left.

Standing in the hallway before the doors to her room, golden light from a flickering sconce had illuminated his sensual mouth, the amber flecks that danced in his eyes. And once again she had seen something like hope in his expression.

"I'll never be able to show my gratitude to you, Tony. It seems you're always there when I need you," she had told him.

He had leaned forward and brushed her cheek with a light, butterfly kiss. "I love you, Laurel."

Words that should have caused her joy had only given her pain. She hadn't been able to say she loved him, not when she carried another man's child, not when she didn't know if she would ever see that man again. Where was he? Who was he? Tony had tried to discover the truth for her, but to no avail. For a fleeting moment she wondered if the man in the bayou really mattered.

Instead of a wedding night learning the pleasure of love, the wedding night of which she had always dreamed, she had told Tony to give her time. Perhaps one day . . .

Then she had closed the door, leaving him standing outside. She still remembered the way her heart had thumped in her chest, wilder than a stallion's hoofs. She had almost wrenched open the door to throw herself into his arms, but she had resisted. Seconds later, she had heard him walk to his room, then the click of his door.

Their wedding night had been spent apart.

It was only now, as Laurel began to think about the last few weeks, that she realized how much Tony had actually given to her when he made her his wife. Not only the material things, but the chance to start over again, to decide when she was ready to become his wife in all ways. The memory of her kidnapper was fading, and if it weren't for the child she carried, she would have believed he had been part of a dream. But he had existed, and she wondered if he would return for her.

She wanted desperately to forget that night and lead a normal life, but she couldn't until she learned the truth about the man who had kidnapped her. Oh, what good did it do to have a handsome husband who loved her if she couldn't be a true wife?

Rising from the table, she left the dining room and walked through the breezeway connecting the kitchen to the house. She found Essie stirring a pot of red beans over the fireplace. The pungent smell of bay leaf and onions permeated the room. Pauline finished chewing a biscuit and scampered off a stool to stand beside Essie.

"Can I help you, ma'am?" Essie asked and quit stirring.

Laurel nodded. "I'd like to know if either of you are familiar with a small, old black woman who wears a turban. She has a son who is quite tall and strong."

Essie and Pauline shot each other a quick look. Essie shook her head. "I don't know anybody like that. Do you, Pauline?"

"No, I don't either," Pauline mouthed, somewhat inaudibly.

"Could these slaves live at Clermont?"

Both women shook their heads in unison. "We know all the people there, and there ain't no slaves like them," Essie intoned. "Would you like some more breakfast, ma'am?"

"No, thank you. I'm quite finished." Laurel gave them a quick smile and left the kitchen to go to the barn and question Tony's driver about the two slaves. He, also, had no idea who they might be and inquired if she was feeling well. He told her that the night she had been kidnapped had caused him moments of fright.

Other people on Petit Coteau answered her questions politely, but no one knew of two such people. Laurel even strayed in the vicinity of the Dauzets and was offered tea by Madame Dauzet and held the baby while they conversed. But, again, these two people weren't familiar.

"Are you certain?" Laurel asked Madame Dauzet.

"Oui, very certain," the woman said, but Laurel noticed she hesitated a moment, almost as if she longed to say something else.

Walking across Petit Coteau was tiring. Her feet hurt, and she felt the whole morning had been wasted in this futile attempt to gain information that either no one knew or didn't want to tell her. She hadn't realized that she had reached the edge of the property until she saw the small shanties of the people Tony had termed "white trash." A swirling trace of smoke rose from a chimney, and on one of the porches sat two men holding wine bottles. They were watching some dirty children play in front of the house.

Pity for the children pulled at Laurel's heartstrings. There were four little girls and two small boys, and each one looked as though a bar of soap hadn't passed over their faces in a year. A young girl of about fourteen appeared in the doorway, and when she saw Laurel, she stepped onto the porch. From where Laurel stood, she could see the girl was about five months pregnant and also very dirty and scantily clothed.

Laurel raised her hand in a wave, but the girl only

watched her, a hardness in her eyes, and didn't wave back. Moving away from the fence line, Laurel decided that she must do something to help these people. She didn't think it was right of Tony to condemn them. No matter how they lived, they were still human beings. She had so much, and they had practically nothing.

A plan formed in her mind, but she wouldn't tell Tony anything about that now. In fact she didn't have to tell him about everything she did with her money. Before the wedding, they had drawn up a contract whereby he had no say over her money. She had expected him to want the same stipulation, but to her surprise, he hadn't. He had told her that what was his was also hers.

Tony was generous to a fault, it seemed. One more reason why her heart managed to thump so hard lately. Was she falling in love with her own husband? Did she have what it took to keep him?

"If only I could be a bit more like Lavinia or even Simone Lancier," she mumbled and made her way back to the house.

When she was going to her room to change for a drive into Washington and seek out Denise, she stopped before Tony's door. She listened a moment and heard his snores. An insane desire to see him propelled her into the dim room. The sun was high in the sky, but the heavy green drapes were drawn tight across the windows. Still Laurel made out Tony's nude body, resting atop the sheets in a massive bed.

Her heart hammered in her ears. Never before had she seen a naked man. Even the man who had made love to her had been clothed in darkness. There was enough light in the room for her to plainly see that Tony was quite well endowed. Moving closer to the bed, her eyes feasted on his body. He lay spread-eagled on the bed, and nothing was hidden from her eyes. His broad shoulders appeared broader, and his arms more powerful and muscular in a reclining position. Her eyes drifted down to his hairy chest and lower, past the lean hips to taut and well-muscled thighs. And then again to that part of him that drew her eyes like a magnet.

A ragged sob rose in her throat. She wanted to touch him, to hold his manhood in her hand. An aching need to give him pleasure pulled her hand toward his shaft, but she couldn't make herself touch him. Fear of his rejection knifed through her heart, and she dropped her arm, holding it to her side with her other hand to keep from moving it. Would he reject her? She didn't want to find out. The pain would be too great if he should tell her he had a mistress now and no longer wanted her.

She drew back into the shadows of the room and found her way to the door. She managed to convince herself that things should remain as they were for the time being.

When the door closed softly behind Laurel, Tony opened his eyes. A deep sigh escaped him, and he muttered a profane curse.

He had known she was in the room and had even managed to catch a peep of Laurel as she stood beside the bed. The breath had nearly died in his throat when he thought she was going to touch him. If she had, he would have pulled her down beside him and made love to her then and there and hang the stupid agreement he had made with her! He had only told her she didn't have to come to his bed until she felt ready, to make her feel comfortable with him. He had expected the marriage to be consummated long before now.

It seemed she would never come to his bed now. He found his sheet at the bottom of the bed and threw it onto the floor. Clearly agitated and aroused by Laurel, he got out of bed and began to dress. He knew he had to calm down before he saw her again, but it was just so damn hard not to grab her and shake some sense into her beautiful head. He wanted her so much he could barely concentrate on anything else.

As he pulled on his boots, he muttered, "Just how long does she think I can stand this?"

The thought had occurred to him long ago to take a mistress, even to seek out Simone. But he didn't want Simone or any other woman. Only Laurel. Always Laurel.

"*Chérie,* I think you have a great problem," Denise Abadie told Laurel. She stirred her tea, sitting on a large divan in the DuLac parlor, and smiled at Laurel. "But I don't believe your problem is insurmountable."

Laurel wrinkled her nose. "It is, Denise. I . . . think . . . Tony has a mistress. And if he does, I can't compete against such a woman. Especially if she's Simone Lancier, who is quite beautiful and very skilled where men are concerned."

Denise raised an eyebrow. "So? Are you not skilled also in these ways? You're having Tony's child, are you not?"

A red blush colored Laurel's cheeks, and she glanced down at the skirt of her blue taffeta gown. She felt very close to Denise. Although they had only met shortly before her marriage to Tony—

Jean's sister lived in Vermillionville—they had become fast friends. But the honey-haired Denise knew nothing of that night in the cabin. Laurel simply couldn't bring herself to confess the truth. She didn't think Tony could live with such gossip. But Laurel had to confide in someone, and why not Denise? She knew her secret was safe with her.

So Laurel told her everything that had happened, beginning with her meeting with Tony on the *Cotton Blossom* and ending with her growing love for her husband. But there was still the child. Another man's child.

"Oh, my dear Laurel," Denise said with tears in her eyes. "You've been through so much. But tell me, if this man who kidnapped you should come for you, what would you do?"

Denise moved closer to Laurel on the divan and placed a comforting arm around her shoulder. "Your night with this man was rapturous. Have you given any thought to your feelings for him?"

"Oh, yes," Laurel said, clearly stressed by the whole conversation. "I've thought of nothing else for over two months. I live in constant fear that he shall return and fear that I'll never feel such rapture again. But, Denise, I'm Tony's wife now. This man can mean nothing to me."

"*Bien*. You've already started to put that night behind you. The time has come to truly become the wife of Tony Duvalier."

"I'm not sure I know how to do that."

Denise laughed. "*Chérie*, with me as your tutor, you shall soon have the man panting for you, and you will no longer be shy. Remember, I was married for ten years before my Pierre died. He taught me very well how to please a man, how to respond to his moods. As Tony's cousin, I shall tell you that he is a man of many moods, but a good man." Denise stopped chattering and considered Laurel a long moment. "I think it is time you had a proper wedding ball. This would be the perfect night to turn your charms on Tony, to consummate the marriage. But you mustn't look too eager. That is the first rule. The wife shouldn't appear too eager for the husband."

"But why?" Laurel demanded.

Denise laughed. "Because I know men, especially Tony. He will want to pursue you, to think that he is wooing you, seducing you. Such things give men a sense of power, *chérie*. Their egos are easily bruised, and we women must let them think they are the seducers, *n'est-ce pas?*"

"If you say so," Laurel said, warming to the whole idea. "But how do I get Tony into my bed?"

"Very simple. Petit Coteau will have many guests that night. All the rooms will be filled, even Tony's. After all, as Tony's devoted cousin, I shall require special accommodations. He will give me his room and occupy your bed."

"You make it sound so simple."

"It is, *chérie*." Denise nodded and giggled. "We shall have a beautiful new gown made for you. Mrs. Pratt is the best dressmaker in Washington, and you shall look like a seductress in one of her creations. And a nightgown of lace, something so sheer that Tony's eyes will pop out of his head, and his hands will not be still under the covers."

Laurel blushed anew, but a feeling of happiness washed over her. "Do you think Mrs. Pratt can arrange for a fitting now?"

Denise got up. *"Mais, oui.* Come along, Laurel. Before this day is over, you shall be well dressed and well versed in the art of love."

* * *

The large candelabra in the center of the snowy tablecloth on the dining room table highlighted the warmth on Laurel's face that evening. Tony sat across from her, and in the golden glow, she noticed sparks of desire dancing in his eyes for her. Taking a puff from his cheroot, he smiled at her and appeared more relaxed and at ease than she had ever seen him.

Laurel picked up her wineglass and brought it to her lips, tasting of the sweetness of the red liquid. Her lips were tinted a deep shade of rose, and Tony had the urge to sweep her into his arms and rush upstairs with her. He wanted to make passionate love to her, to leave her breathless and spent in his arms. But again he resisted and wondered how much longer Laurel was going to tempt him.

"How are the arrangements for the ball progressing?" he asked.

"Very nicely." Laurel toyed with the rim of her glass, unable to tear her eyes away from Tony's handsome face. "Denise had been a great help."

In more ways than one, Laurel thought. Denise had told Laurel about the intimacies of her own marriage that had shocked Laurel at first, but she had learned quite a bit that she intended to put into practice on the night of the ball.

Laurel glanced down at the white tablecloth, afraid Tony would read her thoughts and guess how much she wanted him. Yet, a part of her was unsure about his feelings for her. Though she sensed he wanted her, she wondered if he ever gave a thought to the man who had claimed her body in the cabin. Perhaps she was wrong, and he had married her only because he somehow felt responsible for what had happened. Perhaps he didn't love her at all. What if he still loved Simone Lancier? She couldn't be certain he hadn't been sneaking out at night to see the witch.

Tilting her head to the side, she looked at him. "Would you object if I didn't invite Simone Lancier to the ball?"

"Yes."

His response startled her. "Then I suppose I shall have to invite the tart!" she declared and abruptly stood up. She felt like crying to think that Tony actually did feel something for Simone. He *did* want her on the guest list. If he felt nothing for Simone, he would not want her at their wedding ball.

Laurel felt tears slipping past her lashes. She would have rushed past Tony to seek the solace of her room, but he was already standing and blocking her exit to the stairs. Instead, she twisted around and ran onto the veranda.

"Laurel!"

Ignoring his voice, she sought the darkness of the night. She felt like the biggest fool to plan on becoming a true wife to him, and all the time he wanted Simone. A desire to flee, to put everything behind her, washed over her, and she would have run in the direction of the fields, had she not felt Tony's strong hand on her arms.

Laurel felt pinioned to the spot, but she resisted and attempted to ward him off.

"Where are you going?" His voice sounded harsh, and he had to shake her to make her stop pushing at him.

"I'm . . . leaving . . . you," she sobbed, feeling as if her heart were breaking. "I don't want to stay here any longer. I . . . want to . . . go to . . . San Antonio and be with my family, people who love me."

"I thought you had gotten over that, Laurel. You're not going anywhere. You belong here, at Petit Coteau with me."

She hated the possessive quality she heard in his voice. Tony, she knew, enjoyed feeling that he owned things and people, but she would be damned if he thought he owned her. Anger surged through her, overcoming the pain. He may want Simone, but she didn't have to put up with their little affair.

"I belong wherever I want to belong!" she stormed. "If I want to go to San Antonio, I will, and you can't stop me. Just because you married me isn't reason enough to keep me here like a hothouse flower. You never take me anywhere, not even into town. I think sometimes that you're ashamed of me . . . and my baby. Evidently you care more for Simone's feelings than for mine. If you want the witch to be invited to the wedding ball, then invite her, but I won't be here!"

"God, you're beautiful!"

Laurel blinked in surprise, not certain she had heard the pride in his voice, and the blatant desire. But when a cloud passed, revealing a sliver of a moon, and she could see Tony's face, she saw he was grinning at her.

"Am I such an object of amusement, Tony?"

"Oh, Laurel," he said, fairly groaning her name and pulling her toward him. "You talk too much sometimes." He grabbed a handful of hair in his hand and moved her head near his until their lips met in a kiss that stunned her and took away her breath. His tongue traced the velvet softness of her lips to seek entry and entwine with her own tongue. A wild, swirling sensation settled in the pit of her stomach and caused her to lean weakly against him. Her arms escaped the locklike hold he had, and she wound them around his neck to keep from falling, to pull him closer toward her until she felt consumed by a fierce need to be carried upstairs and loved like the greedy wanton she always became in Tony's arms.

With each kiss, each touch, she gave in to the savage desire to experience finally the delights of the flesh they could give to one another. She felt his hands slip to her buttocks, enclosing her rounded softness in each palm and drawing her closer against his male hardness. She purred like a kitten when he groaned and fanned her ear with his breath. "I want to love you tonight, Laurel. Let me love you, please."

His mouth grazed her tender earlobe, and hot flames shot through her. She had intended to wait until the night of the ball to come to him willingly, but there was no difference if she gave herself to him this night. The night would still hold sensual delights. But did Tony love her or Simone?

"Do you love me, Tony?" she whispered. "Or do you want Simone?"

"I love you, Laurel. You know that. Simone means nothing to me."

Large, green eyes gazed up at him. "Then why do you want her at the ball?"

He kissed the tip of her nose. "Because, my love, I want her and everyone to realize how happy I am that you're my wife."

A cry of joy escaped her, and he crushed her closer to him.

"I want you, too, Tony, more than I ever thought possible to want anyone."

His eyes darkened with desire. "Anyone, Laurel? *Anyone?*"

She knew he was alluding to the man in the cabin,

and she whispered against his lips, "More than anyone, Tony."

Pure triumph shone in Tony's eyes. Sweeping her into his arms, he carried her through the veranda doors and past Essie's surprised face as she cleared away the dishes in the dining room. At the staircase, he took two steps at a time and was soon entering Laurel's room with his prize in his arms. He kicked the door shut behind them and gently placed her on her feet. Still he held her against him, somewhat afraid that if he released her, she would flee.

The scent of rose water drifted from Laurel's hair and mingled with her womanly scent, intoxicating him and further arousing him. He wanted her with such a fierce passion that the evidence of his need was clearly visible beneath the material of his trousers.

Laurel noticed his need. Her head swam with Denise's teachings, and her own body grew heated and ached with her own desire. More than anything, she wanted to pleasure Tony, to prove to him how much she had come to care for him. When his lips sought and found the line of her neck, she quivered and felt a melting sensation between her thighs. Moaning beneath his kiss, she splayed her hands across his broad chest. Long, caressing fingers slipped into the vee of his shirt to trail sensuously through the mat of dark hair. This time she felt Tony shudder.

"I want you so much! I love you so much, Laurel."

Her gaze drifted to the bed, and she smiled to see that the covers had already been turned down by Gincie. She slid her eyes back to Tony just as he began to unbutton the pearl buttons on the front of her gown. Gently she halted him with a hand on his fingers.

"I want to undress you, Tony," she breathed in a wind-soft whisper.

"God, Laurel, do you have any idea what you do to me?"

"I have an idea." A seductive smile split her lips at the very moment her fingers began to fiddle with the buttons on his shirt. Her mind raced to Denise's tutorings, but she couldn't seem to remember anything the woman had told her about how to seduce a man. Laurel's mind was clouded with desire, but she realized that the slow removal of his clothes would arouse Tony unbearably. The actual participation in such an act, she was discovering, was quite different from hearing about it. Tony's musky scent, the feel of his arms around her waist, the salty taste of his skin where her lips planted tiny kisses next to each buttonhole caused her breathing to become irregular until she was afraid she would actually pant from wanting him. She wanted to rip the shirt off his back, but she resisted. From the dark passion she discerned on his face, she knew he was enjoying her wanton and wicked display of undressing him.

At last all the buttons were undone, and she trailed slow and burning fingers over his flesh as she helped him remove his shirt. It billowed to the floor like a white sail to land by their feet. In the candle-lit room Laurel couldn't help but appreciate her husband's handsomeness. In fact not only did she worship him with her eyes but also with her hands as they slid along his dark, furry chest, across the steel-hard shoulder blades, over his back, then once again around to his chest where her fingertips traced a fiery path to the expanse of skin just above his belt buckle.

They hovered there for a moment. Laurel could

hear Tony's heart beating a wild staccato when he sucked in his breath. He stood so still, resembling a bronze statue, until she yanked open the buckle. Then he breathed once more, and his eyes blazed with heat, seeming to singe her image within their amber depths. She began tugging at the pants, but he stopped her a moment with surprisingly steady hands.

"What?" she asked.

Tony grinned. "My boots have to be removed first."

Laurel giggled. Denise hadn't mentioned boots. But the problem was easily overcome when Tony supported his long frame on a chair and pulled them off. When he stood up, he grabbed her hand and led her to the side of the bed.

"You may continue," he invited.

Laurel's pulses beat hard. The tip of her tongue caressed her lips as she unbuttoned Tony's pants. She felt so lewd, so deliciously wanton. With trembling hands, she pulled the pants down the hairy expanse of muscled thigh until Tony kicked them away in an impatient gesture. In the flickering golden light Tony's attributes were more than evident. A tiny gasp died in her throat at the awesome power of his emboldened manhood, ready to make her his own in the most intimate way possible.

She felt attracted to that part of him, almost as if her hand were a magnet. Fingers of cool velvet encircled his shaft of hot steel, moving sensuously along the length and enclosing the sensitive ridge in her palm.

A groan of pure ecstasy slipped from Tony's lips. He pulled her against him in a fiery embrace and possessive kiss that left Laurel weak and panting.

"You're a seductive witch, wife, and have almost

pushed me beyond a mortal man's endurance. But it's time for you to sample a taste of your own potion. *Now,*" he said in a husky growl that sent delicious shivers up Laurel's spine.

With sure but gentle hands, Tony released the many buttons on the front of Laurel's gown. "You're going to have to wear a dress without so many of these damned things," he muttered and kissed the hollow of her neck when her ivory flesh was bared to his hungry gaze. "Makes a husband have to do extra work."

The dress fluttered to the floor and lay at Laurel's feet like a large, ripened peach. As she gingerly stepped out of it, Tony scowled. He fingered her corset. "And this insanity isn't needed at all." He untied the stays like a trained lady's maid, and Laurel flashed a beguiling smile up at him.

"It seems you know quite a bit about a lady's undergarments."

The restraining corset fell away, and Laurel's breasts broke free to be instantly captured by Tony's hands. "I won't lie to you, Laurel. I've had more than my share of undressing females, but you're the only woman I want in my life now. I want you forever."

Tears misted her eyes as she stood before him, dressed now only in her pantalets and stockings. She didn't deserve such a man for a husband. Tony was much too good to her.

For the first time she verbalized what her heart had felt for the last few weeks. "I love you, Tony. I truly love you."

A sigh of happiness escaped him, and he clutched at the top of her pantalets, his fingers seeking the tender flesh beneath the gauzy material. "I'll never love anyone but you, Laurel. Always remember that, *chérie.*" His mouth covered hers in a hungry kiss. Wild swirls of ecstasy shot through her. Burning lips began an exploration of her throat and sought lower until they meandered through the valley between her breasts, leaving hot molten kisses in their wake. Finally Tony's tongue found the rosebud tips of her breasts and suckled until Laurel thought she would go insane unless the hollow ache between her thighs was filled. She arched her body against his, only mildly aware that he had pulled down the confining pantalets and was lifting her up and out of them.

He carried her to the bed and laid her gently in the center, then took her foot in his palm. His other hand snaked across the length of her leg and slowly began to peel back one of her silk stockings. The breath caught and died in Laurel's throat when he turned his attention to her other leg by first planting a kiss, filled with white heat along the inside of her thigh, before taking off the stocking and tossing it onto the floor to meld with its mate.

Tremors shuddered through her when at long last his hard and naked body touched hers. She felt the well-muscled contours of his chest and thighs pressed against the softness of her breasts and lower body. His aroused staff, cushioned by the dark love nest at the junction of her thighs, pressed intimately against her. She was ready for him when his hand caressed the velvety soft mound of her femininity, causing gasps of pleasure and increasing frustration to echo in the quiet room. "I want you, Tony," she sobbed aloud.

"I know, but I want this night to blot out everything that has gone before. I want us to remember this night as the beginning of us and our love. I want you to remember the pleasure I shall give you tonight and for all the nights to come. I want you to know how much I love you."

His name died on her lips when his tongue began a renewed exploration of her body. She writhed beneath him as it probed gently into her womanhood, bringing her to the edge of fulfillment. Her nails raked at his back when he lifted her buttocks from the bed to taste her more deeply.

She wanted him to stop, not to stop. Never in her life had she experienced such ecstasy and frustration. Her body was poised on the brink of climax, longing for the inevitable earth-shattering feeling to inundate her but also afraid to let Tony's tongue discover such an intimate explosion.

"Tony, please . . ." she cried and tried to urge him up toward her, but his head held firm beneath her fingers, and he clasped her wrists in one of his large hands. She couldn't move, and suddenly she knew it was too late. Spears of sharp heat had built to such a degree that even if Laurel had wished to stop the swirling pleasure that now washed over her, she would have been unable to halt the unbelievable sensations that rocketed her over the edge into oblivion.

The explosion against his mouth left her wet and warm. Tony pulled her against him and muffled her gasps of pleasure with his lips. "Did you like that?" he asked her seconds later, a Cheshire cat grin on his face.

Laurel smiled, dewy-eyed. "What if I told you I didn't like it at all?"

"I'd say you were a very poor liar. The night is still young. And I want you now more than ever."

"Oh, yes," she whispered when she felt him lift up and begin to enter her. She wound her arms around his neck and arched her hips, meeting his first thrust.

Laurel didn't believe anything could compare to

her pleasure of minutes before, but when Tony filled her with his massive strength, her body responded. His hips ground into hers, and his hand and lips worked their magic once more over her fevered body. Moonlight spilled through the window and encased them in silver. She hoped this night, the sensations pulsating through her body, would never end.

The pleasure built slowly, but finally she clutched at him when the end was near. His lips found hers. Desire washed over her, scorching her with its intensity. Then she felt the hot liquid of Tony's release and heard Tony shudder atop her. He groaned her name over and over, almost like a litany of love.

Both lay gasping in each other's arms, then laughing. At last they were truly husband and wife. On this night nothing else mattered, and the man in the cabin was finally forgotten.

Chapter Fifteen

Though contentment reigned at Petit Coteau, the same couldn't be said for Clermont. Simone Lancier held the gold-engraved ball invitation in her well-manicured hands and tore it into pieces before tossing the paper on the bedroom floor.

"How dare they invite me!" she ranted to Flossie, her maid, before throwing herself on the bed in a huff. "Tony only wants to see me humiliated. Everyone will stare at me and mumble, 'Poor Simone. She couldn't get Tony Duvalier to marry her.' I can't bear it!"

She hit the pillow with her fists, and Flossie stepped over to the bed with a sly look on her face.

"Now, missy, ain't gonna do no good to get all bothered 'bout Mr. Tony and his fancy city wife. I know somethin' 'bout her that you don't."

Simone sat up and narrowed her eyes suspiciously. "What could you possibly know about Madame Duvalier?"

Flossie's white teeth gleamed in her young face. "Old Cidra, Monsieur DuLac's housekeeper, is my aunt."

"Heavens, Flossie! All of Washington knows that."

Flossie continued as if Simone hadn't interrupted. "Old Cidra told me she heard Mrs. Duvalier talkin' to Denise Abadie 'bout Mr. Tony."

"And?" Simone prompted when Flossie grew quiet, annoyed at the girl for dragging out the story.

Sitting beside her mistress, Flossie shot Simone a big white smile. "Seems that Mr. Tony ain't been sleepin' with his wife, that the missus is fearful he's taken up with you again. Mrs. Abadie told her she should give a ball to spur Mr. Tony's interest in her. If all the rooms done be filled, then he'll have to sleep in his wife's bed."

"Hmm. Quite interesting," Simone observed and wondered how she could profit from such information. Her pulses quickened, and a delighted grin appeared on her face. So, Laurel Delaney was jealous of her. Perhaps Tony might succumb to her charms yet, if she could think of another angle to win him back.

"But that ain't all, missy. Mrs. Duvalier is havin' a baby."

"I knew that already!" Simone snapped. "All of Washington knows that Tony is going to be the proud father."

"But all of Washington don't know that the baby ain't Mr. Tony's child. Seems Mrs. Duvalier got herself pregnant by another man."

Simone sucked in her breath, unable to believe what Flossie was telling her. Such news was unbelievable! Absolutely shocking! Wonderfully delicious!

She grabbed Flossie by the arms and shook her. "You better not be lying to me, girl, or I'll—"

Flossie cut her off, fear in her large black eyes. "I ain't lyin', missy. Old Cidra will tell you what she heard."

"But Cidra is half-deaf. How do I know she heard correctly?"

The girl shrugged. "I only know what she told me."

"Get out of here," Simone commanded and pushed the girl off the bed. Like a frightened puppy, Flossie scampered from the room.

Simone rose from the bed and paced the room. If old Cidra had heard correctly, then she must plan well. She had to win back Tony and expose Laurel Delaney for the trollop she was. Evidently Laurel had lied to Tony and told him the child was his, and the big fool had accepted her story. Simone seethed. To think that he could have married her, a Lancier, one of the most respected families in the parish, or the family had been respected until her father took to the bottle. However, a bride from an old established family was better than marrying a woman whose ancestors were born in, of all places, Texas. What could Tony expect? she wondered. Laurel Delaney may have been born in New Orleans and educated up North, but her heritage left much to be desired. After all, Tony knew nothing about her family or about her.

"The bastard got what he deserved!" she ground out between clenched teeth. But Simone still wanted to be Tony's wife. She needed his wealth, and more than that, she craved his perfect male body. The nights were so unfulfilling since Tony met Laurel Delaney. No man could give her the ecstasy Tony had.

She stopped her pacing. Her eyes flew to the torn remnants on the floor. A plan for vengeance swam in her brain like a large fish in a small bowl, eager to swim free. She knew Tony hated scandal. And if the news about Laurel and her child became public knowledge, he would hate Laurel, too. He might appear duped to his friends and neighbors, but Simone felt he deserved some retribution for throwing aside her affections. How could one not look foolish in such a situation? Besides, Laurel and Tony weren't sleeping together, and whatever the reason, Simone was grateful.

An unattractive, high-pitched laugh escaped from her. She picked up the pieces of paper and danced around the room like a witch before a cauldron.

This was one ball she definitely wouldn't miss.

"Damn!" Tony muttered and kicked at the soft earth with the toe of his boot. Glancing up at his foreman, his brow furrowed. "What's the matter with you, Rabelais? Can't you keep an eye on my herd? This is the tenth cow I've lost in the last few months."

Leon Rabelais's tanned face paled beneath Tony's black gaze, and he appeared sheepish as he sat on his horse, nervously rubbing the reins between his hands. "I'm sorry, Monsieur Tony. I covered the south forty last night, and the rest of the men kept an eye on the northern prairie. There is a crafty thief afoot."

"Evidently craftier than the likes of you and the rest of the men I pay to guard the herd." Tony flicked his riding crop and leaned an arm against the fence post. "Double the patrol tonight," he ordered. "And if one head is missing in the morning, you're all out of a job."

"*Oui,* monsieur," Rabalais stiffly intoned and

swiftly rode away.

Tony's eyes traveled to the endless plain of green and yellow-gold prairie, topped by a brilliant blue, late spring sky. In the distance the cattle grazed on the sweet grass. He wondered how long these thefts would continue. For months now the prairie area had been plagued by them, but it was only within the last three or four months that his herd had been singled out. Thankfully, not one of the Brahmans had been stolen, but Tony didn't relish the idea of a thief stealing him blind, right under his very nose. Each head was precious to him, and he vowed that not another theft would occur. He would find this thief and bring him to justice.

He had a suspicion that the Jeanfreaus, the family who inhabited one of the shanties on the other side of his property line, were responsible, but he couldn't catch them in the act or prove they had stolen the cattle. Sometimes he would sit his horse and watch them, hoping to intimidate them. Other times, he would sneak out of the house at night after Laurel was asleep and wait under cover of darkness for the Jeanfreaus to make a move. He had thought he could count on his men to help him. He had enlisted the aid of young Hippolyte Dauzet to spy on the family for him when he couldn't. So far, according to Hippolyte, the Jeanfreaus were innocent.

Tony cursed again, aggravated with himself. Last night he should have been on watch, but he had been with Laurel. Thinking about her washed away the scowl with a smile. Each night for the last week, they had shared glorious passion, and he no longer discerned that strange haunted look in her eyes. In fact he believed that the night in the cabin had been dissipated from her mind. He felt momentarily disappointed that she had forgotten that night, but he believed it was for the best. The night that mattered was the one where she became his wife in the true sense of the word, and for all the nights to come, Laurel was his now.

Still, things would not be perfect until the thefts were stopped. Well, he reasoned philosophically as he headed back to the house to find Laurel and entice her into bed for a morning tryst, he no longer worried about her discovering he had kidnapped her. One day, perhaps, he would tell her, but not now. Their relationship was still blossoming, and he didn't want to ruin it.

Laurel lay in Tony's arms, oblivious to everything around her but the sound of Tony's steady breathing, the feel of his skin beneath her hands, and the warm flush staining her body from Tony's possession. She was happy, probably happier than she had ever been in her entire life. And she was having a child, a child that Tony accepted as his own.

Her hand crept to her still flat abdomen and stroked it lovingly. No matter who the father of this child was, she loved her baby already. She realized that with Tony raising her baby, the child would never be unloved or want for anything. At last, Laurel had found a place where she belonged, and that was right here in Tony's arms.

Her contented sigh drifted on the midmorning air. Tony stirred and glanced up at her. Their eyes met in a mutual smile.

"You look like a well-fed kitten," he commented and kissed the tip of her nose.

She stretched luxuriously. Her arching back lowered the bedcovers to reveal her beautiful and well-shaped breasts to Tony. "I feel as contented as one."

Warm fingers played across the globular curves and caused heat to gather in the center of Laurel's womanhood. She moaned and settled herself beneath his hands for further exploration.

"I think I've married a wanton woman," Tony joked. "Don't you ever get enough?"

Green eyes, glazed with growing desire, peered into his dark ones, which already spilled over with hot passion.

"Not of you, my Tony, and I never will."

He removed the sheet entirely, and his large body covered hers. Wrapping her legs around him, Laurel was ready for his entrance into her moist, soft center. Spearing her with a heated shaft that held the promise of uncontrollable pleasure, he whispered raggedly, "Then we're evenly matched, *chérie*. I can't think of anything but your luscious body writhing beneath mine."

Laurel wiggled her bottom, urging him to take her more deeply. With quick, sure thrusts he did and both of them found fulfillment so intense that each lay panting and spent in the other's arms until sleep overtook them.

"You know very well what I'm doing, Gincie. I told you about this the other day."

"I know you been gatherin' clothes together for that 'white trash' Mr. Tony told you to stay away from. He ain't goin' to like this one bit when he hears 'bout what you plannin' to do."

"You're becoming quite tiresome," Laurel lamented. "You'd think Tony was a god or something the way you do everything he says. Anyway, Tony doesn't have to know anything about this. What I do is my own business, and I'd wish you'd remember that."

Laurel stood up and pulled the crate out of the chifforobe, then placed it on the floor. "Go get Picard and tell him I need some help carrying this and then to get the carriage ready."

"I won't! I ain't gonna help you with nothin'." Gincie folded her arms in a defiant gesture, which Laurel had seen her do for years when she wasn't about to be persuaded to do something she felt strongly against.

Knowing there wasn't much sense in trying to persuade Gincie, Laurel only shrugged. "If you intend to be so bullheaded, then I suppose I shall have to go for Picard myself. But remember that the ball is less than a week away, and I have a great deal to do. I suppose I'll have to ask Pauline to help me, especially when it's time to iron my gown."

Gincie's eyes narrowed. "You don't mean that, Miss Laurel."

"Yes, I do."

"That French girl don't know nothin' 'bout takin' care of ladies' dresses. She made a mess of those pretty new ones you bought in New Orleans before you left. I can't have people sayin' at the ball that the mistress of Petit Coteau ain't properly looked after by her maid. I wouldn't be able to hold my head up when I come across the darkies from the other plantations."

"Well, Gincie, you know what you have to do."

Gincie disentangled her arms. "Aw, shucks!" she declared. "I'll go get that Picard for you."

"Thank you, Gincie, dear." Laurel smothered a laugh as she put on a large straw bonnet and tied the yellow ribbon beneath her chin.

Half an hour later, the crate was loaded in the buggy, and Laurel, with Gincie by her side, cantered along the road to the shanties. Picard had tried to insist he drive her, but Laurel had refused, believing that the fewer people who knew about her mission of mercy, the better off she would be.

Surprisingly, no one was on the porch, but a mongrel dog began to bark at the buggy, and soon Laurel saw a few faces peering at her from the open doorway.

A man of about fifty appeared, one of the same men who had been on the porch a few weeks earlier, drinking wine, and dressed in hardly anything better than rags. She barely recognized the man now, because instead of the raggedy pants and shirt he had worn, he now sported a pair of new trousers, held up by suspenders, over a white shirt, though his shirt was stained with fresh wine. He made an incongruous picture however, for his feet were bare and caked in mud.

Laurel reined in the horse and stopped before the man. "Hello," she said and offered him her hand, which he didn't seem fit to take. Nonplussed by this slight, she smiled at him. "I'm Madame Duvalier.

"Oui, I know that already."

"What is your name, sir?"

"Denis Jeanfreau," he said. "What you want here?"

Laurel glanced back at the wooden shanty, seeing the form of an older woman, surrounded by children, in the doorway. She swung her gaze back to Jeanfreau and motioned to the crate on the back seat of the buggy. "I brought some clothes, which the children might need, and some for your wife and the young girl I saw here a few days ago."

"I got clothes," he said harshly.

Gincie tugged at Laurel's arm. "Let's leave," she whispered, but Laurel ignored her plea and kept her eyes on Denis Jeanfreau.

"I see that," Laurel said, "but I noticed that your children needed some warmer clothes. Winter will be upon us in a few months. There's also some lightweight clothes to see them through the summer. And there's a very pretty gown for your wife, and I have a nice pink dress for your daughter, which I think can be altered for her figure and then fixed after she has her baby."

"Where'd you get these clothes?" Jeanfreau asked in suspicion.

"Some of them are mine," Laurel said and almost faltered under the man's condemning expression. "The children's clothes are clean and serviceable. I got them from Petit Coteau."

"You got 'em from those niggers, you mean. I won't let no clothes worn by niggers touch these children's backs. You get away from here. Now!"

The man's eyes shot dark fury. At that moment a younger man came out of the house with a wine bottle in his hand. He was similarly dressed to the older man. Laurel couldn't help but wonder how the men had gotten the new clothes.

"We don't take no niggers' leavings," the younger man said. "Tell your husband that we don't care nothing for his plantation or anything else." However, from the lustful way this dirty-faced young man ran his eyes over Laurel, she wondered if she might be the exception. She shivered despite the warmth of the morning.

"But surely you can't deny the children—"

Laurel's words were cut off by the sudden appearance of the young pregnant girl she had seen once before. The girl's hair was neatly combed, and she wore a very pretty blue print gown with a white lace collar and cuffs. The gown had been altered to accommodate her advanced state of pregnancy. Following behind her was the older woman and the children. All of them wore new clothes, but they still were in need of a good bath.

"Don't talk to this woman, Jacques." The girl spoke harshly to the young man, though her gaze stung Laurel with its venom. "She is married to Duvalier."

Jacques shrugged, not about to take his eyes off Laurel. "So, Roselle? I hand it to Duvalier. He has a good eye for pretty women." He took a long swill of wine and wiped the back of his hand across his mouth. "And Madame Duvalier is the prettiest of them all."

Laurel turned her attention to the girl named Roselle. "I waved to you once. Perhaps you don't remember me."

"I know who you are!" Roselle spat. "And that is why I didn't wave back. Why should I want to be friendly with the wife of the man who causes trouble for my husband and brother-in-law? Always he thinks we steal from him, but we don't. We've seen him watching us from across the fence, sitting on that black horse of his like Lucifer himself. No, madame, we have no wish to be friends with either of you. Leave now and don't insult us again by bringing clothes. As you can see, the children are wearing new clothes and want for nothing."

"Except a good bath," Laurel stated. Laurel glanced at Denis Jeanfreau, ignoring the lecherous Jacques. "Is your daughter getting decent medical care? I can have Doctor Fusilier examine her, to make certain her child is fine."

Jeanfreau's face grew redder than a radish, and he looked about ready to explode. "Roselle is my wife!" he barked. "Now leave here, madame, and don't come back."

Laurel didn't care for the threat she heard in his voice, almost as if he had a secret he didn't want to be discovered. Apparently she had made a mistake in coming here. Clearly her efforts weren't wanted or appreciated.

Grabbing the reins, she turned the buggy in the opposite direction and urged the horse into a trot. As she left the yard to seek the road, Jacques ran alongside the buggy. A nasty smirk was on his face. "If ever you grow tired of your rich husband, think of me, Madame Duvalier. I shall come to you!" His right hand waved the wine bottle in the air as Laurel whipped the horse into a gallop. The buggy flew down the road.

"I done told you not to go there, Miss Laurel."

Gincie's voice held no condemnation, only an acute sadness. Laurel realized Gincie had been right all along. Thank God that Tony wouldn't discover what she had done.

Laurel was unaware of the handsome, fair-haired man with his hat slung low over his forehead, who lounged against the post in front of Mrs. Pratt's Dress Shop. She breezed past him once she was out of the buggy, Denise by her side, and began to enter the shop. The two women were halted by the exit of Simone Lancier, followed by a dutiful Flossie.

Laurel managed a tight hello to Simone's surprisingly ebullient greeting.

"Why, Madame Duvalier, how pleased I am to

see you again. May I call you Laurel? Such a pretty name. I gather you're here for your last fitting before the wedding ball. Mrs. Pratt shall deliver my gown tomorrow and declares that it is the most beautiful dress she has ever fashioned. I hope you won't be too put out by it. After all, it is your night to shine."

"I intend to look my best," Laurel told the green-silk-clad beauty.

Simone stifled a chuckle. "I'm certain you shall. Please convey to Tony how much I'm looking forward to this celebration. Good day to you. And to you, Madame Abadie." Simone grabbed her billowing skirts and swept past them.

"What do you think got into that one?" asked Denise.

"The devil probably," Laurel observed.

"Be wary of Simone Lancier, *ma chérie*."

Laurel turned to Denise, unaware that the man was listening, though he seemed to have his attention centered on the departing figure of Simone. "I don't give her a thought. Simone can't hurt me. I have Tony, and she must realize the futility of trying to win him back."

At that moment Mrs. Pratt opened the door and gestured them inside.

So, that was Laurel Delaney, Seth Renquist thought and whistled lowly as he turned and watched her disappear into the shop. She was much more beautiful than Lavinia had led him to believe. Given Lavinia's jealousy of any woman, it was no wonder he had no idea that her cousin was the actual beauty in the family. Seth cursed under his breath. Because of Lavinia's stupidity, he had lost the gorgeous Laurel and her money.

He had arrived in Washington two days earlier with the intention of gaining information about Tony Duvalier and his new wife. As luck would have it, he had happened to be standing outside the dress shop at the time of Laurel's fitting. Perhaps that was a fortuitous omen, he decided.

From the conversation he had overheard, he realized that Laurel was extremely happy with her new husband. Her happiness was obvious in the rosy bloom in her cheeks. Laurel might be contented now with her domestic arrangement, but from the dislike he had seen in that little blonde hellcat's eyes, Laurel wouldn't be happy for long. Apparently the woman known as Simone Lancier had a passion for Tony Duvalier.

Seth decided that before he paid an unexpected visit to Petit Coteau, he had better learn all he could about this Simone. And what better way to do that than to introduce himself. Simone Lancier might pretend to be a lady, but Seth had been around enough women to know when one had an itch for a man . . . and Simone certainly had one he intended to scratch before turning his full attention to the beautiful and wealthy Laurel Delaney Duvalier.

Moving away from the dress shop, he crossed the street to follow after the woman and her slave.

By that evening Simone was prettily ensconced in Seth's bed at the Garland Hotel. Her many charms and her expertise with her hands and body delighted Seth. She was all woman, more than most men could handle, but he prided himself on not being like most men.

Simone sat up after an exciting but strenuous romp with Seth. Her long, blond hair hung in charming tangles down her back, and her large, blue eyes, which usually burned with unquenchable lust, were now calm. Clearly, she was a woman well satisfied at the moment.

Seth pulled her down by him, evoking a delighted squeal from her.

"*Chéri,* you cannot mean to want me again. I have to go home. My parents will be quite concerned over me."

"Make some excuse." He nibbled on her ear. "I'm certain you never wanted to hurry away after Tony Duvalier finished with you."

Simone's flushed face turned white. "What do you know about Tony and me?"

Flashing her an impish grin, Seth toyed with one of her nipples. "Only that you're hot to have him, but since he married, you can't get him back. It seems that his wife has captured his heart."

"You're quite a clever fellow," Simone said suspiciously. "Why have you been checking up on the Duvaliers . . . and me?"

"Let's just say that I have a stake in whether the Duvalier marriage lasts or not. Believe me, I would derive great satisfaction if it fails."

Simone was beginning to catch on to this handsome man's game. She had discerned that he had a motive in being in Washington in the first place. She had also realized he wasn't too well off. His tip to the waiter at their lunch after he had introduced himself to her had been quite frugal. And his room was on the third floor of the hotel, almost the attic. Too bad he wasn't rich enough for her. Still, Seth Renquist was a fine figure of a man and had made her forget Tony for an hour. In fact he was almost as good a lover, but not quite. Tony Duvalier excelled in love play.

A wicked smile played about her lips. "You wish the marriage to break up for your own ends, I see. I won't ask you why, Seth, but I want more than anything for Tony to leave this woman." Her fingers trailed lightly over the taut muscles of his chest. "Let's just say that as of tomorrow night when the wedding ball is over, the marriage will be over. Our alliance promises fruitful results. You will just have to convince Laurel that she needs a strong shoulder on which to cry in her coming times of trouble."

Seth laughed out loud and gathered the curvaceous Simone into his arms. "You're a mighty fine woman, Simone."

"And you are one delightful lover."

He fitted her on top of him, and without preliminary, in a haze of savage passion, Seth slipped inside Simone and took her to a rapturous paradise she had only experienced with Tony.

Chapter Sixteen

Simone's plan, so cleverly and subtly hatched, had already been set in motion, but this wouldn't be the cause of the trouble that happened on the night of the ball. However, Tony and Laurel knew nothing of the events to come as they dressed.

Tony, dressed in a black frock coat with matching pants and boots, a white ruffled shirt covering his broad frame, was breathtakingly handsome. He waited in the parlor, after he had finished dressing, for Laurel to descend the marble staircase of Petit Coteau and greet their guests together, as husband and wife. Anticipation seeped through him, eager for the dancing to begin when he could take his beautiful and bewitching wife in his arms and waltz her across the floor. He felt like a schoolboy suddenly and laughed at this image. Even as a lad he had possessed an eye for beautiful women, and Laurel was the most beautiful of any woman he had ever known.

Shortly before the first carriage rolled up the drive to the house, he saw Laurel standing on the landing. Tony gasped, unable to draw adequate breath. Never had he beheld such a heart-stopping vision as Laurel dressed in an ivory satin gown in an off-the-shoulder style. As she descended the stairs, holding out a slender hand to him, the yards of silk, encrusted with seed pearls surrounded by chips of sparkling emeralds to match her eyes, billowed around her. The soft swish of the gown was the only sound heard in the foyer other than the hard pounding of Tony's heart.

A gentle and loving smile beamed on her lovely face, framed by wisps of hair. Her long tresses were pulled away from her face and held in place by ivory combs. Curls cascaded down her back like a rippling waterfall of dark brown locks. In her right hand Laurel held a white rose bouquet and reminded Tony of a bride. His bride. Never had he felt such love for anyone.

"My, you're a handsome one," Laurel whispered and kissed him tenderly when she reached the bottom step. "I can't wait until we're alone tonight. You know Denise and I conjured up this ball to bring you to my bed. But as fate would have it—"

He didn't allow her to finish the sentence as his lips sought hers again and plundered them in a greedy kiss that promised much. "I knew you were a witch," he breathed against her hair. "But you didn't need a ball to lure me into bed. I'd have crawled on my hands and knees if you'd wanted me to."

"I prefer you in quite another position altogether."

"Laurel Duvalier!" Tony exclaimed in mock shock. "I've created a wanton."

They laughed together and walked into the double parlor that had been turned into a ballroom for the night. Roses and early summer flowers, plucked fresh from the garden and placed in large vases, graced the mantel and tabletops. Green garlands of ivy were entwined around the chandeliers and doorframes. Servants bustled about, placing platters of warm ham, chicken, turkey, salads, and such varied concoctions of rich and creamy sweets that the nearby dining room was turned into a cornucopia of mouth-watering scents.

The small orchestra Tony had hired began to tune up in one section of the parlor. Tony called to them to play a certain French tune, and he formally bowed to Laurel and offered her his arm for a dance.

In a swirl of ivory satin and black silk, they whirled around the room, having eyes and ears for no one but each other. Laurel felt that she was a princess in a fairy story, and Tony was her prince who had stolen her heart. How she loved him. The music drifted through the empty rooms, and they would have continued dancing if it hadn't been for the sudden appearance of Jean and Denise.

"Go away," Tony muttered and buried his face in Laurel's luxurious hair. "Can't you see we're busy?"

"Tony, I'd like a word with you." Jean's voice broke the spell.

Laurel stood in Tony's arms when they stopped dancing. "Later," he whispered to her.

Laurel immediately welcomed Denise with a kiss, and the two women stood together. Jean beckoned Tony outside and met him on the veranda. Jean's face was beet red, and he wiped his perspiring brow with his kerchief.

"I thought to never get here!" Jean burst out. "The carriage wheel broke, and that had to be fixed, but I wanted to arrive before anyone else."

"Your timing is impeccable," Tony groused good-naturedly. But he grew serious when he saw the worried look on his cousin's face. "What's wrong?"

Jean sighed. "I don't know how to say this to you, Tony, but I must warn you before your guests start arriving. A terrible, horrible rumor is circulating among the slaves and has leaked to the plantation owners, to your friends. The rumor says that Laurel is pregnant with another man's child. I don't know how such a malicious rumor began, and I tried to track it down to the source. But you're being made to look like a duped fool."

Tony felt as if he had been punched. Who would start such an ugly rumor? Then anger grew within him when he realized that Laurel might hear it and become upset. He must protect her in her pregnancy from any distress for the sake of her health and the child's.

"I'll kill the first man who utters such a profane rumor in my house!"

Jean patted him on the back. "Calm down, Tony. I told you not to upset you but to warn you. You have a right to know what everyone is gossiping about."

"Say nothing to Laurel," Tony commanded and turned on his heels as the first of his guests began arriving.

Tony joined Laurel in the foyer, and he introduced each guest to her. Laurel was charming, beautiful, and sweet, but Tony immediately sensed everyone's unease and noticed the moving lips behind gaily colored fans and hands. Rumors directed at him, at his Laurel, at his child. As much as he had looked forward to this evening, he now wished the night would end. He had purposely shielded Laurel from the social life of Washington, afraid that someone would slip up and mention Auguste St. Julian to her, but he had agreed to the ball, feeling that Petit Coteau was the proper place for Laurel to meet his friends. He knew he could control a situation in his home and expel anyone who mentioned his poor uncle.

However, this situation might prove more than even he could handle. Everyone watched Laurel in fascination, mixed with open condemnation, and even lust showed on the faces of some of the gentlemen present. He saw a look of bafflement settle on her face when he swept her onto the dance floor. Again, he blamed himself. If not for his plan to avenge himself on Lavinia, Laurel wouldn't be in these circumstances now.

"Tony, why is everyone staring at me so oddly?" she whispered to him. "Is something wrong with me? Have I done anything offensive?"

"No, *chérie,* you've done nothing wrong. You're imagining that."

She shook her dark head. "I'm not, Tony. These people dislike me."

The dance ended, and Laurel and Tony stood in the center of the room, alone. No one joined them on the floor when the music began to play anew, and Laurel realized they were being snubbed.

"Please, come dance," Laurel invited everyone, but no one made a move to join them, except for Denise and Jean. Laurel's cheeks grew red with embarrassment and humiliation, tears stung her eyes when Tony claimed her for the dance. Condemning faces twirled past her, but the only one she seemed to notice was Simone, who watched in malevolent glee from across the room. When the waltz stopped, the kindly Doctor Fusilier moved forward and asked Tony if he could have a dance with Lau-

Affix stamp here

ZEBRA HOME SUBSCRIPTION SERVICES, INC.
P.O. BOX 5214
120 BRIGHTON ROAD
CLIFTON, NEW JERSEY 07015-5214

Get a **Free** Zebra Historical Romance

a $3.95 value

——— F R E E ———

B O O K C E R T I F I C A T E

ZEBRA HOME SUBSCRIPTION SERVICE, INC.

YES! Please start my subscription to Zebra Historical Romances and send me my free Zebra Novel along with my first month's Romances. I understand that I may preview these four new Zebra Historical Romances Free for 10 days. If I'm not satisfied with them I may return the four books within 10 days and owe nothing. Otherwise I will pay just $3.50 each; a total of **$14.00** (a $15.80 value—I save $1.80). Then each month I will receive the 4 newest titles as soon as they come off the press for the same 10 day Free preview and low price. I may return any shipment and I may cancel this arrangement at any time. There is no minimum number of books to buy and there are no shipping, handling or postage charges. Regardless of what I do, the **FREE** book is mine to keep.

Name _____
(Please Print)

Address _____ Apt. # _____

City _____ State _____ Zip _____

Telephone ( ) _____

Signature _____
(if under 18, parent or guardian must sign)

Terms and offer subject to change without notice.

MAIL IN THE COUPON BELOW TODAY

To get your Free **ZEBRA HISTORICAL ROMANCE** fill out the coupon below and send it in today. As soon as we receive the coupon, we'll send your first month's books to preview Free for 10 days along with your **FREE NOVEL**.

GET FREE GIFT

ACCEPT YOUR FREE GIFT
AND EXPERIENCE MORE OF
THE PASSION AND ADVENTURE
YOU LIKE IN A
HISTORICAL ROMANCE

Zebra Romances are the finest novels of their kind and are written with the adult woman in mind. All of our books are written by authors who really know how to weave tales of romantic adventure in the historical settings you love.

Because our readers tell us these books sell out very fast in the stores, Zebra has made arrangements for you to receive at home the four newest titles published each month. You'll never miss a title and home delivery is so convenient. With your first shipment we'll even send you a **FREE** Zebra Historical Romance as our gift just for trying our home subscription service. No obligation.

BIG SAVINGS
AND **FREE** HOME DELIVERY

Each month, the Zebra Home Subscription Service will send you the four newest titles as soon as they are published. (We ship these books to our subscribers even before we send them to the stores.) You may preview them *Free* for 10 days. If you like them as much as we think you will, you'll pay just $3.50 each and save $1.80 each month off the cover price. *AND you'll also get FREE HOME DELIVERY.* There is never a charge for shipping, handling or postage and there is no minimum you must buy. If you decide not to keep any shipment, simply return it within 10 days, no questions asked, and owe nothing.

Zebra Historical Romances
Burn With The Fire Of History—

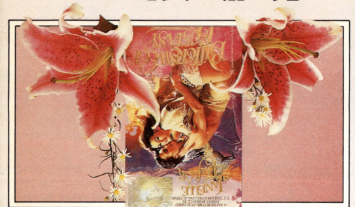

No Obligation!

a $3.95 Value

FREE

IF YOU ENJOYED READING THIS BOOK, WE'LL SEND YOU ANOTHER ONE

Zebra Historical Romances
Make This Special Offer...

rel. Tony bowed and started to walk past, but Madame Fusilier's voice blared through the ball room like the sound of a trumpet.

"Alphonse, if you dance with that wicked woman, I shall not speak to you again!"

Alphonse Fusilier's face turned three shades of red, and he stood beside Laurel, poised in indecision. He motioned to his wife to be quiet, but she pushed past the guests who blocked her way. She was a small, thin woman, but she stared daggers into her husband.

"Don't try to quiet me, you worm! You know very well why we're here. You're afraid that if you didn't show up, you'd displease Monsieur Duvalier, and he'd take his aches and pains elsewhere. Well, let him." She turned her flashing and condemning eyes on Laurel. "I don't want my husband ministering to a whore, to a woman who bears a child that isn't her husband's. It's a sin!"

"Oh!" Laurel's gasp was audible throughout the room, and she would have fallen if Tony hadn't caught her in his arms. But she stiffened her backbone and tried to stare down the woman and think of something to say in her own defense, but nothing came to her. She was guilty of everything Madame Fusilier said, of what everyone must think.

Some titters and jeers circulated through the room as Laurel opened her mouth to speak, but Tony's voice cut through the air like a butcher's knife.

"I am very shocked and surprised by you all," he spoke with surprising calmness, but Laurel could feel him trembling. "You come to my home to be entertained by my wife and myself. You come here as hypocrites, people who, I thought, were my friends. Worst of all, you believe a malicious rumor, something so untrue as to be an abomination. My wife is carrying a child. My child, and I would swear to this on a stack of Bibles that the child is mine. However, I won't give any of you the satisfaction." He called to the butler. "Show my guests out," he demanded.

Then in one fell swoop, he captured Laurel in his arms and carried her upstairs to her room. He sat in a chair, cradling her in his arms while the tears she had suppressed fell onto his shirtfront.

Denise knocked on the door and inquired if she was all right, but Tony assured her that Laurel was fine and that she and Jean should retire for the night.

With overflowing eyes, Laurel looked at Tony. "Denise planned for her to take your bed tonight. She said the house would be filled with guests. You could have your choice of any room now. I'm . . . sorry . . . Tony. I've caused you embarrassment, made a fool out of you."

He stroked her head, wanting to tell her the truth, and he almost did except her next words stopped him. "You were so wonderful to stand up for me like that. I'll never forget what you did tonight, Tony. Never." She kissed his neck. He felt her stiffen in his arms, and anger washed over her face. "I wish to God that man in the cabin never existed! He's the reason for all of this, and I hate him."

Tony smothered a groan. Yes, you should hate me, he thought. Gincie tapped on the door then and entered the room.

"My baby will done feel better after she gets ready for bed, Mr. Tony. Just you wait when you see her in that pretty gown Mrs. Pratt made for her. You'll both forget that nasty business that happened here tonight."

Tony nodded and kissed Laurel on the head before leaving her to Gincie's ministrations. As he left the room, he knew he would never forget this night. And later, he was proved correct.

Simone seethed as her carriage returned her to Clermont. Never had she been so upset. Her scheme had backfired. Instead of Tony becoming enraged and turning against Laurel, he had instead whisked her up the stairs to the seclusion of the bedroom. His attitude about the whole situation puzzled Simone. She couldn't believe he had stood there and, with a straight face, proclaimed the child as his own. Such loyalty was unbelievable to Simone—unless the baby Laurel carried *was* Tony's child.

Her mouth set in a grim line. When she reached home, she would beat that stupid Flossie until the girl was black and blue. Imagine the dumb thing believing anything old Cidra said. The woman could barely hear. What was worse, she, herself, had believed the tall tale. Simone had allowed the rumor to circulate about Laurel through Flossie, even ordering the girl to tell every slave she met for miles around, knowing the gossip would eventually reach the ears of the plantation owners.

Everything had gone exactly as planned until this evening. Tony had become the fly in the ointment, ruining all with his protective attitude.

"Oh, why couldn't he have gone into a rage and slapped her face in front of everybody!" she ranted to herself.

A shiver racked her. She had told Seth that her plan was foolproof. Now she would be the one to look foolish. Calming down a bit, she thought about Seth Renquist. He wanted the same thing she did, and she wouldn't question why.

When Laurel Duvalier was out of Tony's life forever, Simone would breathe easier. Indeed, Seth would prove most useful to her in her new plan. She must depend on him now to woo Laurel away from Tony. The fact that Laurel was having Tony's child didn't matter to her. Accidents did happen. Women miscarried babies everyday.

Once that stumbling block was out of the way, she could turn all her energies into winning Tony and becoming the next Madame Duvalier.

"My, but you look pretty tonight!" Gincie beamed at Laurel who stood in the center of the bedroom, arrayed in a pink negligée that was barely more than a web of lace at her breasts and gauze elsewhere. A lace robe swirled around her in diaphanous folds and skirted the floor. She had unbound her hair, and the dark, silken strands hung down her back in a riot of soft waves.

However, Laurel didn't feel pretty or even care how she looked at the moment. Her heart was heavy and fairly bursting with emotion. Tony had been humiliated over the incident with Madame Fusilier. Now everyone knew the truth, and she couldn't bear to think that he had had his nose rubbed in it in such a devastating way. Tony valued his privacy, and that had been destroyed. But she would never forget the way he had reared up to his full height and stared everyone down, defending her honor. He had lied to protect her virtue, and there was no adequate way she could ever repay him except to love him. And she did love him.

"Is Tony still downstairs?" she asked Gincie.

"He's in the study, havin' a drink with Mr. Jean. Should I go fetch him and tell him you're ready for bed?"

"No, Gincie. I'll wait up for him."

She dismissed Gincie for the night and was just about to get into bed when a tiny knock sounded on the door. Pauline entered at her summons, holding a black silk shirt in her hands.

"I heard you were looking for old clothes, madame. I have one of Monsieur Tony's that was on the floor of his chifforobe. It is torn and a button is missing. I could mend it for you if you would like to give it to someone."

"That's kind of you, Pauline. But the people I thought were in need of the clothes didn't need them. Perhaps you might like to give it to one of the servants."

"*Oui*. I shall do that. *Merci, madame*."

Pauline turned to leave, and Laurel caught the glimmer of gold on the shirt front. Something caused her to stop Pauline in her tracks. "Wait, Pauline! Let me see that shirt a moment."

The woman handed the silken garment to Laurel. Laurel's hands shook as she saw the row of gold buttons reflecting the candlelight. She barely glanced at Pauline, her attention riveted on the shiny objects all engraved with the initial *A*. Pauline spoke to her, but Laurel didn't hear her, and after a few seconds, Pauline fled the room, thinking that Madame Duvalier was acting rather strangely.

The blood rushed to her head and deafened her with a pounding that surged through her brain like a storm at sea. She walked to her dressing table and opened her jewelry box with trembling fingers. She pulled out the velvet lining and searched until she found the button she had hidden so long ago — the button that perfectly matched the ones on the shirt.

"*A*," she spoke dumbly, unable to comprehend her own stupidity. The initial stood for Antoine. Antoine Duvalier. Her husband. Tony. The man she loved. The man who had kidnapped her.

A low moan gathered in her throat. How stupid she had been, how trusting. Of course the man who had kidnapped her had been Tony. She hadn't connected his first name to the letter on the button since no one ever called him anything but Tony. Never in a million years had she thought Tony was the man who had plucked her from the carriage because she had expected him to be at Petit Coteau in Simone's arms. Instead he must have changed his shirt, and since she hadn't expected him to be thundering down the road in a violent rainstorm, she hadn't realized he was the man who had loved her in the cabin, had saved her life only to now cause her untold misery.

She should have known it had been him by the smell of smoke that surrounded him, the way he had disguised his voice. Who else would have had reason to lure her to Petit Coteau and then to spirit her away in the dark of night but Tony?

Yet she must know for certain if he was the man related to Auguste St. Julian, the man who had wanted to harm Lavinia. Throwing the shirt on the bed, Laurel ran down the hall to where Denise slept in Tony's bedroom. She threw open the door and nudged Denise, who was sleeping soundly.

Sleepy eyes settled on Laurel, and Denise looked up at her. "What? What's wrong?" she asked.

Laurel didn't waste words. "I want to know if Tony is related to Auguste St. Julian."

Denise yawned. "St. Julian? *Oui, chérie*. St. Julian was married to Tony's aunt, his mother's sister. But the old man died some months ago. Why?"

A bitter sob gathered and died in her throat. Barely able to speak, she shook her head and left, closing the door behind her. When she reached her own room, she found Tony already there.

His powerful muscles rippled as he threw off his shirt, and he looked like the figure of a Greek god she had seen in a museum once. But Tony was far from godlike, and a bitter pain entombed itself in the pit of her stomach.

His black eyes danced when he beheld her. Laurel was so beautiful that his hands and arms reached out for her, ensnaring her in a viselike embrace. He nuzzled her ear. "I couldn't wait to get up here. Jean can talk a blue streak when the mood moves him."

His breath held traces of brandy, Napoleon's brandy to be exact. The same brandy she had smelled on her kidnapper's breath. Her heart hammered in her chest, and her mind screamed. How could he have done this to her? He had kidnapped her, made love to her, and given her a child. Yet, he hadn't told her that he had been the one to whom she had given her love. Would he have ever told her? she wondered.

"No response, *chérie?*" he asked and tilted her chin. His fingers traced the teardrops that spilled onto her cheeks. "Don't cry, Laurel. What happened tonight is done."

She broke away from him. "You think it's all ended. You're wrong, Tony, or should I say Antoine? I had forgotten that was your given name since everyone addresses you as Tony. If I had remembered that then, I would have realized the truth about this!" Laurel picked up the shirt from the bed and threw it at him.

"My shirt," he said, not comprehending. "So?"

"A button is missing."

"Sew it back on."

"Don't you recall how the button was lost? Think, Tony, think." She walked over to him and opened the palm of her hand to show him the button she had saved. "I've kept this button ever since that night in the cabin when I ripped the shirt from my lover's back. A memento of a glorious night of passion, of ecstasy. I wanted to know who the man was who had shown me paradise, but you couldn't discover his identity. I thought it strange that you weren't able to find my kidnapper; now I know why. Tell me this shirt isn't yours, that you didn't lie to me. Tell me!"

Her fists pounded against his chest, and tears streamed down her face. "I hate you for what you've done! You wanted to punish Lavinia but got me instead. Your stupid plan went awry. And now you're married to me, and I'm having your baby. The only thing you've ever admitted to is the baby. I thought you were so noble to lie downstairs tonight, and all the time you were telling the truth. I *am* having your baby!"

Tony lunged for her, dropping the shirt on the floor. "Laurel, I love you. I wanted to tell you the truth." He reached out to her, but she twisted away and ran to stand on the opposite side of the bed.

"Why didn't you?" she spat with so much venom that his heart flip-flopped in his chest.

"I was afraid I'd lose you. I hadn't intended to harm you. I honestly believed you were Lavinia."

"Of course, Lavinia. I suppose you would have made love to her, but since I was the only female available, you took your perverted vengeance out on me. Should I consider myself fortunate?"

"Dammit, Laurel. I love you."

"You don't know what love is. For months I've felt guilty about what happened that night, and all the time you let me believe a lie. I won't ever forgive you for this, Tony. Never!"

Something in the tone of her voice caused him to halt and abandon his plan of forcing her into his arms. He had never heard her sound so hurt and angry, or look so betrayed. Her green eyes stared like two warning beacons, seeming to defy him to touch her. A sinking feeling gathered in his chest.

"You can't mean that," he mouthed.

"I can and I do." Laurel spoke firmly, though she trembled violently and clung to the bedpost for support. "I'm leaving you, Tony."

"Like hell you are!"

"Try and stop me."

"You're my wife, Laurel, no matter what has happened. I won't allow you to leave Petit Coteau with my child growing inside of you. Promise me you won't do that."

Laurel was ready to shriek that she would do what she damned well pleased, but a thought occurred to her, and she nodded much too quickly. "I promise I won't leave Petit Coteau with your child growing inside of me. And that is the only promise you'll get from me, Tony Duvalier. As far as I'm concerned, our marriage is over. We sleep in separate rooms from now on. You may take as many mistresses as you wish. I don't care."

His dark eyes narrowed. "I don't believe anything you just said."

"Believe it!" she shot back. "Do you remember the agreement we signed before our marriage? Well, now we make a new contract. I will stay here, Tony. You have my word on that. I want you to live up to the terms I just set forth about the sleeping arrangements, and the fact that I shall stay here because I'm carrying your baby. Do you agree?"

Tony felt as if he had just been buffeted by a raging hurricane. He had never seen Laurel like this, so vindictive and hurt, but he would have done anything to appease her and perhaps win back her love. For the moment he wasn't thinking straight, and he promised to abide by the new agreement.

"Good," she whispered through a voice filled with tears. "I truly have your word?"

"For now, but you're a passionate woman, Laurel. I doubt you'll stay away from me for long."

"And you're much too arrogant, Tony! *I'll* honor our agreement to the letter, and I expect you to honor it, also. I'll preside over Petit Coteau as mistress; I'll see to the dinner parties, the running of the household. In front of people I'll allow them to think that we're happy, the perfect couple. But at night we sleep alone, or you may sleep with whomever you choose. I don't care." Tony winced, but Laurel continued on. "I'll raise our child here and will love this baby with my whole heart. This child will be more mine than yours! I'll see to that."

"Over my dead body!"

He made a move toward her, but she held up a warning hand. To judge from the fire that flared in the depths of her eyes, he was wise to halt.

"You promised me you'd abide by the terms. Are you going to renege and prove to me what a loathsome man you truly are?"

She had him there, and he knew it. He wanted to make all up to her, but he knew it was too soon.

Her hurt and ire must abate. Determination welled within him to win her and their child.

"I'll agree to any damned thing you want!"

"Get out of my room, Tony. Leave me alone."

"Laurel?"

"Get out!"

Reluctantly he grabbed a shirt and stalked from the room. He was determined to make Laurel want him again and somehow make things right between them. However, the hard, unyielding woman he had just left presented a great challenge, and for the first time in his life he didn't know if he could overcome *this* woman's resistance.

After Tony left, Laurel's bravado disappeared, and she slumped onto the bed like a limp rag doll. The storm of tears she had managed to quell now spilled forth in a vicious assault upon the bedcovers.

"I hate him," she sobbed over and over, but she couldn't convince her heart of that.

Chapter Seventeen

"Carriage comin' up the drive."

Gincie's voice roused Laurel from a light doze as she sat on the gallery. The summer heat became more intense with each passing day and, coupled with the fact that Laurel was farther along in her pregnancy, caused her to feel doubly miserable. Even dressed in a thin calico print dress of pink rosebuds on a cream background, she still felt perspiration beading on her forehead. Gincie stopped fanning them with the punkah that was attached to the ceiling.

"Guess I'll go make some more lemonade for your company," Gincie said and picked up the empty glass pitcher and glasses from a small, round table. She went inside just as the carriage rolled to a halt before Laurel.

A well-dressed Seth Renquist stepped hesitantly out. He wore a deep-blue frock coat over tan trousers and boots, and on his head was a tan wide-brimmed hat. He looked exceptionally dapper.

"Excuse me, ma'am, but I was told this was Petit Coteau."

Laurel inclined her head. "It is, sir."

A flashing white grin streaked across his handsome face. "Then you must be Laurel Duvalier. I'm Seth Renquist, Arthur Delaney's stepson. Lavinia told me you were charming but didn't do justice to your beauty."

"How pleased I am to meet you!" Laurel flew from her chair and ran the short distance to embrace Seth. "I had no idea you were coming. Is Lavinia or Uncle Arthur with you?"

"No, sorry to disappoint you. I came alone."

"I'm sorry but I'm not the least bit disappointed to see you. When did you arrive?"

"Yesterday," Seth lied smoothly. "I've taken a room at the Garland Hotel. I just had to speak to you, Laurel. I hope you don't mind my arriving so suddenly. Lavinia told me you were quite upset over Arthur, and I thought you should know about his condition."

"Uncle Arthur is worse?"

"His illness *is* physical, but I believe it's more of an emotional one. May we sit down somewhere to talk?"

"Forgive me. Let's sit on the porch. It's quite the coolest place this time of day." Taking his arm, she led him to the porch, but then remembered the carriage and the waiting driver. "You may send the driver back to Washington, Seth. You will stay at Petit Coteau and not the hotel."

"I couldn't impose on you, Laurel."

"Nonsense. I'll instruct the driver to return for your luggage."

As Laurel issued the instructions, she missed a

wicked smile splitting Seth's thin lips. She had fallen in with his plan, having no idea that his bags were packed and waiting in the lobby of the hotel, so certain was he that she would invite him to stay at Petit Coteau.

Returning to her chair, Laurel sat, and Seth took the other seat. Gincie returned with the lemonade and poured a tall, cool glass for each of them.

"So you're the famous Gincie," Seth said pleasantly. "My sister, Lavinia, told me all about you."

"Bet they weren't pleasant things," Gincie muttered.

"Now that isn't true, Gincie, and you know it," Laurel playfully scolded. "Lavinia liked you a great deal."

"True," Seth said and smiled ingratiatingly at the old woman.

"Hmph!" Gincie muttered and went inside.

"You must excuse Gincie sometimes. She speaks her mind and is quite vocal on her likes and dislikes." Laurel took a sip of lemonade. Seth laughed pleasantly.

"We should all be as honest as Gincie." He grew pensive and tapped a fingernail on the side of his glass and gave Laurel a penetrating and serious look. "I came in person to see you, Laurel, to beg you to return to San Antonio with me. Arthur will never admit he feels remorse about the incident with your parents some years ago, and I'm not quite sure what happened. But he wants to make amends to you. Though he has never admitted anything to either Lavinia or myself, we believe he feels quite badly about not taking an interest in your life."

"Lavinia more or less told me that, and I was on my way to San Antonio, but as you can see I was sidetracked."

This time Seth laughed a not too friendly sound, but his words belied what he really felt. "I hope you're quite happy. Will I get a chance to meet your husband tonight?"

Laurel glanced down, something Seth immediately deduced as hesitation on her part. Simone had gotten wind of a rumor from a Petit Coteau servant via Flossie that happiness and joy weren't brimming over at the Duvalier house. Apparently that was true. When Laurel glanced up, an unaccountable sadness was mirrored in her eyes.

"My husband has been in Vermillionville for the last week. I'm not certain he'll be home today."

"I'm sorry. I should like to meet him soon."

"I know he'll be overjoyed to meet you, Seth. I do wish Lavinia had come with you, but I understand why she couldn't. Indeed," she said harshly, "I do understand."

Laurel's thoughts drifted to Tony for a few seconds, and she wondered why he spent so much time in Vermillionville. But his presence made her uncomfortable, and she guessed he was tired of being ignored by her. Probably he had found a woman to take his mind off his troubles at home. This bothered Laurel a great deal, though she told herself over and over that she didn't care.

"Laurel, did you hear what I said? You seem to be a million miles away." Seth's voice brought her out of her reverie.

"I'm sorry," Laurel apologized. "What did you say?"

Seth smiled indulgently and spoke to her as if she were a little child. "I said I hoped you'd give thought to returning with me to San Antonio."

"Oh, Seth, I don't think I can. I'm having a

child, and the traveling will be too much, I'm afraid."

His eyes hardened for a brief instant, but then he smiled. "Give it some thought. Arthur would be pleased." And so would I, he thought, covertly eyeing Laurel's beautiful, well-shaped body as she stood up. He sensed there was trouble in paradise, and he was going to do his damnedest to break up the Duvalier marriage. First, however, he had to discover what sort of trouble there was and the easiest way to bring Laurel to heel.

"We'll see," Laurel told him. "Now let's take you to your room where you can freshen up for supper. Essie is fixing a spicy meat pie, which is quite delicious, and a peach cobbler for dessert, Tony's favorite," she said and bit her lip as she remembered Tony probably wouldn't even be home for his favorite meal.

Laurel and Seth had just finished eating and were sitting in the parlor when Tony entered unexpectedly. Their laughter over a childhood incident when Lavinia had mounted a bronco after she had been commanded not to, and then had landed unceremoniously on a small cactus ended as Tony scowled from the doorway. Seth immediately stood up and extended his hand.

Laurel rose and made the introductions. The pulse at the base of her throat beat hard to see Tony again. In the week he had been away she had almost forgotten how darkly handsome he was. Seeing Seth and Tony together, she had no doubt that Tony was far more handsome than Seth.

"I arrived quite unexpectedly," Seth explained. "I do appreciate your hospitality, Mr. Duvalier. Laurel has been a gracious hostess."

"Call me Tony." Dark eyes, an amber spark in their black depths, fixed on Laurel in her gown of violet organza over a matching silk underdress. It was an almost expectant look, hoping for forgiveness to be bestowed upon the man who hid trembling hands in his pockets. But Laurel barely glanced in Tony's direction as she poured coffee into a demitasse for Seth.

"Seth has been regaling me with stories of Lavinia as a child." Her tone was polite, civil, quite detached and unemotional.

Tony threw himself into a chair, realizing he would receive no forgiveness from that quarter. "That should be quite interesting."

"Did you meet Lavinia?" Seth asked Tony and noticed Laurel tensed.

"A few times."

"Is that all you have to say, Tony? Usually men praise her beauty to the extreme. Lavinia would be quite offended if she knew you weren't taken with her beauty."

"I found her too wild for my liking," Tony grated out from between clenched teeth.

Folding his arms, Seth sensed the strained undercurrent between Laurel and Tony. Whatever was wrong between them involved Lavinia in some way. Had the tart thrown herself at Tony who had responded, only to have Laurel find them together? That would account for Lavinia's arriving home without Laurel. But he dismissed the idea. Apparently Tony simply disliked Lavinia, but something must have happened to cause such silent friction between the Duvaliers.

Seth cleared his throat and shot Laurel an appraising smile. "I agree with you there, Tony. Personally I prefer dark-haired women."

Tony didn't miss Seth's perusal of his wife. The man might be Arthur's stepson, but he wasn't Laurel's blood relation. He realized Laurel might be quite vulnerable now and decided he would have to keep an eye on Seth Renquist.

Laurel tossed and turned upon the sheets, hoping for a cool breeze to stir the curtains, but the night air hung heavy and black as a velvet cloak. Rising from the bed, she pulled at her chemise, which stuck to her body in the heat. Never had she felt so warm, and she wished for the cooler nights of Boston when she used to crawl beneath the blankets, wrapping herself into a warm cocoon. But if she had never left Boston, she would never have met Tony.

She shook her head. "Maybe things would be better had I never laid eyes on him!" she mumbled and walked to the window where she drew back the lace curtain. "If it hadn't been for Lavinia and her love affair with Auguste St. Julian..."

Laurel stopped herself, realizing that nothing would change the past. She had a future ahead of her, no matter how dismal. Soon she would bear a child, someone she could love and who would love her in return, someone who wouldn't cause her pain. A wish, unspoken, surfaced on her lips. She should never have extracted such a promise from Tony. Granted, he was going to leave her alone while she raised their child and presided over Petit Coteau as his wife. Yet was that what she truly wanted? The years ahead would be lonely and unfulfilled ones. An ache grew within her to realize she would never experience passion in Tony's arms again. She tried to convince herself that she hated him, but her traitorous body gave her away. She lovingly stroked her abdomen. She wanted his baby so much.

The sky held no glittering stars tonight. Outside was pitch black. In the distance she thought she discerned a firefly, but the distance was too great and the golden light threaded through the darkness, coming closer. It was a torch, illuminating the way. The sound of a horse's hoofs grew louder, and she saw Tony ride into the yard and go to the stable. Drawing slightly away from the window, she watched him walk toward the house, then she heard his feet coming up the stairs and down the hall.

Her breath stopped in her throat. The sound of his boots ceased by her door. Was he going to open it and come inside? Did she want him to? As much as she thought she hated him, Tony could still make her body uncomfortably aware of his nearness. And damn, she found herself silently swearing, she would probably melt into his powerful arms if he touched her.

But whatever her response might have been, Tony continued on to his room. She heard his door close and let out a long breath of relief or disappointment or a combination of the two. He definitely was keeping to their agreement. Had he gone to Simone's tonight or some other woman who found favor in his eyes and satisfaction in his perfect male body?

She hated to think about Tony with another woman. Such thoughts plagued her until she wondered if she was going mad.

Laurel started to move away from the window, but a flicker of movement across the yard caught her attention. Then she heard the muffled sound of running feet across the grass. She looked but saw nothing and was about to forget it when the discernible creak of the barn door sliced through the quiet night like a knife.

Someone was in the barn. None of the servants slept there, so who would be sneaking into the barn at this time of night?

The flicker of a candle in the tack room caught her eye, then wavering shadows on the wall. She wondered if she should get Tony but changed her mind when she saw the barn door being opened again. Though the night was dark, she made out the figure of Hippolyte Dauzet by the slight limp in his walk. What was Hippolyte up to, and why was he not at home?

She traced his outline to the kitchen at the back of the house where she watched him stealthily slip inside, then after a few minutes, he came out and made his way to the barn, carrying a bucket in his hand.

Laurel's curiosity got the best of her. Though she knew she should summon Tony to look into the matter, she didn't want the Dauzets embarrassed if Hippolyte was up to mischief. Tony would make certain they knew their son was sneaking around at night as a way of keeping him out of trouble. She didn't think that Hippolyte was a bad sort of young man and guessed that he might not look kindly upon Tony's speaking to his parents and could think it interference.

She threw on her robe and quietly descended the stairs at the back of the house, then made her way across the yard to the window where the candle burned.

As luck would have it, the window was open. Voices drifted to her. She discerned Hippolyte's voice and that of a young woman's. Clutching her robe around her, she peered into the room. On a pallet sat Hippolyte with Roselle Jeanfreau. Tears streamed down the girl's face, and even in the dimly lit room Laurel could tell that her cheek was red and swollen and that her lip was cut and bleeding. Hippolyte dipped a white cloth into a bucket containing water and held it to her mouth.

"I'll kill that filthy swine, Roselle. I'll cut out his heart for doing this to you!"

"No, please, don't do anything you'll regret, Hippolyte," Roselle begged. "Denis is very strong."

"He's an old man, and I am young."

Roselle's gentle laughter drifted through the window to Laurel. *"Oui, chéri,* but Denis is a bull of a man still. He is far from weak."

"I don't want you living with him. Leave him and marry me. The child you carry is mine—"

Roselle silenced him with a finger on his lips. "Never say that aloud, for if Denis learns of it, he shall kill you. I couldn't bear for you to be hurt. I love you so much. You know I only married Denis to keep a roof over *Maman's* and the little ones' heads. We had no place to go after Papa died, and Denis wanted to marry me. Your parents would never have agreed to us marrying, and you know it. My family is beneath yours."

Roselle grew quiet a moment, then glanced up at Hippolyte with fearful eyes.

"Jacques suspects this child is not his brother's. I think sometimes that I fear Jacques more than Denis. His cruelty is not with fists but his mind. He pretends to be stupid, but he is not. He is cunning. How else would he get you to steal Monsieur Duvalier's cattle and turn them over to him? Monsieur Duvalier has no idea that you're the one who is actually committing the thefts. And I don't think he'd care that you're doing it to protect me and my mother and brothers and sisters."

Hippolyte grabbed Roselle's hand. "Run away with me! Then I won't have to steal."

Roselle shook her head, tears brimming in her eyes. "I can't, though I want to be free of Denis, of Jacques. *Maman* and the little ones would be at their mercy. I must return home before Denis awakens from his drunken stupor and comes looking for me, and Jacques returns from town. No one but *Maman* will know I was here. I just had to see you once more." Her voice cracked. "I . . . love . . . you."

She kissed him quickly, then rose from the bed. Hippolyte implored her to stay, but her voice came out in a breathless sob. "There is no hope for us!"

She slipped out of Hippolyte's grasp and out of the barn. In the darkness Roselle didn't see Laurel as she ran in the direction of the prairie.

Hippolyte cursed and blew out the candle. When he stepped outside, Laurel's voice halted him.

"I think we have something to discuss, Hippolyte."

Laurel had lighted the candle in the barn and motioned to Hippolyte to sit upon the pallet while she stood. She hoped that she would give the impression of a stern plantation mistress, though she shook inwardly. However, when she spoke, her voice was surprisingly calm and held no condemnation for the crime Hippolyte had committed.

She laced her fingers together and coolly surveyed the young man. Laurel could tell he was afraid, perhaps more than his countenance expressed, but he, too, was pretending a calm he didn't feel. She cleared her throat.

"I heard everything you and Roselle said and am deeply touched by your love for one another." Hippolyte looked up from the floorboards, surprised. "But," she continued, "I can't condone what you have done to protect your secret. You've stolen cattle from my husband, a man who cares for you and your family. This is unforgivable."

"Do you have to bring in my family, madame?"

"No, but I think that just their knowing your crime would be sufficient to shame you."

Hippolyte stood up, dwarfing Laurel. He might be only sixteen, but he was fully grown, and if he had wanted, he could have pushed her down and run away. Instead he waited before her with downcast eyes.

"I will wait here until you get Monsieur Tony and the sheriff comes for me." He looked up. "I promise I won't escape."

Laurel nodded. "I know you won't run away. You're going to help rectify your crime, and free that pretty girl you love, along with her mother and family, from those horrid Jeanfreaus."

Hippolyte's face expressed utter shock and disbelief. "I don't understand. Monsieur Tony will insist the sheriff be called in, and my family will be shamed. What are you telling me?"

"I'm not going to tell Tony what you have done. The cattle you stole can be replaced, but Roselle's and her family's lives are in danger as long as she lives with the Jeanfreaus. Once she is gone from them, Jacques can't force you to steal for him any longer. I wondered where they got the money for those new clothes. He sells the cattle to someone else, doesn't he?"

"Yes, a man from Opelousas. But I still don't know what you're planning to do, madame."

Laurel shot Hippolyte a knowing look. "Yes, you do. We're going to arrange a kidnapping."

Chapter Eighteen

The kidnapping wasn't as difficult to achieve as Laurel had originally imagined. Luckily, Hippolyte discovered that the Jeanfreaus had gone into town for a night of drinking and revelry, evidently celebrating the sale of the last cow they had stolen from Tony. Thus, Roselle, her mother, and the children were left alone. Laurel had decided the best escape route was across the prairie to the servants' quarters. A cabin, set apart from the others, had recently been swept clean by Laurel and Gincie. Freshly laundered sheets covered the cots, and Laurel hoped the family would be comfortable there. She had no clear-cut idea how long they would stay, but Hippolyte had told her he would take responsibility for all of them and would keep them out of sight. Especially out of sight of Tony.

On a clear, star-filled night Laurel restlessly paced the veranda. Her eyes wandered in the direction of the prairie, hoping against hope that Hippolyte and the others would steer clear of the house. Glancing in Tony's direction, she saw that he calmly smoked a cheroot and read the latest edition of the Opelousas *Courier*. Seth swallowed down a bourbon, his eyes on her every movement.

"You seem quite overwrought tonight, Cousin Laurel. Is everything all right?"

Seth's question took her unawares. Her gold silk gown swished around her ankles as she turned in Seth's direction, the torchlights attached to the house flickering over her. She gave him a wan smile. "I suppose it's the heat that agitates me."

Tony put down his paper. "How do you feel?" he asked, concern on his face.

Involuntarily she stiffened as she did so often in Tony's presence lately. "I'm fine," she snapped. "Must everyone comment on my every movement?"

"We think only of your comfort, my dear?" Seth smiled an ingratiating smile, which set Laurel's nerves on edge worse than ever. Tony said nothing more, puffing on his cheroot and watching her like a cat silently inspecting his next mouse.

Realizing that she was making a spectacle of herself and worried that her plan might go awry, she flounced into a white cast-iron chair and fingered the leaf motif on the edge of the arm. If only she could have personally supervised Roselle and her family, but Hippolyte had suggested that things would be better if she wasn't seen on Jeanfreau property. He insisted that he could convince Roselle and her mother to flee to the safety of Petit Coteau. Laurel hoped so. If the girl was forced to endure another beating at the hands of that beastly husband of hers, she might not survive.

The minutes slowly ticked by. When she thought she could no longer stand Tony's silent perusal of her and Seth's constant talk about San Antonio and the large profit the Little L had turned that year,

Hippolyte appeared. He waited before Tony with hat in hand on the pretext of informing him about the cattle on the north forty, but Laurel knew his presence was to assure her that all was well.

"I hope you've passed a nice evening," she told the young man.

"Oui, madame. Very kind of you to ask." He bowed, then started to walk in the direction of his parents' home, but Laurel guessed that once out of sight of the main house, he would take the small gravel road in the direction of the cabin where he had hidden Roselle and the others.

Laurel felt as if a great burden had been lifted from her shoulders. She felt quite happy and spoke almost breezily to Seth. "Now, what was that you said about Uncle Arthur's herd?"

"I thought you might be bored, Cousin Laurel. You didn't seem to be paying attention."

"Oh, piddle. Of course, I was listening, Seth. The whole thing sounded quite fascinating. Please repeat the story for me."

Laurel didn't fail to miss the glimmer in Seth's eyes now that he had her attention at last, or the assessing look Tony threw her way.

The house was silent when Laurel sneaked down the staircase. The large grandfather clock in the foyer chimed the hour, and she stood on the last step, breathless. No one appeared on the upstairs landing. She let out her breath and continued into the hallway and out the back door until she stood under the breezeway connecting the kitchen to the rest of the house. Pulling her black lace shawl over her head, she ran across the lawn, then down the road to the hideaway.

Once on the porch of the small Acadian cabin, she knocked gently on the door. "It's Madame Duvalier," she assured the occupants.

Slowly the door opened, and Roselle stood there with her mother behind her. Both women were illuminated by a lone candle on the table. Laurel entered and nodded to them. Her glance swept swiftly over the children, asleep on the cots.

"I hope you're comfortable," Laurel said, practically cringing under Roselle's stonelike countenance.

Roselle's mother came forward and offered Laurel her hand. "I am Delphine Moray, Madame Duvalier. I thank you for your help. You have no idea the horrors my daughter has been forced to endure the past months. Denis Jeanfreau is an animal, and I think his brutality would have extended to me and my little ones if Roselle hadn't borne the brunt of his wrath. I would liked to have saved her, but with these children and my own poor health, I was unable to stop Denis from harming her. I blame myself for her marriage to that man. If only—"

"Maman!" Roselle cried. "Please don't humble yourself to Madame Duvalier. You couldn't do anything to stop Denis's rages, nor could you risk injury yourself." Roselle glanced at Laurel. "My mother is very ill, and she is quite weak."

Laurel squeezed the thin hand of Delphine Moray. The woman was quite fragile, and she realized that Roselle had probably married Denis only to keep a roof over this woman's head and to protect her brothers and sisters. A warm smile engulfed Laurel's face, encompassing all of them. "I understand you love your children very much, Madame Moray. You needn't apologize to me."

Delphine Moray smiled tiredly and sank into a

chair. "My mother must rest," Roselle said.

"Yes, I'll leave now. I wanted to know if you have everything you need. If there is anything you want—"

"I'll ask Hippolyte for it."

Roselle's frosty attitude puzzled Laurel. She didn't seem to care for Laurel at all.

"Good night," Laurel mumbled and was barely out of the door when Roselle closed it with a heavy thud and bolted it. Roselle was a strange young woman, she thought and apparently didn't mind taking refuge at Laurel's expense and wasn't even grateful for it either.

Retracing her path, she went inside the house and up the stairs. Just as she reached her door in the darkened hallway, she heard Tony's voice.

"Where in the hell have you been?"

She turned to see him leaning against the wall, arms folded across his chest in a gesture of disapproval. Her throat was as dry as a desert, and she couldn't utter a sound.

"I asked you a question, Laurel. I presume you know what time it is?"

"Of course I know what time it is!" she snapped, finding her voice at last. He looked so handsome, standing there in a dark-blue robe that matched the highlights in his hair. So big and bold and unafraid of anything or anyone. Just looking at him caused her to feel wobbly, and so she pretended outrage to keep from throwing herself into his arms.

"Explain to me why you're sneaking into the house at two in the morning." His tone held a challenge.

"I took a walk."

"You're lying!"

"I did take a walk," she hissed. "And where I go

and what I do is my own business, Tony. Remember, we have an agreement. I don't appreciate being badgered by you."

"So you weren't alone."

"I didn't say that."

He grabbed her arm, hurting her. "Who were you with, Laurel? Who did you run off to meet? Was it Seth?"

"No. Why would you think such an absurd thing? Anyway, if I were meeting him, do you think I'd take off in the middle of the night? He happens to sleep only down the hall," she reminded him and attempted to shrug off his hold, but his hand clamped down tighter.

"If I ever get wind that you've been seeing another man, I'll kill him."

"Big, brave bully." Laurel trembled not from fear but from her own traitorous thoughts at realizing that Tony's lips were inches away. "Your bullying tactics leave me cold."

Even in the darkness she saw the flame kindle in his eyes. "Do they? Let's see how you take to this then."

Without any warning, his mouth captured hers and devoured her lips in a hungry, punishing kiss. She pushed clenched fists against his granite-hard chest, refusing to allow herself to feel anything for Tony. However, her body wasn't of the same mind. Without meaning to, her fists unfurled and her fingers, fiery and satin smooth, splayed across the downy surface of taut pectoral muscles.

This response didn't go unnoticed by Tony. "I know you want me, Laurel. You can't live up to our agreement in the same way that I can't. I want you now and will have you."

The passion that had built within her dissolved at

his words. She wanted him, and she knew he wanted her, but he had to learn that he couldn't manipulate people because he deemed it so. Especially not her.

With a strength of will she pulled back, and lifting her hand high, she slapped his cheek.

"You won't bend me to your will! As far as I'm concerned, our agreement stands." Twisting around, she rushed into her room and slammed the door behind her.

Outside she heard Tony's loud curse, then his own door hitting the doorframe so hard the house seemed to shake.

"The object of your affection isn't sharing a bed with his wife." Seth leaned back on his elbows and watched in fascination as Simone sat up from the blanket spread on the grass. He had never known a woman more unself-conscious of her nudity than this one. Even the whores he had frequented in the last fifteen years of his thirty-one years didn't possess her nymphlike beauty or stroll as unabashedly before him with only her long blond hair for cover. She pirouetted like a graceful ballerina and shot him a most engaging smile. If he wasn't careful, he could fall in love with such a creature. However, Simone lacked the necessary requirement to win his heart. Money.

"Are you quite certain of this? If this is true, then Tony is as good as mine right now. I can feel that gold wedding band on my finger at this very moment." Simone giggled as Seth pulled her down into his muscular arms.

"Do you always have to mention Tony Duvalier? I get tired hearing his name. It's bad enough that I have to live in his house, but I hate hearing about him when I'm with you."

Golden sunlight bathed Simone's ivory body, which lay atop Seth's tanned one. She ran her fingernails along his muscular thigh. "Do you know that when you make love to me, Seth, that I imagine you're Tony?"

"Bitch!" He grabbed a handful of hair and pushed her onto her back until she lay half on and off the blanket. "I've got enough to worry about trying to win that cold-hearted wife of his away from him, but I thought you'd at least do me the courtesy of not thinking about him when I'm inside of you. God, Simone, I can't stand it!"

Her eyes glowed with a feral light. Seth's dark anger, the way he could break her in two with his powerful arms, the wonderful sensations he aroused within her when he made love to her, set Simone's pulses to pounding. Seth Renquist wasn't Tony, but he had the ability to drive her over the edge of ecstasy. She had lied to him. When she was in Seth's arms, Tony's image disappeared from her mind.

"Don't you think of Laurel when you make love to me? I can't believe you don't wonder what it will be like when she's your wife and all that wonderful money is yours at last. Tell me you don't think such a thing even a little bit?"

Simone was right. He did dwell on bedding Laurel, but more importantly he couldn't wait to get his hands on her fortune. Soon, he convinced himself, he would take her away from Tony and marry her. Then everything he had ever wanted would be his. The problem was how to handle the situation. An unborn child stood in his way, and though he wasn't certain, he felt this was the reason Laurel stayed at Petit Coteau. Tony, he realized, had done something unforgivable as far as Laurel was concerned, and this prevented her from going to Tony's bed.

However, he would have to say farewell to Simone when he did win Laurel's love, and leaving this blond-haired and lusty woman might prove harder than he expected. He couldn't help smiling in triumph when she arched her body and her lips found his, tracing delicious patterns with her tongue. This was a woman who matched his passion and desires in all ways. The day would come when he would leave her and they would both win their dreams, but for now she belonged to him.

"You're a heartless vixen," he mumbled as his lips found the throbbing peak of a nipple.

"Oui, chéri, but you adore me." She made purring sounds like a cat and wrapped her slender legs around his waist, eager for Seth's first strong thrust. Seth didn't disappoint her.

Essie ran into the parlor, her eyes as big as two ebony saucers and interrupted Laurel's tea. Denise and Jean were there, and Tony was drinking brandy and stood by the mantel.

"Monsieur, madame," Essie began, out of breath. "That dirty Denis Jeanfreau and his brother are very angry. They've just been to the Dauzets, lookin' for Hippolyte, and now they're comin' here."

Laurel jumped up, immediately knowing the reason why. Denise and Jean made sounds of surprise and disapproval, but Tony only glanced in a laconic fashion. "Is that all, Essie?" he asked.

"Oui, monsieur, but they're comin' with guns—"

Tony broke in. "Thank you. You may go."

Essie fairly scudded from the room to take refuge at the back of the house.

Jean stood up and went to the cabinet in the corner of the room that contained Tony's pistols. "Perhaps you should open it," he suggested to Tony.

"Why? I'm not afraid of Jeanfreau and that slimy brother of his."

"Maybe you should be," Denise said, backing up her brother. "Those Jeanfreaus are a nasty twosome."

Tony laughed and placed his brandy glass on the mantelpiece. "The day hasn't come yet when I'll allow riffraff to enter Petit Coteau and intimidate me."

Laurel stood uncertainly by, twisting her fingers together.

"You haven't expressed your opinion," he said to her. "What do you think I should do?"

She lifted her head. "I believe you're formidable enough to scare even the Jeanfreaus away if you wish without benefit of firearms. Your black mood lately is frightening to behold."

"You know exactly why I'm in a black mood, as you so eloquently put it. But you're not scared of me, are you, Laurel?"

"No, Tony, I'm not," she said and meant it. "However, I'm not usually drunk like the Jeanfreaus. Their wits may not be about them today, and I wouldn't put it past them to use a gun. Jean might be right about arming yourself."

"I think we're missing something here," Denise told Jean, who instantly nodded his head.

As Tony was unlocking the cabinet, loud cursing could be heard on the front gallery. The knocker on the door clanged harshly and reverberated through the house. Instead of rushing to the sound, Tony calmly loaded the pistol, and when he was ready, he waved away the butler and opened the door himself.

Laurel watched from the foyer as the Jeanfreaus attempted to push their way into the house, each brandishing a pistol. Tony, in turn, pointed his own pistol, the ominous click stopping their further entrance. "What do you want here?" Tony growled like a panther.

Both of the men appeared to have been drinking. Stale wine stained their shirts, and they also smelled of cheap whiskey. A startled look crept across their faces when they noticed the large, gleaming silver pistol pointed at them. For a moment the bravado that liquor gave Denis Jeanfreau deserted him, and he faltered under Tony's hard and unflinching gaze. He knew that if provoked, Tony wouldn't hesitate to shoot. Jacques, noticing his older brother's hesitation and not about to be intimidated by the high and mighty Tony Duvalier, attempted to push past Tony.

"Come one step closer, and I'll shoot you where you stand, Jeanfreau."

This time Jacques understood Tony meant what he said and slowly lowered his gun to his side. He knew he could kill Tony Duvalier just as easily, but he would still lose. The law would hunt him down and shoot him like a dog. Not a pretty death, by any means. He had only meant to scare Duvalier with the gun, but now it appeared that he was the one to be frightened. And if he did try to kill Duvalier, he couldn't rely on Denis to back him up. His brother was still half drunk.

"We want Hippolyte Dauzet. Where is he?"

"I haven't seen Hippolyte all day," Tony answered. "Now get off my property."

"Not until we find that thief and discover what he did with Roselle and the rest of her family."

"I don't know what you're talking about," Tony said smoothly.

At this point Denis's courage seemed to return, and he lunged forward, only to be halted again by the pistol aimed straight at his heart. "I want my wife. Hippolyte has taken her away, and I'd bet anything he brought her and that scrawny mother of hers and those brats here and hidden them somewhere."

"On Petit Coteau? You're mad, man! Now get off my land, the two of you, before I shoot you through for trespassing."

"I want my wife!"

"Jeanfreau, if the girl has run away from you, I wish her all the luck in the world."

Tony's statement caused the man to scowl. "You think you're such a big man, Duvalier, but I got you where it hurts. In the moneybag, monsieur, where all you rich men hurt. None of you bleed like regular men and have no feelings except for gold. You think you can look down your nose at me and mine, but you can't. I've taken something of yours and—"

"Denis, come with me!" Jacques grabbed his brother by the arm and yanked him from the porch toward his horse.

Denis attempted to rush past Jacques, but Jacques was stronger and whispered something to him that immediately caused Denis to mount the nag. Before he and Jacques rode away, he cried, "I've had my revenge on you and your kind, Duvalier! And keep that meddlesome wife of yours away from my property. I don't want her bringing me and mine old clothes like we were trash!"

They rode away. When the two riders had disappeared, Tony closed the door and saw Laurel standing nearby, a red splotch on each cheek.

"So, you've been ministering to the needy, I see, even after I told you not to bother with those people."

"Yes." Defiance shone in her eyes, which he couldn't miss.

"Have you done anything else I should be aware of?"

"If I have, Tony, you would be the last person I'd tell."

She turned around and entered the parlor, the gentle swishing sound of her green-and-white-striped skirts echoing in the foyer. Tony stared after her, feeling as if she had punched him in the gut.

The next morning after Tony was long gone from the house, Seth insisted that Laurel accompany him on a buggy ride around the plantation. Laurel readily agreed since she was bored with staying in the house.

Denise and Jean had stayed the night; and just as Laurel and Seth were leaving the house, Denise called to Laurel from the top of the stairway.

"Where are you going?" Denise asked.

Laurel tied her bonnet around her chin. "We're going for a ride around Petit Coteau."

"How nice. May I go with you? I'll only be a moment while I fetch my shawl. I freckle in the sun."

"Of course."

Denise shot them a beguiling smile and headed for her room.

Laurel followed Seth onto the veranda where he impatiently pulled a cheroot from his vest pocket. Until now, he had been affable and his usually cold eyes had been lit by an inner fire. Now he gazed at her in stony silence. She wondered if this transformation had something to do with Denise accompanying them on their ride, and she voiced this thought.

"I hope you don't mind Denise inviting herself, Seth, but she is my dearest friend."

He lit the thin cheroot and held it between his fingers. "I had hoped to be alone with you."

She didn't care for the sound of that. His voice was a low growl, almost as if he were more than upset, almost desperate even.

"Why, Seth? Have you had word from Uncle Arthur? Is he worse?"

"No. Yes. I don't know, Laurel. I don't know if I'm coming or going when I'm around you." He grabbed her hand. "I've grown quite fond of you, and I think you're unhappy—"

The sound of Denise's bubbling laughter broke into Seth's words, and Laurel noticed him scowl. But when Denise appeared, he smiled pleasantly and took both women's arms to help them into the buggy. Laurel wondered what was the matter with Seth. She hoped he hadn't been about to tell her that Arthur Delaney was worse, but no matter what her uncle's condition was, she couldn't leave Petit Coteau now. She had promised Tony she would have their baby here, that she would remain his wife. Perhaps after the baby's birth, she would go to San Antonio, but not now. She promised herself she would ask Seth later what he had been about to say before Denise interrupted them.

Seth guided the buggy leisurely around the plantation. Laurel halted him when they reached the Dauzets. Madame Dauzet sat in a rocking chair on the porch and shelled peas while she watched the baby play in the grass before the cottage.

"How have you been?" Laurel called to her from the buggy.

Celeste Dauzet stood up and smiled wanly, her face white and pinched with apparent worry. "Fine, Madame Duvalier. All is well. Monsieur Tony was just here. He and Hippolyte have joined my husband in the fields."

She sounded so sad at the mention of Hippolyte's name that Laurel's ears pricked up. But just then the baby began to chew on a stick, and the woman's attention was distracted. Laurel waved in farewell. Something was wrong at the Dauzets, she thought. She could feel it.

"Petit Coteau is so beautiful. Don't you agree, Monsieur Renquist?" Denise smiled sweetly up at Seth. She was sitting between Seth and Laurel on the leather seat. Seth agreed that it was, but he didn't seem too pleased by Denise's presence. "Perhaps I'll visit your Little L one day," Denise said.

"Sure," Seth answered abruptly, reverting back to the impatient man Laurel had seen at the house.

Denise sighed in contentment, then pointed toward the herd of Brahman, grazing in the fields. "How large and powerful they are!" Denise exclaimed.

"Tony's pride and joy." Laurel couldn't help but appreciate the sturdy and rugged breed. Tony doted on his stock as if they were children. In the morning sunshine she saw Tony riding swiftly across the prairie toward their buggy, his seat confident upon his stallion. Even at a distance he had the power to make her heart speed up, her face flush with anticipation. Denise noticed Laurel's rosy cheeks.

"Such adoration for one's husband causes my romantic heart to flutter, *chérie*."

Laurel's blush intensified as she said, "Please, Denise." Seth did not look pleased, and Denise giggled, seemingly satisfied that she had made her point to Seth Renquist.

When Tony halted the horse beside the buggy, Seth was polite and gentlemanly. "Cousin Laurel was showing me your Brahmans. I'm quite impressed."

Tony nodded at Seth's compliment, but his dark eyes were on Laurel. "The summer heat might be too much for you. You should go back to the house, Laurel."

"I'm not hot at all, and my bonnet keeps me quite cool," she lied. Actually, she felt the heat beating down upon her and the perspiration trickling along her rib cage, but she wouldn't allow Tony to dictate to her. Fluffing her yellow dress around her, she resembled a daffodil.

Tony shrugged. "Have it your way. I have work to do." Turning his horse around, he rode back across the prairie to rejoin his foreman and his other workers who were grouped in a cluster. Laurel wondered what Tony was speaking about as the others listened. Laurel saw that Hippolyte and his father were in the group. This was odd because Monsieur Dauzet had nothing to do with the cattle.

"It is dreadfully hot. Let's return to Petit Coteau for some of Gincie's refreshing lemonade." Laurel's suggestion was immediately followed, and soon Laurel, Seth, and Denise were sitting on the front gallery with a frosted pitcher of lemonade on the table.

Seth had removed his coat and rolled up his

sleeves to reveal muscular and lightly haired forearms. Laurel thought him handsome enough with his whitish-blond head of hair, but he wasn't Tony. She nearly cursed under her breath. Must she always think about that wayward husband of hers and constantly compare other men to him?

She did notice that though Seth seemed affable enough, he often glanced in aggravation at Denise, who didn't seem the least bit inclined to leave Laurel's side. Within half an hour of their arrival home, Jean appeared on the gallery with two valises.

"Time to go home, Denise."

Denise glanced up. "I'm not ready to go yet, Jean. I'm quite enjoying my visit with Laurel and her charming cousin."

"Have you forgotten that you must be in Vermillionville this afternoon? Monsieur LeCompte will be waiting for you."

"Mon dieu! I had forgotten." Denise stood up and smiled her apologies to Laurel. "My lawyer wishes to go over some papers with me. I arranged this consultation quite a while ago." She kissed Laurel's cheek and looked uncertainly at Seth, then back to Laurel. "You will be all right while Tony is in the fields?"

"Of course," Laurel answered.

"Certainly, Cousin Laurel will be all right with me. I assure you that I'll take special care of her, Madame Abadie."

Denise pursed her lips. "I'm afraid of that, Monsieur Renquist." Denise appeared to want to say something else, but Jean hurried her along, insisting they would miss the steamboat.

"I wonder what Denise meant by that last remark." Laurel said as she waved farewell at Jean's departing carriage. It rolled down the gravel drive onto the road and disappeared from view.

Seth settled himself comfortably in his chair and leaned over and took Laurel's hand. "I believe Denise was playing watchdog for your husband. She must believe I have designs on your affections and wishes to protect you from me."

"That's ridiculous."

"No, it isn't. She's right. I love you, Laurel."

Seth's grip tightened on her fingers, and Laurel started to pull away. "Don't joke about such a thing."

"I'm not joking," he said urgently. "I do love you. I've loved you from the moment I saw you. I think I've even loved you before I left Texas. Just listening to the way Lavinia spoke about you in such glowing terms, I knew you were the woman for me."

Laurel extricated her hand and rose from the chair. "You mustn't say such absurd things to me, Seth."

Seth got up, too, and moved around the table to ensnare her in a viselike embrace. "I say them because they're true. I know you're not happy here with Tony. Something is wrong between the two of you, and I think you need someone to love you. I can give you that love, Laurel. Let me love you."

If Laurel had been like any of the women he was accustomed to, he would have plundered her lips with his mouth, but Laurel was different. Seth knew he must woo her gently, but not so gently as to cause her to think he wasn't a real man. Instead of the long, brutal kiss he wished to inflict upon her, he kissed her with a heated but restrained passion. When he broke away, his eyes blazed in triumph.

But Laurel felt somewhat defeated and slightly dizzy. She knew she should slap him, but somehow his kiss didn't repulse her. And this frightened her. She wondered if she was so lonely, so starved for affection, that any man's kiss or caress filled her need, or was she attracted to Seth? Suddenly she felt unable to think straight.

Pushing away, she made for the doorway. "I have to rest now," she said without turning around.

"Do that, my love. I want you well rested. Maybe then you'll give thought to my feelings, and to your own."

In her room, she lay on the bed, feeling unbearably weary. For some unknown reason she felt caught in a snare, but she wasn't certain how she had gotten trapped. She only knew that if the man on the gallery had been Tony instead of Seth, she would not have pushed away.

Chapter Nineteen

Laurel was worried about Roselle and her family. They had been hidden in the old cabin for two days, and though Gincie had brought food for them and declared that everyone was fine, Laurel felt a nagging fear about Roselle and her mother. Delphine Moray was in poor health, and Roselle, in her advanced state of pregnancy, might not be able to tend to her mother properly. So after nightfall on the third day, Laurel surreptitiously slipped from the house and prayed the whole distance to the cabin that Tony wouldn't come to her room and discover she was missing.

Not that such a thing was likely to occur, she found herself thinking as she hurried down the winding path to the cabin. She had barely seen him the last few days, and when they did happen to meet at the dinner table, Tony was always extremely polite because Seth was watching them. Otherwise,

Tony acted distantly. She hated to admit that his presence in the house still had the power to disturb her. However, he hadn't slept in his bed the last three nights. Laurel ached at the thought that he passed his time in the arms of another woman.

"Silly fool," she muttered under her breath and pulled her black lace shawl over her equally dark clad shoulders. A passing cloud, skidding across the crescent moon, obscured Laurel's way. Low overhanging Spanish moss tangled in her hair as she made her way to the edge of the clearing where the cabin stood. A flickering candle on the window sill guided Laurel, but she stopped dead in her tracks when a loud wail emanated from inside the cabin, quickly followed by a piercing scream.

Running up the steps, she entered the cabin, heedless of her own safety. Somehow she expected to see Denis Jeanfreau, but instead, she saw Roselle writhing on a cot and holding onto her mother's hands. The children cowered in the corners with large frightened eyes, and the youngest girl was crying.

Delphine glanced up at Laurel. Her face was white, and she appeared about to faint. "Roselle's time has come, madame. The child is about to be born."

Pulling off her shawl, Laurel laid it across Delphine's shoulders and gently helped her to a chair. The woman looked more frail than the last time Laurel had seen her and was in no condition to help deliver a baby.

"Maman!" Roselle cried. "Please hold my hands. I am frightened."

Delphine would have risen, but Laurel kept her in place with a restraining hand on her arm.

"Your mother is in no condition to help you. She

needs a doctor as do you. How long have you had pains?"

"I don't want a doctor or you here! Get away from me, Madame Duvalier!"

"Roselle, please," Delphine weakly admonished. "Madame Duvalier wishes to help you, and I . . . cannot."

"I know how her kind helps people like us. They cheat us and steal away our land like the Duvaliers cheated *Grand-père*, and—" Roselle's words were broken by a shrill scream. *"Maman,* I hurt!"

Laurel went to the writhing girl and knelt beside her. "Take my hands, Roselle. Hold onto me."

Roselle twisted her head from side to side. "No. You're married to a Duvlaier. I can't take help from you."

"But you already have. You and your mother and brothers and sisters are here. I gave you refuge on Petit Coteau. I don't really know what my husband's family did to cause your family and you such anguish, but I will help you, whether you want my help or not."

Laurel's voice held determination, and she grabbed Roselle's hands in a firm grip. "Now hold tightly and scream your head off if you wish, but I'm not going to leave you."

At first, Laurel thought Roselle was going to try and break free of her grasp, but a hard wave of pain washed over her, and she squeezed Laurel's fingers so tightly that Laurel thought she heard them crack. Roselle's scream split the air, causing the one little girl to cry harder and the others' eyes to widen like black holes in their tiny faces.

As the pain subsided, Roselle gasped, "Damn that Hippolyte Dauzet!"

A soft laugh came from Delphine. "Damn all

men at a time like this. Labor is long and hard. Roselle has been in labor since yesterday afternoon."

Laurel paled.

"Yesterday?"

Delphine nodded.

Laurel wondered why the girl hadn't delivered yet. Surely the contractions were hard enough to bring down the child. She didn't know anything about having children, having already decided that she would put her faith in Doctor Fusilier when the time came for her to have her own baby. But Roselle had no one competent here with her, not even a midwife.

"I'll summon Doctor Fusilier," she said out loud.

"Doctor Fusilier won't come for the likes of us," Delphine spoke harshly. "He didn't come when my husband was dying of the cough, though I went to his house and begged on bended knee. The man caters only to the rich, not to people with no money."

"He'll come if I tell him," Laurel stated emphatically.

"No! Roselle shall not be in the care of such a man."

Delphine's eyes glittered, and for the first time Laurel noticed color rising to her pale cheeks. Yet such a slight outburst seemed to sap Delphine's strength because she took a long, sighing breath.

"Please don't send for Fusilier. If anyone must help Roselle, there is a woman who lives near the Dauzets. Lulubelle is her name. She delivered my third child and is a kind person who doesn't look down upon us." Delphine lifted her eyes to Laurel. "You may send for her."

"I remember her," Laurel said, her mind being

unwillingly drawn to the night of the Mardi Gras dance when Lulubelle had helped her dress in the gypsy costume and to what had happened afterward. "I'll send one of the servants to her."

Laurel softly laid Roselle's hands on her swollen abdomen and then left and ran from the cabin. She went to Essie's where she entreated Essie's husband, Malcolm, to fetch Lulubelle and bring her to the old cabin in the clearing. Then she made her way back, with Essie beside her, to Roselle.

The night wore on, and by the time Lulubelle arrived, Roselle lay weak and gasping for breath. Lulubelle's dark eyes immediately took in the situation and ordered the children away. After Essie had departed with them, she examined Roselle who shrieked in pain. She turned to Laurel and Delphine.

"The feet are coming first, *mesdames*."

Delphine uttered a little cry. "Is that bad?" Laurel asked.

Nodding, Lulubelle got up and poured some water into a kettle, which she placed in the fireplace to boil, her wide girth entirely obscuring Laurel's view of the flames licking at the pot's bottom. She turned and faced them. "You know what must be done, Delphine."

Delphine's hands shook, and she glanced at her gasping daughter with pain-filled eyes, *"Oui."*

"Then let's begin. I need your help, Madame Duvalier, because Delphine is much too weak to hold onto Roselle."

"I'll do anything you ask," Laurel said, "but what is going to happen?"

"I'm going to save this baby and Roselle, but there will be much pain for the girl. I hope you're strong enough to hold her down, madame." Lulubelle eyed Laurel warily, not entirely convinced Laurel would be able to do the job.

Laurel mutely nodded at Roselle, who seemed oblivious to what was going on. With Lulubelle's instructions ringing in her ears, Laurel positioned herself at Roselle's head and, linking their hands, brought them high above Roselle. Roselle's fingers lay limply in Laurel's until Laurel felt them tense when Lulubelle situated herself before the girl's straddled thighs and began to probe.

Lulubelle's voice was gentle. "I'm going to turn the little one, Roselle. You'll feel pain, but soon this shall all be over, *chérie*. Soon your baby will be in your arms, and this will seem like a bad dream. Don't fight me though, it will hurt. It has to hurt, and I am sorry to do this to you."

Though Laurel could tell that Lulubelle was being as gentle as she could, Roselle began to whimper and try to pull away from Laurel. As each whimper became a scream, Roselle tugged more vigorously at the hands that held her pinned. Laurel had thought Roselle was exhausted, but now she writhed and moaned and then shrieked in such excruciating pain that Laurel didn't know if she could hold her grip. Her fingers felt crimped from the pressure she exerted on Roselle's. Then an agonized scream, unlike anything Laurel had ever heard, ripped through the room and momentarily deafened Laurel, and all grew quiet except for the ringing in Laurel's ears.

"Push, Roselle."

Lulubelle had spoken, and Roselle obeyed. Without another sound issuing from Roselle's mouth, she forced her son into the world.

When Laurel left the cabin, Roselle's baby was sucking contentedly at her breast. The sight of the infant's fuzzy head nestled at his mother's bosom was one that Laurel would carry with her for the rest of her life. Tears misted her eyes at the beauty of birth. For the first time she realized what the future held for her and knew that her own child would more than make up for the pain of birth and the pain of Tony's deception.

Few stars sprinkled the heavens as she hurried back to the main house. She had been gone for hours and wondered if she had been missed. Turning her head toward the fields, she saw a flickering light in the distance, then other orange-red spots gathering into a group.

Something was happening on the prairie.

Voices were raised in loud shouts and then stilled by the sound of a gunshot. Tony! Tony! Her mind beat out the name her lips weren't able to form. Had Tony been hurt? She remembered him returning to the house one night with a torch in hand. Her only thought now was to discover if he had been shot, if he needed her.

Her feet flew across the grassy expanse of fields, her eyes on the torchlights in the dark night. In her chest her heart felt about to explode. Her legs seemed wooden, and she wondered if she would ever reach the circle of men who bent over a man's prone figure on the ground. As she rushed forward, no one noticed her except for one man who stood a few feet away.

With a sudden lunge, the arms of Jacques Jeanfreau ensnared her against his chest and held a knife against her throat. She couldn't speak, couldn't utter a sound. The men before her didn't see what had happened. All she heard was the voice of Leon Rabelais say, "He's dead."

An agonized wail ripped from her throat for

fear the man meant Tony. She felt herself being pulled backward into a copse of trees, the knife cool and sharp against her flesh. Tears now blinded her eyes, and she no longer thought of her own safety. She struggled to escape to see if the prone figure was Tony.

Twenty pairs of eyes glanced up in shock, and more than one man went for his gun. She heard Jeanfreau's voice scream in her ear. "Come after me, and I'll kill her!"

Out of the shadows strode the tall broad-shouldered figure of Tony Duvalier. Through her teary eyes Laurel saw him in the light of the torches, and a shudder of relief swept through her. But her relief was short-lived. Jeanfreau's knife at her throat was an ever-constant threat to her own life. She mouthed Tony's name, but he didn't appear to see. His attention was solely on Jeanfreau.

"I guess you have me at a disadvantage, Jacques. You have my wife in your power. I know how good you are with a knife. I've seen you skin animals, and I admit you know how to wield a blade."

"Oui, that I do," Jacques uttered proudly. "I know also how to wield something else that your pretty wife might find quite interesting before I kill her."

Laurel felt sick at Jacques's words. It was clear to Laurel that his cattle-thieving days were at an end, and he wasn't above using her as a hostage or for anything else he had in mind. Her eyes implored Tony to save her, but once again, he was watching Jacques, not her. Tony had stiffened an imperceptible degree, Laurel saw, but Jacques didn't.

"Don't you care what I might do to your wife, Duvalier? Or is it that your tongue still hangs out for Simone Lancier? Such a way you have with the ladies." Jacques's arm tightened around Laurel's waist, and the blade teased the soft flesh of her throat. Just a slight movement of Jacques's wrist and he would slice into her. She would die, she knew it.

Tony shrugged his shoulders and shot Jacques a rather amused look. "You always were jealous of my prowess with the ladies, weren't you, Jacques? I used to catch you staring at me, and any lady I happened to be entertaining from the bushes by the house. Evidently you needed tutoring in the art of love, my friend."

"Shut up, Duvalier, or I slit her throat right now. I will unless I get a horse to escape from here. I'm not going to end up like my stupid brother over there, lying dead on the ground before your polished boots."

"I'm not giving you a horse," Tony said stubbornly.

"Then I'll kill your wife."

"If you kill her, Jacques, and I know you can, you won't escape me. Before God, I swear I'll track you down, and you won't die as quick a death as your thieving brother. Have you ever seen cowhides tanned? I know you have, and you know what a tedious process it is. One must add saltpeter, hot water, and various other salts to the skin, which is then left out for a few days to dry. I pride myself on making the finest leather in the area and shipping it to New Orleans. Now, if you harm my wife in any way, I assure you that I'll find you, and your hide will be a cushion for some rich man's carriage. Maybe even one of my own."

Laurel had never seen Tony's eyes so black, so hard, or had heard his voice filled with such uncompromising vengeance. Jacques's hand on his knife shook a bit, and she heard him mutter a low curse. Before she was aware of what was happening, she found herself being pushed to the ground.

"Get him!" Tony waved his men toward the retreating figure of Jacques Jeanfreau. The men mounted their horses and galloped off and within seconds they surrounded Jacques.

Tony's arms encircled Laurel in a protective ring. She was crying as he picked her up and held her against his chest. Hippolyte stepped forward suddenly and inquired if she was all right.

She nodded she thought she was, then she told him in an unsteady voice that Roselle had borne him a son. Hippolyte immediately rushed away to the cabin.

"Are you really all right?" Tony asked her over and over.

She rested her head against his chest as he carried her home. She was so tired that she didn't care that she should be hating him. It felt so wonderful to be held by Tony again that she had stopped crying before they reached the house.

Gincie, roused from sleep by all the commotion, insisted that Laurel be served tea and a warm bath be prepared. Laurel smiled gratefully to Gincie when the teacup was in her hand and leaned her head against the back of her chair. Dawn was breaking, and soft strands of gray light stroked the interior of Laurel's bedroom. "My poor baby," Gincie repeatedly intoned and saw to it that the water Pauline poured into the copper tub was just the right temperature.

Seth knocked on the door and inquired about Laurel with a worried frown, but once she had assured him that the whole ordeal hadn't harmed her, he nodded and left.

"That man's been hangin' round here long enough," Gincie flatly stated and helped Laurel off with her gown. "It's time he left for home."

"Yes, I suppose so." Laurel settled herself into the warm water and sighed in contentment. She should have felt keyed up and overwrought by the events of the last few hours. Instead a delicious languor had taken hold of her, and all the tensions of the last weeks had disappeared. Was it because Tony had come to her rescue, held her in his arms once again? She knew she should hate him for what he had done to her, but her heart didn't.

Lathering herself with a lilac-scented soap, she watched as the golden beams of dawn warmed the room and touched her skin with a golden cast. She rinsed off as Gincie lay out her nightgown. Her eyelids were growing heavy, but the abrupt opening of the door caused her to come instantly alert.

"I should wring your neck."

Tony stood before her. His hands were placed on his hips, and his stance was spread-eagled. An ominous black cloud hovered in his eyes, replacing the warmth and concern she had seen earlier. He motioned to Gincie to leave the room, and when they were alone, Laurel gazed innocently up at him.

"Have I displeased you?"

"God, Laurel! You could have been nearly killed tonight. Don't pretend you don't know what danger you were in. Jeanfreau would have killed you if I hadn't frightened him about the consequences of such an action. Do you have any idea how shocked I was to see you appear from nowhere? I thought you were in bed, not gallivanting around the plantation. Hippolyte told me you've been hiding Roselle and her family, after I told you to stay away from the Jeanfreaus. I know they needed protection, but it wasn't up to you to do it, Laurel. Hippolyte also admitted the truth to me about the cattle thefts, that he was the one who was stealing and that you knew it. Don't get that questioning look in your eyes. I'm not going to turn him over to the sheriff. He's suffered enough. But, you, walking into the trap we'd laid for the Jeanfreaus...Well, you acted like a muddleheaded fool."

"I was helping Roselle deliver her baby." She hated sounding defensive, but Tony was beginning to anger her. What right did he have to barge into her room and say such an insulting thing to her? "I hope you've unleashed all your anger, Tony, because I'm not going to listen to you another minute. I'd appreciate it if you left now so I can finish my bath and go to sleep."

"Sleep!" he exploded. "You could have been killed, and you're worried about sleeping."

"Yes, I want to go to bed."

The cloud in his eyes disappeared, and a flame flickered in their black depths. "I want to go to bed, too. But not to sleep."

Tony's meaning was clear, and a becoming pink blush suffused her face and traveled to the ivory globes that gently bobbed beneath the surface of the water. Laurel had no idea of the enticing picture she presented to Tony, with a green ribbon tied around her long tresses and wisps of hair framing her face. The tips of her nipples, barely concealed beneath the liquid surface, beckoned to him. An ache grew in his loins to think of suckling them, and more than anything he wanted to taste her flesh with his lips, to feel her satiny legs wrapped around his waist as he took them both to their private paradise. It had been so long since he had made love to her that Tony couldn't restrain himself.

Barely aware of what he was doing, he reached out for her and pulled her wet, slick body from the tub.

One of his arms wrapped around her waist, and a hand massaged the gentle swell of her buttocks as he pinned her against him. "Don't fight me, Laurel." His voice was a seductive whisper against her cheek. "I want you so bad I think I'm going to go crazy if I can't have you again. You're all I think about."

"Put me down."

Her voice pierced through his passion, but he didn't intend to let her get away from him again. "No. You're mine right now. I'm not letting you go."

"I know, Tony," she breathed, and her hands began to fiddle with the buttons of his shirt. "Your clothes are getting wet."

Tony groaned in a purely animal fashion and held her tighter. "Damn the clothes!"

A liquid current, fast moving and hot, coursed through Laurel's body. No matter what this man had done to her, she couldn't deny that she wanted him with a fierceness that surprised her. By the time he had laid her across the bed, she was helping him pull off his shirt and pants, urging him to hurry. No preliminary kisses were needed between them this time. Just the feel of Laurel's silken flesh against Tony's body, which felt as hard and hot as freshly forged steel, sent them both into a passionate frenzy of wanting. Soft, warm breasts met a fur-planed chest. Tony's hand pulled the green ribbon from her hair, and Laurel's tresses fell thick and wild about her shoulders.

"I love touching your hair," he whispered into her ear as his hand became entangled in the mass of dark brown curls. "I love touching every part of you."

Satin fingertips trekked the length and breadth of Tony's chest before snaking over his hip to his powerful thighs and hovering dangerously close to the center of his pulsating shaft. He grasped her wrist before she could move further. "Another movement could get you in trouble, lady."

Laurel licked his ear. "I hope it does."

"Wanton woman," Tony intoned and guided her hand to his heated manhood. With gliding motions Laurel pleasured him until quickening gasps issued from Tony's mouth. Pulling her up to him, he grabbed a handful of hair and brought her lips to his, searing her in a fiery kiss that shot through Laurel like an arrow. She moaned against his mouth when his hands massaged the roundness of her buttocks. Laurel writhed on top of him until the throbbing peak of her femininity was positioned against Tony's desire.

His hands cupped her breasts, and Laurel moaned with mounting passion. "Love me, Tony. Love me now."

Her legs parted and she straddled him, bringing him into her with an unashamed eagerness. Tony filled her with an urgency that only Laurel could quench. They rode the exquisite path of ecstasy, reaching higher and higher until both of them thought they would burst. In one swift motion Tony rolled her onto her back as he thrust into her. Laurel clung to him, reveling in the sudden explosion of his passion, feeling her own body careen over the edge of sanity. Slowly, Laurel and Tony became aware of the tick of the clock, the birds chirping outside the window sill.

Drained of desire and emotionally spent, Tony pulled the covers over them, and they fell asleep in the circle of each other's arms.

Chapter Twenty

"It must be past noon," Laurel mumbled and buried her face deeper into Tony's shoulder. The midsummer sun streamed into the bedroom and, with it, heat, which caused Tony to pull back the sheet. Laurel clutched at it in a vain attempt to cover herself again, but Tony held it fast and grinned.

"I've seen you naked before this, *chérie*. You don't have to be embarrassed."

Her face lifted at the sound of his voice until she found herself staring into the ebony pools of his eyes. "I feel so wicked to be in bed at this time of day."

"Wicked, is it?" His finger stroked her chin. "Nothing we do together is wicked, nor is when we do it. I love you, Laurel. I'll always love you."

Laurel's heartbeat speeded up. Tony's touch always caused her body to respond. She knew that if she didn't get out of bed, they would make love again, that she would disgrace herself and beg him to make love to her. But she couldn't will herself to sit up, to leave him. No matter what had happened in the past, she hoped this might be a new beginning for them. Had she forgiven him for what he had done to her? She wasn't certain. All she knew was that, without Tony, she was incomplete.

"Can we try again?" she heard him ask. "I'm not made for the monk's life I've led the past few weeks. I can't bear not touching you, kissing you. What I did was unforgivable, but I promise you that I'll never hurt you again. I want your trust, your love, the little one you carry. Without these things, I'm nothing."

He placed a gentle kiss upon her lips. She kissed him back, feeling his arms wrap around her in a protective embrace. She wanted to tell him that, at this moment, she loved him with her whole heart and that she was very close to forgiving him. The pain he had caused her had lessened, and she no longer felt its sting. But there was time for talk later, she decided, when a windstorm of passion swept her away.

A warm evening breeze gently stirred the leaves of an oak tree as Simone, on a white gelding, rode toward Seth. With a long leg propped against the tree, Seth smiled at her when she stopped the horse by him and helped her to dismount. But there was no welcoming smile on her lips for him. She eyed him with a hint of contempt in her face.

"Flossie gave me your message," she began but refused to sit on the blanket he had placed on the grass for her. "What do you want?" She sounded impatient.

"I think the time has come to make some sort of a move where Laurel and Tony are concerned. I've been at the house for a while now, and I can tell you that my presence has not caused any dissension in their lives. In fact, I wouldn't be at all surprised if Laurel asked me when I'm returning home."

Simone considered Seth a moment, then said, "What about telling her that your stepfather has worsened?"

"I thought of that already," Seth countered, growing aggravated at Simone's apparent coldness for him. "She won't leave now, believe me. Laurel and Tony went into her bedroom this morning and have only come out within the last hour. When I saw her, her face was flushed, and she had eyes for no one but her husband. She won't leave him now."

"Damnit!" Simone paced up and down, hitting at the air with her riding crop. She turned her anger-filled eyes on Seth. "I thought you were going to seduce the witch. Can't you even accomplish such a simple task?"

Seth grabbed hold of her shoulders. "Be quiet, you stupid whore. No one talks to me like that. No one, not even you, Simone. I admit your beauty has bewitched me, but compared to such a viper as you, I'll take Laurel anyday."

Simone's mouth trembled, and tears formed in her eyes. "You're a cad. I'm carrying a child, and all you can do is call me names. Because of your bungling I'm going to lose Tony."

"A child? Whose baby is it? Is it mine?" he asked, a part of him hoping the child was his. He had always wanted a living, breathing reminder of himself.

She shook her head and gave a tiny sniff. "I don't know whose baby it is. That's the problem. It could be yours, but what good would that do me? You don't have any money either. A fine pair we'd make together. The father could be one of three other men, and none of them is wealthy."

Seth felt deflated at how cold and calculating she could be where he was concerned. "Could the baby be Tony's child?"

"No. Tony hasn't slept with me since before he met Laurel. He stayed the night at Clermont in my bed when he was very drunk, shortly before he married her, but he was so inebriated he couldn't make love to me."

"Does Tony remember that night?"

"How could he, Seth? I told you he was drunk and passed out. He hurt me, too, the next morning when he insisted that nothing had happened."

A faint glimmer of light began to sparkle in Seth's brain. Simone's pregnancy might be the answer to his prayers.

He looked at Simone and saw not the woman he thought he had loved, but a woman who would grant him the means to an end. "I think I know how to get Laurel to leave for San Antonio with me. Arrive at Petit Coteau tomorrow morning and appear pale and sick."

"I won't have to *appear* pale and sick. In the mornings, I am quite ill. Seth, what are you planning?" Her eyes began to brighten, somehow surmising Seth's plan already. It was too bad they were both without money. She and Seth were perfect together. They even thought alike.

The next morning, after a rapturous night spent in Tony's arms, Laurel agreed to accompany Seth on a buggy ride around the plantation. The rosy flush of love still glowed on her face, and she marveled anew at Tony's prowess and the care he took with her because of her pregnancy. She finally had admitted to herself that she loved him and forgave him for everything. She still had to admit it to him, and she would, just as soon as they returned to the house.

Seth held the reins in his hands and smiled sadly at her. His voice brought her back to the present and away from the delights that awaited her in the future. "I wanted this time alone with you to tell you that I'm returning to San Antonio next week."

"I'll be sorry to see you go." Laurel touched his hand. "Please don't worry about Uncle Arthur. I'm sure he'll be all right."

"I'm not convinced of that," he spoke somewhat harshly, then tempered his words with, "I had hoped that you'd come to love me as I love you."

This was the second time Seth had proclaimed his love. She couldn't allow him to think there was hope for anything other than friendship. "Thank you for caring, but I love my husband. I'll always love Tony. No one else."

"Yes, Laurel, I'm aware of that, but you can't blame a fellow for trying." He fell silent.

The horse clip-clopped along, and Seth returned them to the house. Simone's carriage was parked by the front steps as they came up the drive.

"What does she want?" Laurel asked out loud.

When they entered the foyer, Laurel could hear loud weeping coming from Tony's study at the end of the hallway. She made her way to the open door and saw Simone Lancier sitting in a chair, her face in a kerchief, and sobbing piteously. Tony stood above her, watching her with uncertainty and dismay.

"You're lying, Simone. I know you are," Tony spoke to her.

Simone glanced up, her eyes a washed-out shade of blue, her face pale and pinched. "Why should I lie to you, Tony? I tell you that I'm having your child, and you accuse me of lying. Ask Doctor Fusilier. He'll confirm my pregnancy and how far along I am."

Tony blanched. Could the child be his own? he wondered. That night when he had been so drunk he hadn't known which end was up, and Simone had insisted they had made love. But how could he have made love to her? All he remembered was blackness until he woke the next morning.

"What do you expect me to do? Marry you? I already have a wife."

"The honorable thing would be to divorce her and to marry me."

"You conniving little baggage—" Tony was interrupted by a flash of blue taffeta outside the door. Laurel! He rushed after the retreating figure heading for the stairs. Seth attempted to block his way.

"I heard what that Lancier woman said to you, and I think you're a pig!" Seth stated and made a lunge for Tony.

Tony sidestepped him, causing Seth to lose his balance a bit, and dashed past him. Halfway up, Tony ensnared Laurel with a large sweep of his arm.

"Let me go! Leave me alone, Tony. I don't want anything to do with you."

"You heard what Simone said?"

"Of course I heard her! Do you think I'm deaf as well as stupid? How could I have allowed you to worm your way back into my bed after all you've done to me? I must be crazy!"

"None of it's true. I love you."

"Is there a chance that Simone could be carrying

your child? Answer me."

"Yes, there might be, but I was drunk and—"

"Get your hands off of me! I'm leaving you."

Laurel twisted away. She wanted to go to her room, but Tony held her fast.

"Remember our deal," he hissed. "You remain at Petit Coteau as my wife. I won't have my child growing up away from me."

"I wish to God I had never become pregnant. I wish that night in the cabin had never happened. I wish I didn't have to see you again."

Laurel pushed at him with a strength she didn't know she possessed. Free of him suddenly, she ran up the next step, but the toe of her shoe entangled in the hem of her gown. She tottered, and for a moment she thought she could right herself or that Tony would catch her. But Tony's gaze had shifted to Seth and Simone at the bottom of the stairs. He didn't see her falling backward and was too late to catch her.

Laurel bumped on each step as she fell. The last thing she saw was Seth's stricken face as she landed by his feet.

Seth puffed impatiently on a cheroot and watched Simone as she poured a cup of tea in the parlor of her Clermont home. She shot him a Cheshire cat grin. "Don't look so down in the mouth," she scolded. "Laurel isn't dead yet."

He stubbed out the cheroot on a small golden tray and stared accusingly at her. "It's easy for you to be calm and cool over her accident. You have nothing to lose if she dies or recovers. Either way, you'll be able to latch onto Tony, the poor sucker."

Simone laughed her delight. "I think I played my

part very well. I was quite upset over my pregnancy, but now since Laurel has lost her baby, Tony will turn to me to fill the void. I shall soon be Tony's wife and quite wealthy, I should add."

Simone's complacency grated on Seth's nerves. He wondered how he could ever have been taken in by her. She was selfish through and through and a first-class whore to boot. But it wasn't the fact that she was so pleased with herself that upset him. He worried that he was now back to where he had been when he arrived in Lousiana. Potentially penniless unless Laurel lived and he could convince her to leave with him and then marry him. What blasted luck!

"I better go back to Petit Coteau. Tony hasn't left her bedside, hoping she'll wake up. I'd like to be there if anything happens."

Simone lay on the divan and stretched languidly, blowing him a kiss. "I hope all works out for you, Seth, darling. My future is assured no matter what happens to Laurel. If she lives, she won't stay with Tony now. If she dies, well . . . What can I say?"

"Cold-hearted bitch," Seth muttered and left a giggling Simone for the return trip to Petit Coteau.

For the first time in years, Tony prayed. Sitting by her bedside with Gincie in attendance, he knew that if Laurel died, he had no reason to live either. Their child was gone, and though Doctor Fusilier had said Laurel would have other children if she lived, Tony knew she would never want another child of his. Agony was imprinted on his face whenever he looked at her. She lay so still, and her face was ashen beneath the purple bruises from her fall. Her whole body was bruised, and he felt responsible. If only he hadn't gone to Simone's house those long weeks ago. He doubted the veracity of the woman's story, but he couldn't prove the child Simone carried wasn't his own. He would most probably never be able to prove that nothing had happened. And what was worse, Laurel would never trust him again.

Gincie lightly patted Tony on the shoulder. "There's nothin' to be done for my baby now, Mr. Tony. You been sittin' up with her for two days now. You got to get some rest."

Tony stroked the stubble on his chin. "I won't leave her. I'll wait until she wakes up."

"Mr. Tony, she may never wake up."

"She will!" Tony insisted. "Laurel will be all right."

That night Laurel still hadn't come out of the coma. Doctor Fusilier came and checked her and then rested in a bedroom down the hall until there should be some change. But when the next afternoon arrived and Laurel still hadn't woken up, he reluctantly left. Tony was unaware the doctor had gone as he continued to sit at Laurel's bedside and ate only light meals in her room. Gincie grew worried over Tony's bedside vigil and his haggard appearance. The man loved Laurel, that was certain. What would happen to Mr. Tony if Laurel died? Gincie wondered, and she didn't like to think about that.

That night Tony was dozing in his chair, attuned to Laurel's every breath. At midnight he heard a slight movement on the bed and instantly came alert. Laurel's eyes were open, and she was looking at the candlelight flickering across the ceiling, apparently disoriented.

"Thank God you're awake," Tony breathed and kissed her hand. "I thought I had lost you."

Laurel's gaze drifted to him. Her eyes focused on his face, and she saw tears streaming down his cheeks. She wondered why Tony was crying when she was the one who felt so awful. Then her mind cleared, and she suddenly felt lucid and wide awake. "I had an accident, didn't I?"

He nodded. "You're going to be fine. I knew you'd come back to me."

"How long have I been sleeping?"

"A little over three days."

"My head hurts," she said. "Every inch of me hurts." She grew silent for a few seconds, feeling the warmth of Tony's hand in hers. She remembered the fall down the stairs and, more importantly, recalled the scene in Tony's study. Her hand touched her abdomen. The past few weeks she had noticed a roundness there. Now she felt a hollow emptiness. She had said right before her fall that she wished she had never become pregnant. Now her wish had come true.

"I lost my baby."

A strangled sob rose in Tony's throat, and all he could do was nod.

She felt unable to cry, unable to summon the appropriate emotion for the circumstances in which she found herself. "I should have known things were suddenly too perfect not to be destroyed. People I love have died without warning. I'm alone again."

"You're not alone, Laurel. You have me. I love you. Doctor Fusilier insists you can have other children. I'll take care of you. You belong with me, here at Petit Coteau."

Her emerald eyes fastened on him, impaling him. "There's nothing to keep me here any longer. The baby is gone. When I'm well enough, I'm leaving with Seth for San Antonio. Don't try and stop me, Tony. This time, I *am* going."

He knew she meant to leave him. He had lost her because of a stupid indiscretion, something he didn't even remember, something he wasn't certain had ever happened. Suddenly he was too tired and weary of life to try to convince her to stay. He had gone through a living hell the last few days. Retribution for his revenge against Lavinia Delaney was staring him in the face. His life was over.

Standing up, he sighed. "Do what you will, Laurel. I won't prevent you from leaving. Go to San Antonio with Seth, make a new life for yourself. Forget I ever existed."

"You'll take care of all the . . . arrangements." She meant a divorce but couldn't say the word.

"Whatever you want."

He turned his back and didn't look at her again, as he closed the door behind him.

Chapter Twenty-one

After a long and arduous trip, the stagecoach pulled alongside the Plaza House in San Antonio to let the passengers disembark. Laurel, with Seth's supportive arm around her waist, got off before Gincie. Their clothes were covered in dust, and Laurel was glad she had purchased sensible calico gowns in New Orleans all those months ago. Her good dresses would have been ruined. She couldn't wait to bathe and wash away the weeks of accumulated dirt and grime. The way stations had been few and far between and the facilities had been inadequate. Now she eagerly awaited decent accommodations and the chance to sleep in a comfortable bed. Although she felt suddenly very tired, she glanced with curiosity at the plaza containing the golden-colored limestone facade of the Alamo, now occupied by the United States Army. She also noticed a brewery and the beginnings of an elaborate hotel.

On the street, carts and carriages moved at a leisurely gait, and she even saw a herd of cattle being driven through the plaza by vaqueros on horseback.

"You feelin' all right?" Gincie asked as she followed Laurel and Seth onto the covered porch of the hotel out of the blistering summer sun.

"Just weary," Laurel told her.

"You shouldn't have left Petit Coteau until you felt stronger." The admonishment in Gincie's tone didn't go unnoticed by Laurel, or by Seth, who tightened his grip on Laurel's waist and shot Gincie a chilling look.

"Laurel will feel better once she's rested. Tomorrow we'll start for the ranch, and she can regain her strength there."

Gincie grew quiet and wrinkled her nose in distaste, her dislike for Seth evident on her face.

Inside the hotel, Laurel welcomed the sudden coolness of the interior, and once in her room, she ordered up a bath. Seth said he would return at six to escort her to supper, and she promised she would be ready by then, but she really didn't want to go. She wished she could just crawl into bed.

Though she was appreciative of Seth's company and his solicitous concern for her health, she sensed he would press his suit of her affections in earnest now that they were in Texas. She didn't care for him in that way and doubted she ever would. It was Tony she still loved and would love for the rest of her life.

Damn him! she silently cursed and laid her head against the back of the tub. He had disappeared the day she woke from her accident and she hadn't laid eyes on him since. Essie had told her he had gone to Vermillionville. Laurel had half-expected him to return for the marriage of Hippolyte and

Roselle, followed by their son's baptism, or at least before she left for San Antonio. However, by the time she was sufficiently recovered to travel, he hadn't come home.

Denise had arrived unexpectedly from Vermillionville and told her that she had seen Tony in a lawyer's office and he looked awful. This had been Laurel's first indication that Tony was filing for a divorce. Denise had begged her to reconsider, but Laurel had been adamant. There was no hope for a reconciliation. Too much had happened between them. She couldn't trust him. Their relationship had been doomed from the start. Denise had listened sympathetically, but in her parting words to her she had professed that Laurel was making a mistake in leaving Tony.

"Well, it's my mistake," she mumbled to herself and picked up the soap and began to lather her arms. She felt she had no alternative but to leave Tony. A raw, nagging ache filled her to think that Simone Lancier could be carrying Tony's child. Would she ever get over the empty feeling inside her? Even yet she had not shed a tear over her miscarriage or leaving Tony. Something must be wrong with her, she briefly realized, but couldn't dwell upon anything but reaching the Little L. Starting a new life and seeing her uncle were her priorities now.

Gincie bustled into the room and laid out a pink taffeta gown with white rosettes on the low neckline. "This dress is too revealin', Miss Laurel. That Seth's eyes are gonna pop out of his head. Why don't you wear that respectable green dress with the lace collar?"

"Because, dear Gincie, I'm going to do things with a flair from now on, and hang what people think."

"You're still hurtin' and not thinkin'. Remember before you left New Orluns, you wanted to change your life. Well, you did. You got a good man back in Louisiana. You ought to go back and claim your man before that nasty Simone gets her claws in him too deep."

Laurel ignored Gincie's advice and continued bathing until Gincie realized that nothing she said was going to sink into Laurel's brain. Half an hour later Laurel was attired in the daring pink gown and walked down the stairs to the dining room on Seth's arm. Every eye was trained on her as they were seated, and she had a sense of déjà vu. She recalled wearing a daring dress the night Tony had first kissed her and how she had melted into strong arms. Pain flickered across her face, and Seth patted her hand.

"Would you rather go upstairs? We do have a long trip to the ranch in the morning."

"No, I'd like to order our supper now. I'm not tired at all." Suddenly she wasn't physically tired, just emotionally spent. Seth's concern for her well-being touched her. He didn't seem to be a bad sort, yet she couldn't help being suspicious of him and his motive for coming to Louisiana in the first place. However, she had no reason not to believe that her uncle was the force that drove him to come for her. Still, something she read in his eyes disturbed her. They contained a guarded look, a dark possessive quality when they settled on her face.

Yet, when Seth smiled at her, she discerned a lusty gleam flare in those blue orbs. With a start, she realized she didn't find his attentions totally undesirable. Perhaps in time she might come to care for Seth if only she could forget Tony's dark handsomeness. At that moment when Seth took her hand and kissed her fingertips, she was desperate enough to try.

Before dawn the next morning they left San Antonio, Seth seated on a spirited roan, riding alongside Laurel and Gincie's carriage. As the veil of night lifted, the countryside opened into a panorama of rolling green hills and ancient trees, bathed by the first rays of a golden morning. Laurel caught her breath at the untamed, virginal beauty. Mexican junipers, evergreen and lush, dotted the roadside as well as tall stalks of white-blossomed yuccas.

The road followed along cypress-lined rivers, dipping down to the water's edge and causing moments of unease for Gincie as the carriage precariously crossed to the other side. Passing farms of various sizes, Laurel couldn't help observing that the cattle and sheep grazing nearby in vast stretches of green farmland, interlaced with wild bluebonnets, appeared contented and well-fed.

The coolness of the hill country morning caused a peaceful feeling to flow through her, the first she had felt in weeks. She realized why Lavinia and her uncle loved Texas. It was a place of enchantment. Seth glanced down at her from his horse, his face partially obscured by his wide-brimmed hat, and gave Laurel the opportunity to see him as the Texas cowpoke he thought he was. In a comfortable plaid shirt tucked into Levis and with boots on his feet, he no longer resembled the dandy who had arrived at Petit Coteau.

"What do you think of Texas so far?" he asked her and grinned.

"I think I've already fallen in love with it."

"I hope that's not all you fall in love with." The charming grin revealed even teeth as he spurred his horse and galloped before the carriage.

"Watch out for him, Miss Laurel. That Seth ain't like Mr. Tony."

Laurel grimaced. "I hope not! And please, Gincie, don't mention Tony's name to me again. I want to forget I ever knew him. I'm starting life over again. Something I should have done months ago if it hadn't have been for him."

"Yes, ma'am," Gincie muttered, though she sounded unconvinced.

By the time the carriage rolled past the German settlement of Fredericksburg, the sun was setting. An orange glow had settled over the Cross Mountains in the distance when Seth pointed to a large ranch house at the base of the mountains.

"The Little L!" he shouted back.

Laurel craned her neck to get her first appreciative view of the Delaney ranch. A piece of wood, suspended across two thick fence posts, held a large wooden *L* surrounded by a circle in place. Beyond that, beneath a blood-red sky was the two-story ranch house built of gray granite from the nearby boulder-strewn hills of Bear Mountain. Some fifty feet away she discerned a barn and various smaller buildings, which she assumed were bunkhouses for the men who helped her uncle work the Little L. Farther away, the descending twilight began to obliterate the forms of the cattle on the open range.

"Isn't it beautiful?" Laurel gushed to Gincie, who didn't seem the least bit impressed.

"I still think Petit Coteau is where you belong."

"Do be quiet," Laurel chastised her as the driver halted the carriage before the house. Seth jumped excitedly down from his horse, and grabbing Laurel's hand, practically pulled her onto the porch.

"Father will be so pleased to see you," he told her and pushed open the door to lead her into a large foyer with a highly polished wooden floor. A middle-aged Mexican woman glanced up in surprise from the flowers she was arranging in a vase on a round mahogany table in the foyer's center.

"Señor Seth, we didn't expect you. Your father will be much happy to see you again."

Seth introduced the woman to Laurel as Rosita and inquired where Arthur and Lavinia might be found.

Rosita's face clouded over for an instant. "Señor Delaney has felt unwell these last two weeks and has taken to his bed. Senorita Lavinia is upstairs reading to him."

A subdued Seth escorted Laurel into the large parlor. A fireplace took up one half of a wall, and a leather-cushioned sofa, flanked by two matching brown chairs, stood in the center of the room. Red drapes framed the long windows on another wall and were pulled back to reveal the fiery peaks of the mountains. Rosita followed behind them, and Seth instructed her to see to Gincie's wants. When Laurel and Seth were alone, Seth glanced up the stairway to the open balcony. His eye was trained on a large oak door in the middle of the hallway.

"We better go up and see Father now. I had hoped he'd be better, but I think he may be worse."

Laurel gently touched Seth's arm. "Would you rather see him alone first?"

Nodding, he began to ease his way up the stairs. "Wait here for now, while I see if he's feeling up to seeing you."

Laurel watched Seth enter Arthur's room. She

was standing by the sofa when Lavinia left Arthur's room and closed the door behind her. Touching the smooth, polished surface of the handrail, she surveyed Laurel for a moment before descending.

Lavinia stopped in front of Laurel. "So you've really come. You left that handsome Tony Duvalier to come here. I can't believe Seth accomplished that."

The seriousness in Lavinia's face and overall demeanor surprised Laurel. She thought her cousin would be pleased to see her at last. "You knew when we left New Orleans that I wanted to see Uncle Arthur. I don't know why you should stare at me in such disbelief. I have finally arrived."

"But I don't understand why you're here now, Laurel. You're married to a handsome and wealthy man. What could have possessed you to leave him for this trip?"

Laurel threw down her reticule and sat on the sofa, gazing into the cold ashes in the fireplace. "Tony and I are getting divorced. I came here because I don't have anywhere else I'd rather be."

"No! How did Seth manage that?" Lavinia blurted out, without thinking what she said.

Laurel looked at her with a quizzical expression on her face. "Seth didn't manage anything. I don't know what you're talking about. Tony and I had insurmountable problems. Seth has nothing to do with our divorce."

"Really?"

Lavinia didn't sound as if she believed her. "I assure you, Lavinia, that your stepbrother has been a gentleman at all times."

"I just bet," Lavinia mumbled under her breath, as Seth came out of her father's room and ambled down the stairs.

"Father would like to see you," he told Laurel, "but don't stay for too long. He's not very strong. He had some sort of an attack. His lungs are weak, and he coughs a great deal, but he insists he wants to talk to you."

Laurel rose from the sofa and nodded that she understood. She walked up the stairs and opened the door to her uncle's room.

The bright flame from an oil lamp on the bedside table cast a golden glow over the thin man who lay in the large four-poster bed. A patchwork quilt atop him almost drowned his slight form in a sea of color. Laurel tensed and wiped her perspiring hands on the calico material of her pink and white gown as Arthur Delaney lifted his head slightly from the pillows supporting him.

A thin hand beckoned to her, and her feet moved until she stood beside the bed and gazed down at the gaunt face of her uncle. She saw that his hair, though predominantly gray, still contained streaks of red, and his green eyes were alert as he looked at her.

He pointed to her bonnet. "Take . . . it . . . off." His voice was no more than a whisper.

With trembling fingers, Laurel removed her pink bonnet, and her hair fell in long, cascading curls around her shoulders. Arthur smiled. "You . . . look like . . . Emily."

"Not as beautiful, I'm afraid," Laurel told him and sat in a chair near the bed.

"Just like her."

"I don't want to overtax you, Uncle Arthur. If you'd rather I go . . ."

"No. Stay. I wanted to see you again. I haven't been a . . . good uncle to you."

"Don't speak about the past now. You must rest.

When you're feeling better, we can talk."

She began to get up, but his hand weakly grabbed at her arm, "Don't go yet."

Sitting back down, she noticed a book on his bed and picked it up. "Would you like me to read to you for a while?"

Arthur nodded, and Laurel began to read aloud as he watched her until he drifted off to sleep.

Seth sat on the porch and watched night descend. Lavinia stood behind him, half-leaning on a stone pillar. Her eyes locked with his when she spoke.

"You accomplished the impossible, I see. Congratulations, Seth."

Seth laughed and acknowledged her compliment with a nod. "I told you I'd break up their marriage."

"How did you do it? Laurel was in love with Tony Duvalier. I think she still is."

"Don't ask questions, Lavinia. The conditions surrounding the breakup are unimportant. Besides, the marriage was in trouble when I arrived at Petit Coteau. I helped things along, that's all."

"Laurel isn't going to fall in love with you."

Seth's eyes hardened to an ice blue. "She better, or we're both going to be out in the cold. The old man is very ill, probably going to die soon. I can't see him rallying this time. Then where will we be? We'll have to sell the ranch, and I know you don't want to let go of the Little L, nor do I. That leaves Laurel to provide the money. She'll simply have to marry me. At the very least provide some funding to keep the ranch afloat if Arthur dies. I spoke to Tom Evans a little while ago. He said the Kansas market isn't interested in our stock because of last year's cattle fever. Arthur won't admit there's a problem, but Tom said he and the other men are thinking of leaving us and working for other ranches because we can't meet our payroll. Now, tell me, Miss Know-It-All, that Laurel won't fall in love with me and marry me."

Everything Seth said was true, but she hated this cold and calculating side to him and detested that she too sometimes viewed life in the same fashion. She doubted if Laurel had ever seen this side of Seth. If she had, Lavinia doubted she would even have come to Texas with him. But Lavinia didn't want Seth to think he had gained the upper hand and wished to wipe that cocky smile off his handsome face.

"I didn't say Laurel wouldn't marry you. I said she'd never fall in love with you. There's a difference there, my darling stepbrother. A very large difference."

Lavinia turned and went inside, slamming the door after her. Seth threw down his cheroot in disgust and watched the flame burn away.

Seth's prediction that Arthur wouldn't rally again proved wrong. Two days after Laurel's arrival, his cough abated and his appetite increased. By the end of her first week at the Little L, Laurel saw a definite filling out in Arthur's face, and he felt strong enough to sit on the porch with her in the evenings. Each afternoon, just before sunset, Tom Evans, Arthur's foreman, would help the ailing man to the porch and sit with them to watch the sunset. One evening Seth helped Arthur when Tom didn't appear.

"What happened to Tom?" Laurel asked.

Arthur heaved a disappointed sigh. "He gave his notice to me the other day. He took a job at a ranch closer to San Antonio and is probably packing his duds."

"Wasn't he happy here?"

"Sure, but—"

Seth interrupted. "Don't talk ranch business with Cousin Laurel, Father. I doubt she's interested in the help."

"I'm very interested in the Little L," Laurel said icily, not caring about Seth's deciding her interests. "Tom told me that he has worked for you for over ten years. I can't believe he took another job. I know how much you trust and rely upon him."

"That's true," Arthur said, "but Tom's pretty young yet and has to make a living. He's planning to get married. Got a girl from San Antonio he's been courting for a few years now. Guess he wants to live there and make more money. I can't pay him or the other hands what they're worth right now. Ever since the cattle fever struck last year, I've lost a number of my herd, and the Kansas markets don't want my stock. Unless I get a buyer for my cattle, the Little L is going to go under."

This was the first Laurel had heard of her uncle's financial plight. She had thought the business reversals she had heard about last year had taken a turn for the better. Apparently not. Why hadn't Lavinia told her about this? Surely she had known when she was in New Orleans. Was that why she was so eager to wed a wealthy man like Auguste St. Julian? And why hadn't Seth told her about the Little L's financial condition?

She stole a glance at Seth, who turned his back and sat on the porch railing. Arthur pulled the light blanket resting on his legs tighter about him. "Are you chilled?" she asked him.

Arthur admitted he was and that he would like to go inside. Seth hauled his long legs from the other side of the railing and got up to carry his stepfather to his room. Laurel went with them, and though he dismissed Seth, Arthur requested her to stay.

She sat beside him on the bed when he pointed to the spot and took her hand, squeezing it gently. "You've been very sad since you got here. Would you tell me what's wrong? Maybe I can help you."

"No one can help me. My problems have nothing to do with you."

"You're sad because of your husband."

Laurel sighed. "You're very astute, Uncle Arthur."

"I know what it's like to be sad over a lost love, Laurel. Now tell me what happened."

For some reason, Laurel felt quite at ease with Arthur and knew he genuinely wanted to help her. Not that he could, but by the time the story of her meeting and subsequent marriage to Tony tumbled out of her, she was crying tears she had held inside her for the past miserable weeks. Arthur tenderly pulled her head against his chest and stroked her hair.

"Now, now, don't cry," he said soothingly. "Nothing's as bad as you think. Believe your fath . . . your uncle when I tell you that. Everything works out for the best." He lifted her tear-stained face to look into eyes that matched his own. "Believe me when I tell you that, Laurel. One day you'll forget all your pain."

"I'm going to try." She wiped her eyes with her fingertips. "Thank you for listening, for caring. I feel much better now." Laurel kissed his cheek quickly and left the room.

"That's what fathers are for," he said to himself. Arthur rang the little bell beside his bed, and when Rosita appeared, he asked her to fetch Tom Evans from the bunkhouse. He had a telegram to send.

Chapter Twenty-two

Laurel tucked her plaid shirt in the top of her jeans and surveyed herself in the mirror one last time. She nearly laughed aloud at the sight of herself dressed like a cowpoke. The expensive, flat-heeled leather boots she had purchased in Fredricksburg the day before pinched her feet a bit, but the clerk had assured her that the boots would outlast her. She placed the wide-brimmed felt hat on her head, conscious of Tom Evans's words that without its protection, the sun would play havoc with her fair skin under the Texas sky. Laurel thought she looked quite different and unrecognizable, though the clothes molded to her curves in a manner that men might find distracting. However, Laurel couldn't do anything about her physical attributes. But Gincie was dismayed by her less than feminine attire and insisted she tie back her hair with a red ribbon, and Laurel had bowed to this one touch of femininity.

"A lady doesn't wear men's clothes." Gincie eyed Laurel in distaste and stood with arms akimbo beside Laurel's bed.

Laurel turned from the mirror and grinned. "Lavinia dresses this way."

"Miss Lavinia ain't no lady."

A sound from the open doorway drew their attention. "I heard that," Lavinia said and sniffed the air. She entered the room, dressed in a like manner to Laurel and critically surveyed her cousin. "You'll do." Lavinia sounded almost grudging in her compliment. "Tom is downstairs waiting for you. I don't know why you insist on being shown all of the Little L. You're a guest here, Laurel. We don't expect you to take part in roping and branding."

"I want to see how everything is done," Laurel insisted. "Since I'll be here for some time, I may as well get used to the environment."

Lavinia pursed her lips. She would rather Laurel got used to Seth's company, but Seth had ridden into San Antonio the day before yesterday, no doubt to visit one of his whores and probably to gamble Little L money, which he could ill afford to lose. What the stupid fool should be doing was courting Laurel, or at least making an attempt at courting her. However, it always seemed that Seth's vices got the best of him.

"Then I'll go along with you and Tom." As Lavinia started to follow after Laurel, she stopped for a moment and poked her tongue out at Gincie and laughed in devilish delight at Gincie's shocked mien before joining Laurel and Tom on the porch.

Shortly thereafter Laurel was settled on a spirited chestnut mare named Starfire. She broke into a gallop beside Tom's dark stallion and Lavinia's She Devil, a high-stepping filly, which Laurel couldn't help but think suited her cousin perfectly.

"Where'd you learn to ride, ma'am?" Tom asked Laurel, an appreciative twinkle in his gray eyes for her expert horsemanship, as they headed for the open, rolling countryside.

"My father taught me when I was a child. He was Arthur's brother, you know, and grew up in the Texas wilds. I spent long hours on horseback during the summer months at our plantation."

"Well, your father taught you right good."

"There's nothing that my cousin can't do." Lavinia's voice dripped venom, and she spurred her horse. Her long hair flew like a comet's tail behind her as she rode swiftly ahead of them.

"Don't take Miss Lavinia too personal, ma'am. She's just high-strung and worked up over her pa being sick."

Laurel caught Tom's eye and smiled kindly. "I know. Lavinia feels things deeply and doesn't always show her feelings. Instead she acts brattish." She rode alongside Tom in companionable silence for a few minutes before speaking again. "Uncle Arthur told me you were leaving the Little L. He hates to see you go. He relies on you."

Tom nodded. "I don't really want to leave, but I've got me a fine woman I aim to marry. She won't live any place but San Antonio, so I have to be where she is. Besides, times on the Little L ain't the best right now. I promised Mr. Delaney I'd stay on a while longer until he gets some business settled." Tom glanced downward in a sheepish manner, almost as if he had said something that pertained to Laurel directly and didn't want her to know about it. "I'd do anything for Mr. Delaney. I owe him a lot."

"I'm very pleased you care about him, Mr. Evans.

I've grown quite fond of Uncle Arthur, and I'm worried about his health. The last day or so he's been coughing more but won't send for a doctor." She grew quiet a moment. "Uncle Arthur is dying, isn't he?"

"Reckon so, ma'am. We're all dying a little each day, but Mr. Delaney don't have much time left. That's the real reason I'm staying on. He made me promise not to leave until after . . ." His voice drifted away, and for the rest of the ride Tom Evans said nothing else.

When the horses crested a small hill, Tom pointed to a large group of cattle, grazing by a slow-moving stream. "Mr. Delaney's pride and joy," he said, smiling proudly at Laurel. Spurring their horses onward, they galloped across the dewy grass until they drew to a halt near a circle of men, mounted on what Tom told her were cutting horses. These riders would ride into the herd and cut from it those cows that needed to be branded.

Lavinia had gone ahead and was already there. She sat on her horse a slight distance away from Laurel. When the cutting horses headed for the herd, Lavinia joined them, surprising Laurel with the ease with which she separated a calf from a cow and roped it before dragging it to the branding fire. In fascination Laurel watched while her cousin and one of the men held down the struggling calf. A second man applied the red-hot branding iron to the calf's flank, quickly and carefully burning it with the *L* marking. The calf bawled loudly, and while Lavinia spoke soothingly to the animal, the man who had branded it took a sharp knife and earmarked it for identification.

"Why are the calf's ears cut?" Laurel asked Tom.

"Well, a cow without earmarks is called 'slick ears.' If the cow wanders onto someone else's range without the earmarkings, it's rounded up and becomes that outfit's property. The branding and earmarking help to make certain that the animal is the Little L's property. If we find a number of marked cows on our range, we herd them into a stray herd until the outfit's foreman comes to drive them back to their own range."

The whole procedure of branding repulsed and fascinated Laurel. She slid from her horse and for the next few hours watched Lavinia and the men go through the same process of roping, branding, and castrating most of the bull calves, except for the ones judged to be prime specimens and set apart as breeding stock. Laurel lost count at one point of the number of animals that were roped and dragged, struggling and bawling, to the branding iron. Tom, however, told her that Arthur had lost quite a number of cows to the cattle fever last year, and that the number of cattle that now grazed had been substantially reduced.

Laurel remembered what Tony had said about his Brahman breed's sturdiness in resisting the ravages of drought and fever. Perhaps the Little L could profit from Tony's knowledge, she wondered, but quickly dismissed the thought of Tony from her mind.

When the sun was high in the sky, the hollow ringing of a cowbell summoned them all to lunch. A grizzled old man named Rusty, who had lost a great many teeth but possessed a large, warm smile, handed plates of warm stew topped with a hard piece of bread to everyone. The men waited in line for their helping, but when Laurel appeared, they insisted she be served first. No one stepped out of line for Lavinia.

Laurel sat beneath a cottonwood tree and began to eat her lunch, imitating the men by using the bread as a spoon. Lavinia, with plate in hand, plopped down on the cool grass next to Laurel.

"Are you enjoying yourself, Cousin Laurel?"

"I'm learning a great deal. I hadn't realized that ranching could be such backbreaking work."

"Hmph! A lot you know about ranching."

Laurel caught the unmistakable hint of scorn in Lavinia's voice. "I'd like to learn. The men are quite skillful."

"The hands are putting on a grand show for you."

"I don't understand."

Impatiently, Lavinia pushed strands of auburn curls away from her brow, which was misted with perspiration. "Don't pretend you haven't noticed how they all look at you, how they've gone out of their way to be deferential. More than one has asked about my beautiful city-bred cousin. They want to know if you're available."

"Lavinia, I think you're jealous."

"I've never been jealous of any female in my life. I can have my choice of any man."

"I'm certain you have," Laurel said, taunting Lavinia with her innuendo about her stormy past. "However, you're acting catty and spoiled. I'd advise you to stop, because you appear quite unattractive when you're not the center of attention."

Anger gathered in Lavinia's eyes and sent blue fire in the direction of her cousin. "Really, Laurel. Who are you to give advice? You forget that because of me you wouldn't have met your husband.

Evidently you weren't woman enough to keep him. Something I'll never be accused of."

Laurel's mouth fell open. She couldn't believe that this nasty woman was the woman she had protected from Tony's wrath. How dare Lavinia insult her. She had been through too much these last months to have her own cousin sit there and insinuate that she somehow was less of a woman because she and Tony were divorcing. She would love to wipe that smug smile from Lavinia's face by informing her that Tony was the St. Julian relative she feared, that she might still need to remain on her guard. For all anyone knew, Tony might have his revenge on her yet. But she didn't say these things to Lavinia, couldn't summon the words to hurt her. Lavinia was jealous of her, and this surprised Laurel. Here she was, safe and secure within the loving bosom of her family and knowing she had a place to call home while Laurel was still adrift with no one to love her.

Laurel stood up, and she calmly appraised Lavinia, but her voice sounded cold. "Don't ever make assumptions about me or my marriage. Never mention my marriage again."

Laurel strode away, too angry to speak to Lavinia further and only calmed down when Tom took her aside to show her a rope trick.

With trembling fingers, Lavinia wiped away a tear that threatened to spill onto her cheek. She hated herself for acting jealous, but Laurel's presence at the ranch upset her. True, she had wanted Laurel to come home with her and had plotted with Seth. Now that Laurel was finally at the Little L, Lavinia found she couldn't cope with not being the center of the hands' attentions any longer. If that wasn't bad enough, her father doted upon Laurel, spoke of her constantly as if he were a proud father. He already had a daughter, she thought resentfully, a daughter who had done almost anything to win his love and save the ranch by making a rich older man fall in love with her. What more could she do?

She watched Laurel, surrounded by Tom and a few of the men. No doubt about it, Laurel was quite beautiful in a soft and gentle way that she lacked. None of the men ever took the time to treat her like a lady. She remembered Gincie's words that morning and grimaced. The old biddy was right, but she could never act like Laurel. A streak of wildness as deep as a canyon ran through her. The only man who might have tamed her was Jim Castille, and he had betrayed her.

But I'm just as beautiful as Laurel, she thought in defiance and shook her auburn hair about her shoulders.

She could have any man she wanted, even Tony Duvalier if the opportunity had presented itself. But she had been eager to be gone from Lousiana and didn't want to become involved with another man. A small smile played about her mouth to think that she could have taken Tony from Laurel if she had put her mind to the task. A very pleasant task, too, she couldn't help thinking. Now it was too late. She would never see Tony Duvalier again, and neither would Laurel. That thought made her feel instantly happier. Yet the pressing problem of money still weighed down her mind.

She might resent Laurel, but Laurel was the means of saving the Little L. Lavinia had no doubt that her cousin, if pressed, would loan or give some cash to help the ranch. That solution, however, was only temporary at best. Yet if Laurel married Seth, the money problem would be settled once and for all. Yes, that was the answer as it had been from the beginning. Laurel and Seth must marry, and very glad she would be over the marriage. Laurel might not deserve a greedy scoundrel like Seth for a husband, but Lavinia didn't think she deserved to lose her father's love to Laurel.

Walking over to Laurel and Tom, she shot them a winning and engaging smile. Lavinia had already decided that she would be kind to Laurel until after the ceremony. Then she would put her beautiful cousin in her place with Seth's help. Any twinge of conscience over the gentle Laurel marrying her conniving stepbrother dissipated because Laurel had stolen her father's love.

The night hung dark and heavy as a quilt over San Antonio. Not one star glittered in the moonless heavens. Seth walked with quick strides through the area known as La Villita with his head down, purposely not glancing at the Spanish-speaking passers-by. His strides took him well past the small Mexican *jacals,* or huts, made of posts driven into the ground and tied together with rawhide and chinked with mud. He didn't want to go back to that section of town tonight, not after he had just lost a great deal of money in one such dwelling.

He cursed himself for being stupid and entering the poker game in the first place. But when Raphael Ortega had approached him about the game earlier, he had been feeling no pain. He had just drunk a great deal of tequila and had bedded

Dolores, a beautiful whore, in Ortega's bedroom. Ortega, the slimy bastard, always knew how to make him feel at home on his trips to San Antonio.

Not that this was the first time Seth had lost at the poker table. He had spent many previous hours in Ortega's parlor, cards clutched in his sweaty hands, while Ortega's and the other men's crafty eyes dared him to fold. But he had always bluffed them and come away from the card table with some cash in his pocket. But for the last few months his luck had run out. He had lost, and Ortega had accepted his promissory notes.

However, this night, Seth sensed a difference in Ortega. He no longer seemed as affable or as willing to accept another note. The man's brown eyes flickered in disdain over Seth as he signed the note, and Seth felt a coldness creep into his stomach. When Ortega left the room to escort another player to Dolores, Seth wasted no time in leaving. He wanted to return to the ranch where he felt he would be safe.

Seth's horse was tethered to a lamppost, and he had nearly reached it when he bumped into a wiry figure. "Excuse me," he said and lifted his head. His breath made a hissing sound when he recognized the grinning face of Raphael Ortega. A cigar dangled from between Ortega's teeth.

"Ah, Señor Renquist, how pleased I am that I caught you before you left. You didn't bid me farewell. And Dolores is quite broken-hearted that you didn't kiss her good-bye."

"Sorry, Ortega, but I have to get back to the ranch. My sister is having a birthday tomorrow, and guests will be arriving in the morning." What a lame excuse, he thought to himself. He didn't give a damn about Lavinia's birthday, but he did care about what might happen to him. The red light on the tip of Ortega's cigar burned as brightly and menacingly in the dark as the flame in Ortega's eyes.

"*Sí*, the ranch. The Little L, I believe, is the name. I've heard it is a fine spread, much cattle."

"Yeah, so?"

"You're growing impatient, Señor Seth. I don't like impatience, nor do the men who work for me. Do you remember Claudio?"

Seth nodded, recalling Claudio as a man who possessed shoulders as broad as a window and huge muscular arms. He had seen Claudio squeeze a man to death once for nonpayment of a debt to Ortega. A cold sweat broke out on Seth's brow.

"*Bueño*. I see that you do." Ortega looked amused. "Claudio takes care of my business associates when their debts are in arrears, as are yours, Señor Seth."

"I'm going to pay you your damn money!"

"*Sí*, I know you are, because I am going to collect. Now if you will return to my humble home with me, we can work out the details of repayment."

Seth would have punched Ortega. He knew he could knock the small man unconscious and gain enough time to get to his horse and race for home, but Claudio appeared and placed a warning hand on Seth's shoulder. Instead he found himself turned around, positioned like a corncob between a pig's jaws, headed for Ortega's hut.

Tony's hands, filled with fire, cupped her breasts

and brought them to his mouth. He suckled the rose-tipped buds until desire flared within her. Then his mouth left them to be replaced again by his hands, and his lips trailed lower upon her writhing flesh. She felt the softness of his mouth against her inner thighs, arched her body to meet his flicking tongue. But then he was atop her, gazing at her in love and passion, driving into her with subtle strokes that threatened to consume her in white heat.

Her body swirled in a heated mist, pulsating and trembling for fulfillment. Her fingernails dug into the taut flesh of his back, deeper and deeper, pulling him closer and closer against her, until the moment of exquisite release was near at hand . . .

"Wake up, Miss Laurel. Folks done started arrivin' already for Miss Lavinia's party."

Gincie's voice cut through the room, causing Laurel to waken with a start. Early morning sunshine streamed brightly onto the bed when Gincie opened the curtains. Laurel sat up, rather disoriented, a pillow clutched in her arms.

"What you done to that pillow, child? There's feathers all over the bed."

Glancing at the sheets, Laurel saw she was surrounded by wisps of duck down. Her fingers were embedded in the pillow, and when she withdrew them, she noticed that two long thin lines streaked through the soft linen material. Her cheeks turned beet red.

"I-I don't know, Gincie," she stammered and pushed the pillow away.

"Lordy me, but you must have been havin' one strange dream. Must have been a nightmare to account for such goin' on."

Laurel blushed deeper and quickly got out of bed in a rising cloud of down. She stood near the window, as Gincie began to take the sheets off the bed, careful not to disturb the feathers further. Below her, outside people gathered on the front lawn, where tables and chairs had been set up for the cook-out in honor of Lavinia's twenty-third birthday. Carriages and riders on horseback could be seen rolling and cantering up the road to the house. They exchanged greetings, and a spirit of joviality filled the air. All sorts of friendly people waited downstairs, but Laurel felt alone.

She held the curtain between trembling fingers. The dream haunted her, its memory filling her with an ache so painful and deep from wanting something she didn't care to admit to, denying to herself that Tony's phantomlike presence in her dreams had unsettled her. She didn't want him! She didn't love him any longer! Why must her own body, her mind, betray her, even in sleep? she asked herself and nearly cried aloud from the pain that tore through her as she realized that she would never quench the need within her own body. Tony was the man she ached for, but she must forget him, forget him as if he had never existed.

With resolve in her eyes, she left the window and began to dress before Gincie could offer to help her. She threw on her best petticoats and over these donned a blue-and-white-checked gown with a deep ruffled flounce and a low, off-the-shoulders neckline. Instead of pulling her hair atop her head, she had Gincie pull the sides back with white combs and brushed to such a gleaming brightness that it hung in reddish-brown waves to her waist.

She pirouetted before the mirror, pleased with the

result. Would Seth like what he saw? she found herself thinking in an attempt to drive Tony and her dream from her mind. She imagined herself in Seth's arms, responding to his kisses. She was determined that today she would forget Tony Duvalier forever.

Chapter Twenty-three

Arthur sat in the shade of the porch and watched his friends and neighbors milling about. He saw Laurel standing beneath a spreading oak tree. She was looking fresh and lovely, as she talked with some women. He smiled, seeing that she appeared to be enjoying herself. His eyes searched for Lavinia. She was nowhere in view, and he hoped she wasn't getting into some mischief. Lavinia had been acting rather pettishly lately. A deep frown creased his wrinkled brow, as he realized his stepson hadn't yet returned from San Antonio. It was just like Seth to miss Lavinia's party, Arthur decided. The two of them had never gotten along, and he wondered if their dislike of each other was because of him. Had he treated Seth differently because he was his stepson? He hadn't meant to, but then again, he had sent Lavinia away because he couldn't bear to look at her after the sordid incident with Jim Castille.

Either way, each of his children could attest to the fact that he hadn't been the best of fathers.

Especially Laurel. He let his eyes settle upon her again, feeling the same bittersweet pain he always felt when he looked at his beautiful younger daughter. She resembled her mother physically and also reminded him of Emily in other ways. The way she would tilt her head at an angle when she listened to a person, as if she were truly listening and not just pretending to hear. So many times he had seen Emily staring at him in just that way, that seeing Laurel do the very same thing tugged at his heartstrings.

He had loved Emily Delaney with a fierceness he had never experienced before he met her or afterward. Lavinia's mother never made him feel the way Emily had, and certainly not dear Anna, Seth's mother. He had never loved any woman but Emily. From the moment his brother had brought her home with him, he had known that if he couldn't possess the beautiful brunette, he would never be happy. But he was married to Lavinia's mother, and Emily was engaged to his brother. He had thought he would die at Sylvester and Emily's wedding. He still remembered the way he had wanted to grab her from his brother's arms and carry her away on his horse, never to be seen again by anyone.

He hadn't said anything to her, however, and had never told her how he felt until after his wife had died from childbirth fever. By that time he and Sylvester had started the Little L, named for baby Lavinia. Emily had taken care of his daughter, loving her as her own mother would have loved her. Sometimes, when he returned early from the range, he would find Emily alone, cooing softly to the auburn-haired baby in her arms. At these times, he would pretend that Emily was his wife, and Sylvester didn't exist. Guilt at loving Emily had torn at him. He had wanted her so badly that one day he couldn't contain himself and grabbed her, kissing her with a violence that stunned her as well as himself. She had slapped him and run away. At supper that night, he was unable to look at her or Sylvester. Arthur would never forget how Sylvester had accosted him after Emily had gone to bed. His brother had witnessed the whole incident and told him never to come near his wife again. The only reason they stayed at the ranch had been because the child needed a woman to look after her, and Lavinia filled an emptiness in Emily since she had been unable to conceive. And Arthur stayed away from Emily, though thoughts of her were always with him.

One night Sylvester and Emily had argued, though Arthur had never known why. He had been asleep in his room on the other side of the house, but the loud voices had woken him. Minutes later Sylvester had left, riding off into the night, and hadn't returned home that night or the next. Emily had been beside herself with worry until one of the hands told her that Sylvester had been spotted at a fancy house in San Antonio. Arthur remembered the way her face had fallen, how shattered she had looked. He would never forget how she had turned to him, took his hand, and led him into the house to her bedroom.

None of the women he had bedded in his lifetime could compare to the one night he had spent in Emily's arms. He had loved her and hoped she loved him, but then Sylvester had returned, and once again, Emily had become the proper wife. He had felt he was living a nightmare, unable to cope with Emily's desertion of him. When he asked her to leave Sylvester, she had refused. She had told him that she cared about him but she loved her husband and would never leave him. In fact they had decided to head for Louisiana where Sylvester wanted to buy a plantation. They could all start over again, and he must forget her and the night they had shared.

Not until the day Emily left had he learned from Sylvester of her pregnancy. In his heart he had known she carried his child, not his brother's, by the way she hadn't been able to look at him or do more than nod at his congratulations about the baby under Sylvester's watchful eye. After they had gone, he had found a letter under his pillow from Emily.

She had told him that she cared for him, but she couldn't leave Sylvester. They had shared one night, a night she would treasure all her life. He had given her a child, she wanted him to know about the baby, not to torment him but to allow him to rejoice in her happiness. If he loved her, he would not contact her again and would never tell anyone that she had borne her brother-in-law's baby. She loved Sylvester and would never leave him, so nothing he might do would matter in the end.

Emily hadn't been heartless. Though he wanted to believe she was cruel, he would never hurt her. Truly, she and the baby were better off in Louisiana, living in luxury rather than the hard life of ranching. It hadn't been until five years later, when the ranch finally began to turn a profit, that he hoped he had done the right thing in doing nothing.

Now his fondness for Laurel was expressed by the slight smile on his lips. He hadn't felt well that day, but just seeing that she was happy and beautiful, so like his Emily, caused him to feel better. His lawyer, Carson Turner, joined him on the porch and noticed the soft, loving gaze Arthur sent in Laurel's direction.

"Everything's all taken care of," Carson said and heaved his bulky frame into the chair next to Arthur's. "All of your children will be well taken care of in the event of your death."

Arthur nodded. "Good. I don't expect to be around much longer."

"You say that everytime I see you. You'll outlive me, you old goat."

Arthur didn't dispute him. He felt death was near, but he wasn't frightened of it. "When will the new buyer be here?"

"Funny you should ask that." Carson withdrew a piece of paper from his shirt pocket and handed it to Arthur. "Received this telegram at my office yesterday. Your buyer will be coming within the next month, as soon as things are settled on his end."

Arthur read the terse message and handed the telegram back to Carson. "You keep it. I don't want this to get in the wrong hands before then."

"You're afraid Seth might read it."

"Yes, but I don't want Laurel finding it. She might get cold feet and skedaddle out of Texas. Remember, Carson, it's imperative that she know nothing about the Little L's new owner until he gets here, or until after I pass on, whichever comes first. Promise me."

Carson smiled, thinking that Arthur would be around for a long time. If ever there was a man who could recover from physical setbacks, it was Arthur Delaney, his old and dearest friend. "You've got my word, old friend."

* * *

Leaning against the post of the corral, Lavinia watched Buck Dawson, one of the ranch hands, attempt to break in a wild stallion. The blood pumped swiftly through her veins, and excitement grew within her. At that moment, nothing could compare to the engrossing combat of one man's will against that of this magnificent beast. The stallion was ivory in color, and a more beautiful animal Lavinia had never seen. She knew Buck was trying to impress her, but when the horse reared up and deposited Buck unceremoniously on his backside, she sent up an inward cheer for the horse.

Buck looked sheepish as he limped to the gate and joined her on the other side. "That horse ain't never goin' to be tamed," he said and brushed the dust from his pants with the brim of his hat.

"I thought you told me you knew all about taming animals."

"I do. I can tame any filly of the two-legged variety. Horses just take a mite longer."

Lavinia sidled up to him, drawn to Buck only by the fact that he was an attractive male. It had been a long time since she had been kissed by a young, handsome man. "Do you think you can tame me?" she asked in a breathy, suggestive whisper.

"Honey, I'll have you purring like a little kitten before you know it."

Grabbing her around the waist, Buck planted a wet kiss on her lips. His hand fumbled with a button on her lawn gown. Instinctively Lavinia realized that Buck was probably all talk and didn't know much about pleasing women, but she decided it might be fun to teach him a thing or two. Just at the moment she was about to close her eyes, she noticed a man on horseback watching them. She broke away from Buck almost as if she hadn't invited his touch.

"Who is that?" she asked Buck.

"Huh?"

"The man on that horse over by the barn."

Buck turned in aggravation to look at the man. A weather-beaten hat hung low over his darkly bearded face, and long black hair reached his shirt collar. Lavinia couldn't see his eyes, but she knew he was watching them and took no pleasure in their kiss. But as he leaned forward to observe them, his broad shoulders blocked the sun, and he appeared in no hurry to glance away.

"That's Jamie somethin' or other. I'm not real sure he has a last name, or if he does, he don't seem to know it. Tom Evans hired him on when he was in San Antonio last week. He's a good worker, I guess, but don't say nothin' to nobody. Just minds his own business."

Lavinia's heart beat faster. He was watching her, only her, and he knew she was aware of his gaze upon her. He seemed to be taking mental inventory of her body, causing an unfamiliar flush to scatter across her flesh. Her legs felt wobbly, and for a moment she thought she was going to fall. Something about him was familiar, so achingly familiar that she couldn't put a name to it. She felt drawn to him, almost as if this stranger was beckoning her to come to him. She made a movement forward, but Buck held her arm.

"Where you goin', Lavinia? Don't start trouble with that fellow. He may be quiet, but I think he's mean. I don't want no trouble with the likes of him."

Buck's warning stalled Lavinia. She would have gone to him, but the man turned the horse around and galloped in the direction of the open range.

Somehow his leaving caused her to feel slighted.

Buck hugged her to him. "Now that nobody's watchin' us, let's say we go in the barn and roll around in the hay."

"What?" Lavinia barely heard him. Disentangling herself from Buck, she shook her head. Any flicker of desire she might have felt earlier for Buck was now dead. "I have a headache," she protested when Buck tried to kiss her again. "Maybe some other time."

Maybe never, she thought and ceased to think about Buck. She barely realized he had stomped away. Her sapphire eyes followed the man on horseback until he became a speck in the distance.

Seth came charging down the road and halted his horse by the front door. Still in a hurry, he jumped off with barely a civil nod to Arthur and Carson Turner. Laurel, standing nearby in the company of some of Texas' most handsome and eligible young men, heard Arthur ask, "Where you been, boy?"

Seth, his face half hidden beneath the brim of his hat, replied, "San Antonio." Before Arthur could say another word, he entered the house in a flash of dust and grime.

Arthur shook his head in seeming dismay, and Carson Turner pretended to take an interest in a piece of barbecue chicken. Laurel politely broke away from her group of admirers and went around to the back entrance of the house.

Inside, she made her way up the cool, shadowed passage of the kitchen staircase to the upper landing that ran the length of the downstairs parlor until she came to Seth's door at the end of the hallway. The door was slightly ajar, and she saw

Seth standing, shirtless, at the washbasin and wiping away the vestiges of his trip. She entered unannounced, intent upon berating him for his terse reply to Arthur, for not having had the courtesy to arrive sooner, knowing that Arthur wanted his whole family together for Lavinia's birthday celebration. But when he heard her enter and turned to face her, a gasp escaped her. Seth's left eye was a patchwork of blue and purple, streaked in places with red. It was so swollen that only a tiny slit remained for him to see.

"What happened? Did you get in a fight?"

"You might say that," Seth remarked, his movements quick and agitated as the washrag skimmed across his bare chest. "How's the party?"

"Very nice." Laurel realized that his eye must hurt unbearably, but he was giving a good show of a rough and tough cowpoke. Her hand touched his, stilling his movements. She took the rag from him and pointed to the bed. "You better rest for a while. I'll take care of your eye."

He appeared about to protest, but he wearily lay on the bed. Laurel dipped the washrag into the large porcelain basin. She wrung out the excess water before placing it on Seth's swollen eye. He grimaced. "I don't mean to hurt you," she told him.

Seth held the cloth in place. "You didn't. Sit beside me and talk to me for a spell."

He appeared so pitiful that Laurel sat down, her blue-and-white skirt billowing about her. "Who did you fight?"

"Just a fellow with a big fist."

"Does he look as awful as you?"

Seth barely nodded. He couldn't tell her that Ortega hadn't laid a finger on him. Claudio's large fist had done the damage, and that was all it had taken to convince him to pay off his debts to Ortega. He dreaded to think about how he had agreed to repay the bastard, but he would do it and do it gladly. He knew he would die at Claudio's strong hands if he defied Ortega's orders, and he was too much of a coward to resist.

The night had passed for him in a haze of pain, but now just looking at Laurel, so beautiful and dainty with her hair falling with abandon around her bare shoulders, eased the ache in his eye. Desire for her flared within him. He doubted she would be as fiery or well tutored in the art of love as Simone, but she must have learned something from her marriage to Duvalier. He decided that the sooner he seduced her, the better and safer his own life would be.

One second Laurel was gazing at Seth, and the next he had dragged her down, pinning her body against his. She made a weak attempt to push away, but Seth held her tightly, seemingly not concerned over his injury any longer. With one arm around her waist and the other hand cupping a breast, his mouth devoured hers in a kiss that left no doubt in her mind that he wanted her then and there. Her early morning resolve to supplement Tony in her mind with Seth washed away. She had been determined to respond to him, but now she found his kiss and embrace too possessive, and she began to struggle. So many times Tony had loved her in the same way, and she had reveled in his passion, eager and willing to be taken. This time the knowledge that Seth wanted her and would have her unless she put some distance between them lent fury to her fear.

Laurel's hand shot out and raked the other side of his face with her fingernails. Seth yelled in pain and sat up as she bounded from the bed to take a position behind a rocker. "What in the hell did you do that for?" Seth cried and used the wet cloth to staunch the blood on his cheek. "I wasn't going to rape you, for Christ's sake."

"It seemed that way to me." Laurel trembled and clung to the back of the rocking chair for support. "I'm not some sort of whore that you can bed and then forget, Seth."

So that was it, he thought. She didn't want to be used and cast aside. He had no intention of doing that to Laurel, at least not yet, not until he got her to trust him and to give him the money he needed. Ortega's advice about how to pay off his debts wouldn't yield him as much as he could get in one fell swoop from Laurel. But he must tread carefully with her. If she could love the way she fought, he didn't want to lose her money *or* her body. His cheek stung and inwardly he cursed her, but outwardly his face expressed surprise and concern.

"How can you think I'd be such a cad? Haven't I been a gentleman?"

"Yes . . ."

"I'll have you know that my intentions are honorable, but Texans just go about things differently than other men. We're a breed of men who like our women willing and full of fire. I'd never take you against your will. You have to know that."

After Seth got up and went to the washbasin to clean his cuts, Laurel felt terrible. He looked so hurt and helpless that she inched her way toward him and took the cloth to daub at his wounds. "I'm sorry. I behaved badly."

Laurel's apology instilled a sense of hope and daring in Seth. Not wanting her to see his pleasure, he showed a face of pain. He went to his bureau, took out a leather box and placed it on top of the bureau. Removing an emerald ring surrounded by tiny diamonds from the box, he held it out to her.

"This was my mother's engagement ring from Arthur. I want you to wear it. I . . . want . . . you to marry me." Just the right amount of hesitancy in his voice, he decided, to sway Laurel's cold heart.

Her eyes widened, and she shook her head in disbelief. "I can't marry you. I'm not sure how I feel about you, Seth. My divorce from Tony isn't even final."

"I know all that." His voice overrode her objections. He grabbed her left hand and slipped Tony's wedding ring from her finger and replaced it with his mother's. Gazing deeply into her eyes, he smiled a boyish and beguiling smile, certain that he would charm her into accepting his ring.

"You can't grieve over Tony Duvalier forever. I want you to marry me."

"I can't accept—"

"Don't say another word. Hear me out. I do want you as my wife, but I don't press for your answer now. Just wear the ring for me. Regard it as a symbol of my love and loyalty for you. If you feel later that you still can't accept my proposal, you can give back the ring. But I am willing to bet that you won't take that ring off your finger, Laurel. You have to start loving again, and I'm as good as any man you'll find around these parts."

I don't love you, she wanted to scream. Yet she didn't want to hurt Seth and decided that wearing the ring wouldn't do any harm. Who knows? she asked herself. She just might learn to love him. Seth wasn't unattractive, and she didn't find him physically repulsive. The only strike against him had nothing to do with him. He just wasn't Tony.

"Besides," she heard him say, "I think Father would be pleased if he thought we were going to be married."

Laurel didn't deny what he said. She glanced down at the ring, which flashed streaks of green across the ceiling and walls as it caught the sunlight, then at her gold wedding band on the bureau. A sob rose and died in her throat to think of what that golden band had meant to her not so long ago. It signified pain to her now. Perhaps with Seth she would finally forget Tony. However, she knew it would take a long time. Would Seth be willing to wait?

She gazed at Seth through watery eyes. "I'll wear the ring as a token of your affection. I can't answer you yet, but if you'll wait until I'm ready—"

He broke off her words by gently enfolding her in his arms and tenderly kissing her. "Anything you want, my darling. I'll wait for as long as it takes you to make your decision." But not too long, he found himself thinking.

Laurel broke away. "We should see to your father. He's very worried about you."

"I'll finish cleaning up and come downstairs right away." Seth took her hand and kissed the ring before turning his attention to the bureau drawer from which he pulled out a clean shirt. When he was putting it on, Laurel grabbed her golden wedding ring and slipped it into the pocket of her gown. She stole a quick glance at the flash of emeralds and diamonds on her left hand, almost overpowering her small finger. She decided that the simple, golden band had looked richer.

Just as Laurel and Seth were leaving his room, Gincie hurried down the hallway, calling to them. "Come quick," she gasped, unable to draw an adequate breath. "Mr. Delaney's taken real bad."

Racing down the stairs, Laurel and Seth were halted in their strides by Carson Turner and another man as they carried Arthur into the parlor and laid him on the leather cushions of the sofa. Lavinia rushed in behind the men, followed by some of the other party-goers, concern written on their faces. Laurel watched while Lavinia placed a large red throw pillow beneath her father's head.

"You'll be all right, Papa," Lavinia crooned softly, but unguarded fear covered her face.

Arthur was deathly pale and coughed up blood into a kerchief that Carson Turner held to his mouth. Laurel made her way through the people who stood silently by, almost as if they knew Arthur's end was inevitable and didn't know what to do.

Laurel tapped Carson on the shoulder. "Can't anything be done?"

"Just to make him comfortable, Laurel. I think that's all I can do for my old friend now." Carson gazed at Arthur through blurry eyes.

When Seth came into view, towering above Laurel and Lavinia, Arthur had stopped coughing. His green eyes fastened on the three of them, and a little smile turned up the corners of his mouth. He spoke to Carson in a such a feeble voice that Laurel barely heard him.

"Make certain . . . my children . . ."

Carson nodded. "I told you everything is taken care of. Don't worry, Art. Just rest now, rest."

Somehow these words seemed to ease Arthur's mind. Then he gave a contented sigh, and his soul slipped from his body. For a few moments no one could believe that Arthur Delaney was truly gone. Laurel and Lavinia stood transfixed. It was Lavinia who broke the spell by flinging herself across her father's body.

"Papa, Papa, why did you leave me? You were the only one who ever loved me!"

Lavinia's piteous weeping caused a sob to overpower Laurel. Pushing her way through the crowded parlor, she found herself outside. The evening air washed over her as she headed for the barn. Once inside the cool and shadowed nook of a stall, away from the curious and sympathetic faces of everyone, she sank onto a pile of hay and allowed herself the luxury of tears.

Chapter Twenty-four

Carson Turner laid down the legal document on the black oak desk in Arthur's study. He folded his hands and leaned forward, his gray eyes critically examining each of Arthur's children. Needless to say, they all appeared astounded, and he couldn't judge which one was the more surprised.

"Those are the terms of Arthur Delaney's last will and testament, drawn up by me and duly witnessed not two weeks ago."

"I can't believe it. It isn't possible . . ." Lavinia mumbled.

"The old man must have been out of his mind! He was crazy! There must be a way to declare the will invalid!" Seth paced up and down the room, the heels of his boots scraping harshly across the wooden floor. "Did the old coot think I was working my fingers to the bone, taking care of ranch business, just to discover that he had sold it? I don't believe any of it. The will's a fake."

"Sorry, Seth. The will is quite legal. This is what Arthur wanted. You can protest it, but you'll only be wasting your time and incurring a number of legal fees." Carson peered at Seth over his horn-rimmed glasses. "I'd advise against such action. In your present situation you'd be quite foolish to make more debts."

"But this is still our ranch, Mr. Carson," Lavinia protested. "Papa would never have sold it without telling us. Why did he do such a thing?"

Carson's gaze slid to Laurel for a second, then back to Lavinia. "He wanted his children to have some cash from the ranch's sale. He felt that you, Lavinia, would be better off away from here, and that Seth, because of his extravagant life, was ill suited to ranching. He only wanted the best for you."

"This is the worst thing that ever could have happened to me. I love the Little L!" Lavinia's protest was drowned out by Carson's voice.

"There's more to the will. You should all be quiet and listen."

Seth threw himself down in the chair beside Laurel. His face was a thundercloud, and he shook from intense rage, but he was quiet, in fact engrossed, when Carson began to read the rest of the will. The lawyer no longer directed his attention to Seth or Lavinia, but to Laurel.

"In the event of my death," Carson read, "I wish the running of the Little L to be turned over to Laurel Delaney Duvalier. She shall execute decisions of ranch business and see to the handling of any monies. I request that she oversee the Little L until such time as the new owner arrives, and for a period of six months thereafter, she shall advise the owner in any capacity he deems fit."

Carson stopped reading. Laurel jumped up, her hand clutching her throat. "There must be some mistake, Mr. Turner. My uncle couldn't possibly have requested such a thing. I don't know anything about ranching."

"No, she doesn't!" Seth interjected. "Father's illness must have made him insane."

"I assure you that your stepfather was completely sane," Carson rebuked him, growing annoyed with Seth. "I'm finished with you and Lavinia. I have something to say to Laurel. Now you both leave us alone."

Lavinia, almost in tears, and Seth, who looked more than puzzled, fairly glared at Laurel as they left the room. When the door was shut tight behind them, Carson turned a warm face to Laurel.

"Sit down, my dear, and don't be so shocked. Arthur knew what he was doing when he appointed you to take care of the Little L. I think it has something to do with your father and mother." He took a small key from his vest pocket and opened a drawer in Arthur's desk. Withdrawing a folded piece of paper, he handed it to her. "This explains everything. I'll leave you to read it alone. Then when you want me, I'll be right outside."

Carson smiled kindly and left the room. She began to read Arthur's letter.

Dearest Laurel,

I know that you shall find my request strange, but if it hadn't been for your father's differences with me, the ranch would have been partly yours. I'd like to think that if Sylvester and Emily hadn't left Texas, you'd have grown up wild and free, able to throw aside the restrictive life you now embrace. You're a woman of passion, Laurel. I can sense that in a woman. Soon, you'll meet someone just as passionate as yourself. I predict that with a certainty. Don't turn away from passion and love when it comes, my dear. You'll be forever sorry.

A long time ago, I fell in love with a beautiful woman. I've loved her all my life, but she didn't love me. Still, fate was kind to both of us. The one night of our love produced a child . . . a daughter I dearly love. The woman I loved wished me never to tell our child that I am her father. I kept my promise. But if you're reading this, I must now be dead. I don't think there's harm in telling you that the woman I hold dear in my heart was your mother, and you are that child.

Laurel stopped reading. Her hands trembled so badly she didn't know if she could read on, but the desire to know the truth overrode her shock.

If Emily had stayed with me, things would have been different. Lavinia wouldn't have had to turn to men for affection. I admit I was busy. My life was ranching. Perhaps I've been neglectful of you, but only because your mother wished for you never to know. She didn't want me to interfere in your life, and I haven't until now. I want to believe that as you read this, Emily and I are together and she knows why I've told you, why I'm giving you the responsibility of running the ranch and showing the new owner the ropes. None of the profits of the sale are to be passed to you. I know you're a wealthy young woman in your own right. But Seth and Lavinia need the kind of life that the money can bring — if only they use it wisely.

I am giving you nothing of material wealth, Laurel. Once again you may think I'm not looking out for you. I assure that this time I am taking very good care of you, my daughter, in a way which won't be clear at the present moment. Wait and have faith.

If you never believe anything else in your life, little Laurel, believe that I love you. Know that I'm giving you a gift beyond price.

The letter was signed in Arthur's scrawly handwriting. The paper shook in Laurel's hand. Tears filled her eyes and threatened to spill over onto her cheeks. She stared in numb disbelief at the wall. She was Arthur's daughter and Lavinia's half-sister! She couldn't comprehend any of it. All these years she had lived a lie. An aching pain gathered in her breast, and she felt unable to breathe. In fact she wanted to scream, to lash out at Arthur Delaney for what he had done to her, at her mother for not telling her. But the more practical side of her nature reflected upon this deception and realized that the decision to have her grow up as Sylvester Delaney's child had been the right one. She would never have met Tony otherwise.

Laurel groaned. Must all her thoughts, her feelings, be centered on Tony even at such a time as this? Rising from her chair, a vision in black taffeta, she faced Carson when he entered the room.

"You've finished reading Arthur's letter, I see. I have a list of instructions he wanted you to follow pertaining to the ranch. Tom Evans left for San Antonio this morning with a recommendation for a new foreman."

"Mr. Turner, you seem quite certain that I'll accept the responsibility for the Little L."

He cocked his head. "Haven't you? I don't see you swimming in a vale of tears, which leads me to think that Arthur made the right choice. You're a level-headed woman, Laurel, and Arthur Delaney's daughter. Don't forget that part of this ranch could have been left to you, but Arthur had other reasons in mind when he sold it."

"Yes, I understand all of that."

"No, not yet you don't." Carson motioned to her to sit again. He took a place in the chair next to her and took her cold hand in his. "It's time to discuss the running of the Little L until the new owner arrives. Are you up to it?"

Was she up to it? Probably not, but she felt she owed Arthur something for all the years he had loved her mother, for the years he must have loved a child he had never known. The responsibility of the ranch was his way of making amends with her. And wasn't that the reason she had wanted to come to San Antonio in the first place?

Laurel straightened her spine and wiped away any hint of tears from her face. "I'm up to the task. Brief me on the Little L, Mr. Carson."

Financial conditions of the Little L were far worse than Laurel had feared. The ranch hands hadn't been paid in full for almost three months, and the little they had received had sent some of them away in search of a better opportunity. Some had stayed, and to pay them, Laurel dipped into her own funds, not expecting the new owner to reimburse her.

Creditors, when hearing that money again flowed at the Little L, arrived with outstretched palms, which Laurel promptly filled. The livestock had to be fed, the barn needed a new roof, and the bunkhouses could use a coat of paint. She was surprised that most of the stores in Fredricksburg had given Arthur credit, but apparently the store owners had held her father in high regard.

As often as she tried to think of Arthur as her father, she found she couldn't. Sylvester Delaney would always be her father as far as she was concerned. Still she couldn't dispel the knowledge that Arthur had been her father; Lavinia was her sister. She longed to tell Lavinia this but resisted. Ever since Lavinia learned the ranch had been sold and Laurel was running things until the owner arrived, she hadn't bothered to hide her hostility. Laurel believed that she and Lavinia would never be close friends, much less sisters.

Seth, however, was more than pleasant, apparently reconciled to the fact that Laurel now ran the ranch and controlled the money. She had learned from going over the account books that Seth had accumulated a large number of debts. She understood why Arthur had decided to sell the ranch. The debts must be paid, but she realized that Seth's share of the profits from the ranch's sale would barely cover the clothing debts to San Antonio stores and to a person known as Ortega.

A week after the will's reading, Laurel asked Seth who Ortega was.

"Just an acquaintance of mine, darlin'."

"This 'acquaintance' requires quite a bit of money. What sort of debt is that?"

Seth shrugged his broad shoulders, holding his hat in his hands. He reminded her of a small schoolboy standing before the schoolmarm's desk. "Don't worry about it. I'll pay him off when the ranch is sold."

"You'll be lucky to barely cover this debt with the money." She held up numerous bills from the stores. "And what about these clothing establishments? They need their money, too. How do you intend to pay them?"

"Aw, sugar, don't bother your pretty head over those nasty bills. I'll take care of them." Walking around the desk, he pulled Laurel to her feet and wrapped his arms around her waist. "I just want to know when your divorce is final."

She found herself imprisoned in his embrace, not certain she cared for it. Though Seth had never been outwardly unpleasant to her, there was always a guarded quality in his eyes that disturbed her, and she wondered if he had a cruel streak. Pushing him away, she managed to break his hold.

"I imagine the divorce will take a while longer to come through. Tony is handling the details, and I expect to hear from his lawyer any day. In fact, Carson has agreed to represent me." Seth reached for her again, and Laurel once more managed to separate herself from him. "Please, Seth, I'm busy now."

His eyes hardened like blue ice, but she decided that Seth hadn't done an adequate job of running the ranch during Arthur's illness. It was up to her to take charge, and she didn't want to be deterred from her duties. Picking up the bills, she opened the desk drawer and placed them on top of some greenbacks and pieces of gold kept there for the purpose of having ready cash in the house. She locked the drawer with a tiny key and slipped the key into another drawer.

She had expected an argument from Seth for putting him off, but he smiled at her. "At least you're still wearing my ring. I'm full of hope, Laurel. Really, I'm bursting with it."

He left the room, whistling a happy tune. Some minutes later a knock sounded on the door. The man to whom she bade entry strode into the room and waited on the other side of the desk. He *didn't* remind her of a naughty schoolboy. Over six feet tall, his long jean-clad legs were spread-eagled in their stance. His light-blue shirt was covered with a layer of fine dust as was the hat he had recently removed. Long, dark hair hung in shaggy waves to his shoulders, an equally black beard and mustache covered most of his face, and ebony eyes were fringed with long dark lashes. She had the impression that he was probably part Mexican, maybe Indian, or a smattering of both.

He threw his hat on a chair by the desk and sat in the one opposite when Laurel motioned to him to sit.

"You're Jamie Castle, I believe."

The man nodded. "Yes, ma'am."

"Tom spoke highly of you. He said you were hired in San Antonio. Have you had any ranch experience?"

"Sure."

"Well, where, when?"

"No place you'd know of, ma'am."

"Try me."

He hesitated a minute. In one swift motion he stood up and grabbed his hat. "I don't think you'd want me as a foreman once you know. So, I better be moving along. I'm surprised nobody's caught on to me yet, but Tom thought I was a good worker and hired me on. I guess it was stupid to come back here, but I needed the work."

"I don't understand any of what you're saying,

Mr. Castle. Do sit back down and explain."

A muscle jumped alongside his eye, but he sat down, and Laurel waited patiently until he began to speak.

"My name's not Jamie Castle but Jim Castille. I worked on the Little L about eight or nine years ago. I'm a good worker and honest despite what Seth Renquist says." He sounded bitter. "I know you're going to marry him, but I didn't do what he said I did. I didn't steal from Mr. Delaney. I liked and respected him too much for that. Somebody stole the money, and Seth said I did it. I didn't do it. I swear I didn't do it."

"I see," she said, showing nothing by word or deed to infer that she did or didn't believe him. She sensed he had suffered a great deal in his life and deserved another chance to make good. "Tom Evans thought very highly of you, so highly that he risked Arthur Delaney discovering you were back on the ranch. Why do you suppose he'd take such a chance?"

Jim Castille lifted his hands in a gesture of disbelief. "Tom's a good guy. He wants to give everybody a second chance."

"Then I will, too, Mr. Castille. If Tom thought enough of you to hire you back, he must have known you were innocent of stealing. You are now foreman of the Little L." Laurel extended her hand, and Jim took it, not quite certain he had gotten the job.

"You mean it, ma'am?"

"Yes, I do. If you'd rather not use your real name, I understand that, too. I wonder why Seth hasn't recognized you."

Jim grinned and stroked his full beard. "My own mother wouldn't recognize me now, but I'll use my own name. I swear to you I didn't steal that money, and I don't want to hide for the rest of my life."

"Good. If anyone gives you any trouble, let me know. I assure you that my word is the law here until the ranch is turned over to the new owner in a few weeks. And just to set the record straight, I'm not officially engaged to Mr. Renquist."

"I'm glad to hear that. Thank you, ma'am. You're real kind."

As Jim turned to leave the room, he put on his hat and then nearly bumped into Lavinia. He stood stock still, keeping his head lowered and mumbling an apology. He was gone before Lavinia could utter a sound.

"Who was that?" Lavinia asked, remembering seeing him the day of her birthday celebration, which would forever be linked to her father's death.

"The new foreman, Jim Castille."

"Jim . . . Castille?" Lavinia's voice cracked. Her limbs quaked, and she sank into the chair Jim had recently vacated.

Laurel glanced up from an account book. "Do you know him? He said he worked here years ago. Lavinia, are you all right? You're so pale."

Shaking her head, Lavinia jumped up. "He's a thief! I won't tolerate Jim Castille being here on the Little L. Papa ran him off with a shotgun. He stole from us, he stole—"

"Yes, I know. What else did he steal?"

My heart, Lavinia almost said, but instead, she twisted around and headed for the door. "We'll see just how long that thief stays on the Little L. I'll fire him!"

"Don't you dare!" Laurel bellowed. "I hired Jim Castille, and I believe him when he said he didn't steal anything. I think he's a decent, honest man."

"In a pig's eye! We'll see what Seth says."

Laurel strode across the room to Lavinia. "I don't care what Seth says. I hired the man and he's staying. If either one of you interferes in whatever I do on this ranch, you both can move off. Understand?"

From the fiery gleam in Laurel's eyes, Lavinia did understand. "Whatever you say, boss lady." She whirled away, leaving the room in a flash of blue Levis and auburn hair.

Laurel leaned tiredly against the doorframe. She had thought the major problem in ranching would be the ranch, not the people on it.

Running the distance from the house to the ranch foreman's bunkhouse, Lavinia reached the porch, breathless and flushed. The scuffing sound of her boots on the wooden floorboards was the only indication to Jim Castille that someone was outside. When she opened the door, pushing it back loudly against the wall, she saw Jim sitting on the edge of his bunk, calmly polishing his best boots to a high sheen. He barely glanced in her direction, infuriating her further because he didn't immediately acknowledge her presence.

Her blazing blue stare finally forced him to glance up. "I was wondering how long it would take you to get here. No more than fifteen minutes. Must be some kind of a record."

"You arrogant, nervy bastard! How dare you show your face around here! I can't believe that even you'd have the gumption after what you did."

Jim glanced down, seemingly absorbed in his boots. "I didn't steal from your father, Lavinia. If you had loved me at all, you'd have trusted me."

"Don't put the blame on me. I wasn't the one caught with Father's gold pieces on me. I still don't know how you could have sneaked into my house, into Papa's study and stolen from him. You're a thief, Jim Castille. A thief. Look at me, you thieving bastard. Put down those damn boots and look at me!" Lavinia grabbed the boots from him and hurled them across the room.

In a fluid pantherlike motion, Jim rose up and pinioned her wrist between his large hands. She nearly cowered beneath his dark and penetrating stare that stripped away her haughty facade and saw her soul. That was the main reason she had fallen in love with Jim Castille all those years ago. He had a way of seeing beneath the surface and stirring up her emotions. But right now she didn't want him to see how his very presence, his masterful touch, affected her.

"Let me go." She struggled, but Jim only gripped her more tightly. "You think because you're bigger that you have power over me. You're wrong. I stopped wanting you when you robbed my father."

"You were always a poor liar. You want me now."

"I hate you."

"I'll prove you wrong, and you know I can." With deliberate slowness, Jim lowered his head until his lips locked with hers in a heated kiss. Lavinia felt her body respond to the feel of his mouth on hers, and when his tongue sought entry, she found that her own willingly and wantonly met his. Her breasts met the hardness of his chest, and she ached for him to touch her. For a few dizzy seconds she forgot that she had sworn to hate Jim Castille. Instead she found her traitorous body had no will of its own. No longer was she the inexperienced girl who had loved him, and he definitely wasn't the young boy who had loved her and who had risked Arthur Delaney's wrath to possess her.

Their bodies seemed to fit together so perfectly, she thought as her throbbing pulses beat a wild cadence—almost as if they were made for each other. No man had ever made her feel the way Jim could with a just a kiss. She knew she was like clay in Jim's arms and always had been. She had loved him for so long and had fought that love. At this moment, she didn't want to fight any longer. She wanted Jim Castille.

"I know you want me, Lavinia." His breath grazed her ear and sent delightful shivers down her spine. "Tell me you want me, that you want me to tame you, my wild blue-eyed temptress."

"Yes, oh, yes. I want you. Only you, Jim."

He pushed her from him. Through passion-laced eyes she watched as the lips that had kissed hers with such desire now curled into a sneer.

"I'm not like Buck Dawson or one of the others always panting around you. Your tempting lips, soft body, have no hold over me any longer, Lavinia. Maybe *this* time, *I* don't want *you*. Why don't you seek out one of your other men for satisfaction? You're as ready as a mare in heat."

Jim dropped her wrist almost as if he found her loathsome. Tears gathered in her eyes. She hadn't felt this abandoned since the day her father had chased Jim from the ranch. That day she vowed never to be hurt again, to hate Jim Castille for the rest of her life. Now, at this moment, the vow renewed itself within her. Lifting a hand, she slapped him and was rather surprised when he just stood there and took the torrent of her rage.

"I was right about you. You are a bastard! I hate

you! If you ever come near me again, I'll kill you. I swear, I'll kill you."

She ran out of the bunkhouse, running without direction. Finally she stopped and found herself on the grassy, green knoll where her father was buried beside her mother and Anna. Dropping to her knees, Lavinia felt the tears streak down her face, and she sobbed long and hard. She hadn't cried in such a way since the day she had given birth to Jim's still-born baby daughter.

Chapter Twenty-five

The heat of summer gave way to a pleasant chill in the air as the autumn breeze swept over the countryside, awash with indigo-blue and scarlet wildflowers. Life at the Little L had picked up its pace since Laurel took over. Because the men were being paid on a regular basis and needed repairs had been made on the barn and the outbuildings, everyone was in a much better mood with the exception of Lavinia. Laurel couldn't fathom what was wrong with her. She realized Lavinia had been quite upset over Arthur's will and had grudgingly started packing for the move to heaven only knew where, but there was more to her disquiet than that. Laurel couldn't put her finger on what was bothering her, but she didn't have time to analyze Lavinia. The ranch required most of her energy.

Each day she woke early and dressed either in her blue denim pants or a split riding skirt to comb the range with Jim Castille, looking for strays. She had thought Lavinia would have tagged along, but she hadn't. Laurel discovered that she enjoyed Jim's companionship, finding him to be quite well educated. He told her that his mother had been a schoolteacher from Kentucky who had come to Texas on a visit to her priest brother. While in Texas, she had fallen in love with Jim's father, a Mexican from an old and noble house, but all had been lost after Texas had gained independence from Mexico. His father, unable to bear the strain of being poor and without his lands, had committed suicide. His mother had died soon afterward, and Jim had become a young drifter until he found work at the Little L. However, his happiness had ended when someone planted evidence that he had stolen from Arthur Delaney.

By the bitter tone in his voice, Laurel assumed he was referring to Seth. "Do you think Seth had something to do with the whole incident?" she asked him.

"Yes, ma'am, I do," came the quick response. Jim reined in his horse and stared at Laurel. "Seth never liked me. He was always trying to start trouble for me. I think he had a hankering for Lavinia, and this was why he wanted me off the ranch."

"I'm certain you're wrong. Seth is Lavinia's brother." Laurel looked as shocked as she felt by such frankness from Jim.

"Seth is her stepbrother, and if he married Lavinia, the Little L would have been all his. You see, ma'am, Lavinia and I . . . Well, we loved each other, and Seth couldn't stand the idea that she loved a half-breed. He never loved her for herself, mind you, only for the ranch and Arthur's money. Yeah, I think he framed me. Seth stole that money, and one day I'll see that he pays me back."

Lavinia wondered if Jim spoke the truth. Could Seth be as deceptive as Jim was leading her to believe? Was that why she had never completely trusted him when he came to Louisiana? She knew Seth had accumulated a large amount of debts. Was this the main reason he had wanted her to return to Texas with him? Did he see her as some sort of salvation for his ailing bank account and want to marry her only for her money? Though she had known Jim for a short time, she trusted him more than she could ever trust Seth. Somehow she would learn the truth. She wasn't going to be such an easy mark, as Seth would soon discover.

"Has Seth spoken to you about your return, Jim?"

Jim nodded. A grin split his lips. "Seth's not too happy to see me. He told me he'd fire me off the Little L if he could, but since he won't be here much longer, he knows he can't do anything. And he also knows that I know he framed me."

Laurel said nothing else as she pondered all Jim had told her. By the end of the day they had found a number of unmarked strays, which the hands branded with the Little L mark. When she returned to the house, she was dusty and dirty. Her hair, which Gincie had neatly coiled at the nape of her neck that morning, lay in long curls down her back. The soft cream-colored blouse tucked into her tan riding skirt was smudged as were her cheeks. She looked a sight but felt exhilarated by the day's activities. A part of her would definitely be sad when the day came to leave the Little L.

Entering the house, she heard voices coming from the parlor, one clearly the booming tones of Carson Turner. Laurel turned a corner and nearly bumped into Lavinia. In a flamboyant peach-colored dress, cut indecently low and edged around the neckline and hem with white daisies, Lavinia was strikingly beautiful. Her eyes were alight with mischief, and she almost purred when she greeted Laurel.

"We have guests," Lavinia told her.

"Who? Is Carson here?" Laurel began to move forward, but Lavinia stopped her.

"Yes, and he brought the new owner with him."

"For someone who has been moping around the house for the last few weeks with such a long face, you seem quite pleased. I thought you hated the thought of leaving the ranch."

"I do. But I might not have to leave now. Come into the parlor and meet the man. He's quite handsome, Laurel."

"I have to change first."

"No, come now."

"Lavinia . . ." Laurel protested, but Lavinia, with a Cheshire cat grin on her face, practically dragged her into the parlor. Carson Turner sat facing her and rose immediately, inclining his head to the man who sat in the high-backed tufted chair facing away from her. Seth stood at the fireplace, a none-too-pleased expression on his face. He would have gone to her at her sudden and bedraggled appearance in the parlor, but the man in the chair rose and blocked his way.

The fading light from outside lent the room a misty quality. Laurel was about to suggest that the lamp be lighted as her gaze focused on the man who slowly turned toward her.

Her pulse raced, then almost died, slowing to an imperceptible beat. A weakness seized her, and she would have fallen if Lavinia's hand hadn't tightened on her elbow. She felt barely able to speak and couldn't mouth the name that stuck to her tongue like resin.

"Hello, Laurel. I've been looking forward to seeing you again."

"It's Tony, Laurel. Don't you have anything to say?" Lavinia prodded.

Tony! Of course, I know it's Tony, you silly dolt! she screamed inside her brain. Who else but Tony could reduce her to a quivering mass of jelly? Who other than Tony had eyes that impaled her and drew her to him? She couldn't think or move at the moment. If Lavinia hadn't pushed her onto the couch, she would probably have stayed in one spot like a stone statue.

This position was worse than standing. Tony towered over her, but she couldn't seem able to do anything but stare open-mouthed at him. Seth came and sat next to her, taking her hand in his. Laurel was too shocked to notice that Tony saw this proprietary gesture and the emerald and diamond ring sparkling on her finger.

Seth glared at Tony. "Laurel's had a shock. You should have given us warning that you were coming, Duvalier. God, you should have told us you were the new owner." He shot an equally baleful glance to Carson. "You knew all the time."

"I admit I did," Carson intoned and took his seat again.

"Why didn't you tell us?" Laurel asked, surprising herself with her own questions.

Tony fielded that question. "Arthur didn't want anyone but Carson to know the circumstances of the sale. I'm really sorry you're so shocked, Laurel, but maybe you deserve to be shocked."

"What a cruel thing to say to me!" She shoved Seth's hand away and rose from the sofa. Green fire flared in her eyes. "I don't deserve such treatment from you. Ever since the day I've met you, you've manipulated me, and you know what I mean. Just don't think you're going to play your dirty tricks on me again, Tony. I won't allow it. I absolutely will not stand for your manipulations and deceptions again. I won't stay another minute in this house with you."

"You have to, Laurel. The will says you must be at my beck and call, give me lessons in ranching—"

"I don't give a fig about the will!" she shot back and prepared to leave the room, but Tony grabbed her arm.

"Then I won't buy the ranch. The deal isn't final yet."

"Don't buy it. I don't care."

"Who else will buy it? Arthur asked me if I'd buy it to help him out, seeing that he was your relative and knowing that you'd wish the profits to go to Lavinia and Seth. I know just how much this ranch owes, and I know who owes it." His eyes momentarily traveled to Seth, then back to Laurel. "The Little L has a bad reputation among cattlemen. The livestock needs improving in the bloodlines. I intend to breed the Little L's cattle with my Brahmans. This type of crossbreeding has proved quite profitable along the Texas coast. There's quite a bit of money to be made. Now, if the sale isn't completed, you've got yourself an unproductive ranch here. The Northern markets won't buy your cattle any longer, but they will if I take over. Think about it, and you'll admit I'm right."

Tony's lips were inches from hers. She longed to kiss him, to throw her arms around him, but nothing would be gained by such a display. She had thought she had forgotten him, but she hadn't been able to think about him as much because she had been busy with the ranch. She knew, however, that he meant everything he said. He wouldn't buy the ranch, and no one else would either. The Little L was no longer held in high esteem by businessmen, but under Tony's guidance and knowledge, the ranch would once more prosper. That was the one thing she couldn't stand about Tony. He was always right. She had to help Lavinia and Seth. Arthur had appointed her as head of the ranch, knowing that she had their interests at heart. She couldn't disappoint her father now.

Pulling away from him, she said, "You've made your point. Will Simone be joining you?" She sounded shrewish and hostile to her own ears.

Dark clouds seemed to gather in Tony's eyes. Had the very mention of his love upset him? The thought crossed her mind that he must love Simone very much. "I'm tired. Can you show me to my room?" he asked abruptly.

"I will," Lavinia chimed in and possessively took Tony's arm to lead the way. Her auburn head tilted up, and her eyes peered into Tony's. "We're going to become very good friends, I think."

"Lavinia's on the prowl again," Seth noted.

"Be quiet," Laurel ground out and sank onto the sofa, holding her suddenly aching head in her hands.

Carson patted her gently on the back. "I wanted to tell you, but Arthur made me promise not to say anything."

"I don't know why he did this to me, but I can't live here with my soon-to-be ex-husband."

Carson cleared his throat and lifted her chin. "I don't know how to say this, Laurel, but Tony and you are still legally married and will be for some time. He never filed for divorce."

* * *

"Miss Laurel, you can't stay in Mr. Tony's room lookin' like this. You ain't bathed yet. You look like somethin' the cat dragged in while Miss Lavinia is all prettied up. What will Mr. Tony think?"

"I don't give a damn what Tony thinks, and stop harping on how I look. A little dust never hurt anyone."

"Hmph! I remember a time you cared about wearin' nice dresses. This ranch has changed you."

"Get out, Gincie!" Laurel slammed the door of Tony's room and paced restlessly. The faint glow of evening dimly silhouetted the furnishings. A large four-poster bed, covered with a colorful patchwork quilt, stood against a wall, a braided rug on the floor beside it. At one point she nearly tripped during her frantic pacing and, in a rage, kicked it away with the toe of her boot. Catching a quick view of herself in the mirror, bedraggled looking and dirty, she cursed at realizing that Gincie was right. She looked terrible. What a study in contrasts she was from Lavinia in her frilly, pressed gown. She was dressed like a dirty urchin.

Unconsciously Laurel rubbed at her dirt-streaked face with her fingers before finally settling down and sitting in a rocker near the window. Her gaze strayed to the mountains, hoping to find peace in their majesty, but all she could do was impatiently tap her foot and grit her teeth and talk to herself.

"How dare that arrogant bastard not file for a divorce. He told me before I left Petit Coteau he'd take care of all the arrangements. Like hell he did! I should never have believed him. He's lied to me since the day I met him. But I'll find out the truth even if I have to sit here all night and wait for him and Lavinia to come back. Ooooh!" She folded her arms in a huff.

Earlier in the parlor Seth had been quite disturbed by the news that Tony hadn't filed for divorce. After Carson left for home, Seth had been ready to run upstairs and bring Tony to task. Laurel had stopped him, insisting that Tony was her problem. She hadn't agreed to marry Seth yet. His eyes had turned a dark shade of blue when she told him this. If he had given her any hint of trouble, she would have smacked him and thrown his ring in his face. As she headed up the stairs to Tony's room, he had said nothing.

Gincie had met her on the landing to tell her that Lavinia and Tony had sneaked down the backstairs for an evening buggy ride. This news had only served to fan Laurel's anger higher. She wasn't certain if she was more angry with Lavinia for spiriting Tony away, or with Tony for leaving without speaking to her about the divorce.

Now as she rocked back and forth in the chair, a sense of rivalry with Lavinia surfaced. Why had Lavinia and Tony gone off together? Did Tony think he could reenter her life, still her husband, and carry on with Lavinia? He was a notorious womanizer, as she well knew. However, to think of Simone at Petit Coteau, swelling with child and believing herself secure in Tony's love while he gallivanted around the ranch with Lavinia, gave Laurel a great deal of perverted pleasure. But she was also wary. Tony had professed to hate Lavinia. Why was he now suddenly taking an evening buggy ride with her?

She waited until the clock in the foyer chimed nine. Her anger had long ago given way to agitation, and she was about to go to her room when she heard Lavinia's flutey laugh, followed by Tony's deep voice, ascend the staircase. His room was now in darkness, but when he opened the door, light from the wall sconces in the hallway spilled into the room.

"I had a delightful time," Laurel heard Lavinia say. "I was silly not to bring a shawl. Thank you for keeping me warm. Maybe we can do this again another time." A husky laugh followed.

"I'll look forward to it, Lavinia." Tony moved, and before Laurel's startled gaze, Lavinia threw her arms around Tony's neck and kissed him. Tony's arms went around her waist, and Laurel felt as if her heart were being squeezed.

Lavinia moved her lips away. "I've wanted to do that all evening. No, I've wanted to do that since the time I saw you on the steamboat, but you were quite taken with Laurel."

"Yes, well . . ." Tony disentangled her arms from around his neck. "See you in the morning."

The door closed, and Laurel heard Tony groping for the oil lamp on the bureau top. When the room was finally bathed in a soft, orange glow, Laurel startled him when she spoke.

"Are you going to tell Lavinia that you're a man she should fear? Because if you don't, I will."

"You are the quiet one," he said and threw her a smile as he pulled off his jacket. "Does your presence in my room mean you've come to seduce me?"

"I wouldn't touch you if you were the last man on earth. I want to know why you never filed for a divorce." Her voice was so detached, so unemotional, that she wondered if she were really speaking. Tony seemed to hear the aloofness and replied in a crisp tone as he yanked open the buttons on his shirtfront.

"I didn't have the time to pursue it, Laurel. A

large rainstorm nearly drowned the crops. Then Jean was in a carriage accident and broke both his legs—"

"Is he all right?" Laurel interrupted him.

"Yes, but for a while he was at Petit Coteau since the accident happened on a rainy night after he left the house. Since he was so close by, I had him carried to a guest room and sent for Doctor Fusilier. Then Denise showed up to care for him, and she turned the household upside down. So, you see, I had a full house."

"Simone was there, I presume."

He pulled off his cufflinks, saying nothing. An icy chill permeated the room. "She was there, wasn't she?" Laurel persisted.

"I'd rather not talk about Simone."

"Of course," Laurel stated haughtily, feeling foolish and hurt. "A gentleman doesn't discuss his paramours with his wife."

Rising from the chair, she stood with arms akimbo, not the least bit bothered by the fact that Tony was taking off his shirt. Anger boiled within her, pushing aside any embarrassment she might have felt.

"I'm damned mad that you never filed, Tony. If I had known, I would have gone to a lawyer."

"I did go to a lawyer. Remember old Mr. Dabadie in Washington. Well, I spoke to him about handling the divorce, but he died two days later. I guess he never got around to it."

Laurel groaned. "Just my luck to still be tied to you."

Tony stood before her, shirtless. His hairy chest was only inches from her, as were his arms, his lips. An insane desire to be gathered in his strong embrace and held against his beating heart, to feel the soft fur against her cheek, was quelled when Tony's hand grabbed the wrist of her left arm, wrapping his fingers around it like a steel band. His dark eyes filled with unbridled rage as the ring on her finger caught the light and flashed green and silver fire.

"Seems that Seth wasted no time. When is the wedding to be, or did you start the honeymoon early?"

"What do you care? I'm certain that you and Simone weren't waiting until the divorce was final. So don't judge me." She wrenched her hand away, aware of his strange silence again when Simone was mentioned.

Tony took a deep breath. "Laurel, we must come to some sort of an understanding. I agreed to buy the ranch because Arthur Delaney begged me. I haven't any desire to ranch here, but the man was desperate. He couldn't sell his cattle, and he knew he was dying. If I didn't buy the ranch, he'd be leaving his children an operation that would surely fail."

"How noble of you." Laurel moved away from him, keeping all hint of emotion from her face.

Tony shook his head. "No, it wasn't. I would have refused him except for one very important fact he mentioned in his telegram to me. He said he was your father."

Laurel's chin trembled. She held onto the bedpost for support. She had never wanted anyone other than her father and Carson Turner to know that. She hated the sympathy she saw in Tony's eyes for her.

"Now you know I'm the bastard child of Arthur Delaney. My mother never even loved him. She loved Sylvester all her life." He made a move to touch her, but she jerked away. "I don't need pity, Tony, especially not yours. She managed to compose herself. "Tell me your plans for the Little L."

He considered her for a moment before speaking. "For one, I'm going to make this the best damned cattle ranch in Texas. I've arranged to have some of my Brahman shipped here to crossbreed with your Texas cattle. It's been done quite successfully in other parts of Texas and seems to eliminate cattle fever, which is the main reason the market up North folded for Arthur. I spoke to Lavinia about it, and she's quite enthusiastic over the idea."

"I just bet she is."

"Now, Laurel, don't show your claws. Lavinia is your sister."

"Something which I haven't told her, and don't you tell her. What's the second reason?"

A flame danced in Tony's eyes. "I'm going to use this experience as a way to get you back. I'm glad old Dabadie didn't file for a divorce. I love you, Laurel. I want you to come home with me."

Her face grew white with shock, and she shook her head in utter disbelief. "You're crazy! I'll never return to Louisiana with you. Have you forgotten your pregnant tart, waiting like a vulture at Petit Coteau?"

"I haven't forgotten Simone," he said slowly. "I can never forget her." He glanced away in seeming distraction, then focused on her again. "You're my wife and will stay my wife. No man will ever have you but me."

Tony leaped forward, and Laurel found herself ensnared in his arms. She struggled against him, but he held her two arms behind her back. His lips descended to quiet the curses that sprang from her mouth until she grew quiet. He sensed more than felt her surrender, as she held herself rigidly against him. But her lips softened and seemed to blossom under his kiss, almost as if she were inviting him to plunder the dark recesses of her mouth with his tongue. He would have willingly gone further, but her surrender was all he wished for now. The rest would come later when he had won her love and trust.

Laurel's legs almost gave way when Tony released her. She fell onto the bed and gazed up at him with eyes so bright and green they resembled a clear mountain stream.

"I hate you," she muttered through clenched teeth. However, she wasn't certain if she hated Tony or herself for responding to him.

"You liked that very much, *chérie,* but are too cowardly to admit it. Now, I'd bet that Lavinia would never say such a thing when passion overwhelmed her."

"What does Lavinia have to do with any of this?"

"Lavinia is my means of getting you back into my bed and my life again. She's an unwitting pawn, so to speak."

Laurel jumped off the bed, her face red with rising anger. "I told you that I haven't told her she's my sister. You can't mean to blackmail me into returning to your bed. I'll simply tell her the truth."

Tony wagged a finger at her. "No, no, no. You misunderstand. I don't care if she knows you're her sister, but *you* care about her to protect her from me. Remember how you protected her from Auguste St. Julian's vindictive relative? You went to great lengths to keep her safe. She eluded me because of your help, Laurel, but I'm on the Little L now. Hell, I own the Little L! Lavinia Delaney is at my mercy, trapped in a corner where she should have been long ago."

"Don't harm her, Tony!" Laurel pleaded.

"I won't, *chérie,* if you become my wife again." He leaned into her, his breath fanning her face and sending shivers of warning and desire down her spine. "And that means sleeping in my bed again, giving to me what Seth has been getting."

"Seth means nothing to me," she found herself saying, not quite sure why she wanted to convince him of that fact. But she clamped her mouth shut and surveyed him as a predator, a hunter. His eyes contained a feral gleam, and a slight smile split his sensual lips at her statement. Damn! she silently cursed. Why couldn't she have kept her mouth shut. He would think she hadn't given in to Seth because she still ached for him—which was true, but he didn't have to know it.

Tony was manipulating her again. She had thought she was done with him, and here he was again, spinning a web of revenge and enchantment about her. She had no alternative but to give in to him. Clearly, he might harm Lavinia.

Laurel backed away and walked to the other side of the room. "If I agree to this preposterous bargain, you'll leave Lavinia alone?"

"I promise I will."

Laurel sneered. "I know how you keep your promises. I'll think about it and give you my answer later." She started to walk past him, but he grabbed her upper arm and twisted her around to face him.

"I want your answer now, Laurel. This minute. I'm not a patient man, and you know that."

"You're hurting me."

He dropped her arm, but his gaze rooted her to the spot.

"What's your answer? Do you share my bed again, or do I start my revenge against Lavinia in earnest on the morrow? And never fear that I will make her life miserable."

Laurel shook, knowing he would finally have his chance at Lavinia. What had happened to the gentle man she had come to love? She had been wrong about Tony from the beginning. He was wild and untamed, thinking only of himself and not of others, especially not her. Sometimes Lavinia aggravated her so much that she would have gladly clobbered her, but Lavinia was her sister, and that meant more than when she had thought they were cousins. She must protect Lavinia from Tony's wrath, even if it meant humbling herself and becoming his wife again.

"Lavinia will rue the day she walked into my uncle's life," Tony reminded her.

"Damn you and damn your threats!" Laurel hissed. "Fine, I'll be your wife again, but don't expect me to like it."

Tony laughed. "My darling, I promise you that you'll eat those words. Where are you going?" Tony asked, seeing that she was starting for the door.

"To get a bath and go to bed," she shot back.

"I'll have Rosita pull out the tub and fill it for you. Then Gincie can bring in your gown, but I doubt you'll need it."

"What! What do you mean? I'm going to my room."

Tony opened his arms and gestured around the bedroom. "This is your room, my love, as of this night. You won't need the other one. In the morning I'll tell Gincie to put your clothes in the wardrobe in here. From now on, you bathe in here and sleep in here, and do whatever I say in here. We made a bargain, Laurel. You're a person who expects others to keep their word, so don't you renege now."

"But—"

He shot her a warning glance, and she knew he meant that their deal would begin that night. He took her hostile silence for acquiescence, and within half an hour, Rosita was carrying pails of warm water upstairs for Laurel's bath.

When the tub was filled, Laurel stripped off her clothes, grateful that Tony had had the decency to leave the room. Rosita left her, and Laurel settled into the water, which lapped over her like a warm summer's tide. She washed herself with soap that smelled of wild violets and washed her hair, rinsing it by dipping her head under the water. She heard the door open and close and, thinking it was Rosita, asked for the towel before she opened her eyes. Dutifully the towel was presented to her, and Laurel's eyes flickered open to settle on the person who stood above her.

It was Tony, practically leering at her. His gaze lazily perused her swelling breasts, the rose-tipped nipples hard and protracted and quite visible beneath the water's surface, to follow a path past the creamy globes to the hollow of her neck and upward to her face, framed by a swath of dark, wet hair, hanging over her left shoulder. Then to her chagrin, his eyes moved again to her breasts and seemed to see that part of her body that lay hidden beneath the liquid. Laurel felt herself coloring.

"You can put your eyes back in your head, Tony," she found herself saying icily. "My body is old news to you now."

"Far from old, *chérie*." He had the good grace to sit on the bed, against the headboard, and remove his rapacious gaze from her. But this was only momentary. No sooner had he stuffed a pillow behind his back than he watched her again. "Don't let me disturb your bath."

"I won't!" She sat in the tub and dried her hair vigorously with the towel.

"Are you going to stay in that tub all night, Laurel?"

"I'm waiting for you to be a gentleman and leave the room so I can get out and dress." The water had grown cold, and goose flesh rose on her arms. She began to shiver.

"You know I'm hardly the gentleman where you're concerned. I advise you to get out. If you sit in there all night, you'll look like a prune in the morning. The choice is yours, but I'm not shutting my eyes or leaving the room." Tony clasped his hands behind his head and settled deeper, making himself quite comfortable and Laurel very uneasy.

She searched the room for something to cover herself, but all she had was the skimpy towel she had used to dry her hair, and it was wet. She would barely be able to cover part of her torso with it. As always, Tony had won, leaving her no alternative but to rise from the tub with the wet towel hiding as much of her as possible. But before she did, she grabbed the washcloth and hurled it at him, hitting him in the center of his chest.

"Damn you!" Her epithet was met by a chuckle of amusement.

"Texas has spiced up your vocabulary."

"Go to hell," she intoned. Laurel rose, water dripping in silver rivulets down her golden pink body. Clutching the towel to her upper body, she managed only to cover her breasts and the dark triangle at the top of her legs. However, she didn't realize that the flimsy cloth only enhanced her attributes by clinging wetly to her curves and emphasizing the parts of herself she wished to keep hidden from Tony.

She didn't hear his intake of breath as she stepped gingerly out of the copper tub, but the desire flaring in his eyes was unmistakable. Nervously, she scanned the room for her nightgown. She knew Rosita had gotten it from Gincie earlier because she had seen it on the bed. Now it was gone.

"Looking for something?"

"My—my gown," she stuttered, feeling the room's chill settling over her body.

Tony turned his head in two directions, then said innocently, "I don't see any gown. Perhaps Rosita didn't bring it."

"I know she did. I—saw—it." Her teeth began to chatter. "Please go get Rosita—for me. Or knock on Gincie's door. I need—my—gown."

"Stop it, Laurel!" Tony ground out. "You didn't sleep in a gown at Petit Coteau. You don't need the pristine piece of cloth now." He opened the bedcovers to her. "Come to bed and warm up before you turn into an icicle."

She shook her head. "I won't."

"Stop being such a bullheaded female."

"I—am not a—bullheaded female."

"Damn if you aren't!" Tony growled lowly. He sprang from the bed and pulled the wet towel out of her tight clutch. He scooped her up into his arms, while she flailed at him and protested, but he didn't heed her angry words. One second he held her against the warm fuzz of his chest, and the next she was plopped onto the bed and he was pulling the covers over her.

"I thought you were level-headed, but Texas has

made a hellcat out of you. I arrived none too soon, Laurel. You've been on your own for too long now. You need a man to tame you."

"And I suppose you think you're that man!"

Tony bent over her, his breath ruffled the tousled strands of her hair. "I better be, because I'll kill any man that lays a hand on you. Including that conniving Seth."

"Seth has been a gentleman," Laurel protested.

"I hope for his sake that he has. If not, he'll wind up no better than a castrated bull."

"Tony! You're being ridiculous now."

His mouth twisted in a wry grin. "That includes any other man who might get any ideas in his head about you. You're my wife, and no man takes what's mine."

"Why, you pompous, arrogant . . ." Her voice drifted away to nothing when Tony didn't seem to hear her. Moving away from her, he went to the bureau and turned down the oil lamp until the only light in the room was from the large Texas moon outside. Laurel pulled the quilt up to her neck, watching as he walked around to his side of the bed and began to undress.

Her pulse raced, and she found herself shivering beneath the warm blanket, not from cold but from a sudden surge of desire that twisted warmly in her stomach. If just seeing Tony's perfect nude body in the moonlight could do this to her, what might happen if he touched her? But she couldn't turn her gaze from him. It had been so long since she was wrapped in his strong embrace or stroked the rippling muscles of his arms and back that she grew dizzy with the thought of it. She had fought this absurd bargain between them, but now that the moment was at hand, she admitted she didn't want to fight if he touched her, kissed her. She knew she would melt the moment his lips found hers. Tony possessed a power over her body, her senses. No matter what had happened in the past between them, Tony was still the only man she would ever love. But she vowed she wouldn't give him the satisfaction of knowing that. She would fight him if he touched her and retain some pride.

Laurel turned her head away. When the bed ropes creaked and the mattress dipped from the weight of Tony's body, she found she was actually trembling. When Tony's thigh came in contact with her right leg beneath the covers, she jerked it away, almost as if she had been burned. A second later she found her chin held in the cup of his hand, and he forced her to look at him. In the silvery moonlight, his eyes held a pain that she couldn't help but see.

"Don't jerk away from me when I touch you. Remember our agreement. Lavinia is in my power, Laurel, and you know it. I can begin to make her life miserable on the morrow."

"Why must you use threats? I agreed to this, but I don't have to like it. Maybe I jerked away because I hate your touching me. Why don't you just rape me and get it over with now?"

"I've never raped a woman in my life. I don't have to rape a woman, and we both know that I don't have to force you to respond to me. What's got you all riled up is the fact that you do want me to touch you but can't admit it."

"I don't! I hate your touch."

"Liar." He breathed into her ear, causing her head to spin. "I'm going to prove you wrong, Laurel, once and for all."

His lips descended and placed a gentle kiss upon hers. Laurel attempted to keep them tightly closed, but his tongue lapped at them until she was forced to open them, unwillingly inviting his entry. His tongue probed the dark recess of her mouth and entwined with hers. A flame ignited within her belly, growing higher and brighter, when his right hand moved beneath the cover to skim lightly across her rib cage. His palm moved upward to her breasts, full and ripe for his possession. Each one was in turn cupped in his hand, and the aching nipples massaged by fiery fingers.

Her moan of surrender was muffled by Tony as his kiss deepened. All thought of fighting fled Laurel's mind. A part of her knew that to fight was futile; she didn't want the wonderful sensations his hands produced upon her wanton flesh to cease. If she fought him, she would be fighting herself as well. With mind-drugging skill, Tony's wandering fingers began a journey downward from her breasts to the indentation of her waist, the curve of her hip, finally settling on her silken leg and trailing lazily to the soft area of her inner thigh where they hovered, dangerously close to the pulsing peak of her womanhood.

His fingers stroked the satiny flesh of her leg but didn't move further. Laurel writhed against the mattress in an attempt to move his fingers to the part of her that burned for his possession, but still they waited, almost singeing her with their heat. Finally she parted her thighs and arched upward, unable to speak, for Tony's mouth still covered hers.

Tony moved his lips from hers and whispered huskily, "Tell me you want me to touch you, Laurel. Tell me."

Desire beat out a wild cadence in her heart, and she could barely speak from the liquid sensations coursing through her, setting her on fire. She couldn't wait another second to feel his hand upon her. "Touch me, touch me . . . touch . . ."

Once again his mouth found hers and stopped all conscious thought. Laurel became a creature of sensations, no longer able to concentrate on anything but the pleasurable pulsing at her core, the fingers that trailed liquid fire in their wake as they finally found their destination. The breath died in her throat when each one slipped inside her moist warmth, then withdrew only to be plunged into the satiny depths over and over.

Desire pulsated through her. She felt weightless. Golden and silver lights danced before her closed eyelids, threatening to blind her if she opened them. Nothing mattered to her but the shimmering point of light at the center, which grew brighter and brighter until her whole being was consumed by such ecstasy that she cried out against Tony's lips.

Her body trembled with her climax, having been thrown over the edge of sanity but coming to rest on a cloud, carried by a warm breeze. Slowly Laurel came back to reality and realized that Tony held her in his arms. Her eyes opened, and she gazed up at him in wonder at the full impact of his power over her. She expected him to love her completely then, for she could feel his rock-hard desire against her thigh. At that moment she wouldn't have refused him anything. In fact she craved his complete possession of her.

His hand stroked her naked thigh, and he gently kissed her. "Never tell me you don't want me to touch you again. I believe I've just proved you wrong."

Bestowing a kiss on each of her nipples, he grinned at her, and to her absolute surprise, he let her go and turned on his side, away from her.

"Tony," she mouthed his name, but no sound was forthcoming. She lay there, wide-eyed, for hours until tears slipped from under her lashes. Tony had proved a point by making her respond to him, a point that Laurel decided was quite clear. He could take her to paradise whenever he felt like it, even at the expense of his own pleasure, to show her his mastery over her body. At that moment she would have preferred him to rape her rather than force her to admit her weakness for him.

Chapter Twenty-six

When Laurel woke the next morning, Tony was gone. Gincie tapped on the door before entering with a breakfast tray, just as Laurel was getting up.

"I don't take breakfast in bed," she told Gincie and clutched the sheet about her.

A huge white smile lit up Gincie's face. "Hush, Miss Laurel, and sit back and eat. Mr. Tony done said you'd be hungry this mornin'. You didn't get any supper last night with all the excitement at Mr. Tony's comin'."

Laurel was at first going to refuse the food because Tony had ordered it for her. When Gincie removed the red-and-white-checkered napkin that covered the plate of freshly fried ham, scrambled eggs, and a biscuit still hot from the oven and dripping with melted butter, her stomach growled. Settling herself against the back of the bed, she allowed Gincie to place the tray on her lap.

"Now this is what my baby needs. A good breakfast and not runnin' off after those cows. You got a good man to look after you."

"You would say that. But Tony and I are just living a farce of a marriage, Gincie. Don't expect too much from this apparent reconciliation. Looks can be deceiving."

Laurel swallowed a forkful of egg as Gincie bent down and grabbed a white handful of material from under the bed. "My nightgown!" Laurel cried.

"Yes, ma'am, it's your gown all right. Now you tell old Gincie why your pretty gown is thrown under the bed and you is sittin' there with only a sheet to cover you if you and Mr. Tony ain't together."

Laurel blushed. "That bastard told me he didn't see my gown. *He* put it under the bed just so I wouldn't be able to wear it."

Gincie didn't bother to hide her good-natured laugh. "I done knew Mr. Tony would think of a way to get you back."

"He hasn't gotten me back yet," Laurel professed and put the tray on the table beside the bed. "I'm not hungry any longer. I'm getting up and heading for the range."

"Mr. Tony left for the range hours ago. That Jim fellow came, and they went off together. He told me not to disturb you before ten."

"Is it that late already?" At Gincie's nod of affirmation, Laurel bounded out of bed, muttering curses at Tony for his high-handedness in assuming that since he had arrived, she would no longer take an interest in the Little L.

"I'll just show him who's boss around here," she remarked, once she was dressed in a pair of blue Levis and a sky-blue blouse. "I was left in charge of the Little L until the new owner could adequately take over, and I don't think Tony knows a damn about Texas ranching."

Gincie smirked. "Mr. Tony knows a lot. He done got you in his bed again."

Laurel left her room in a huff. Outdoors, as she walked to the barn for her horse, she ran into Seth. He grabbed her by the arm and swung her around when she barely acknowledged his greeting.

"What's wrong with you?" she bit out, sensing his argumentative attitude.

"You slept in Duvalier's room last night?"

"Yes."

"In his bed?"

"Where did you think I'd sleep? On the floor?"

"Did he make love to you?"

The memory of last night washed over her. She hated to remember what Tony had done to her, how she had responded, but she couldn't stop the rising heat that flooded her face, and this was all the answer that Seth needed.

"Filthy bastard."

"Seth, we have to settle something," Laurel told him gently, having come to an immediate decision. "I'm Tony's wife and can't marry you."

"You're going to divorce the varmint," Seth persisted.

"No. Tony and I are man and wife. There's no hope of my falling in love with you and marrying you. I'm sorry." Taking off the ring Seth had given to her, she handed it to him. She hadn't forgiven Tony for Simone and didn't know if she could accept his hostility toward Lavinia, but one thing she did know was that she couldn't love any man but Tony, the contemptible bastard.

Seth gazed at the ring and buried it in his fist. "You're the one who'll be sorry, Laurel. I guarantee that you will."

He stalked off, leaving her somewhat unnerved by the hatred she saw in his eyes. She knew she had done the right thing. Seth just had to realize that.

Entering the barn, one of the hands helped her saddle her horse, and she rode to the open range in search of Tony, intent on giving him a piece of her mind.

"Rustlers," Jim Castille informed Tony. He leaned forward in his saddle, an arm placed protectively on his gunbelt out of habit rather than necessity. "I didn't want to tell Miss Laurel that we've lost a few head here and there. I don't think that is a woman's concern."

Tony's dark gaze surveyed the pastoral landscape where the cattle were grazing in contentment. His stallion pawed the earth, eager to be off, but Tony gentled him with a steady hand. "How long has this been going on?"

"Hard to say, but I think a little under a month. Not enough head disappeared to notice at first, but since last month the count is down by two hundred. I doubt if that many just wandered off. I'd say they were led away."

"Have you posted lookouts?"

"I did a week ago. Five men are posted on the south forty and five on the north forty. Others scout the rest of the range. I mentioned the problem to Seth Renquist, but he didn't seem too worried about it. He's been taking care of the north forty. Funny thing about it all, though. Most of the cattle that disappeared were from that section."

Tony shot Jim a knowing look, aware of Jim's assumption. He wouldn't put it past Seth to steal cattle from the Little L. He had learned from Simone that Seth had had a hand in causing Laurel to think that the child Simone carried had been his. He wouldn't forget such duplicity. Tony cleared his throat.

"We'll just have to keep our eyes and ears open from now on."

The sound of thundering hoofs drew their attention as Laurel rode into view. Her long hair was unbound and whipped around her face and shoulders like black velvet. She reined in her horse, breathing hard, unaware that the top button of her blouse was undone, exposing part of her heaving bosom.

"What are you doing out here?" Tony practically growled at her, feeling a stirring in his loins and frustrated by last night.

Laurel rose up in the saddle, staring him down. "I'm in charge of the Little L. I don't intend to sleep late and eat breakfast in bed because you deem I should. You're not going to bully me, Tony Duvalier, no matter what we agreed last night." She turned her flashing emerald gaze on Jim. "And you, you traitor. I thought we were friends and you respected my authority, but the moment a man appears, you change sides.

"Hold on now, Miss Laurel—"

Tony broke in. "I asked Jim to show me the spread. He wanted me to bring you along because he knew you'd fill me in on things, but I told him you were sleeping. I'm sorry, I won't overstep my bounds again. You've taken pretty good care of the Little L. I'm proud of you, Laurel."

Tony's quick flash of a smile took her aback. Tony Duvalier had actually apologized to her and commended her on the ranch. She could barely believe it. She didn't dare think that he was finally coming to see her as a capable female rather than a bed partner.

They rode on, saying nothing. At noon, the three of them watered their horses by a clear stream. When Jim was out of earshot, Tony sat beside Laurel, who was resting in a patch of goldenrod. For a brief instant, his hand touched hers, and then he began to fiddle with the brim on his hat.

"I meant what I said about being proud of you. You've accomplished a great deal on this ranch. Jim told me about the improvements you've made, the way you've taken an interest in the stock. You've come a long way from the girl I married." His black eyes were soft and filled with respect when he looked at her. "I didn't make a mistake in coming here. I know that now."

A lump formed in her throat at this admission, which she realized must be quite hard for Tony to say. He was the kind of man who expected his woman to be in one place, a place where he could find her, not running a ranch. On Petit Coteau she had never bothered with anything but the house and hadn't wanted any more responsibility because she knew Tony would handle things much better than she ever could. But here, she was her own person for the first time in her life. No one saw her as the Delaney daughter, or Tony's wife, or the orphaned cousin. She was simply Laurel, simply herself.

"Thank you, Tony. That means a great deal to me coming from you."

Tony plucked a goldenrod and handed it to her.

"Truce?" he said.

Laurel took it from him, her fingers touching his, but she didn't pull away.

"Truce."

* * *

Near sundown, Laurel, tired and dusty, with Tony and Jim beside her, rode into the yard. She had barely slipped from the saddle when Lavinia appeared, resembling a wild violet in a purple gown, edged with green lace on the scooped neckline and elbow-length sleeves. Her auburn hair was piled atop her hair in tiny curls. She sashayed toward them and clutched Tony by the sleeve when he dismounted.

"Rosita has supper ready. I was wondering when you were coming back. I've been alone all day," she said, pouting, and clung tighter to Tony.

"You could have joined us on the range." Laurel moved briskly away, a feeling of jealousy eating away at her. Lavinia looked so beautiful while, once again, her own appearance left much to be desired. And what made matters worse was that Tony smiled familiarly at Lavinia and didn't remove her grasping hand from his arm.

"I didn't feel like it today. I took a long, warm bath in some wonderful violet bath salts from Paris. Do I smell sweet to you, Tony?" Lavinia leaned in closer to him, enabling him to catch a whiff of her scent.

"You smell divine enough to drive a man mad."

Lavinia giggled. Her gaze slid to Jim, who was watching from his horse, seemingly nonplussed by the encounter taking place below him.

Jim called to Laurel. "I'll see you in the morning, Miss Laurel."

"Would you like to stay for supper with us?" Laurel invited him.

"No, ma'am. I think I might be sick from all these fancy smells mingling in the air." He rode toward the bunkhouse, not missing the nasty scowl Lavinia threw his way.

"Where's Seth? I haven't see him all day," Tony asked Lavinia.

"He took off this morning for San Antonio. He said he didn't know when he'd be home. Seems that the sleeping arrangements weren't to his liking." Lavinia's voice dripped venom. "Some people around here can't seem to make up their minds about which bed they fancy to sleep in."

Laurel felt herself coloring and marched into the house before she said something just as ugly to Lavinia. When she reached her and Tony's room, she discovered that all her clothes had been hung neatly in the large wardrobe and that her toilet articles were lined up in orderly fashion on the bureau. The bathtub already stood waiting in the center of the room, filled with warm water, and Gincie had laid out one of her best gowns on the bed.

The dress, a light-rose-and-white-striped silk with a revealing décolletage and a rose pinned to the front, was much too fussy for a simple evening meal. At first Laurel was going to exchange it for a plainer looking gown. She wondered why Gincie had not laid out one of her calico gowns, but she remembered one of their earlier conversations about her clothes. Lately Lavinia's vibrant beauty was much too noticeable, and Laurel had begun to feel homely in comparison. Now that Tony seemed unable to tear his eyes from Lavinia and with Lavinia hanging onto him like a leech, she felt downright dowdy. Laurel took one last lingering look at the gown and began to undress. It was about time that Lavinia got a dose of her own medicine.

After a bath scented with rose water, Laurel fastened her long hair away from her face with ivory combs. Her dark tresses hung simply down her back and curled wispily at her waist. When she was dressed she waited on the open balcony, watching the scene below her in the parlor, until Tony felt her gaze upon him and glanced up.

"King me!" Lavinia cried out in delight as she made a move on the checkerboard. Her delight quickly faded when she realized that Tony was oblivious of her and the game. His eyes were on Laurel.

Laurel moved slowly down the stairs. The light from the oil lamps on tables on both sides of the sofa cast a soft peach glow across her bare shoulders and the swelling curves of her breasts. Her eyes were a vivid shade of green and hadn't yet left Tony's face as she took a seat in a chair across from him. A small smile played about her lips.

"Who's winning?" she asked, not really interested in the game but in the man whose face was taut with desire.

"I am!" Lavinia chimed in. "I always win!"

"Do you really? How nice, Lavinia." Laurel sounded unconcerned, almost patronizing. Lavinia seethed, seeing that Tony had lost all interest in the game. "Tony, I have a king," she said through clenched teeth.

"What? Oh, sorry." Tony topped Lavinia's checker with his own. "Game's over. I lose."

The room was charged with an electric current that ran directly from Tony to Laurel. They gazed into each other's eyes, unaware of Lavinia who fidgeted in her chair, then threw the checkerboard and checkers into a wooden case, practically spilling the round pieces on the floor.

Laurel felt her body come alive and glow. She

hated to admit to herself that she was anticipating the moment she and Tony would go upstairs. Just thinking about tonight in their bed set her heart to racing. Tony wanted her. His eyes held a dark passion that she had come to know well. His lips enticed her to touch them, and she believed she would have, no matter that Lavinia glared at her from across the room, but the sound of booted feet striding through the front door prevented her.

Jim entered the room, a look of apology on his face. "Didn't mean to interrupt your evening, folks, but, Tony, there's a party for Tom Evans at the hands' bunkhouse. He's getting married day after tomorrow, and the boys are giving him a celebration. We thought you might like to come."

"That's kind of you," Tony said, removing his eyes from Laurel, "but I might be busy later."

"Go, Tony," Laurel urged, coming back to her senses momentarily. "This will be a good chance to meet all the hands."

"Do you mind? I could be a little late."

His eyes and voice held a promise in them that Laurel couldn't refuse. "That's fine."

"You'll wait up for me?"

Laurel nodded. Moments after Tony had left with Jim, Lavinia plopped herself down on the sofa. "You know that the men are going to get so riproaring drunk that when Tony does come back, he'll be quite worthless to you."

"Goodness, Lavinia! Let it never be said that you have a way of being tactful."

Lavinia shrugged and leaned her head against the cushions. "I always say what I think because it prevents complications later."

"Then be honest now, pray, and tell me what mischievous thought those blue eyes are hiding."

Tilting her head, Lavinia placed a thin finger on her lips. "I'd say it is more like lascivious thoughts, Cousin Laurel, concerning your husband. I don't know why you're sleeping in his bed again, seeing that you claimed to hate him so much until he showed up again. Now you can't take your eyes off him, but don't think that, because you're acting the part of his wife, he's safe from predatory females."

"Of which you're one," Laurel interjected.

"Certainly."

"Why do you want my husband?"

"That's obvious. Tony is a handsome and virile man."

"And quite rich," Laurel said. "You shouldn't forget that."

Lavinia had the grace to flush as that remark sank in. Rising from the sofa, she made a big to-do over arranging some colorful wildflowers in a vase by the window. "You would say that. You're cruel to even think it."

"I'm being honest with you, but it's time you were honest with yourself. Tony holds a large attraction for you because he's wealthy, and you want to latch onto him as a means of keeping the Little L. But he won't marry you. He doesn't love you and you know that. And what's more, you know you don't love him."

"How do you know that, Miss Know-It-All?"

"Let's say that I have a woman's intuition. I know that Jim Castille is the man you love and that he loves you."

"I hate Jim Castille!"

"Look into your heart," Laurel told her softly. "You'll find the truth there."

Laurel got up and made a move to touch Lavinia, but Lavinia swiped at her. "I wish you'd never come here!" she cried and ran from the room with tears in her blue eyes.

Tears stung Laurel's eyes as well. She felt Lavinia's pain but could do nothing to help her. Somehow, some way, Lavinia had to face up to herself. Suddenly very tired, Laurel went upstairs and had Rosita bring her supper to her room. Then she undressed and slipped nude between the sheets to wait for Tony's return.

Lavinia kicked aside her gown, not caring that it landed in a heap beside the foot of her bed. She finished buttoning the last button on the front of her blue-and-white-checkered blouse and impatiently tucked the shirttail into her denim pants. After sitting on the edge of the bed and pulling on her boots, she pulled the pins from her hair and allowed the red strands to hang in wild abandon down her back. Before she left her room, she surveyed her reflection in the mirror and smirked with satisfaction.

No more acting the lady for her, she decided. She had done more than her share of acting in New Orleans to entice Auguste St. Julian, but she would be damned if she wasted her time on Tony Duvalier, who clearly wasn't interested in her. She wouldn't dwell on the man for one more minute. Winning him over with ladylike etiquette and lowered lashes accomplished her nothing. He loved Laurel, and he could have her. Any plan of wooing him away from Laurel and of claiming the Little L for herself by enticing him into marrying her were now buried. But she was vexed and angry that Tony didn't want her. She felt her charms were slipping, and slipping badly.

She sneaked out of her room and took the backstairs to the yard. A full moon cast silvery fingers across the landscape as she headed toward the corral. From the hands' bunkhouse a distance away, she heard the sound of male voices, laughing and raised in rowdy song, drift through the quiet night. No one seemed to be outside, and Lavinia was glad.

Buck had warned her to stay away from the white stallion in the corral, but Lavinia felt ornery enough not to heed anyone's orders. So far, no one had been able to tame the horse because the horse reared up and threw his rider every time.

"I'm going to tame you," Lavinia whispered to the horse as she stopped by the corral gate. "For once I'm going to succeed where others failed. We're going to be good friends, boy."

Cautiously, Lavinia opened the gate and stepped inside. The stallion appeared oblivious to her, but Lavinia knew he sensed her intentions. His ears perked up, and the muscles in his flanks stiffened. She spoke in a low, soothing voice as she inched closer to him. By the time she lifted herself onto his back, she thought he had come to trust her.

"There, boy, this isn't so bad. You'll get used to me in time." She patted his soft mane, feeling a thrill of triumph surge through her. She had won! The stallion was hers!

"Lavinia! Get off that horse!"

Jim Castille's voice cut through the night. Lavinia turned in the direction of the sound at the same moment the horse reared up. One second she was on his back, the next she was on the ground beneath the powerful hoofs. A sudden, searing pain shot through her right shoulder, and she knew she would be trampled to death, but then she felt strong arms pulling her away from the animal. In a haze of pain, she watched Jim quiet the horse.

Rising to her feet, she clutched her aching shoulder. Jim escorted her outside the gate and shut it with a thud.

He turned to her, his brown eyes filled with fury. "Don't you know you could have been killed? That horse wouldn't let a man ride him. What makes you think you could tame him?"

"Damn you to hell, Jim Castille! I mounted him. The animal accepted me, but you had to scream at me and you spooked him. He was fine until you yelled your fool head off."

"Listen to me, you silly fool, you were inches away from being trampled. If I hadn't come along when I did, you would have been hurt really badly, if not killed. You'd have been thrown whether I was there or not. What in blazes are you doing out here at this time of night?" He didn't wait for her answer. In aggravation he grabbed her arm, not prepared for Lavinia's yowl of pain.

Her face grew white, and her eyes looked like huge blue circles. For an instant her knees buckled beneath her. Jim caught her and scooped her up into his arms.

"Why didn't you tell me you were hurt?"

"You didn't—give me—a chance," she gasped out. "You've got a big mouth."

"Kick me next time," he whispered next to her ear and carried her to his bunkhouse.

"Believe me, I will," she said with conviction.

Barely a minute later, Jim gently set Lavinia on his bunk. He lighted the lamp and surveyed her. She looked like a little girl with her hair all a tumble. A wave of affection for Lavinia swept through him unbidden, but Jim repressed it. She had hurt him too much.

"Let me take a look at your arm," he said brusquely.

"I don't need you to look after me. I don't like it here anyway. I'm going back to the house." She started to get up, but sank down on the bunk as the pain shot through her and made her dizzy.

"Lie down, Lavinia." Jim plumped up the pillow and helped her lie down. "Your arm might be broken. Can I take a look at it?" His voice was suddenly gentle, and Lavinia nodded. "You'll have to take off your blouse."

Lavinia's eyes bored into Jim's. "Could you please undo the buttons? I can't . . ."

He nodded in an impersonal way, but Lavinia noticed his hand trembled when the buttons began to give. In the lamplight he swallowed hard as his fingers grazed the swell of her breasts, the soft flesh of her stomach. When the last button was undone, Lavinia sat up for Jim to help her remove the right sleeve. Then she attempted to pull the blouse across her full right breast as a sort of shield.

Jim shook his head in amusement. "I've seen more of you than that in the past. No need to hide from me. You don't have to play the modest lady with me."

Lavinia flushed. "You should know all about ladies," she snapped. "You trail after Laurel like a little lost puppy with its tongue hanging out. And what makes you think I want to be a lady anyway? Or that I care what you think about me? I don't give a damn for your opinion. If your preference is for a lady, then you'd better seduce Laurel fast, because I think Tony may have already beat you to it."

She would have said more, but a throbbing ache caused her to be silent when Jim bent down and examined her arm and then made her move it. "No bones broken," he said. "Just a slight sprain. I think you'll live."

"No thanks to you!"

"You can be a shrew."

"And you can be a bastard." Lavinia tried to pull her blouse on, but she had trouble getting her arm into the sleeve and was forced to accept Jim's help. His hands felt warm, and an uncomfortable heat gathered in her abdomen and spread to her lower body, causing her to practically spring from the bunk. She knew that melting sensation well. She had felt it many years ago when she and Jim had made love. During the intervening years, Lavinia had had quite a few men, but none caused her to feel the way Jim could with only a touch. She must get away from here, she told herself. Otherwise, she would be unable to resist Jim, and too much had happened between them for her to ever let him love her again.

"You're in the devil's own rush to get out of here. What's the matter, Lavinia? My humble place isn't good enough for you?"

She didn't stop as she made her way to the door. "You're not good enough for me anymore. Go find Laurel and bring her here. Most men want ladies, and you're no different. I'm tired of being a lady, acting like some priss with lace on her drawers. Being a lady had gotten me nowhere."

Lavinia's hand clasped the doorknob when Jim's came down gently upon hers and stilled her.

Turning her face to his, he showed in his expression all the passion she felt. "What makes you think I want a lady, Lavinia? Maybe you're all the woman I've ever wanted."

The throbbing pulse at the base of her throat matched the irregular beat of her heart. She gasped when a second later Jim enfolded her in his arms. Guttural sounds of pleasure escaped unwillingly from her when he picked her up, carried her to the bunk, and placed her gingerly on the spot she had just left.

He joined her, stretching his long body beside hers, careful not to disturb her arm. His hand slid beneath her blouse and stroked the soft curve of her waist and moved upward to find the swollen tips of her breasts. His touch felt like fire upon her skin, and she shivered with the deep, burning ache of wanting him again and knowing that she wasn't going to fight him.

"Don't hurt me, Jim," she breathed. "I couldn't bear for you to hurt me again."

"I didn't hurt you years ago, and I never will. You believed a lie about me, something Seth set up to turn you and your father away from me. None of you let me explain anything, but I thought you'd listen to me." He stroked her cheek with gentle fingers. "I sneaked back to the ranch to see you, believing that you didn't think I'd stolen the money from your father's desk. But when I sneaked in and asked Rosita if I could see you, she said you weren't here, that you'd gone to Louisiana with your father and would probably be gone a long time. So, I left. You did think I stole the money, didn't you?"

"Yes. But you didn't. I know that now." A strangled sob spilled forth. "If only I had trusted you, believed in you, everything would have been so different. I've done some terrible things since I left here with Papa . . . the men I've known—"

His lips silenced hers. "I don't want to hear any more. What's past is done. I haven't led a spotless life either. I've made a lot of mistakes. But one thing I know and have always known, though I didn't want to admit it. I love you, Lavinia, and I always will. No woman has ever had my heart and my love but you."

"Me . . . too." She choked on her words and would have said more, but at that moment Jim's lips descended once more against hers, and she was lost in a spiraling labyrinth of desire. They removed their clothes and lay in each other's arms, delighting in the feel and scent of one another. The years melted away with each kiss, each heated caress until both Jim and Lavinia blended into the light at the end of a velvet tunnel and found the rapture that had eluded them since the day they parted.

They lay spent in each other's arms, listening to their twin heartbeats, thrumming in time to each other. Lavinia's auburn hair, spilling across Jim's chest like a red and gold fan, caught the lamplight. She lifted her face up to his and smiled.

"I never thought I could be this happy again."

Jim squeezed her. "Me either." A long silence stretched between them. Finally, he said, "Lavinia, I want to ask you something. You don't have to tell me, because it doesn't make any difference. But did you ever have a baby?"

Her breath died away. "Why?"

His hand massaged her abdomen. "There are faint marks a woman gets when she's borne a child. I know a lot has happened in the past eight years, and I don't condemn you, but . . . Hell, maybe I shouldn't have asked. You're starting to cry. I'm sorry."

She sat up, shaking her long hair about her

shoulders. She viewed him through a haze of tears and pain she thought she had buried along with her baby. "When I left here with Papa, I was carrying your baby, Jim. Papa sent me to Uncle Sylvester's, thinking it would be better for me to have the baby there. But it was lonely. I was away from my home, my family . . . from you. It was awful, and I was sick most of the time. The baby was yours, and I so wanted that baby." She sobbed the moment Jim sat up and enfolded her in his arms. "We had a baby girl. She was stillborn. The slaves helped me bury her in a little cemetery along the River Road. I'm sorry she died. I can't do anything right, not even give you a child."

Lavinia's sobs gushed forth, and she found she couldn't still them. For so long, she had held herself in check. Just to be in Jim's arms, to know that he still loved her, was more than she could bear. She had never been able to unburden herself of this pain with anyone. Believing Jim was lost to her had made the baby's death unbearable. But now, he held her and stroked her hair, his tears mingling with her own, and she felt cleansed of the past, of the pain. He kissed her when she began to grow quiet and held her face between his hands.

"My brave love. I never thought or imagined you'd gone through all that alone. I can't make it up to you, but I'll try. I will. We can have other children one day. Will you marry me, Lavinia? I love you so much that I hurt to think you might not want me."

She threw her arms around him, and her face glowed with happiness and love. "Yes! Everything's all right now. I love you, too. I do." Lavinia rained warm kisses over his face, his body, until the flame was rekindled again.

As Jim lay later with her curled like a kitten in his arms, he didn't think everything was fine.

Seth Renquist had spoiled their chance for happiness by framing him for a robbery he hadn't committed. Because of Seth, Lavinia had been sent away to live in Louisiana and had borne a dead child among strangers. Perhaps if she had stayed at the ranch, if Seth hadn't told Arthur he had stolen the money, Lavinia would have married him and not have been put under this terrible strain. Maybe their daughter would have lived.

Jim's eyes slid to the gleaming gun in the holster belt hanging over the headboard of the bed. Jim decided at that moment that a debt had to be paid. One of the bullets in the gun was engraved with Seth Renquist's name.

Chapter Twenty-seven

"Tony!"

Laurel woke, her sleep disturbed by a vague feeling of uneasiness. Dawn's soft light filtered in through the lace curtains at the window. In a half-wakeful state, she moved her hand to Tony's side of the bed and felt a cold emptiness.

Getting out of bed, she dragged the sheet with her and wrapped herself within the linen folds and went to the window. Soft fingers of light caressed the tops of the hills in the distance. In the yard below and in the direction of the bunkhouse, nothing stirred. A strange silence permeated the ranch. She wondered if Tony was still at the bunkhouse, sleeping away a night of drinking and merrymaking with the hands. He had told her he would be back, and she felt an unwilling degree of disappointment. Though she had shared Tony's bed for only a few nights, she had gotten used to his presence beside her — something she had vowed to fight against. But she knew she was weakening where Tony was concerned.

Clutching the edge of the sheet in her hand, Laurel didn't know if they had a future. She had agreed to a stupid bargain, believing that he would make her play the wife in all ways, but so far, he hadn't. Was he attempting to win her favor again by going slowly with her? She knew he could very easily have seduced her and she would not have put up a fight. All Tony had to do was touch her, and she was lost, beyond all reason, in his arms. But she couldn't deny to herself that she wanted him again or that perhaps she was using the threat against Lavinia as an excuse to be his wife.

A little smile snaked across her mouth as she realized that Lavinia had nothing to do with her coming to Tony's bed. It was clear to her now as it had always been. She loved Tony and would tell him so, but first he had to forget this silly revenge against Lavinia before *she* decided to allow him to make love to her.

"I'll find him, and somehow we'll make everything all right," she mumbled and lit the oil lamp to search for her clothes. Tony's jacket was lying on the rocking chair on top of her pants. She reached for the pants, but the jacket fell onto the floor, and a piece of wadded paper tumbled out of the pocket. Laurel's curiosity got the best of her, and she unfolded it, smoothing out the wrinkles with her hands, until she deciphered Jean's name at the bottom of the letter. She moved closer to the lamp and began to read the letter, which was dated two days after Tony had left Louisiana.

Dear Tony,
I hope you arrive safely in Texas. The past weeks haven't been happy ones for you. I am

mending nicely at home. Denise keeps me quite busy with books and newpapers and her constant chatter. Doctor Fusilier doesn't think I will be able to walk for at least another two months. The breaks weren't as serious as he originally believed. Still, I don't like being the invalid.

Monsieur Lancier visited me yesterday. He'd gone to Petit Coteau and found you gone. Needless to say, he was very upset. To my surprise, he was sober. Madame Lancier didn't come as she is still in mourning and refuses to leave the house. Simone's death was hard on both of them, and I doubt they will ever fully recover. Simone's tragedy isn't your fault. You must believe this and not hold yourself responsible. Monsieur Lancier told me that he knows you were blameless, that Simone was headstrong. I didn't tell him about the child she carried, and neither did Doctor Fusilier. What is the point of bringing more grief on the Lanciers? Simone is gone.

Tony, I write this letter to express in words that which I couldn't do in person. No matter your feelings for Simone, you must put her memory to rest. I know you are in pain, but you must go on with your life. Laurel is the answer you seek, and I'm pleased you've gone to Texas to claim her. Heaven knows you don't need a ranch, but you do need the lady. As you've always told me, Laurel is yours and will be your wife forever, no matter about Simone. Bring her back, *mon cousin*. I'm fond of her, and you've been hell to live with the last few months!

Express my devotion and love to Laurel.

Denise also sends her best.

> Your cousin,
> Jean DuLac

The paper shook in Laurel's hands. Utter shock at the letter's news held her rooted. She wanted to laugh and weep at the same time. Tony was playing her for a fool. No wonder he couldn't bring himself to speak about Simone. The woman he loved, the woman who carried his child, was dead. Such stoic grief from anyone else would have touched her heart, but instead she felt her heart shattering into jagged shards. She had thought she might have a chance to win him from Simone, but she couldn't fight such a bittersweet memory.

Tony hadn't come to Texas only to help Arthur. He had come for her, not because he loved her but because she was a possession to him. What would have happened had Simone not died? Would she have been forced to share Tony with the woman, live in the same house with her and her child? Was that part of the reason behind this bargain not to harm Lavinia? He had known she would do anything to protect Lavinia from his wrath. Had he concocted this scheme before Simone died and decided to bring her home to Petit Coteau even after Simone's death to prove a point?

"Damn him!" she railed through tears of anger. "He won't manipulate me anymore." She threw off the sheet and hurriedly dressed, eager to confront Tony once and for all. She would let him know she wasn't returning to Petit Coteau with him, that she would buy the ranch and run it herself. There was no way in hell that she was going to take second place in his heart or live with Simone's memory for the rest of her life. And as far as harming Lavinia, just let him try.

Buck Dawson was waiting in the parlor when Laurel descended the stairs. She was dressed in Levis and a plaid flannel shirt to ward off the chilly morning air. Her hair hung loose and wild around her shoulders, and a buff-colored wide-brimmed hat hung on her back, held in place by a string at her neck. With each step, her hair and hat bobbed slightly.

"What is it?" she asked him brusquely, intent on seeing Tony and setting him straight.

"I—I—" Buck stammered, not used to Laurel's abruptness. "Today's payday, ma'am."

"Oh, yes, it is. I'm sorry to snap at you. Come into the study." Buck followed her into the room. "I thought Jim paid the hands."

"Usually he does, ma'am, but he was called away around two this morning. He and Mr. Duvalier and some of the other hands left quick like. Those rustlers have struck again, and we heard tell that one of the hands on the north forty was shot."

Laurel looked blank. "Rustlers?"

Buck nodded. "Yeah, the ones who done been stealing some of the Little L's herd the last few weeks. Mr. Duvalier and Jim are going to catch them and string them up. I know you'll be real glad when they're caught."

"Yes, I will." Laurel looked down, unwilling to allow Buck to see that she didn't know what he was talking about. She had never heard anything about rustlers, and she had ridden with Jim and Tony. Evidently neither one of them had seen fit to tell her about what was happening on the Little L because she was a woman. A new wave of anger rushed over her at the realization that Tony, for all his mouthing off that he was proud of the job she had done on the ranch, believed she should be protected from this vital information. The arrogant man! Who did he think he was to hide such knowledge from her? Her resolve to find him today and take him to task redoubled.

She found the key to open the desk drawer where she kept the loose cash. To her amazement the drawer was empty of greenbacks and gold pieces. She had been robbed! To hide her surprise and dismay, she flashed Buck a weak smile.

"I hope you and the other men can wait until tomorrow for your pay, Buck. I have to send Jim into town to the bank. I forgot that an expense came up the other day, and I used all the cash."

Buck's face fell, apparently disappointed. "I'll throw in a bonus for all of you for all your help in tracking down the rustlers," she offered. Buck smiled his pleasure.

"Sure, ma'am, that's fine. Most of the fellows are on the range with Jim and Mr. Duvalier anyway. Nobody will be looking for anything tonight but a good long sleep."

Laurel thanked Buck, and after he sauntered out of the room, she heaved a huge sigh. No one knew where she kept the key to the drawer but Jim and now Buck, who hadn't known until now. And Seth. It didn't take her long to analyze the situation. Seth had stolen the cash and taken off. Why he left without waiting to collect on his part of the ranch was a mystery to her. However, he apparently hadn't left empty-handed.

At the moment, she couldn't concentrate on Seth and his crime. She went to the kitchen and had Rosita make her a small breakfast, which she hurriedly ate under Gincie's admonishing stare. When she was finished, she saddled her horse and rode to the open range, intent on finding Tony and joining the search for the rustlers.

By the time Laurel came into view of Tony and Jim, with Lavinia riding beside him, the morning sun had receded behind gray clouds. A crisp, wild wind blew across the range, and Laurel noted that toward the west, the sky was nearly black. Some of the hands rounded up the steers and others branded the unmarked strays. When her roan sauntered toward Tony and stopped beside him, she shot him a look of venom.

"I suppose it's fine for Lavinia to know about the rustlers, but I'm to be excluded. Thank you for your trust and confidence in me, Tony. And you, too, Jim. I appreciate it." Her voice dripped sarcasm. Jim flushed and Tony stared stoically ahead.

"I had my reasons for not telling you." Tony shifted his weight in the saddle, the only indication Laurel had that her wrath caused him to feel uncomfortable.

"Miss Laurel, don't blame Mr. Duvalier," Jim quickly interjected before Laurel had a chance to say anything else. "It was my idea not to tell you just now."

Laurel's eyes slid to Lavinia, and Lavinia smiled a warm rich smile that lit up her sapphire orbs like the most exquisite jewels. "I was with Jim when the news came that one of the hands was shot during a rustling. Otherwise, I doubt I'd have been told anything either. I tagged along with Jim. So, don't send me those killing looks. I'm as much in the dark as you."

Laurel decided the best tactic was to forget Tony's slight for the time being. He appeared to be in no mood for a confrontation, and she decided that she would wait until they were alone before she offered to buy the Little L and send him packing. She truly didn't want Lavinia to learn that Tony was the man who had vowed revenge upon her. She would insist that Tony leave the ranch and remain mute on the subject of Auguste St. Julian. Especially now. Something in the way Jim leaned toward Lavinia, and the answering motion of her body, the way they intimately exchanged secretive looks, told Laurel that Lavinia had found her true love again. Nothing and no one would spoil Lavinia's newfound happiness, she vowed to herself. Not even Tony.

Tony's voice pierced through Laurel's thoughts. "We better get a move on if we're going to track down the rustlers. I don't think the women should come along. Things could get dangerous."

Both Laurel and Lavinia reared up in their saddles, about to protest. Tony grinned wryly, seeming to realize what was to come, and shook his head. "But I wouldn't think of insisting that the ladies stay behind. Please" — and he made a formal gesture with his hand — "lead the way, ladies."

Laurel spurred her horse forward, and Lavinia followed. Jim and Tony trailed behind until they came to a grassy hillock where the cattle grazed peacefully. For the next two hours they took count of each head until they stopped to rest.

Thunder rumbled in the distance, and the sky darkened with impending rain. Jim was thirty feet away, tending to his horse, and Lavinia helped him. Her long auburn hair blew about her glowing face like a crimson flame. Laurel had never seen her look more beautiful.

Tony noticed her interest in Lavinia. A scowl marked his mouth. "Lavinia's found a new man to keep her busy. The poor devil. Maybe I should tell Jim what she's like."

Laurel positioned her legs beneath her on the soft, cool grass and watched Tony take a swig from his canteen. The hard angles of his face seemed harsher this morning, and Laurel sensed a restlessness about him. Only last night he had been calm and so totally charming that she had waited for him, ready to become his wife in all ways again. Now his attention was focused on Lavinia and Jim. She realized that the thought of Jim and Lavinia upset him because of his uncle. He must think that Lavinia was going to use Jim, but Laurel knew better. Lavinia loved Jim Castille. She would make certain that Tony didn't interfere in the relationship.

"I wanted to speak to you about Lavinia earlier, Tony." Her eyes bored directly into his. "This vendetta against her must stop. She had nothing to do with your uncle's sudden death."

"Do you know that for a fact?"

Laurel hesitated. "No, but . . ."

He put his canteen away. "For all you know she may have caused his heart to fail. Look at her with Jim. She's all arms and hands, practically falling all over him. The guy doesn't have a chance with a spider like that one. Before long she'll have pulled him into her web, and he'll be just another victim."

"Jim knows what he's getting into with her. He and Lavinia loved one another years ago. Jim told me that Seth framed him for theft, and Arthur ran him off the ranch. It was after this that Lavinia came to stay on my father's plantation. They deeply loved one another and still do. Don't try anything to turn Jim away from her, because I don't think you can. He knows Lavinia isn't perfect, and I don't think he expects her to be."

Tony considered Laurel for a long moment, almost as if he were thinking things through. Pulling off his hat, he ran a hand through his thick, black hair. "You might be right, but I sense that you want to say something else to me. You were in a hell of a mood this morning when you rode up. What's on your mind?"

Storm clouds gathered and hung over the range, and the wind grew brisker. Laurel felt buffeted by the stiff breeze, and her own emotions warred within her. She ached to touch Tony, to tell him she loved him, but she remembered his anger toward Lavinia and his love for Simone. No longer could she allow Tony to dominate her life. The moment of freedom was at hand.

She took a deep breath and spoke in a rush. "I want to buy the Little L and run it myself. I'm not returning to Louisiana with you. And don't try bullying me with threats against Lavinia, because they won't work. I'll simply tell her the truth about who you are, and if you attempt to harm her, I'll retaliate. I want my freedom, Tony. I don't want to be your wife."

Tony's mouth fell open. Laurel had never seen him look more surprised or stunned by the bluntness of her words. At that moment she wanted to return to Petit Coteau with him, but this senseless vengeance, the thought of taking second place in his heart forever, gave her the courage to eye him steadily and not waver in her resolve.

"Auguste St. Julian was my uncle," Tony reminded her, keeping eye contact with her. A shadow fell across them that neither of them noticed. "I want to know how he died. I want Lavinia to pay for his murder."

"I assure you, Tony, I didn't kill your uncle," came Lavinia's shaky voice from behind them. "Why didn't you just ask me what happened? I'd have told you the truth."

Tony rose to his feet, and Laurel quickly followed suit. "I doubt you'd know the truth if it hit you in the face." Tony stared down Lavinia, but Laurel noticed that though Lavinia shook, she squared her shoulders and her sapphire gaze flashed fire.

"You might not believe this, but I cared for Auguste. I'm not proud of trapping him into an affair. He was a lonely man, a man who'd gone too long without a woman's love. His wife was cold to him and had long since stopped sleeping with him. Yes, I wasn't truthful with him. I wanted his money, position. I needed to save my father's ranch, as I needed someone to love me. And Auguste did love me and knew I wasn't wildly in love with him, but he didn't mind. We gave comfort to one another, and he loved me enough to risk the scandal. I'd have made him a good wife. I owed him that much.

"But I didn't kill him, as you think. If I'd known who you were long ago, I'd have told you that. Auguste died in his sleep. I don't really know what happened to him. He'd been strong and healthy only an hour before. I didn't harm him, Tony, and I won't get on my knees and beg your forgiveness. I've already suffered more than any punishment you could mete out to me."

A lump of pride stuck in Laurel's throat at seeing Lavinia stand up for herself. Somehow she doubted that Lavinia would have been able to do this before now. Evidently the strength of Jim's love had sparked courage in Lavinia. The cowering woman who had begged Laurel to accompany her to Texas and agree to a disguise to save her life was gone. In her stead was a fearless, strong woman.

Lavinia stood with shoulders thrust defiantly back. Tony was quiet and regarded her with a quirked eyebrow, seemingly not certain she was telling the truth but impressed with her nevertheless.

An uneasy silence fell across them broken only by the sudden crack of gunfire. Tony pushed Laurel to the ground and instantly covered Lavinia with his body as a bullet whizzed past their heads. Before Tony could draw his gun, Jim had pulled his rifle from his saddlebag and fired at the fleeing form of the gunman. The man dropped to the ground and lay lifeless beside a large rock.

Tony waited until he was certain no other gunmen watched from the hillside or waited behind equally large hiding places before he helped Lavinia and Laurel to their feet. He made certain they were both all right before he and Jim went to examine the dead man.

"Who is he?" Laurel asked when they returned to the women.

"He's a Mexican named Pedro, one of a group of hired guns who worked for a man named Ortega in San Antonio," Jim explained and gathered a trembling Lavinia in his arms. "Evidently he had orders to stop anyone on the rustlers' trail."

"Seth owed money to a man named Ortega." Laurel remembered the listings in the account ledgers. "Seth is involved in all of this," she said. Tony nodded.

"Jim and I believe he has been rustling cattle from the Little L for Ortega as a means of paying off his debts. Seth needs cash, and that's where the problem comes in. If Ortega is taking the cattle, then what is Seth going to do for money? He left the Little L in a hurry."

"No. Seth stole the money I had in the drawer in the study. But it wasn't that much. He should have waited for the sale of the ranch to go through."

"Wouldn't be enough." Tony strode to his horse and untied the animal from a tree. "He owes Ortega money, but he'll need a lot more to get out of Texas and make a life for himself. I'd bet he has another plan altogether and is just waiting to set it into motion. You and Lavinia are to ride back to the house before the storm breaks. We'll post men there for your safety."

"I'm not going back to the ranch. I'm going with you," Laurel insisted. "Arthur gave me the responsibility of running the Little L. I'm in charge here until the sale is final."

Tony's stormy eyes swept across her face like the black clouds in the sky. "You're going home, and that's the last I want to hear on the subject."

"I'm going with you!"

"It's too dangerous for a woman."

"Damn it! Forget I'm a woman. In your eyes I'm only good for one thing."

Tony smiled seductively, his dark eyes glowing with feral light. "You said that. I didn't."

"You're an impossible man, Tony Duvalier. But this is one time I won't let you manipulate me or have your way. You can't stop me from going with you. I intend to buy the Little L from you, and my interests are tied up until the rustlers are caught. If you don't let me ride with you, I'll simply follow you on my own. Either way, I'm coming with you."

Before Tony could say another word, Laurel strode to her horse and climbed onto the saddle.

She turned in Tony's direction and waited until he mounted. Tony breathed a heavy sigh of resignation and told Jim to take Lavinia back to the house before the storm started, that he and Laurel would no doubt return before nightfall if the rustlers' trail proved cold. Then they rode toward the open countryside.

Chapter Twenty-eight

Unable to outride the approaching storm, Tony and Laurel took shelter in a ramshackle hut an hour after leaving Jim and Lavinia. The large raindrops pelted the tin roof and streamed steadily through the overhead cracks to wetly splotch the hut's mud floor. Laurel sat huddled in a corner, and Tony crouched near where the front door had leaned.

The late afternoon appeared nightlike. Jagged lightning strokes crisscrossed the blue-black sky. Thunder barreled in the heavens to echo across the sodden range.

"We should have returned to the ranch," Tony commented.

"Then Seth and his cohorts would have gotten away."

"Maybe for now. Seth's time is numbered in days, because I'm going to make him pay for what he's done."

A hard edge crept into Tony's voice, and it

chilled her. Not even in his vengeance against Lavinia had he sounded so cruel and calculating.

"What has Seth done to upset you, Tony? I know he's probably involved with the cattle rustling and stolen cash from the Little L, but I think there's something you're not telling me."

"That's right" was all he said, and Laurel noticed he gritted his teeth.

She wasn't going to ask him anything else. Evidently he didn't want to tell her the reason he hated Seth. She felt suddenly chilled and clasped her arms around her to ward off the cold dampness that surrounded her.

"Let me unroll the blanket for you," Tony offered, immediately attuned to her need. He withdrew a bedroll containing a rough, woolen blanket from his saddlebag and also a small sack of biscuits, now hard and stale, from that morning's breakfast.

Laurel hadn't eaten lunch, and a ghost of a smile hovered on her lips as she gratefully took a biscuit from Tony. She devoured it as she watched Tony smooth out the bedroll in a dry area of the room.

"If I didn't know any better, I'd swear you smiled at me, Laurel. Could it be that you're softening up a bit?"

"Maybe," she replied noncommittally and wiped the crumbs from her mouth with slender fingers.

"And just why is that?"

"You know very well why."

Tony finished the bedroll and sat upon it. Dark hair spilled across his forehead, emphasizing the ebony eyes, fringed by even darker lashes. His pale blue shirt was opened and revealed the curly mat of black hair on his chest, which disappeared beneath the silver buckle of his belt. Laurel caught her breath at the wakening response of her own body. She wanted to look away from him, but she felt powerless to tear her gaze from his.

"Tell me," he said in a silky voice.

"Because . . ." She found herself barely able to speak and heard her heart hammering in her ears. She was only able to continue by taking a deep breath. "You saved Lavinia's life today. She might have been killed if you hadn't thrown yourself across her. I know you dislike her, and maybe your reasons are valid, but Lavinia is my sister. If she'd died, I think part of myself would have died with her. Thank you for saving her, Tony. God knows, you didn't have to risk your life for her."

Tony watched her intently. "Perhaps I was wrong about Lavinia. Believe me, I think she can be a conniver when the situation warrants it, and I still think she only wanted my uncle for his money and would have taken advantage of him if they'd married. But I don't think she killed him. Auguste died of causes other than Lavinia. She wasn't responsible."

"I'm glad you realize that now.

"I realize something else, too."

"What?"

"I love you, and I won't let you stay in Texas without me."

"But Simone—"

"Forget Simone, forget all of it. Hell, Laurel, if I'd loved Simone, do you think I'd have come all the way to Texas just to humor a dying man I never knew? I came for you. I don't know what you believe about Simone any longer, but I never loved her and wasn't her child's father."

Tony had told Laurel this after she lost their baby and had continued to tell her, but she hadn't believed him. Why, suddenly, did she know he was telling her the truth? But the letter from Jean gave the impression that Tony grieved over the woman's sudden death. Was there something more to the whole incident with Simone, to her sudden tragedy, that Tony hadn't yet told her?

Tony opened his arms to her. "Come to me, Laurel. Trust me. I love you and that love can't hurt you. If you love me, and I think you do, you'll come to me now. This time you must decide."

Her body shivered from cold and growing passion. Tony's arms held warmth and desire. She realized that his revenge against Lavinia was over, and Simone was dead. No matter what had happened with the woman, Tony loved her. She knew that now. More importantly, her own life, her future, was tied to him as it had been from the moment they met. They were two parts of the same whole, and without the other, each was adrift in the world. Only in Tony's arms did she possess a sense of belonging, of coming home. Since her parents' deaths, she had been alone, but in Tony's embrace, she was never lonely.

Sliding toward Tony, Laurel was soon pulled into his strong arms. He wrapped her in an embrace of steel tempered with tenderness. Lips of fire and velvet joined in an all-consuming kiss. The beating of their two hearts sounded as loud as the thunder overhead, and their desire glowed in brilliant sparks, competing with the lightning that flashed across the heavens.

The beauty of the moment shook them with its intensity of feeling. His tongue parted her lips, and a low moan of pleasure broke from Laurel. Threading her arms around his neck, she pulled him closer to her as a deep burning ache grew within her. They kissed for a long moment before Tony's hand slipped beneath her shirt, and then he broke away.

"You'll come home with me, Laurel. Tell me you will, *chérie*."

"Yes, yes, I belong only with you."

Pure love and desire shone within the depths of Tony's eyes. His hands moved deftly along her rib cage to seek the aching fullness of her breasts. Each breast filled his palms when he cupped them, nearly driving her mad with his touch. Laurel wanted all of him and needed him quickly. It had been so very long since they made love that just to imagine such pleasure was enough to rouse her passion.

With trembling fingers, she reached for his shirt, already open, and removed it from his broad shoulders. Her fingers trailed a wanton path filled with fire and promise along his shoulder blades to the taut muscles of his upper arms before snaking across to the hairy expanse of pectoral muscles. He grabbed her wrists before she could move lower.

"I think it's my turn to take off your shirt."

His words sent shuddering spirals of delight down to her toes. Deftly he unbuttoned her blouse, and within seconds it lay beside her. His mouth then sought the valley of her breasts and gently placed a kiss there before moving to the target of his passion. Each coral-tipped nipple was gently laved with his tongue in endless circling motions. Laurel held onto Tony's shoulders as rapturous waves built within her.

His kisses upon her flesh were like a heady wine and set her body aflame. Never had Laurel felt so feverish to have him inside her or know of such ecstasy building within her that she thought she would burst before he took her completely. Her lips trailed answering kisses along the side of his neck and across his shoulder blade. She thought she would die if he stopped kissing her breasts, but she knew she couldn't wait much longer for him.

With a husky moan on her lips, she broke away and kissed his forehead. "I can't wait much longer, Tony. I want you now."

Tony's dark head lifted from the creamy globes. His eyes filled with amber lights when he looked up at her. Without a word he began removing his pants, and Laurel followed suit, fumbling with the buttons on her own pants until both of them were naked and clasped in each other's arms. By some unspoken consent Tony sank onto the bedroll, taking her with him. Laurel's hands stroked his thighs and wantonly moved to the warm, hard shaft of his manhood. Tony's groan of pleasure told her that he enjoyed her touch and would have welcomed more, but Laurel needed his length within her now, needed to know that he was as starved for her as she was for him.

Moving from his embrace, she straddled his thighs. Her fiery fingers reached for his hardened desire and sheathed his manhood within the silken folds of her body. He filled her eagerly, holding her hips in place as she rode him, her dark head thrown backward in ecstasy. The lightning flashed around them like a million fireflies, and Laurel resembled a silver goddess, naked and uninhibited as she took her pleasure. Finally in one swift and searing plunge, Tony arched toward her and drove deeply within her. She ceased moving and her eyes grew wide, almost totally unprepared for the undulating waves of intense rapture that lapped through her as Tony spilled forth his love.

Their moans of completion were smothered when

Tony pulled her head down and their lips met in a molten kiss. It seemed that hours passed before their hearts stopped their erotic beating, but their hands were never still on each other's bodies. Once more they were in passion's paradise, somewhere above themselves in the heat of the storm.

"The rain's stopped," Laurel mumbled, feeling saddened that their time together had come to an end. By nightfall they would have returned to the ranch, the rain having washed the rustlers' trail away. She felt certain that their earlier passion would ignite again when alone in their bedroom. But would Tony hold her to their agreement to return home with him? She had more or less agreed in the heat of desire. Yet she didn't know if she could forget Simone.

Somehow reading her thoughts, Tony gently turned her face away from the open doorway. He gazed at her with troubled eyes. "You're not certain any longer that you want to come home with me."

"Yes."

"I told you that I hold nothing against Lavinia now. She's safe from me. I was stupid to try to hurt her, to hate her as I did. I can't change the way I felt, but believe me when I tell you that I'm sorry—"

Her fingers on his lips stilled his words. "It's not Lavinia. It's Simone. I don't want to take second place in your heart, Tony. I don't think I can live in the woman's shadow. You told me her child wasn't yours, but can you be sure? I read Jean's letter to you, and apparently you've been grieving over her death . . . and the child's. If Simone and her baby meant nothing to you, then why do you care so much?

Tony sat up and rested his elbows on his knees.

His hand raked through the thickness of his hair. His eyes were filled with such pain that Laurel shivered in the belief that he had loved Simone.

"I should have told you sooner about what happened the night Simone died, but I couldn't talk about it. In fact I've spoken only once to Jean and even then, I couldn't find the words to say how awful I felt, how depressed."

Laurel didn't know if she wanted to hear more. "You don't have to tell me." She made a move to get her clothes, but Tony stopped her.

"Nothing's as you think, Laurel. Hear me out."

She became quiet, and satisfied that she wouldn't leave, Tony continued, a frown marring his forehead.

"The night Simone died, a very bad rainstorm passed through the area. It was late, and Jean and Denise had dined with me. They were getting ready to leave when a pounding started on the door. It was Simone. She'd ridden from Clermont in a fragile buggy and was drenched and chattering from the cold. I offered her some tea, but she refused. In front of Jean and Denise, she accused me of taking my responsibility lightly as far as she and her child were concerned.

"I was dumbfounded and aggravated with her lies. Up until this night I wasn't certain whether I had fathered the child or not. I believed I hadn't, but she kept insisting I had made love to her. I had been so drunk I didn't remember, yet I knew that if I had been that drunk, I wouldn't have been able to make love to her or any woman. I attempted to reason with her, but she became enraged and acted like a mad woman. She threw an expensive vase at my head, called me all sorts of names. I truly think she wanted to embarrass me so much that I'd have admitted to anything just to shut her up."

Tony took a deep breath here, almost unable to go on. He clasped Laurel's hand and stared ahead, lost in his own memories.

"By this time, the rain had stopped. I had had enough of Simone's ravings. I asked her to leave, and she wouldn't. She planted herself on the sofa in the parlor and refused to budge. She said that if I didn't seek a divorce soon and marry her, she'd drag my name through the parish and would cause such a scandal that no one would associate with me. I told her to go ahead, that I owed nothing to her and that the child wasn't mine. This angered her more, and before Jean's and Denise's terrified eyes, she lunged at me with a knife she pulled from her reticule. I forced it from her, and then I picked her up and bodily hauled her from the house to her buggy.

"She was wide-eyed with loathing and hatred. I've never seen such a wild, crazy person. It was as if Simone had lost her good sense. Jean begged me not to cast her into the night like this, but I didn't care. I wanted her gone from Petit Coteau and out of my life. Jean, as you know, is a kind and caring man. He jumped in the buggy beside Simone as she whipped the horse into action. They literally seemed to fly down the mud-slicked road. It was half an hour later that a servant came for me and told me he'd found the buggy overturned on the road. Jean had been injured, and Simone lay unconscious."

"How terrible for all of you," Laurel said and squeezed his hand.

Tony nodded, only vaguely aware that she had spoken. "I rode to the spot where the accident had occurred. Jean was taken back to the house and later found to have two broken legs. Simone was in horrible shape. She was bleeding everywhere and lost her baby that night. Doctor Fusilier told me he didn't have much hope for her. She woke for a few minutes and asked for me. In Doctor Fusilier's presence she told me that the baby wasn't mine. She wasn't certain who the child's father was. It might have been Seth's child for all she knew. She begged my forgiveness for what she'd done by trying to trap me. She admitted that she and Seth wanted you to think that I was the child's father. If not for Seth's involvement with the whole plan, you'd not have lost our child, Laurel. I can't forgive Seth for how he conspired to get you away from me. I forgave Simone because I realized she had no one to love her. However, I can't forgive myself for putting her in that buggy, for speaking to her the way I did. I caused her death as surely as if I'd shot her."

A sob escaped Laurel's lips, and she threw her arms around his neck. "Don't blame yourself. Simone was wild and destined for unhappiness. Her death was her own making. I just thank God that Jean will be all right."

Tony hugged her fiercely and buried his face within the sweet scent of her hair. "I love you, Laurel. I'll always love you. But if you want to stay here, I won't force you to come home with me. I only want you to be happy. I want that more than anything."

"Oh, Tony! You make me happy. I love you, too. I can't stay here without you, can't imagine living without you now that we've found each other again. I'll go home with you to Petit Coteau. I don't want to be anywhere but within your arms."

"Then that's where you'll be, *chérie*. Forever."

Their lips met again, and the kiss was filled with the promise of a new beginning, the start of their life together without deceit. From this moment on, both of their hearts overflowed with happiness and love and trust in each other. Each felt that nothing could mar their joy.

"We better get dressed and head back to the ranch or we'll never leave." Tony grinned and stroked her breasts. "Unless you'd like to stay here a while more."

Laurel made a pretense of pondering this suggestion. "Hmmm, that's a tough decision to make."

"You hard-hearted vixen." Tony playfully nipped her ear. They dissolved in laughter, but Tony made a move to start dressing. "We better go back. Jim will wonder what happened to us."

Laurel sighed. "I suppose we should."

After they had dressed, they kissed and embraced again, then headed outside into the quiet dusky evening with arms around each other's waists, oblivious to everything but their delight in being together. They moved to their horses, but Tony suddenly stopped in his tracks and his head shot up. Laurel's did also, and in that instant, Tony was roughly pulled from her by two Mexican men who seemed to appear from nowhere.

Another man reached for her, and in one fell swoop, she was hauled onto his horse and perched before him. She struggled and screamed for Tony, aware that Tony called her name and attempted to pull away from the men who held him. A long scream dissolved in her throat when one of the men raised a gun and hit Tony on the back of his head, knocking him unconscious.

"Tony! Tony!" she screamed as she saw him fall to his knees and pitch face down onto the muddy wet ground.

"Quiet, *chica*," the man behind her whispered into her ear. "Your man can't help you now." He made a nasty-sounding laugh, chilling her to her soul. "Don't forget the note!" he yelled to one of the other men. Quickly he turned the horse around and spurred the animal in the other direction and rode into the fast descending gloom of night.

Chapter Twenty-nine

The sun blinded Tony's eyes when he woke. The golden orb beat upon him, rousing him from his unconscious state. For a few minutes he lay still, unable to think, feeling only a sharp pulsating pain in the back of his head. Finally he sat up, trying to orient himself. A distance away, his horse grazed peacefully, but something was wrong, very wrong.

Out of the blue the memory of what had happened hit him like a lightning bolt. Laurel! He must find Laurel! Rising to his feet, he swayed unsteadily and started to go to his horse but stopped. The world spun dizzily before him, and for some seconds he felt as if he were on a wild carousel ride. But slowly, by degrees, he got his bearings. At that moment, as he moved his arm to grasp the horse's reins, he heard the crinkle of the paper in his shirt pocket.

He scanned the contents.

Place $10,000 in gold on the porch of the old Montgomery farm. Your wife will be released unharmed. If not, you'll never see her again.

Tony crumpled the paper in his huge fist and cursed. The men who had kidnapped Laurel and knocked him unconscious had been Mexican, but somehow he was sure that Seth Renquist had a hand in this. The time for a showdown was near, and he hoped that Seth was praying in fear of losing his life, because if not, Tony vowed the man would spend an eternity in hell.

He got on his horse and rode quickly in the direction of the Little L to rally the hands together.

"I can't believe Seth would do this," Lavinia told Tony and Jim later that day while the two men saddled their horses for the trip to the Fredricksburg bank to get the money. "He's not a stupid man."

"Just crazy," Tony said through ground teeth. "That makes him more dangerous."

Lavinia looked imploringly at Jim when he mounted his horse. "May I go with you?"

"No!" Both Tony and Jim spoke in unison.

"But Laurel is my cousin, and somehow I feel I should help her. Maybe I can talk some sense into Seth. He can be a nasty, mean person when he's riled. If he sees both of you and the hands, there's no telling what he might do. I've seen him when he's angry, and he's not a nice sight to behold. Sometimes he can't control himself, but I've been around him enough to know how to calm him."

"Sorry, Lavinia." Jim bent down and kissed her. "Stay here."

"But I can help. Laurel has been my only friend over the years. A bond holds us together somehow—"

"Perhaps you feel like that because Laurel is your sister," Tony broke in. He hoisted himself onto his horse and began pulling on a pair of leather gloves, aware of Lavinia's shocked face. "Arthur was her father, too. She didn't want to tell you yet, but I think you should know. If you want to keep her safe, to help her, then stay here and wait for her return. Will you do that for her? Do you understand how important it is for you to remain here and not meddle in something you can't handle?"

Always used to acting on impulse, Lavinia contemplated Tony and mulled over what he had just told her. Finally a shadow of a smile flitted across her face and she nodded. "I understand."

"Good" was all Tony said and knew that for once Lavinia put another person's welfare ahead of her own.

"Do you hear them?" Seth turned to Laurel. His eyes swept over her as she rested against a granite boulder, her hands tied behind her back and her feet tied together as well.

"I don't hear anything!" she snapped. "What are you talking about?"

"The spirits, of course." He sounded as if she were an ignorant child he must educate. He glanced up at the pink granite dome where the sun cast a soft orange glow. "They're talking again the way they do everyday when the sun starts to set."

A large shadow from a nearby rock moved across Laurel's face by degrees. The evening air had taken on a definite chill, and she was glad she was wearing the warm flannel shirt. Last night had been cold, and this night promised to be the same. She would have to huddle against the rock the best way she could and hope that the small outcropping of rough rock behind her would finally break the rope on her wrists. She had been rubbing the rope against it whenever Seth wasn't watching her.

She had to admit that he appeared to be calmer now than yesterday after the Mexican had left her here alone with him. He had paced for hours over the rocky landscape, not giving her time enough to attempt an escape. Whenever she thought she was free of him, he had come to check on her again, foiling any plan she might have.

"The Comanches never come here," he continued. "This spot is sacred to them. They say it's enchanted. But I'm not afraid to come here at night. I found this place years ago and watched the sun set as it's doing now. I've never been afraid." He spoke proudly, almost as if he considered the Indians to be cowards. He turned to her, his blond hair blowing around his face, and Laurel ceased rubbing her rope-bound hands against the sharp edge of rock.

"You don't think I'm a coward, do you, Laurel?"

She didn't know if this was a question or a statement, and it caught her off guard.

"Answer me. Am I braver than Tony Duvalier?"

"No."

"Why you—" He lunged forward and grabbed her arm, hurting her. "Do you know that I could rape you and toss you back to Duvalier like a used washcloth? I bet you'd see what a coward he was then, Laurel. He wouldn't want you, would sooner spit on you than take you back as his wife after I was finished with you."

"Tony isn't like that! He loves me!"

The fire died in his blue eyes. Suddenly he let her go. "Do you know what I wished each time I came here? What I asked the spirits for? I asked for money, a lot of money. I asked for a woman who'd love me, a woman who was a lady, not one of those tarts in San Antonio or a rancher's plain, long-faced daughter. I wanted a woman who always smelled nice, who was kind to everybody, and pretty. But I never got a lot of money or found a woman like that. Soon, however, I will have money, thanks to Duvalier, and I'll have a real lady. You, Laurel. I'd do anything to have you and the money."

"If I have anything to say about it, Seth, you'll end up with nothing."

"Hah!" He appeared amused by her answer. "I'll

have it all! You see, Lavinia was my first choice because she was Arthur's daughter, but she's such a tramp, and I can't marry a woman who sleeps with every man she meets. I also wanted Simone Lancier and thought she was a lady with money, but I learned quickly that she didn't have any money to speak of and most certainly she wasn't a lady. As we well know." Seth bent down and his eyes gleamed with sapphire sparks. "You, Laurel, fit the bill perfectly. Lots of money and a lady to boot. Now I didn't have to ransom you, because I'm certain you'll be more than generous to me eventually, but I like being a thorn in Duvalier's side. I like to see him in a lather."

"Why, Seth? Is it because Tony is everything you'd like to be but aren't? He's polished and wealthy, a true gentleman ... something you'll never be." She practically spat in his face. Seth backed off.

"I could hit you for that."

"But you won't. You're afraid that if you harm me, Tony will kill you. Your actions prove that you're the coward, Seth."

"You don't know what you're saying. In time you'll think differently and know that I'm better for you than Tony. I can be a gentleman, too, with the proper clothes. Then you'll want me."

Laurel shook her head. "I could never want you. How can I after learning that you and Simone tricked me into thinking she was having Tony's child? What was worse was that I believed the lie and lost my own child over it. I hate you, Seth. I'd rather die than give in to you."

Closing his eyes, he then peered at her through tiny slits and stroked a long curl that trailed across her breast.

"Maybe you will, Laurel. Just maybe you will."

Tony and Jim crouched low on the hilltop that overlooked the old Montgomery place. An hour before, they had placed the bag of gold on the dilapidated front porch in full view of any henchmen who sought it. Now they waited for Ortega and his men to claim it, and when they did, Tony, Jim, and the hands of the Little L, who waited on the other side of the hill, were ready to follow in pursuit. The hope was that they would be led to Laurel.

"If that bastard has hurt her," Tony muttered thickly for the tenth time that day, "I'll torture him first before I kill him."

Jim immediately knew Tony spoke about Seth, and Jim had to agree. "Not before I get first crack at him. Because of him, I lost Lavinia."

"Seems like Seth Renquist won't live out the day." Tony's blunt statement caused Jim to nod. After a few moments, Jim nudged Tony and pointed. "Some men are riding down the road to the farm."

"It's Ortega," Tony muttered as the five came closer.

The two men on the hillside watched as Ortega dismounted before the farmhouse, drew his pistol, and sent a wary eye in all directions. When he seemed convinced that no one was watching, he went to the porch and grabbed the bag of gold. Even at a distance, Tony and Jim saw the white triumphant smile flash across his face when he mounted his horse. With wild, gleeful cries Ortega and his men rode swiftly down the road, kicking up clouds of dust in their wake.

Tony motioned for his men, who outnumbered Ortega's group. Soon he and Jim and the others were on the Mexicans' trail. However, the early afternoon sun, which had been so bright and warm hours before, now cooled and started to sink in the western sky. Tony's frown wasn't lost on Jim when they realized that the direction they had expected Ortega and his men to take didn't lead to Laurel and Seth. In fact Tony and the men had doubled back in their pursuit and seemed to be heading in an easterly direction. Finally Tony cursed.

"The bastards are heading for Mexico!"

Spurring his horse forward, Tony galloped ahead, and the men followed suit. Soon they had caught up with Ortega and his bunch. Sliding from his horse, Tony pulled Ortega from his and grabbed the wiry man around the throat.

"Where's my wife? Tell me where she is, damn it!" His balled fist looked large and ominous, and Ortega trembled before the broad-shouldered man with the burning eyes.

"Please, señor, have pity on me. I know nothing."

"Liar! You've got the money. Where's my wife?"

The threatening fist in front of his face caused Ortega to swallow hard. "She is with Renquist by the stone the Comanches hold in reverence."

"Where is that?"

"Enchanted Rock," Jim interjected. "I know where it is. Old legends say that the Comanches used it for human sacrifices to their gods."

"Just great!" Tony exclaimed and threw Ortega at one of the Little L hands. He gave instructions to his men to take the Mexicans to the sheriff in San Antonio. Then he and Jim rode toward Enchanted Rock.

"Where is that slimy bastard Ortega?" Seth stormed as he paced up and down, a large rifle in his hand. "He was supposed to be here hours ago with the ransom money. If he double-crossed me..."

"You couldn't possibly have expected him to come back for you, Seth," Laurel observed. "Ortega didn't even leave you your horse."

She shivered in the cool night air and leaned against the rock where she had sat for the last two days. Seth hadn't given her food, and her stomach rumbled like waves breaking upon a beach in a hurricane. Sometimes he did lift his canteen of water to her mouth for her to drink, but he hadn't eaten either. All he had done was pace like a caged animal, and Laurel grew more fearful that Seth was indeed insane.

"Ortega's got to come back. The ransom money was my idea."

"Don't be absurd. Ortega and his men are probably long gone. There's no reason to keep me here. Let me go, Seth. Untie me, and I'll find my way back to the ranch."

Seth whipped around to face her. A full moon had already risen and was reflected in the depths of his frosty blue eyes, causing them to appear harder and colder than usual.

"I'm not stupid. Even if they did leave me here, I've got you, the golden goose, Miss Moneybags herself. Duvalier will pay a fortune for you, but he won't ever see you again. Somehow I'll arrange to get the money, and we'll slip over the border into Mexico. That should really stick in his craw like a sack of rocks. Duvalier's precious wife in my bed." Seth laughed, a shrill piercing sound that hung on the air and sent shivers through Laurel's body. She knew then without a doubt that Seth was indeed crazy.

She had to free herself. What if Tony didn't find her? Who knew what madness Seth was capable of? She watched him as he began pacing again, his eyes fixed on the distance horizon, barely discernible in the darkness. Pushing against the jagged outcrop of rock behind her, she sawed it against the rope. Over the last two days, she had constantly endeavored to break the rope. Though she couldn't see her bound hands, she felt that the rope had frayed some. It no longer felt so tight around her wrists. If only Seth would fall asleep, she would be free to work on the rope until it broke away. But Seth hadn't slept at all, another reason why she decided he was demented. He appeared unable to relax enough to sit down and doze off.

She watched him continue his vigil while she surreptitiously worked at the bonds on her wrists. A shudder of hopelessness overcame her at times because she didn't feel any further along. Two hours later, the moon was high in the sky, and spilled its silvery light across the rock. Suddenly Laurel felt the rope break free. She made an involuntary moan of surprise. Seth twisted around and faced her.

"What was that?"

"I didn't hear anything." Laurel huddled against the rock, shivering from cold and covering up her triumph.

"I heard a moaning sound." His eyes slid up to the top of the rock. "It's them. They're back."

"The spirits you hear?"

Seth nodded. "They're trying to tell me something."

"They want you to release me. Why don't you listen to them?"

Moving closer to her, Seth's breath fanned her face. "You think I'm stupid or crazy, or both, don't you? I'm not. You're mine now, Laurel, and I don't mean to give you up to Duvalier. I'd rather see you dead first."

He continued to listen to the sounds he heard coming from the rock, and Laurel heard them, too—groaning, queer sorts of sounds. Her heart raced with fear, not from the sounds, which she knew couldn't hurt her, but because of Seth, a man who would.

Laurel's chance for freedom came in the unexpected form of a falling star, gliding through the heavens and disappearing beyond the dome of the rock. She watched as Seth stood transfixed, then slowly began to climb up the side of the smooth, bald stone. He seemed to have forgotten her, to be more interested in the star and the groaning voices that called to him from the top. As he made his way upward, he became a silhouette in the moonlight. Hurriedly she pulled off the ropes around her wrists and untied her feet, which had long ago gone to sleep. When she attempted to stand, she fell and had to wait for the blood to rush into her toes again before taking the tentative and necessary steps to restore her circulation. She then ran in the opposite direction.

She didn't look back as she made her mad dash for freedom. In fact she had no idea which way to run, having become disoriented because of the dark, but it didn't matter the direction she took. All she wanted was to get away. Her breath came in little spurts, and her lungs felt about to burst with the fear and panic of being caught. The cold night air wrapped around her, but Laurel didn't feel its sting, so intent was she on escaping into the countryside and the hope that someone would aid her.

Making her way along the base of the rock, she stayed in the darkness, frightened that Seth would see her. Her heart hammered out the words running through her head. "Get away. Get away. Get away." But which way to go?

A noise nearby startled her, and she nearly screamed into the face of a fawn, who seemed just as frightened as she was. The small animal lifted its tail and scooted away into the night. Knowing that she was so easily spooked gave her the courage to run. She found herself streaking across a rolling landscape, her boots kicking rocks strewn in her path. At one point she fell, twisting her ankle but stood up despite the pain to continue onward. She had no idea how far she had gone but guessed not far enough. She almost imagined she could hear Seth calling her name, and she stood still to catch her breath, to listen a second. It was then she heard the pounding of horses' hoofs coming her way.

Her first inclination was to rush toward the sound and flag down the riders, but she hesitated. Suppose it was Ortega and his men? Immediately she fell to the ground and crawled to a large rock that gleamed like a bastion of safety in the moonlight.

The riders came nearer. Two men were silhouetted against the horizon, growing larger and larger, the sound of their horses racing toward her growing louder and louder in her ears. It was almost as if they saw her and knew her hiding place. Her heart thumped painfully in her chest and felt about to explode. Fear pumped through her, and her legs felt as if they were about to give out beneath her. God, help me, she prayed, help me . . .

"Laurel!" the voice of one of the riders called to her. "Laurel!"

She jumped up, waving her arms. Tears slid down her cheeks. "Tony! Tony!"

Making a move forward, she found herself suddenly pinned against Seth's chest and heard his venomous voice beside her ear. "Shut up, or I'll shoot your loving husband and Castille down now."

Before she could utter a word, Seth grabbed her by the arm and pulled her with him into the darkness. The barrel of his rifle nudged against the small of her back and felt frigidly cold. Laurel could see that Tony and Jim had instantly stopped and waited about five hundred yards away. So close and yet so far!

Seth screamed, his voice piercing the quiet night. "Come any closer and she's dead, Duvalier!"

No sound issued from the two men. Laurel glanced one more time at them before Seth dragged her over the path she had come earlier. Within minutes she was by the rock, towering over them like a foreboding dragon in the darkness.

"Let me go," she pleaded with Seth. "You can't escape. Tony will kill you. I can talk him into—"

"Into what!" He cut her off and sneered at her as he pulled her up the side of the rock. "Into being merciful to me, sparing my wretched life? No, thank you. I've had people's pity all my life. You think it was easy being the son of poor German parents? It was hell. We had nothing. Even my own uncle pitied us. He gave my mother a job in his bakery. He could have done better by her, but he didn't. She never complained and was grateful for each and every thing she got, and it wasn't much. Arthur married her and gave us a home. I worked like a dog to please him, and what did he do? Huh?" He kept pulling her up the smooth granite surface with him as he spoke, not allowing her to rest. "He left the ranch in your care until the new owner took over. Your husband, I might add. Why would he do that? Why?"

"Seth, please." Laurel tried to twist out of his grasp, but Seth was too strong. Her arm felt as if he were pulling it from its socket.

He continued as if he hadn't stopped speaking. "He did that because you're family. The old man never considered me his son. No. He was mouthing off words all the time. I never forgave him for that. I'll never forgive you for not wanting me. You could have given me the money I needed, you could have agreed to marry me, but you didn't. All you ever wanted was Tony Duvalier! You were right about Simone and me and our plan to break the two of you up. I'm glad you lost your baby, because I was determined that Duvalier's kid wouldn't come between us. Now, he's going to suffer for coming here and making you forget me. I'm going you kill you both!"

"Seth!"

A deaf ear was turned to her plea. The long climb up left Laurel winded and weak. When they reached the top, Seth pushed her down on the smooth surface and threw himself on top of her. His hands tore at her blouse until her breasts broke free and gleamed like fine porcelain.

"Duvalier and Castille can't get up here. Only one path leads up here, so I'll shoot them before they see me. But from the bottom, they can look up here and see me violate the haughty wife of a

Cajun bastard before I kill all of you."

Laurel struggled as his hand snaked out and whirled over her breasts. "You can't do this! No!"

She pushed at him but Seth wouldn't budge. Seth's mouth quirked in an evil smile that chilled her to the bone.

"I'll do what I want!" He turned and called out, "Duvalier, do you hear me?"

From below came Tony's agonized voice. "Don't hurt Laurel!"

Seth laughed confidently. "I'm going to make her unfit for you before I kill her. I'm going to make you wonder what I'm doing to her before I toss her over the edge. Then I'm going to shoot you and Castille down like two wild dogs!"

Laurel wondered if she should fight Seth. Perhaps her struggles only enraged him and made him more determined to hurt and then to kill her. She realized that Tony and Jim could shoot from below, but that they were afraid of hitting her instead of Seth. Everything was up to her. She had to find a way to stop Seth.

A low moaning sound came from somewhere within the rock itself. Each evening and all through the night strange sounds had issued from within the rock. Somehow Laurel knew the sounds had to do with the rock's settling after a warm day, but Seth's ears perked up as this sound rolled over them.

She knew now what she had to do.

"I hear your mother calling for you, Seth. She's calling for you."

"You're lying!"

"No. Listen."

Somehow, when Seth quieted and listened, the moaning sound that swept over them did indeed sound like a woman's voice. Chills coursed through Laurel, but a weight was lifted from her when Seth stood up.

"Mother," he called softly and moved to the sound, completely forgetting about Laurel.

This was her chance. Swiftly she sat up and just as quickly she backed away toward the path that led down to the base of the rock. The whole time she kept her gaze on Seth, who appeared dazed. Standing up, she made a move to run down the path just as Tony's shout echoed up to her.

"Renquist!"

Seth turned at the sound, startled, not quite certain which voice to listen to. Instantly his brain seemed to clear, and he raised his rifle in Tony's direction. He was too late. The nighttime stillness reverberated with the double crack of gunfire from below the rock. Laurel watched in horror as Seth bent forward, falling onto his face. She tried to scream but was able to make only a small cry.

His face was turned toward her. His usually cold eyes now contained a strange warmth, and he smiled at her.

"Mother, it . . . is . . . you."

Then he spoke no more.

Laurel turned and flew down the side of the rock, slipping and nearly tripping over her own feet in her haste to get to Tony. When she was nearly to the bottom, she saw Tony and Jim. With arms outstretched to her, Tony dashed forward.

Within seconds, Tony held her, shivering and crying, in his arms.

When she lifted her face to him, his arms tightened protectively about her. They gazed into each other's eyes as Jim silently stole away. At that moment, no words were needed between them.

Scooping Laurel into his arms, he carried her to his horse. When dawn broke, they reached the Little L where Lavinia, crying tears of happiness, embraced her sister.

Chapter Thirty

Petit Coteau, one year later

Jean lifted the champagne glass in a toast. "To Jean Antoine Duvalier, the heir to Petit Coteau."

Tony, Laurel, and Denise acknowledged the toast with their own glasses while the rest of the guests in the parlor followed suit. The clink of fine crystal sang through the room, and merry, animated voices drifted on the air.

The only person who wasn't too pleased was Jean Antoine himself. In Gincie's arms, he let out a lusty cry that Laurel immediately recognized.

"What a way to behave at your christening party," she softly scolded and took the baby from Gincie. "Let's go upstairs and feed you."

With a bright smile for her guests and a secretive wink to Tony, she and Gincie then went upstairs.

Jean patted Tony on the back. "How does it feel to be a papa now? Your son is a healthy little fellow and will do you proud. As his godfather, I shall see that his errant father doesn't teach him bad habits."

"And as his godmother," Denise chimed in, "I shall make certain that his father and godfather don't spoil him unbearably."

"If I know you, Denise, you'll do all the spoiling." Tony smiled into his pretty cousin's face. Denise fluttered her fan.

"That might be rather hard. I think his mother has first priority. All the child does is whimper, and Laurel is there to take charge of him. I have a feeling that you've been displaced in her heart, *chéri*."

"We'll see about that." Tony made a grand display of pretending outrage, but when he left his guests and bounded up the stairs, his face was wreathed in a tender smile. Upon entering the nursery, he was engulfed by warmth at the sight of his child suckling at the breast of the woman he loved more than life itself.

If possible, Laurel, dressed in a gown of yellow and green silk, was more beautiful now than on the day he had met her. Her bodice was pulled low over her breasts as she fed the hungry baby. A sweet smile touched her lips when Tony came and knelt beside the rocking chair.

"He's nearly asleep," Laurel said, gazing upon the child with love in her eyes.

"Jean Antoine is a lucky fellow," Tony remarked, his eyes resting on the lushness of her bosom.

Laurel reached out and stroked Tony's chin. "It's been a long time since we made love."

"Exactly three months, seven days, and eight hours."

"Tony! How can you remember such a thing?"

"Does a hungry man not remember the last time he ate?"

Laurel laughed. "You're a devil, you know that." They sat in contemplative silence and gazed in adoration at the infant in Laurel's arms. "I received a letter from Lavinia today," Laurel said. "She and Jim are planning to visit us next month. She said she adores being an aunt and can't wait until her own baby is born in the summer."

"It's kind of hard to imagine that red-headed vixen as a mother."

"I can picture her very clearly. Lavinia will be a good mother, and Jim a doting father. They'll never be able to thank you enough for turning over the Little L to them. Lavinia said to tell you that again."

"No thanks necessary. The ranch was Arthur's. Lavinia should have inherited it all along."

Gincie came into the room then, a frown of disdain marring her forehead. "Mr. Tony, you ain't supposed to be in here when Miss Laurel's feedin' the baby. It ain't proper."

"Proper? If I'd been proper, this baby you coddle and coo at all day wouldn't be here."

Gincie blushed.

When finally Jean Antoine was fast asleep and stopped suckling, Laurel stood up and tenderly placed him in his crib, leaving him in Gincie's care. As they started out the room, she tugged at the bodice of her gown, but Tony's hand reached out and stopped her.

"Why bother?" he asked.

Laurel was shocked. "Tony Duvalier, we have a houseful of company. How can we dare—"

His lips broke off her words. Laurel found herself clinging to him, aching for his hands upon her body. It had been so long.

He whispered into her ear. "How can we not?"

With a naughty smile hovering around her lips, Laurel cast a sidelong glance at Gincie and nodded to Tony.

A minute later when Gincie left the nursery, she saw the door to the master bedroom close softly behind a yellow-and-green silk skirt.

Gincie didn't suppress the pleased grin that twitched about her mouth. "I always said that Mr. Tony was the man for Miss Laurel."

Down the hall in the huge four-poster bed where she lay wrapped in Tony's embrace, Laurel quite agreed.

SURRENDER TO THE
PASSION OF RENÉ J. GARROD!

WILD CONQUEST (2132, $3.75)
Lovely Rausey Bauer never expected her first trip to the big city to include being kidnapped by a handsome stranger claiming to be her husband. But one look at her abductor and Rausey's heart began to beat faster. And soon she found herself desiring nothing more than to feel the touch of his lips on her own.

ECSTASY'S BRIDE (2082, $3.75)
Irate Elizabeth Dickerson wasn't about to let Seth Branting wriggle out of his promise to marry her. Though she despised the handsome Wyoming rancher, Elizabeth would not go home to St. Louis without teaching Seth a lesson about toying with a young lady's affections—a lesson in love he would never forget!

AND DON'T MISS OUT ON THIS OTHER
HEARTFIRE SIZZLERS FROM ZEBRA BOOKS!

LOVING CHALLENGE (2243, $3.75)
by Carol King
When the notorious Captain Dominic Warbrooke burst into Laurette's Harker's eighteenth birthday ball, the accomplished beauty challenged the arrogant scoundrel to a duel. But when the captain named her innocence as his stakes, Laurette was terrified she'd not only lose the fight, but her heart as well!

Available wherever paperbacks are sold, or order direct from the Publisher. Send cover price plus 50¢ per copy for mailing and handling to Zebra Books, Dept. 2419, 475 Park Avenue South, New York, N.Y. 10016. Residents of New York, New Jersey and Pennsylvania must include sales tax. DO NOT SEND CASH.

ZEBRA ROMANCES FOR ALL SEASONS
From Bobbi Smith

ARIZONA TEMPTRESS (1785, $3.95)
Rick Peralta found the freedom he craved only in his disguise as El Cazador. Then he saw the exquisitely alluring Jennie among his compadres and the hotblooded male swore she'd belong just to him.

CAPTIVE PRIDE (2160, $3.95)
Committed to the Colonial cause, the gorgeous and independent Cecelia Demorest swore she'd divert Captain Noah Kincade's weapons to help out the American rebels. But the moment that the womanizing British privateer first touched her, her scheming thoughts gave way to burning need.

DESERT HEART (2010, $3.95)
Rancher Rand McAllister was furious when he became the guardian of a scrawny girl from Arizona's mining country. But when he finds that the pig-tailed brat is really a voluptuous beauty, his resentment turns to intense interest; Laura Lee knew it would be the biggest mistake in her life to succumb to the cowboy—but she can't fight against giving him her wild DESERT HEART.

Available wherever paperbacks are sold, or order direct from the Publisher. Send cover price plus 50¢ per copy for mailing and handling to Zebra Books, Dept. 2419, 475 Park Avenue South, New York, N.Y. 10016. Residents of New York, New Jersey and Pennsylvania must include sales tax. DO NOT SEND CASH.

Now you can get more of HEARTFIRE right at home and $ave.

Preview Four Brand New ZEBRA Heartfire Romance Novels...

FREE for 10 days.

No Obligation and No Strings Attached!

♥

Enjoy all of the passion and fiery romance as you soar back through history, right in the comfort of your own home.

Now that you have read a Zebra HEARTFIRE Romance novel, we're sure you'll agree that HEARTFIRE sets new standards of excellence for historical romantic fiction. Each Zebra HEARTFIRE novel is the ultimate blend of intimate romance and grand adventure and each takes place in the kinds of historical settings you want most...the American Revolution, the Old West, Civil War and more.

__FREE__ Preview Each Month and $ave

Zebra has made arrangements for you to preview 4 brand new HEARTFIRE novels each month...FREE for 10 days. You'll get them as soon as they are published. If you are not delighted with any of them, just return them with no questions asked. But if you decide these are everything we said they are, you'll pay just $3.25 each—a total of $13.00 (a $15.00 value). **That's a $2.00 saving each month off the regular price.** Plus there is NO shipping or handling charge. These are delivered right to your door absolutely free! There is no obligation and there is no minimum number of books to buy.

TO GET YOUR FIRST MONTH'S PREVIEW... Mail the Coupon Below!

Mail to:

HEARTFIRE Home Subscription Service, Inc.
120 Brighton Road
P.O. Box 5214
Clifton, NJ 07015-5214

YES! I want to subscribe to Zebra's HEARTFIRE Home Subscription Service. Please send me my first month's books to preview free for ten days. I understand that if I am not pleased I may return them and owe nothing, but if I keep them I will pay just $3.25 each; a total of $13.00. That is a savings of $2.00 each month off the cover price. There are no shipping, handling or other hidden charges and there is no minimum number of books I must buy. I can cancel this subscription at any time with no questions asked.

NAME _____

ADDRESS _____ APT. NO. _____

CITY _____ STATE _____ ZIP _____

SIGNATURE (if under 18, parent or guardian must sign)
Terms and prices are subject to change.

2419

ZEBRA HAS THE SUPERSTARS OF PASSIONATE ROMANCE!

CRIMSON OBSESSION (2272, $3.95)
by Deana James

Cassandra MacDaermond was determined to make the handsome gambling hall owner Edward Sandron pay for the fortune he had stolen from her father. But she never counted on being struck speechless by his seductive gaze. And soon Cassandra was sneaking into Sandron's room, more intent on sharing his rapture than causing his ruin!

TEXAS CAPTIVE (2251, $3.95)
by Wanda Owen

Ever since two outlaws had killed her ma, Talleha had been suspicious of all men. But one glimpse of virile Victor Maurier standing by the lake in the Texas Blacklands and the half-Indian princess was helpless before the sensual tide that swept her in its wake!

TEXAS STAR (2088, $3.95)
by Deana James

Star Garner was a wanted woman—and Chris Gillard was determined to collect the generous bounty being offered for her capture. But when the beautiful outlaw made love to him as if her life depended on it, Gillard's firm resolve melted away, replaced with a raging obsession for his fiery TEXAS STAR.

MOONLIT SPLENDOR (2008, $3.95)
by Wanda Owen

When the handsome stranger emerged from the shadows and pulled Charmaine Lamoureux into his strong embrace, she sighed with pleasure at his seductive caresses. Tomorrow she would be wed against her will—so tonight she would take whatever exhilarating happiness she could!

TEXAS TEMPEST (1906, $3.95)
by Deana James

Sensuous Eugenia Leahy had an iron will that intimidated even the most powerful of men. But after rescuing her from a bad fall, the virile stranger MacPherson resolved to take the steel-hearted beauty whether she consented or not!

Available wherever paperbacks are sold, or order direct from the Publisher. Send cover price plus 50¢ per copy for mailing and handling to Zebra Books, Dept. 2419, 475 Park Avenue South, New York, N.Y. 10016. Residents of New York, New Jersey and Pennsylvania must include sales tax. DO NOT SEND CASH.

SHE CAST HER GYPSY SPELL

"You should congratulate yourself," Tony Duvalier growled. "Every man in the room is half in love with you."

"I can take care of myself," Laurel retorted, not quite believing the rude womanizer. Her gaze turned upward to his, as she wondered what game he was playing with her. Laurel was inexperienced with men, but an awakening of her own sexuality had begun this night, a sense of power. Through long, sooty lashes, she fastened her gaze on Tony's full, sensual lips. "Are you half in love with me, too?"

A groan of intense pleasure escaped from Tony. In one motion he pulled her to him, trapping her with an arm around her waist, and with the other hand he grabbed a handful of silky tresses so she'd be forced to render her gaze upward to his.

"I'm not like the others here," he ground out. "I'm not so easily taken in by a beautiful face, a voluptuous body." He laughed hoarsely. "However, my gypsy temptress, I am only a man and you've ignited the spark."

His searing kiss made the world spin crazily for Laurel. She tried to move away from this man and the delicious, forbidden sensations he was provoking in her, but the more she struggled the more closely he held her.

Thoroughly caressing her, he whispered, "You're everything I thought you'd be and more—and I intend to quench my desire for you. I have to."

And though he proclaimed to hate her, Tony Duvalier couldn't help but love the mysterious woman in his embrace . . .

ZEBRA'S GOT THE ROMANCE
TO SET YOUR HEART AFIRE!

RAGING DESIRE (2242, $3.75)
by Colleen Faulkner

A wealthy gentleman and officer in General Washington's army, Devon Marsh wasn't meant for the likes of Cassie O'Flynn, an immigrant bond servant. But from the moment their lips first met, Cassie knew she could love no other . . . even if it meant marching into the flames of war to make him hers!

TEXAS TWILIGHT (2241, $3.75)
by Vivian Vaughan

When handsome Trace Garrett stepped onto the porch of the Santa Clara ranch, he wove a rapturous spell around Clara Ehler's heart. Though Clara planned to sell the spread and move back East, Trace was determined to keep her on the wild Western frontier where she belonged — to share with him the glory and the splendor of the passion-filled TEXAS TWILIGHT.

RENEGADE HEART (2244, $3.75)
by Marjorie Price

Strong-willed Hannah Hatch resented her imprisonment by Captain Jake Farnsworth, even after the daring Yankee had rescued her from bloodthirsty marauders. And though Jake's rock-hard physique made Hannah tremble with desire, the spirited beauty was nevertheless resolved to exploit her femininity to the fullest and gain her independence from the virile bluecoat.

LOVING CHALLENGE (2243, $3.75)
by Carol King

When the notorious Captain Dominic Warbrooke burst into Laurette Harker's eighteenth birthday ball, the accomplished beauty challenged the arrogant scoundrel to a duel. But when the captain named her innocence as his stakes, Laurette was terrified she'd not only lose the fight, but her heart as well!

Available wherever paperbacks are sold, or order direct from the Publisher. Send cover price plus 50¢ per copy for mailing and handling to Zebra Books, Dept. 2419, 475 Park Avenue South, New York, N.Y. 10016. Residents of New York, New Jersey and Pennsylvania must include sales tax. DO NOT SEND CASH.